First published by Elybion Entertainment LLC 2020

First edition 2020
ISBN 978-1-7337384-0-8

Maps by Kellerica
Illustration by Sarah Evelyn
Designed by Anamaria Stefan

Elybion is divided.

With the last empire overthrown, the realm struggles for prosperity.

Five destinies are revealed.

The temple apprentice turned adventurer.

The last empress of the fallen empire.

The neglected bastard of the rebel king.

The glory-seeking twins from the frozen south.

Together, they will face a rising darkness and mysterious pursuers attracted to the Art Stone as they journey through Elybion in search of the truth.

THE
ART STONE

JESSE A. ELLIS

For those who build and protect
the paths artists travel on.

NORTH ISLES

Watertree

Tyfu

Delphinus City   Phys

SWEDAS

NORTH
APTORIA

DELPHINUS

Lothbrooke

Rotho City

Mudkath

Dalveri

Ly Galia

Simb's Point

The Skyfort

Moorquarry

MAGNAVOZ

The Crossing

FANGOUR

SOUTH
APTORIA

Rock Hollow

Alahdih

Enix

ARILAND

Neva

ILLITAWW

Sol-Boski

ELYBION

in the year of 51 AE

N

In the beginning, the goddess gave twelve stones to the four tribes of Elybion. The stones held incredible transformative magic. Whoever possessed the stones would be responsible for the well-being of the world and its inhabitants.

She gave three stones to the builders of the East to form the world in her image. The builders constructed the grandest structures the world would ever know.

She gave three stones to the artists of the North to create beautiful shapes in her honor. The artists molded the natural beauty of the world for everyone to enjoy.

She gave three stones to the travelers of the West to tra-verse the lands and discover the world. The travelers spread the glory of her power across all lands.

She gave three stones to the protectors of the South to guard the rest of the world against anything seeking to destroy it. The protectors guarded the realm from all threats for many generations.

Over time, the purpose of the stones was forgotten. People became greedy and twisted the stones into their own forms of destructive power.

The goddess sent her son to reestablish love and prosperity in the world, but the people rejected him and his promise of harmony. They killed the goddess's son and waged wars against each other for dominion over the world.

Saddened by the murder of her son, the goddess turned away from the people for thousands of years. During these times, her people carved dividers in the land and established laws to subjugate each other. They reversed the laws she had given them, and with the true power of the stones forgotten, they lived short lives filled with suffering and despair.

When she turned back to see what her people had done, she was angry at what they had become. The people saw the goddess and prayed for vengeance against their fellow men. The goddess sent three lesser gods, who were her guardians, to conquer the world and reestablish her rule. If her people wanted to be subjugated, she would be the subjugator. Her word was the ultimate answer.

The guardians conquered the world and established a new one, void of freedom. They took the stones and hid them deep within the earth. The rule lasted for thousands of years until a group of people broke from their ranks and found the stones. With all twelve stones, they were more powerful than the three guardians combined. However, they didn't use the stones for destruction. Instead, they used the combined power to revive the son.

The goddess saw what her people had done, but she wasn't convinced they would continue to do good. Her son begged the goddess to release the people and send the guardians back to the heavens.

"Every time people are free, they steal, murder, and covet," the goddess said.

"*Yes, and some people create and protect the beautiful things you love,*" her son said.

"*If you love people so, it shall be your responsibility to watch over them from the heavens for all eternity. You may never go down to see them, and if the people ever ravage the world again, I will send my guardians to stay,*" the goddess said.

"*Agreed. I will watch over them,*" her son said.

The goddess, the guardians, and the son returned to the heavens. The people remained free to choose their own destinies.

PART I

ECHOES OF
THE EMPIRE

CHAPTER ONE

The Apprentice

Kai

SUMMER L14, 46 AE

A white marble walkway guides us to the temple. A horde of apprentices rushes up the steps before me. Though some are highborn, we wear the same charcoal-dyed robes. The temple doors, taller than five men, swing open to let us in.

"Foyd, Kaison." The young master holding the ledger stares blankly ahead.

Today I begin my apprenticeship at the Temple of Summer's Light. It's the most important day of my life.

"Yes, thank you. I'm Kai." I wave.

"Master NcTully is waiting for you in the East Library," she says.

I weave through the crowd of other young apprentices and exchange a piece of parchment for a smile. I can't believe I'm here. I find myself continually closing my mouth to keep a smile from swimming to the surface and making me look like a fool. The dyed parchment is the first proof that my apprenticeship is real.

Summer's Light is the base of knowledge and civilization for the realm. Seekers of wisdom travel from every nation to visit the beautiful temple and listen to the masters recite text from the ancient scrolls. Most of the apprentices are devout Artians, but it isn't a requirement to attend. Artism is the most common religion in the North and possibly the oldest in Elybion. My mother, a devout Artian, spent her entire life seeking the necessary knowledge to guide me to Summer's Light.

Summer's Light is the grandest structure in a city where greatness can be lost in a sea of pristine architecture. I slide my fingers down the walls as I walk to the libraries. It's the greatest honor of my life to be here. Summer's Light is a polished beacon of wisdom for the rest of the realm. The governors of Delphinus honor knowledge above anything else. The result is a prospering country. Other nations, in the South, invest their resources in armies and war, but Delphinus and the North Isles have little in terms of an organized army. Our people are pacifists who excel in politics, accounting, and city design.

I enter the East Library. Apprentices in burlap robes rummage through piles of loose parchment.

"Greetings. I was sent to meet Master NcTully." I step into the foyer.

The busy apprentices ignore me. Beyond them, a great Fangourian calendar is carved into the wall. I've never seen a depiction so large. My breath shortens as my excitement grows. *I'm in the right place.*

The Fangourian Empire relied on man because they didn't believe in any god. Near the end of their reign, the great minds of the empire developed the calendar, which united the realm under standard days. Not everything the Fangourians made was destructive.

I start to reach for the carved notches representing days of the year, but I pull back. I'm not sure if I'm allowed to touch it, and I don't think I want to. The chiseled art seems like something that should be cherished and protected. The creators divided the year into eight rulers. Each season has two, and each ruler owns fifty days for a total of four hundred. Even rural families memorize the days. Most cherish the days owned by their country. I count the notches and follow them around the circular calendar to find today's ruler. Today is the fourteenth day of Lebonor, who was the first grandmaster of Summer's Light. What role will I have here with this calendar?

"Over here," a scratchy voice calls from somewhere between the shelves.

"Master NcTully?" I say.

"Yes, yes. Now, come," Master NcTully says.

I follow the man's voice down the row.

"Master?" I search between the shelves.

"This way." Master NcTully appears behind me.

His back is hunched so that his freckled white face, covered with a wiry gray beard, sits on his chest. His robe is midnight-blue like most of the masters'. Unlike most masters', his dress is ragged, with many holes.

"This is where we keep the bits about land creatures. It's common for us to get requests on the subject, especially from ranchers in North Aptoria. They seem especially interested in cattle breeding." Master NcTully runs his fingers along the scrolls as we walk.

Bits of dust fall out and waft into my face. My nose scrunches as I try to fight sneezing.

My tightened face isn't strong enough to hold back the sneeze.

"You'll get used to the dust," Master NcTully says.

We make several turns down the winding shelves filled with scrolls.

"What is your name, son?" Master NcTully stops.

"Kai," I say.

"Kai? No. What is your father's name? Your family name?" he says.

"Foyd. My full name is Kaison Foyd, Master. Foyd is the name passed down from my mother, Master," I say.

"I see. Well, that's a rather boring name. I suppose that it's a common name in Ariland. Pity, there aren't any notable historical figures with that name." He pats a large bound book of texts. "This is where we house all the texts about the families of the realm. My name, NcTully, comes from a long line of stewards here at the temple. Our name originates from Master Garth NcTully." He looks back for a response.

"Oh, really?" I say. He wants me to be impressed, and it's not a lie for me.

"Yes, it's true. My ancestors were among the first who rediscovered the North Isles, which is your home, if I'm not mistaken. You can thank my ancestor that you are here." He laughs and pats the book a few more times.

Part of me wants to thank him, and part of me resents his statement completely. I keep my mouth shut and follow him down another row of shelves.

"We have many requests for proof of heritage and family lineages. It is a constant battle and one we never have enough apprentices for. I think I'll start you here," he says.

"Really? That's great. I've studied many of the ruling houses, and I can recite—"

"You'll need to prove your quill speed. We don't have tolerance for a slow print, and I do hope you know your calendar,"

Master NcTully interrupts.

I nod and remain silent. I know everything about the calendar, but he isn't interested in what I know. I hide a sigh and suppress my excitement about the calendar for the time being. Master NcTully is most interested in making sure I know my place.

"Come this way." NcTully waves me on.

My mother's protection trinket brushes my skin underneath my robe as I turn. Then I remember the songs my mother taught me about the calendar as NcTully guides me. I smile, imagining her reaction if she were to see it carved into the white marble.

☽

My work grows as the days pass.

The Foyer of Letters is the most cluttered excuse for a hall in all of Summer's Light. Apprentices crowd the hall to gather letters for themselves and their masters.

"For Master NcTully?" An apprentice hands me a pile of letters.

"Yes." I accept the stack of mismatched parchment.

I examine the letters for the feathered hand of North Aptoria, which I find pressed into blue wax on one of the sealed letters. Each Aptorian family has a unique emblem, but this feathered hand represents the five major families united.

"This is it." I slide the letter to the top of the pile. "Thank you."

"A delivery from Tyfu for Kaison Foyd." A master shakes the roll of parchment in his hand.

"Yes, Master." I wave my hands, full of letters.

"Here, then." He dumps the scroll into my elbow crease.

The red wax seal of Tyfu bleeds through the parchment, but I know the author.

Blessed Kaison,

How are your studies? Perhaps your letters were lost somewhere in the Northern Sea. I know you are safe with the stone, but I miss you. Take a ferry home to visit us during the journey season. Remember your teachings. Art has a plan for you, and she will guide you through the gateways.

Love, Mother—Joleen Foyd

Her signature is scratched at the bottom of the letter. The journey season is the time when Artians travel to sacred sites for prayer and reflection. The season occurs every other year, and the most recent journey ended a few days ago.

I reach through my robe for the leather-bound trinket. What superstitious bundle has my mother left tethered around my neck?

The crowd of apprentices continues to scurry through the letters of the realm. My eyes connect with one of the masters, dressed in white robes. He stares confidently from across the room. His skin is richly brown, like an Arilandic highborn, while his hair is black, contrasting against his undyed hood. His strikingly violet eyes pierce through me. I feel awkward, like I should look away, but my curiosity hooks me to him. Although I've never seen this man, he seems to recognize me.

A group of apprentices rushes between us, and I lose sight

of the man. Master NcTully will note my absence if I linger any longer. I grab the letters and leave.

●

I've spent weeks copying text about the storage and upkeep of honey. A wealthy lord from Swedas requested the bundle, and we have remained busy since. Stagnant dust floats around us as we work. I haven't left the library since the masters assigned the task. I would like to sleep in my hammock, but the climb up the stairs to my chamber is more of a chore than when I first arrived.

The work is grueling, but no one complains. The others are all my age or perhaps younger. There are two young women sitting in front of me. Their assignment is to log all the species of bees. We work together, yet separately. There are too many words for us to read the same scrolls twice, so we share what we find.

I find one section describing which species produces the best honey.

"Here." I lay the scroll in front of them.

"Thank you," Phanelly Mercah says.

Phanelly is a princess of Dalveri, the capital of the North Aptoria region. Like most women from the Northeast, she is light skinned with a petite physique. Her shoulder-length hair frames her face with perfectly blended bits of wheat and barley. She doesn't show any arrogance, which usually accompanies royalty here at Summer's Light. Lord Davon Mercah, the ruler of North Aptoria, is her father. Since the fall of the empire, many of the great houses have adopted loftier titles, such as King or Prime, yet the North Aptorians refused the more extravagant names. I don't know their reasons, but I like when fewer people in the realm call themselves king or queen.

Phanelly's friend is Sanya Samon. She's equally as attractive. Her skin is flawlessly dark, like a carefully stained wood. Sanya is related to the queen of Magnavoz and looks more Magnavozian than most.

At Summer's Light, highborn apprentices are as common as lowborn. We wear the same clothes, and the masters discourage the use of titles. Still, nothing wards off their intimidating looks.

I carry a dry ink bottle to the front of the library, where a large vase of ink sits. Phanelly looks up from her work as I pass them. Her expressions are kind, but I'm uncomfortable.

"Pardon. Do you mind if I take a few drops of ink?" I say.

"Please do," Phanelly says.

Usually the royals don't acknowledge me. Her kindness is as rare as it is genuine. I smile and crank the lever, which pumps the ink out of the vase and through a filtered cloth. As the ink drips through the cloth, I watch Sanya and Phanelly work. Phanelly's elegant script-hand produces line after line of flawless text, while Sanya's hand is quicker and less refined.

"Your ink." Sanya points at my overfilled bottle.

Droplets of ink splash onto the floor. I try to contain the rest, yet a clumsy jerk causes the ink to pour onto my robe. Sanya laughs, and Phanelly maintains her composure.

"Kaison, that's your name, right?" Phanelly says.

My face flushes, and I wipe my ink-stained hands on my robe.

"Uh, yes. I'm Kaison Foyd, but please call me Kai," I say.

"Very well, Kai. Aren't you from the islands?" She writes as she speaks, looking up to me every other line.

"Yes, that's correct. I'm from a little village called Watertree," I say.

"That's a lovely name for a town. I would like to hear more

about it. I'm Phan, and this is my friend Sanya." She points the end of her feathered quill toward her friend.

"Hello." Sanya doesn't look up.

"Hi. It's nice to meet you both," I say.

"Are you going to listen to Master Erwon and Master Yessic on the Plat?"

The Plat is a broad surface raised in the center of the garden. It is a holy place where masters give speeches on their discoveries. Sometimes the masters will have differing opinions, and they settle them on the same stage. During the debates, apprentices, other masters, and city folk form the audience. It is a battle of wits, where words can be as damaging as punches.

"Yes, I suppose I will." I casually shrug, and I walk back to my seat.

"You can sit with us if you like." Phan turns back to me.

For a moment I'm stunned. It seems like too kind an offer.

"Thank you," I say.

When she turns away, I smile. Sanya catches my awkward grin. She frowns and lowers her eyebrows. I casually begin my script, and my smile fades.

"I'm tired of copying text. I thought we would be learning more interesting things by now," Sanya says.

"We will be teaching the next rank of learners soon," Phan says.

"I can't imagine filling any more pages with this boring drivel about bees." Sanya lies down over the table.

"It's not so bad. Look at this line right here." Phan points to the text she is reading from.

I edge closer to see what she is pointing at. Sanya waves her hand to shoo Phan away.

"See this, Kai?" Phan notices me peeking from behind her.

"What's that?" I say.

"Look here. Bees are vital to the success of farms. Locations with bees near are more likely to produce high-yielding crops.

That's pretty special. If you ask me, the bee is a direct gift from Art." Phan rapidly taps her parchment with her quill.

I nod and continue to work, which suddenly seems more gratifying.

Later in the evening, I leave the Plat and journey through the garden to my tower. The debates were lively but long for a group of tired apprentices. As I walk through the fragrant or-chard, exhaustion pulls my back into a hunch. Pigeons coo, skirt away, and circle back behind me. Phan and Sanya were kind to invite me to sit with them. No one talked, because speaking from the crowd is considered disrespectful, but even in silence, it was nice to not be alone in the crowd.

I reach the bottom of the tower. As I peer up the endless steps, lit by wavering candlelight, I exhale a long sigh. I ascend to the top chamber for the first time in weeks. The moonlights are shining through the window and under my door before I enter. I drop my satchel on the ground and stumble over to my hammock in the corner. The chamber is large enough to accom-modate several more apprentices. Empty hammocks hang in each corner. I'm the only apprentice foolish enough to climb to the top of the tower. Giving way to fatigue, I fall into my hammock. It swings and sways as my eyes shutter closed.

I wake to silence. The moonlights have faded, leaving only gloomy darkness. Wooden planks creak from across the chamber. I peer up and across the room to find the source in the darkness. Nothing. My outstretched neck relaxes, and I roll back to the corner.

When my eyes meet the corner, a man with hot breath and

glowing violet eyes is waiting.

I scream and scramble to fight myself free. Something is squeezing tighter around my waist and neck. The hammock? It's wrapped around me. With exhausted lungs and a wildly beat-ing heart, I thrash and scratch until I twist myself into another knot. One end of the hammock tears, and I fall to the ground as it unravels. The trinket unwinds from its pouch on my neck. Herbs sprinkle onto my chest, and a beautiful stone slides across the chamber floor. The moonlights have returned. Their radi-ance seems to flow through the stone like waves into a cove.

The man is gone, or was he ever here? I light candles all around my chamber and lean my back against the bricks. The fear of the man returning keeps me awake.

●

The next morning, NcTully is waiting to give us new as-signments. Phan and Sanya move back to the West Library to aid Master Erwon with a finance assignment. I remain to repli-cate and update family trees. Though I'm surrounded by other apprentices, I feel lonelier without Phan.

My mind wanders to the glowing violet eyes. What magic possessed me? I need answers, but the ever-increasing piles of parchment nag at me.

"Begin. I'll have more for you soon." NcTully scurries away.

I skim through the pile of texts until I find one that inter-ests me.

"Yes. Nagidah." I pull out the black book with crimson stitching.

"Kai." Master NcTully glares at me through the dusty hall.

The hardened leather cover has a sword encircled by roses. Below the emblem, "Nagidah" reads in crimson and gold thread. House Nagidah are the rulers of Magnavoz. Their crown rests at Rock Hollow, which is the largest castle in Magnavoz and the highest structure in the realm. Their castle is planted within and on top of a great mesa on the Magnavozian Plain. The Nagidah family led the rebellion that vanquished the Fangourian Empire. Though Nagidah is not native to Magnavoz, they rule like they have always been there. They are one of the most powerful families in Elybion, and they have a new addition to their family. A third child, by the name of Valisha. The tree shows two older children named Vega and Velvia. They were born one year apart to King Donak Nagidah and Queen Tyra Nagidah. The queen's description has a secondhand addition that shows her maiden name, Samon. Samon is a powerful family with ties to both Magnavoz and Ariland. They have the financial skills of Arilandic tradesmen, while their political prowess matches that of the greatest Magnavozian rulers.

I carefully reproduce the Nagidah tree on a blank parchment. As I dot the last details, Master NcTully slams another pile of books and loose parchment beside me. I shake my sore, ink-covered hand. I can't pity myself. There are many other nations with many other people. Each has their own concerns. I grab the top parchment and continue my work.

CHAPTER TWO

The Empress

Lifia

AUTUMN R49, 47 AE

I sit in the hard wooden throne in the center of the Orb of Dominion. The Orb is gripped by a jagged spire of obsidian at the top of the Evoni Skyfort. In one direction, the canopy of the Okiari Forest spreads wide until it opens to the beaches of the gulf. In the opposite direction, forking roads split the forest. One road snakes back to the beach, and the other rolls west to the Necklace River.

Shifting back and forth, I search for comfort, but there is none to be found. Delicate artwork covers the backrest of the throne, which reaches toward the ceiling. The carvings illustrate the history of our once great empire. Depictions of Emperor Revan are centered at the crest. Revan, the first and last emperor, was the first to unite all the people of Elybion under one rule. The depictions of our history continue down the ridge of the throne, with his daughter standing beside a proud Fangourian tiger. Eiame was the first in a long line of empresses. Though she never married, she bore many children. Her daughters are beside her, each with their own tiger cub. Eiame's eldest daughter, Peiliname, followed in her mother's footsteps, creating our first traditions. She is carved the largest of her sisters, below her mother. Peiliname passed more than five hundred years ago, but we still follow her traditions today.

"Keep your back straight and eyes forward, Lifia. Don't blink unless it is necessary," my mother, Empress Dianame, says curtly.

The empress is slender and strong. Her eyes reflect a version of mine, though wiser and filled with a richer green.

"Yes, Your Imperial Majesty." I practice my plain face.

To show emotion would show vulnerability and give enemies an opening to attack. Now that I know the basics, my mother grooms me for the harsh ways of the world. Politics is the most important topic, yet the easiest to fail.

"That's enough for today." Her shoulders relax as her empress persona fades.

The tension held in my neck releases. My posture returns to its imperfect base to mirror hers.

"What dance shall we practice next?" She smiles with a rejuvenated glow.

"The beautiful dance of the crane," I say.

"Yes." She turns away. "To dance like the majestic crane, you must have perfect balance."

She stands on one foot and stretches her other leg behind her back until it rises above her head. She is nearly fifty, but her body doesn't betray her in the slightest. I have practiced to master my body the way she has, but I'm not as fluid with the movements. I envy my mother's perfect form.

"Your staff?" she says.

Her long, soft hair falls down her back with perfect obedience. Her neck, stretching above her shoulders, is the only bare skin exposed. It is flawless and of the lightest of Fangourian tones.

I reach for the rugged staff my mother bestowed on me years ago. I tap it twice against the marble floor to signify my readiness. Without looking at me, she lowers herself down to the floor in a hitch-free slither, like a serpent. Keeping her eyes closed, she recites her first combat lesson of the day.

"The snake slithering in the stream while she drinks is the only thing a crane fears." She crawls toward me, keeping her chest close to the ground. The movement seems unnatural for a person, but not for the empress of Fangour.

I slap the ground between us as a warning. My staff cracks against the floor, and the sound echoes around the Orb. She switches direction and rolls into a ball, stands on both hands, and splits her legs. I recognize her movements. She has performed a similar tactic against me before. This time, I'm wiser. She steps in and out of my range to lull me into a false sense of security. I keep a plain face and loosen the grip on my staff. She stops and rises to her feet, which causes me to tighten my grip once more.

She resumes a more natural stance. Unfortunately, the empress is far less predictable standing straight with her feet together. To complete the threat, she forms a double fist in front of her chest. She whips her leg at my shins. I'm ready and move away in time.

"Exquisite, Lifia." Her eyes remain closed. "The lesson is simple. Yet it is a lesson you must never forget. You are always in battle, no matter what form or position your adversary takes."

"I understand."

"Good. Now, attack me!" she shouts.

The sudden elevation in her voice rattles my confidence enough for me to second-guess my approach. I tighten my grip as I sneak a step forward. I yell as I swing in her direction. My forearms tense in anticipation of contact, but she veers left. I stop, pretending to study her.

"Have you found a shiny spot peering through the branches?" She holds back a smile.

"Yes, I believe...I have." I swing my staff around in a circular flurry.

Each time my staff's blunted edge comes near, she slips out of range. Every empty attack drains me. I'm breathing harder, and sweat is running down my neck, causing hair to clump together. I pause for a moment. She is a master of deception, but her eyes are closed, and she will not open them. Her hearing is impeccable, but sounds of combat are not always truthful.

I shout a grunt while standing still, to test her reaction. A smile is all she returns. I perform a sequence of quick jabs. Then I stop abruptly in a wide stance. I wait half a moment longer than is natural to swing a side swat. All the while, I maintain my silence and hold my breath. The end of my staff brushes the silk trim of her robe right before she dodges. She reveals deep emeralds for eyes.

"From now on, I will train you while using all my senses. You have learned two of the most important lessons today: never play by someone else's rules, and always be aware of the many forms an enemy can take." The empress returns as my mother's shoulders draw back and her back stiffens.

The throne guards retract their crossed spears as we step down the steps that lead to the skybridges and sanctums below. Each guardsman wears a great hardened shell of armor, covering every part of his body. The taller guard wears the helmet of an elegant snake, while the shorter guard wears a helmet shaped into a snarling ape. Their helmets signify their lineage. Older families wear armor with the markings of animals, while others wear armor marked with their family's tradecraft.

The empress breaks my attention away from the guards with a lecture as she guides me to the libraries.

●

Autumn chills to winter. Many lessons later we are walk-ing in the Okiari Forest. A new year is here. Some of the trees are both taller and larger than the Skyfort. Most trees are too large for four people to reach around and meet each other's hands. The many branches hamper sunlight in reaching the for-est floor. Yet when the branches are situated perfectly, light penetrates through, creating bright spots among the litterfall.

I come as often as I can to visit my greatest ally, Bulba.

However, this visit is different. Today we are avoiding contact with Magnavozian diplomats. A herald informed us of the Magnavozians before we set out into the forest. Their en-campment was seen a few miles into the jungle. The vegetation will impede their pace, but they are still expected to arrive to-morrow.

My mother was surprised when the herald informed us of the sizable Magnavozian party.

"Why did they bring so many? Have we not done enough to accommodate their demands?"

The herald leaned in to whisper in her ear. I was unable to decipher the message. My mother's lip twitched, but only for a moment, before we left for our jungle lecture.

A sudden fleeing of birds ushers in a gigantic creature. Sauntering between the trees, the tiger rivals a stallion in size. He stretches his mouth open, showing fangs like swords.

Before I can brace myself, he brushes his thick crown against me. The creature is my friend, my Bulba, and the last Fangourian tiger. Legends say that the Fangourian tigers are unlike any other creature in the world. They are more intelligent and far better friends to humans than their orange cousins in Ariland. I wouldn't know. As the daughter of the empress, I've never traveled far from the Skyfort.

Our family has always held a special bond with the tigers, and Bulba's mother protected mine for many years. During the peak of our empire, we rode the tigers into battle. They were quicker, more cunning, and far deadlier than any other mount on the field.

"You have done well training him." My mother strokes the other side of the hulking mass of fur between us. Coming from the only other person who understands the tigers, the praise is meaningful. I imagine her relationship with her tiger companion was as strong as mine is with Bulba. I can't believe he was once smaller than me.

We arrive at our special spot in the forest. Small boulders, smoothed by the rain, form a half circle around a larger boulder. We call them the sitting stones. Bulba leaps up onto a branch above us as we settle on the worn flats.

"What are they expecting from us?" I grab my mother's right hand as she puts her left arm around me.

Splintering snaps crackle above us. The branch that Bulba has decided to rest on fractures under his tremendous weight. He abandons his post and hops down to the ground with a light pounce. Circling around us, Bulba finds his favorite seat beside us on the moss. He nuzzles his giant head into my side and rolls over onto his back.

"He may be the largest I've ever seen. It seems fitting for the last of these majestic animals to be the kingliest," my mother says.

We laugh at Bulba rolling back and forth on his back as he

attempts to snuggle closer to us.

"The diplomats." I look at my mother more seriously.

"They want to see you as the empress. They want to see you in power, and me stripped of it," she replies mildly.

My stomach sinks. Am I ready for this? It's not our tradition to unceremoniously change the leader of the empire. Before the war, before the fall, we were true empresses ruling a true empire. Our empire was vast and reached through every home in the realm. The responsibility of ruling only passed to the next empress once the previous had passed away. Now we are political stewards in charge of a diminished portion of the land. Our traditions are meaningless to the tyrant Magnavozian leaders. They only call us empresses to prevent our people from revolting.

"I'm nervous to meet the Magnavozian representatives," I say.

"You will be excellent. I have trained you well in all I know of diplomacy. Remember what I have taught you, and you will succeed as our empress." She lightly runs her fingers through my hair.

"Do you think they are coming for anything else?" I say.

"Whatever they are here for...they will respect us. We are not as weak as they wish us to be," she says.

Her calming voice brings me confidence. I will perform my duties as expected.

"Bulba," I call.

We rise to venture back to the high towers of the Evoni Skyfort. The Skyfort is the husk that seats our hollow empire. It represents everything that we once were. Now we are secluded in our black diamond between the forests.

Bulba follows us to the massive stone walls of our home before he leaves us and returns to his kingdom in the forest.

I'm seated in the carved throne as the Magnavozian diplomats enter the heart of the Skyfort. My mother sits to my
right, in my deceased father's open seat. Our guards wait in the
sanctum below, leaving us alone with the two diplomats. I wait
for the perfect moment to speak.

*Never take your eyes off your guests as they enter, and do
not speak until they are still.*

My mother's words reverberate in my mind.

They are both tall men. One is old, with freckled skin
sagging around his cheeks. He wears a crimson cape fastened
to dyed leather vestments. He carries a small sheathed dagger
with a golden handle. It's a treasure taken from the Fangourian
Vaults. His illegitimate possession of the dagger angers me, but
I won't show it.

The second man has a kind young face and dark tan skin,
like many Magnavozian highborns. He stands to the left of the
elderly man.

"Welcome to the Evoni Skyfort. We are honored to have
you as our guests."

"Thank you for having us, Your Imperial Majesty." The
younger guest bows onto one knee.

The older man dips lazily with a simple lowering of his
head. I resist the urge to look at my mother for guidance. Is this
a sign of disrespect, or has his age tightened his back beyond
bending?

"I'm Commander Lord Pikon Gravesmon, and this is Prince
Vega Nagidah, firstborn of King Donak Nagidah and heir to the
throne." Gravesmon gestures toward the prince.

Never show anger to the enemy.

My mother's teachings continue to guide me.

"I'm pleased to meet you," I say.

"Dianame...how are you faring in your twilight?" Gravesmon looks at my mother.

She rises and bows deeply to both men without uttering a

word. It's essential for my future and our captors' peace of mind for her to be submissive.

"Your beauty has not been exaggerated," Prince Vega says.

He seems to be speaking to me, but I'm taken aback by his forward compliment. I resist giving a response. The prince is well-known for his courage and success in tournaments around the realm. I have heard rumors that he is one of the handsomest men in all Elybion. His bone structure is perfectly carved, with a strong chin, but it doesn't overpower his frame. Below his thick, well-groomed eyebrows, his dark eyes are large and soft. His hair is more Arilandic in style and straightness, while his skin is reddish brown like that of many Magnavozian men. Seeing him now, I understand why the maidens speak so highly of him. I have never been to a royal tournament to witness him or any other dregadin in combat, but I can recognize a warrior when I see one.

Gravesmon jumps right into a rant about finances. Currently we are making progress toward repaying our debt to Magnavoz. He continues to drone on about taxes and other oppressive items on his agenda. However, nothing the diplomat demands seems to be up for debate. I struggle to maintain a presence in the throne room. The prince doesn't appear to be the least bit interested in Gravesmon's agenda. He maintains eye contact with me, offering sweet smiles whenever our eyes meet. It's difficult to maintain composure, so I allow a half smile to creep across my lips. What does he want from me?

Finally Gravesmon wraps up his long-winded lecture with a hard cough. "Which brings us to the most important reason for our meeting," he says.

Vega takes a step forward to me and unsheathes his sword. My hands tighten, and I begin to perspire, yet I maintain my plain face.

"I will be forthcoming." Prince Vega lays his sword down at my feet. "This isn't a regular diplomatic meeting. My father, the king, has commanded me to ask for your hand in marriage, so that we may finally unite our people."

Neither I nor my mother move, but my mind is swirling around in contemplation of what to do next. My eyes shift to my mother in hopes that she can calm the storm.

"We do not follow the same traditions as you do in Magnavoz." My mother shifts forward in her seat.

The prince exudes confidence, even without armor or guards.

"This is not a proposal, Dianame," Gravesmon says.

"I know exactly what this is. If this were a serious proposal, we would be much more inviting." She settles back, away from the edge of her seat.

I lift up from the seat of the throne and glide across the platform above them.

"We are honored to have you here, and your request has been received. It is not our custom to have formal marriages, let alone arranged... However, we will consider your proposal, Prince Vega." I smile down at them.

"You little Fangourian witch. You will not speak of your evil ways to the prince. It is a privilege to marry into the royal family, one you and your family do not deserve." Gravesmon spits at my feet.

My mother is at the edge of her seat again. I search her face, needing her help, but she only returns a look of contemplation.

"That is enough." Prince Vega raises his hand to halt Gravesmon. The prince grinds his teeth as he glares at his subject.

Gravesmon takes a step back, raising his hands and lowering his head to the prince.

"Your Imperial Majesty, I assure you this is a legitimate proposal. Please take my sword, and I will be a pledged king to you and your people." With open hands, he invites me to step down from the carved throne to meet him.

He is persuasive in both his words and his gestures. I want to say yes to him because I don't want Fangour to suffer for us refusing, though I don't fully understand what I am saying yes to. Our ways are changing, and we will need to conform with the rest of Elybion eventually. I never anticipated my duty of marriage arriving so soon.

"We will need time to ponder your request, Prince Vega," I say.

Mother glances at me shortly to inform me that she approves of my response.

"There is nothing to ponder," Gravesmon retorts. "We are uniting our lands. This is the easy way."

Several Magnavozian soldiers begin to flood the throne room.

"What is this? Have you lost all respect?" My mother fades as the empress steps forward. Her voice is eerie and as calm as I've ever witnessed. Tiny bumps rise on my back.

"We aren't asking," Gravesmon says.

Fear breaks my plain face, which I maintained so well before this moment. Prince Vega is still reaching out to me.

"Please, Lifia?" the prince begs with a tremble in his voice, as if he knows the outcome if I say no, and he desperately wants to avoid it.

Before I can decide, Gravesmon steps up onto the raised platform. With the grace of a fox, my mother rises and slides in front of me. I feel the tension rising over a mountain.

"We will ponder your kind proposal." Her hands rest on the back of her hips and grip her hidden daggers.

She is close to striking. I wish this wasn't the day I became the empress. I wish I had more days like before, when I was running in the forest.

"If only we could allow you the time to ponder... Our people need us to unite before everything falls apart. Please." Prince

Vega's hand falls to his side as he accepts the denial of his request.

He takes one last look of pity at me as he turns to walk away. As soon as he steps through the door, his soldiers fill in the place where he stood.

"Mother?"

"Dance as a crane, my daughter," she replies calmly.

"Detain her." Gravesmon points at the coiled cobra that is my mother.

Before he lowers his pointed finger, the cobra slips down beside him. She cleaves his hand from his wrist in one elegant swipe of her daggers. Blood squirts out violently as he grips his wrist to cover the fresh wound.

The sight of blood conjures my training to take over, and I begin to become hyperaware of every movement in the room. I grab the scepter leaning against the wall and follow the cobra into combat without hesitation. The soldiers are swinging at my mother while Gravesmon retreats behind his guards and spits curses at us both.

"Fangourian bitch!" Gravesmon withdraws with a bloody stump where his right hand once resided.

Already my mother is dodging sloppy attacks as she slices through Magnavozian soldiers. They attempt to capture her, but she is untouchable. One soldier gurgles gruesome whispers as he chokes on the blood spilling into his throat. The empress twirls her blades as she dances and cuts them in every vulnerable spot between their armor. Her blade screeches across metal like a fork screeching across a plate before it meets flesh.

I can hear crashes beyond the doors, but I have no view of the battle ensuing outside.

Have you found a sunspot?

My mother's voice continues to guide me.

When two soldiers attempt to grab me, I take the end of my scepter and jab it into one of their throats. He goes down coughing and choking. The other soldier drops her sword, tackles me, and pulls me to the ground. She is a powerful woman who is well trained in the maneuverability of her body. I grunt as I force her off. Before I can completely free myself from her grasp, she grabs me from behind. Then she pushes my face into the cold obsidian floor. My nostrils fill with scents of the sour fruit mixed with vinegar used to polish the floors. Her fingers dig in around my neck. I hear a choking gurgle followed by a hot mist splattering on my neck. The soldier releases her grip as warm, thick liquid replaces the mist pouring down my neck. The soldier falls dead beside me.

"Breathe." My mother pulls me to my feet.

The room is covered in slain Magnavozian soldiers. Our gowns are stained in Magnavozian crimson. Ten soldiers lie dead at our feet, but we hear more coming. I'm stunned by the heavy scent of blood filling the room. My body doesn't want to move, but the Magnavozian soldiers press against our guards outside.

"Come." My mother holds her hand out to me, and I grab it like I did as a child.

We run behind the carved throne to a seemingly solid obsidian wall. She presses in a loose brick with her foot, and it falls into the darkness beyond. Next, rumbling creaks crack from the other side. I raise my eyebrows. Every brick falls through the floor in a perfect cascade, right to the point where the top blocks fall flush with the floor. The transformation ends with a cold, dark hallway open in front of us.

The doors break open, and air drifts in to fill the void. Soldiers crash into the throne room behind us. My mother pulls me with her as she treks into the darkness. When we pass the threshold of the dark, she pulls a lever, and another cascade of bricks falls behind us. We are enclosed in complete darkness.

"The tunnels." I cling to my mother in the dark.

It has been many years since she showed them to me. I almost forgot they existed. We step down a circular flight of stone stairs that ends at another narrow tunnel hidden between the walls of the Skyfort.

"I've shown you all the secrets of the Skyfort as you've grown." My mother pulls me along in the dark. "Our lord, Emperor Revan, built the Skyfort to protect us from invasions like these. Many of the secrets have been forgotten over time, but I've taught you all I know."

Her feet quit shuffling. She reaches out with her hand holding mine, and we feel around on a solid wall with our outstretched fingers.

"How do you finish a throne dance?" she says.

I never remember what the throne dance looks like, but I remember the answer.

"With a right slide, turn left, a right-slide turn back to the right, and end with a left slide." I let my thoughts evolve into words as we twist and slide around walls to match the dance sequence.

A glimmer peeks out from the end of the tunnel. We edge closer and closer to the light. As it dissolves, a canopy of trees begins where bricks form a secret portcullis.

Below us, at the edge of the tunnel, the Okiari Forest is outlined by the setting sun.

"We will meet where Bulba nests." She releases my hand and stares lovingly into my eyes.

She kisses my forehead and brushes away the stray hairs falling into my sight. Then she gestures to a coil of rope before she backs away into the darkness.

"Wait. Aren't you coming?" I call to her before she disappears.

"The Evoni Bow," she says.

The Evoni Bow is our sacred weapon, crafted before the empire was formed. Revan carried the bow when he conquered the realm, and legends say he never released a poor arrow from its string. She won't leave the relic in the hands of Magnavoz.

"Mother," I call out into the darkness.

She's gone. I don't want to go alone, but I need to be brave for Fangour. I grind my teeth as I take the rope, tie it to a branch, and begin to rappel down.

Sliding branch to branch, I descend to the forest floor. The rope length ends as I begin to smell the honey fungus, which only grows near the base of trees. I reach the lowest branch capable of supporting my weight. The ground lies fifteen feet below. I scoot onto the branch, which flexes as it nears the ground. At the end of the branch, I'm swaying in the instability of the narrowing twigs. I wedge the scepter between two of the closest twigs, and I hang down from the edge of the branch. My feet are as close as possible to the ground before I drop.

The scepter is loosened by the branch. It is flung into the darkness, ricocheting off branches above. I tuck and roll onto the surface of the forest.

After gathering myself, I look up to see the deep red horizon shining through the gaps in the branches as the sun makes its own descent.

CHAPTER THREE

The Slayer

Lifia

WINTER S22, 48 AE

The moonlights are shining through the branches when I arrive at the sitting stones. The largest of the rocks is lit the brightest, while the smaller stones are hidden in the darkness cast by its shadow. The trek through the untamed forest was long. I imagined my mother might beat me here, but the glade is empty. How long will it take her to retrieve the bow and meet me?

The temperature drops with the chill of night. The winters in northern Fangour are rarely cold, but tonight is the exception.

I sit on the stone and cover myself with my heavy gown. My body is restless and uncomfortable from the coolness of the rock on my bottom. Eventually, my warmth is shared with the foundation, and I settle in.

A figure rustles in the woods behind me.

"Bulba?"

No. If it was Bulba, he would already be nuzzling his head into my shoulder. The prince slips out from behind one of the massive trunks.

"Prince Vega? How?" I utter with a sharpness in my voice.

"Lifia. You must come with me." He holds out his leather-gloved hand.

"I...I don't understand. How did you find me here? Where's my mother?"

I glide to my feet, away from the prince. My voice trembles as I fear the worst has happened to my mother.

"Please. You don't understand...I will keep you safe, and no harm will come to you or your mother if you just follow me," he assures me urgently.

I can't quite form his face clearly in the moonlights, but I sense no betrayal in his words. Yet he is right. I don't understand. I don't understand why all this has happened. Why are they forcing this marriage upon me?

"Prince Vega, what—?"

An arrow flies over my shoulder and into the prince. My mother, the cobra, saunters up on her thin, padded slippers. She has the Evoni Bow raised in a threatening stance and faced toward the prince. The relief of seeing her alive is quickly replaced by the horror of what she has done.

"Mother!" I scream.

The prince falls to his knees with an arrow wedged below his collarbone. It is a near miss of his heart. It is a miss she would only have made on purpose.

"They want to enslave us and take what is ours. No matter

the kind words the prince shares with you, they are all lies." She maintains her aim.

She is a predator, and the prince is her prey. I want her to stop. I want all this to end so I can awake from this nightmare.

"Our empire was taken long ago." Tears are swelling in my eyes.

The temporary peace in the realm is fading with the events of the night. My mother takes her dark eyes off the prince.

"I am sorry, my crane." My mother relaxes her aim and releases her bowstring gently.

There is sorrow in her voice. She knows I'm right and that she is equally responsible for the escalation of tonight. She steps toward the prince as she lowers the Evoni Bow, but quickly jumps back and pulls her bowstring onto the anchor point on her cheek. Dark figures step up beyond the crouched prince. For a moment, it was over, but now it will never end.

"Kill them both." Lord Pikon Gravesmon appears behind Prince Vega with many soldiers at his back.

"No." Vega chokes on the pain.

Bulba, who was watching from the trees above, announces himself as the ruler of the forest. The vibration of his roar makes bumps sprout down my spine. Branches shake above my head, followed by a thud as he leaps down. With bared teeth, he stomps out one paw after the other, entering the space between the soldiers and my mother.

Bulba poses in all his glory. His fur is as thick as the branches above and as tough as the bark covering the trunks. Some of the men behind the prince gasp and shuffle backward in pure instinctive fear. Bulba notices their retreat and roars a threat at them.

"You dare bring this abomination here to threaten the prince and his men?" Gravesmon shouts.

"We do not enslave our creatures as you do," I cry out.

Our exchange initiates the verbal battle, and Bulba will not be threatened without challenge. He snaps at the air in front of the soldiers with his powerful jaws. His bite can break the limbs of tree or man. Still, I'm afraid for his safety and the lives of the soldiers he may take. Before I have time to decide whether to command him to retreat or attack, Gravesmon shoves his soldiers forward, urging them to kill us.

"Breathe." My mother sings the melody of her calming voice.

She knows where this is going, and she draws the bowstring tight against her flawless face as she takes aim. I straggle behind until my mother's words finally connect with me. I'm revitalized as I inhale longer than is natural and widen my stance on the moist forest floor. We will choose the hard, honorable way, as the Evoni family always has.

"Attack." I click my tongue at Bulba.

His ears twitch. In the next moment, he pounces. An arrow flies into the eye of the soldier in front of the commander, Gravesmon. He steps behind the next line of defense and commands his soldiers to charge. There are more than ten soldiers, but even more await. Reluctantly they move forward into the jaws of Bulba as he begins to shred them apart. He rips off limbs with single swipes of razor-sharp claws. The more they attack, the more ferociously he cuts through their paper armor. The violence that ensues is hard to watch, yet I can't look away from his compelling power.

My mother hands me the Evoni Bow and a stocked quiver of arrows. Then she continues to dance into the fray with Bulba. Without hesitation, I claim the bow and take aim with fluid instinct. The years of practice are engraved into my eyes and wrists. I focus on the other archers as I begin to loose. One, two, three, four arrows and soldiers drop in a row. They are not paying heed to my fatal stingers as I pluck them out with little effort. I am only a nuisance compared to their real focus: the brown beast thrashing in elegant fury. My mother is dismantling the wall of soldiers nearest to Gravesmon as Bulba and I finish our efforts against the archers.

A man shouts as he pushes past the other soldiers. He's wearing a plate helm, mail gauntlets, and no other armor besides thick muscles between him and the air. With his head above the others, he is easy to keep track of.

He charges, leading with his spear. I try to stop him with a barrage of arrows, but he is too swift to be easily taken. He slides out of the way, repositions for his target, and continues running. A hulking shadow collides with the giant soldier before I can aim another.

"Bulba!" I scream.

Bulba roars another powerful declaration as the spear enters his flesh. He swipes the last soldier in front of him and spins around to find the deliverer of the spear. He pounces and slashes straight across the bare chest of the soldier. His paws are like battering rams as he slams the man to the ground. I take aim at him as he falls. I loosen an arrow aimed at the giant's head. It ricochets off his plate helm, splintering into shards. Having stopped the last enemy, Bulba begins to limp away toward a break in the tree line, with the spear still stuck in him.

My grip loosens, and I let the bow relax to the ground. I run to my friend to guard him against further harm. He shifts his weight toward me, and I press onto his blood-matted fur. Before the Magnavoz arrived, he was my baby Bulba. Tonight he is a battle-damaged warrior. I grab his massive head in my arms to hug him as he loses stride and falls.

I turn around as my mother slays the last soldier protecting Lord Gravesmon. Gravesmon retreats through the forest, back toward the Skyfort, but my mother doesn't follow him. From my crouched position, I calmly raise my bow to line up where his throat will be right before he disappears behind the trees.

A man rises from the ground near my mother. I swiftly turn my arrow toward him and release a perfect shot at his shoulder farthest from her. The arrow punctures the man right as he stabs her through the back with a final thrust. My heart falls out into the pit in my stomach. My mother spins around, slicing the man's throat with an elegant dancer's pirouette.

Mother?

It's too late. The entire blade juts out from her chest. She falls to the ground as gracefully as anyone could with a sword in them.

"No!" I release a shrill screech as I drop the bow.

The forest is quiet again. Grasping her soft cheek in my hand, I press my head into hers gently. I wail. My body falls limp with grief as I hold my mother in my arms.

"What do I do?" Tears cloud my vision.

She opens her emerald eyes and reaches to touch her soft hand to my chin. She exhales her last, long breath. I kiss her and rest her gently against the sitting stone.

I don't know what to do or where to go. I lie beside her, in the cool dried blood, crying like a helpless kitten.

Eventually, my grief gives way to my fear of Gravesmon returning. I try to rise, but my aching heart pulls me back to my knees. Is this really happening?

"What do I do?" I ask.

"Survive," she would say.

As I stand, I peer down at the man whose sword is in my mother. Prince Vega lies with two arrows piercing him. An out-pour of his life's blood soaks the forest floor. One bolt is in his collarbone, the other below his neck. A clean swipe across his beautiful throat finishes the image I will never forget.

I stumble over the bodies and clumsily chase after Bulba, looking back once more at my beautiful mother shining in the moonlights.

CHAPTER FOUR

The Akkimon

Marr

WINTER S23, 48 AE

Lined up in the pit below the temples of Sol-Boski, we perform our precombat rituals. Each of us represents a clan. Today we fight and learn together. Next season, we will participate in the trials for a chance to become members of the elite warrior class, the Wrekk-Taww. Everyone is eager for a chance to show off their skills.

Jupp, my brother, shakes his long arms lightly to warm up. He resembles our father. They have round noses and the squared shoulders of a mountain. His coarse black hair has grown out from ten days without a shave. Those who have never seen Jupp might say I resemble our father, but I'm a slighter mold.

Hellahh, of the Unthapp clan, pulls her head to the side to stretch her neck. She is stout and walks with a wide gait. Like many of the Unthapp, her bronzed-brown skin contrasts with the snow wafting around us. Her father was a friend of my father. They fought alongside each other in the war against the North. When her father passed, our father took Hellahh to train her alongside his own children.

Kagg, of the Navijj clan, swings a heavy hammer in each hand. His long, braided hair indicates his high standing in the Navijj clan. I'm not familiar with the Navijj warrior, but many have attested to his skills in single combat. I'm eager to see if the rumors are true. Nestled in solitude in the western valleys of the mountains, his clan created the fighting forms that all clans have adopted.

I practice my breathing to remain calm and conserve as much vigor as possible. I am Marr of Clan Erowkahnn. We are the keepers of the chokworm silk and the leaders of all Illitaww. Before our father rose to power, we were regarded as a weak clan, filled with more den-mothers than warriors.

Our father, King Lakk, and a few others watch us from above the pit. Many clans have not yet arrived. Those of us here are the early arrivers, and we must prepare the city for the other clans. Many people travel to Sol-Boski during winter for trade and fierce competitions. In Sol-Boski our ancestors built permanent dwellings, arenas, and temples, which we make our winter homes. In the remainder of Illitaww, it's uncommon to have a permanent home.

"Marr, keep your shield arm high." Father paces around the pit.

Kagg's blunted sword grazes over the top of my shield and bashes into the side of my head. Flashes of light shine from the back of my eyes, and I'm falling to the frozen ground before I can blink. When I realize what has happened, Jupp has already taken my place in the spar, and he has begun dismantling Kagg's defense.

"When you leap forward to attack, you tend to let your shield arm waver in favor of a more powerful attack." Our father jumps down into the pit and begins to criticize my defense in detail.

Hellahh steps back, lowering her eyes when Father enters.

"You can't throw ice every time, or you will lose control." He waves me over. "Show me your sword grip."

I flip my wrist over to show him my grip on the blunted practice sword. Meanwhile, Jupp avenges my defeat by knocking Kagg unconscious with a brutal slam.

"Good. Hold on as if it were your lifemate. Soft, yet unbreakable," my father says.

The sword hilt sits perfectly in my palm. Nothing has ever fit more perfectly anywhere. Yet the shield is cumbersome, and an unnatural weight against my forearm.

"Now, reclaim the glory that your brother has taken from you." He points at Jupp while keeping his gaze upon me.

Jupp, towering nearly as tall as our father, turns around and waves me toward him in a challenge. Resisting the growing hesitation, I shake my shoulders loose and charge for him. Our swords and shields collide as we trade a series of attacks and blocks.

Shortly, I make yet another mistake. Overextending my shield, in defense against Jupp's long, sweeping attack from above, I leave my blocking arm high. He hits my shield with his own and trips me with his practice sword. Before getting up, I glance toward our father. He remains neutral, refusing to influence either son. I press my teeth together, rise, and charge again.

Slipping the first swing, I manage to drive the end of my sword into his right shoulder. He grimaces as his defense is penetrated. He stomps forward and jabs his sword into my shield again and again. When I find his timing, I swat his blade down and to the side. His blunted edge lodges itself in the leather of my shield strap. He grunts and spews his milky-sweet breath as we become entangled. Jupp is adamant today. He is not holding back, and I prefer it this way.

"Release it!" Jupp tries to headbutt me free.

When he misses, he pulls harder, ripping my shield off with his sword, and both are flung to the opposite side of the arena.

Armed only with a shield, he lunges with sweeping attacks. I roll out of range and toward my departed shield. The strap has been sheared off, so I can't make much use of it. Jupp is leaping at me again. I fling the fractured shield at him and quickly take his sword from the dirt. I hear the shield crack and snap as it bounces off his forearms. Equipped with both blades, a sense of balance overcomes me.

When he comes to me again, I knock his shield aside with my off hand and attack him squarely with my main. I'm faster without the cumbersome shield, so I escape his assault and reposition myself on his weak side. Slash, block, slash. I swing one sword, knock his attack away with the other, and swing the first sword again. Frustration begins to show through his bared teeth. He throws his shield to the ground, clenches his jaw, and lunges for my legs.

Normally, he would have caught my ankles, but not this time. With a clear vision and lighter feet, I jump out of the way. He grunts and reaches again. I throw my feet backward and use the blades to counterbalance my dodge. Jupp lands in the frozen dirt. Earthy scents of fertile dirt break free from the permafrost underneath him.

My swords rise to Jupp's neck in a blizzard of my confidence. This is the first time I've ever beaten him. I want to smile and tease him, but after the many times he has beaten me, he has never gloated. I remain firm and respectful to my brother even though I want to scream of my victory to the gods watching above.

"Stop," our father says.

We both snap to attention, and I drop my swords to the ground in respect.

"Go with Kagg, and make sure he makes it to the healer." Father holds me back with his hand.

"Not bad." Jupp gathers up his shield and slings it onto his back.

Jupp smirks and nods in approval as he walks away. He meets Hellahh, who is helping Kagg out of the training pit. After their exit, my father studies me.

"Do you seek the role?" he says.

Does he mean Akkimon? The Akkimon are the rare, generational warriors who lead the front line into war. Most of the den stories involve one in some regard. Unsure of what he wants me to do or say, I remain silent. Could I be next? I've always imagined Jupp claiming the honor.

"Throughout our history, the Akkimon have held the highest honors of combat. Yet the glory awarded them shorter lives." He gazes toward the sky. "Your mother, my battle maiden, carried the blades. We took them north against those who trespassed. You've heard the tales of her greatness."

There have been many great dual wielders of Erowkahnn, but only a few have carried the Twin Blades. The blades were forged from a rare mineral, given by the gods, for the great Queen Sakk Taww. War and Harmony were names given by the swordsmith. Once they were complete, the queen used the Twin Blades to defeat northern invaders. Her triumph over the North built the legend that initiated the tradition. When she retired from battle, the legendary blades passed on to her trusted guardian, Te-Zaza. He was the first Akkimon. The honorary passing of the Twins flowed from Te-Zaza, down the river of time. One day, the blades fell to our grandfather Eojj. He carried the blades until our mother was strong enough to wield them.

"Yes, I accept."

He takes a step away from me and glances at the ground in a thoughtful manner. His heavy fur coat sweeps across the field when he turns back.

"It is your privilege to claim the Twin Blades, if it is what you desire." Before I speak, he holds his hand up to stop me. "There will be no dishonor in leaving the blades for the next, but you have first claim."

I follow him out of the pit. Once we exit, he wraps his heavy arm around my shoulders. A few chokworms wander pointlessly in front of us while our clan gathers the last silks of the season.

"It must have felt nice to finally best your brother." He grins.

"It did." I smirk back.

He laughs along with me as a flurry of snow gusts at our backs.

CHAPTER FIVE

The Runaway

Lifia

WINTER S26, 48 AE

I peer down at the man from our perch in the tree. Bulba is sprawled out, gripping the thick branches surrounding us to keep himself nestled beside me. He is as watchful as ever but more docile as he recovers. I'm relieved none of his battle wounds are infected. In contrast, the wounds the Magnavozian left in Fangour are aching for revenge. Each time I close my eyes, my mother's face appears, making it impossible to sleep.

We are rooted in the thickest part of the forest. An unfamiliar person could easily get lost here. This advantage has helped keep us free from Magnavozian soldiers. Several days have passed since the night of the attack. Many search parties have combed through the forest, but we have remained out of sight. Several times, I've held Bulba back by a handful of his coat. In reality, I don't have the strength to catch him if he genuinely wants to go. Yet he has the obedience to listen when I tell him to stay.

This man is different. He is dressed in fine Fangourian robes, and he treads lightly on the forest floor.

"Natoni," I whisper.

Bulba tilts his head as my voice tickles his ears. He twitches and lets out a low growl.

Lord Natoni Koki is my uncle, my father's youngest brother. He is short, even for a Koki. My father was the tallest of all Koki men, but average among others. As Natoni draws near, I recognize the emblem of the Koki family. Three black tigers stitched on a scarlet background. It is simple yet elegant. Natoni's hair is straight and black, the color matching his eyes. He lives across the gulf in the sister nation of Swedas. Since my father passed, Natoni has only visited to bring little gifts once a year. However, the gifts stopped arriving a few years ago. Natoni stops and begins to examine our tree.

"Lifia!" he yells.

Bulba's growl grows more ferocious as Natoni approaches.

"Please, call off your guardian. We don't have much time." He takes another step toward us.

Can he see us through the thick branches, or does he hear the rumbling growls of Bulba?

"What are you doing here, Uncle?" I inquire.

"What are you doing up there?" He smiles and steps beneath us.

We climb down to meet him. Bulba lands before me and takes the space between Natoni and me. His teeth are bared and ready for battle if needed.

"Bulba." I try to step around him, but he stands his ground.

"How did you find me?" I pet Bulba down his back to calm him.

"Everyone has been looking for you. Fortunately, they don't know how to track the tigers," Natoni says.

Bulba sits down beside me with his jaws slightly open. Natoni is wise enough to take a step back before continuing the conversation.

"Where is everyone, our guards? Where are the Fangourian soldiers?" I say.

He looks at his feet.

"We weren't prepared, and we were quickly outmatched." He turns his back to me and takes a step to the side.

"What are you saying?" I can't keep my voice from trembling. "Have they taken the Skyfort?"

"Yes. The royal guards are in chains. We weren't much of a fight...without you and Dianame." He chokes on his words.

Sensing my pain at the mention of my mother's name, Bulba rises. He hisses at Natoni. Natoni kicks at the ground, unaffected by the agitated tiger.

"I'm sorry, Lifia. Your mother knew a proposal would come one day. She should have prepared you for it." He glances up at me for a moment, then quickly returns his gaze to the forest floor.

My uncle is a shrewd man. He has many ventures that keep him wealthy, but he lacks the compassion required to be loved by many.

"What do you mean? She did prepare me. She was always prepared. The Magnavozians did not allow us to contemplate the marriage...not even for a day." I feel tears beginning to swell.

Sensing my anger, Bulba steps in front of me again and growls. The hair of his mane is protruding high.

"Enough. Call him off." Natoni raises his hands.

"Bulba." I grasp his fur and tug him back.

"I'm sorry. We don't have time for this. They are still searching for you, and soon they will begin the burns to smoke you out," he snaps.

What would my mother do?

"What are you saying? Are there soldiers in the city? Can we fight them?" I say.

"No. We cannot fight them. Everything is lost. We need to get you out of Fangour," Natoni says.

Leave Fangour? The Evoni family and Fangour are synonymous. This is not the dance I wanted.

"I cannot leave Fangour. We need to gather our armies and take the Skyfort back." I swing the Evoni Bow off my shoulder and tug at its string.

"No. Everyone is dead, and they blame you for taking Prince Vega's life. They won't stop until they find you. I wanted to spare you, but there is nothing left for you here," he says.

A part of me wants to fight no matter the odds. Another part of me wants to die with the other Fangourians. Yet I'm so scared I'll die for nothing, and our family will be washed away by the harsh hands of history.

"Where will we go?" My voice cracks.

"I can smuggle you out on one of my ships, to Swedas." Natoni grabs my hands.

"And Bulba?" I say.

He shakes his head.

"I can't go without him." I grip my forearm with my shaking hand.

Bulba licks my hand. His tongue begins at my wrist and travels up to my elbow in one swipe.

"This is Bulba's home. The tigers have never done well outside the Okiari lands," he says.

It is true, the tigers belong here as much as I do. I can't lose Bulba too.

"He would not survive the voyage," he says.

Soldiers shout in the distance, spooking Natoni.

"Lifia. Meet me at the docks tomorrow morning, without Bulba." He takes three steps backward before turning away.

Natoni disappears before I can give my answer.

"Let's go, Bulba." I tug his fur in the opposite direction.

We travel farther into the thick to escape the Magnavozians. Thin streams cut through the forest like cracks in a wall, but they are challenging to find with the dense undergrowth. This is far enough, and Bulba will never be found unless he wants to be.

Bulba waits with his hind paws in the stream while I wash his wounds. He doesn't mind the water, and he likes having his fur combed. His lips slide back, showing more of his teeth each time I rinse a wound. Gentle pets relax him before I rinse him again. He shakes, sprinkling me with water. Then he tries to reach back to lick his spear wound.

"You need to be careful while I'm gone," I say.

His ears twitch as I speak.

"Stay here in the deep thick, where no one can find you." My voice cracks.

Bulba looks back to check on me. He has always been my protector, but now I must protect him. I don't want to leave. I belong in this forest and in the Skyfort, but Natoni is right. My mother would want me to live.

I can't believe I'm here. This nightmare has extended beyond my worst fears. When did it begin? The Magnavozians must have been planning to take Fangour all along. They were waiting for their children to be old enough to enslave one of us through marriage. Their political alliances taint the beauty of the union. The worst part is that Vega was lovely. There was nothing about him I could not have grown to accept and perhaps even love one day. If they had been gentler, we could have made the alliance.

Bulba flicks the end of his tail down like a whip, shaking

the water off. Silence has filled the gaps in the trees, isolating us from the rest of the realm.

We finish washing and cleaning our wounds. Bulba nuzzles me, signaling his appreciation that the cleaning has ended. Holding nothing back, I hug him around his neck and press my head into him to hide my tears. He smells earthy, like the forest.

"Bulba, stay here." I release his neck and step away.

Bulba leans forward like he is going to follow me.

"Stay." I hold up my hand.

He sits in response. His coat blends with the trees behind him. The forest welcomes him in.

I turn before any more tears can break free.

◗

The next morning, I sneak down to the beach before the sun rises. The moment I arrive, I know my uncle has betrayed me.

The docks are separated from the mainland by a great bridge. The architecture of the bridge resembles the skybridges connecting the Skyfort. Crossing the bridge to the docks requires passing over the water for several ship lengths. There are three columns constructed in the water, which support the bridge to the docks. The columns elevate the bridge high enough that waves never reach the top, yet low enough so that no sailboat can maneuver underneath. For those reasons, local Fangourians refer to it as the Water Walk. The bridge begins at the end of the road that leads to the Grand Market. Most Fangourians reside somewhere between the Grand Market and the docks.

From my vantage point, east of the docks, I watch Natoni. He is speaking to Magnavozians, who occupy the docks. He yells and directs them into position.

The soldiers are dressed in merchant attire and more-exquisite silks, yet their stiff bodies give them away. Typically, traders from Swedas stand nimble and light. On the contrary, these soldiers are heavy-footed and clumsy on the dock. Most are mainlanders who have never sailed. Swedans, in general, are quite suave and value elegance in movement and speech. It is not uncommon for a man from Swedas to wear a frilly gown and sway when he walks. On the other hand, Magnavozians are more known for bold, proud stances. Magnavozian men are typically masculine, and most would find outward femininity embarrassing.

When did Natoni betray us? Was it when the Skyfort was sacked, or long before? I'm out of hearing range, but I can land an arrow in him from here. Here, among the last trees of the forest, I contemplate how to strike.

I can't board Natoni's ship filled with leeches. Yet I can't stay in Fangour, with an active conspiracy hinging on my capture. Who among the Fangourians can I trust? Only days ago, I believed all Fangourians cherished the Evoni rule. That was naive.

Natoni barks more orders before leaving the actors on his ship.

I follow him to a small building beyond the docks. When I enter, I release my veil and allow the door to slowly creak until it is closed behind me. Slipping in, I creep behind the lone occupant.

"I told you to wait. I will come once you have her in hand." Natoni fiddles with trinkets on the merchant's counter.

Typically, this building is the first place a traveling trader would stop, to pay taxes on imports or approve a ledger. Today the only traveler is my treacherous uncle. When he turns to see who has entered the building, his hands shudder, knocking trinkets off the counter. A weight disk, used for measuring coin, falls off the table and rolls to my feet. I'm the last person Natoni expected.

"Lifia. You've arrived," he says.

"Yes, Uncle." I take the bow off my shoulder.

My face is swelling with the warmth of a rage fire.

"Did you see my ship? It's the one with the three tigers on the banner. You know our family emblem..." he says.

"Yes, I remember my father's emblem."

It's an emblem Natoni doesn't deserve to wear.

"Go on. You need to get on the ship. My men are expecting you." He points to guide me outside.

"Your men?" I slide an arrow onto the string.

"What are you doing?" His wide-eyed expression of surprise cracks.

He doesn't have the will to lie. The way he moves and speaks is choppy, like a novice dancer.

"What can I say?" He shrugs his shoulders.

"You can admit you betrayed our family. You can admit you betrayed Fangour," I offer.

Natoni drops his hands. His fake smile and staged gestures have faded. I raise my bow and draw back. My target is his left eye.

"They will find you. No matter where you are, they will find you and make you pay for the prince's life," he says.

"And who will pay for my mother's?" I say.

"No one. She will be forgotten with the empire, and wiser, more diplomatic rulers will rise." He shuffles back to the counter.

"What did they promise you, Uncle? Did you trade our lives for gold or something grander? Perhaps a place on the throne."

"Why not me?" He bows as he flips a coin over the side of the counter. "Do you find me guilty of wisdom and foresight? I'm the only Fangourian who would cooperate with them.

You're a cub starting a fight with tigers. You can't imagine their power. Besides, you're up against more than Magnavoz. There are others pulling the strings."

"What others? Who?" I say.

"You wouldn't believe me if I told you," he says.

"The Illitaww?" I say.

"The frozen warriors? What strings would they pull? You really are a cub."

I contemplate releasing my arrow, but I can't. Fangour has seen too much death. I release the taut string, sliding it gently to a relaxed position. Natoni sighs in relief.

"If you come quietly, we can make your holding more comfortable." He opens his arms, inviting a hug.

I take a step forward. Before we embrace, I step under his outstretched arm to his back and wrap my arm around his neck. He tries to strike me, but I sink my head to the middle of his back to dodge him.

He goes to his knees as I cinch up my arm around his neck and squeeze air out. My right arm is wrapped around his neck while my left hand pushes the top of his head down, tighter into the noose. He kicks a few more times before he passes out.

I don't have much time. Natoni will recover in a few seconds. I sprint to the door to check outside. There's nothing out there besides the actors and a few trading ships. One ship is already beginning its departure. I jump out and dash toward the tree line, following it to the end of the docks.

CHAPTER SIX

The Follower

Marr

AUTUMN R2, 48 AE

Sol-Boski bustles with the arrival of the clans. Large statues of the gods tower into the sky around us. Stairs wind up and
down various paths to individual temples.

"Do you want to visit Madokk's temple next?" Jupp jogs
down the temple steps.

"Yes, we—" a group of young women cross the space between us on their way up the stairs "—should pray for his blessing." Jupp smiles back at me knowingly as my eyes follow the
one with big yellow eyes.

"Or do you want to pray to Kulujj once more?" Jupp nods back up the temple stairs.

"I prayed to Madokk yesterday. He wouldn't want us to pray to him every day." I grin and jog up the stairs to follow.

Madokk is depicted as thin, hairless, tall. The elders say he has the height of five men. Usually he is the god of war and harmony. Elders call him the god of life and death. Our father told us they are all wrong. "Madokk is simply the god of balance," he said.

The Temple of Kulujj is warm. The smell of barley overpowers my other senses as we pass over the threshold. The one with yellow eyes watches us as her friends giggle at traded whispers.

Kulujj is the god of the harvest. He is not a favorite god of Clan Erowkahnn, since we do not sow. Yet Jupp always prays to Kulujj. For him, the god represents good health. Kulujj is a wise god with a long beard that sweeps across his heavenly fields.

Jupp nudges me forward. Inside the temple, I'm less brave.

"Did you forget your tongue outside?" Jupp turns to me so the young women can't see him speak.

They wear longtusk fur and purple silk wrapped around their necks. The dyed purple silk reveals them to be of the Dul-Tonn clan. Their people are hunters who follow the longtusk east to west. They have close connections with the bonecrushers, which aid them in the hunt for the powerful longtusk. The bonecrushers are a rare canine species with massive jaws and ferocious appetites. The Dul-Tonn clan is the only clan to have ever trained the beasts, giving them an edge in hunting and war. Yet their relationship with the animals is not always harmonious. Stories of bonecrushers turning on their handlers are common.

Occasionally their clan will cross ours as we herd the chokworms northward. We trade raw silk for longtusk steaks while we share camps for a time. However, the joining never lasts more than a few days. Here is different. Here we have more time.

Before I can think of what to say, Jupp is walking toward them. I follow behind.

"Hi. I'm Jupp, and this is my brother, Marr." Jupp smiles.

"Hi," one says.

"Jupp, son of Lakk?" another one says.

"Yes. We are of Erowkahnn. Your scarf tells me you are of Dul-Tonn, no?"

Jupp speaks with the girls while I exchange smiles with the girl with yellow eyes.

"Hi." I step to the side to talk to her. "I'm—"

"Marr, son of Lakk. Yes, we all know you are the sons of Lakk," she interrupts me.

"I see. Well, we are of Erowkahnn. And you?" I say.

"Yes, and this is your brother, Jupp. Do you always repeat what he says?" She smiles.

"I'm sorry. We don't meet many from other clans. Is Kulujj your god?" I say sheepishly.

"I've never worshipped Kulujj, but his temple smells the best." She runs her fingers down one of the idols placed on the temple pillar.

The other young women are laughing while Jupp entertains them.

"My god is Madokk. I came here for the scents as well," I lie.

She snorts a giggle.

"Ours is Yevenhi," she says.

Yevenhi, the goddess of the hunt, is an obvious choice. Yevenhi is the most attractive of all the gods. Her long, luxuriant hair and full lips represent the most desired features in an Illitaww woman.

Everyone quiets behind me. A large man ducks to enter the temple. He has the same yellow eyes as the one I'm speaking to, except one of his is cloudy and scarred. He's as tall as Jupp, and wider. His name is Yatzekk, a renowned hunter, fearsome warrior, and leader of the Dul-Tonn clan.

"Come," he orders.

The cute one frowns and slowly follows Yatzekk to the exit. He watches me as she leaves. I stare back, resisting the urge to turn away.

"Mind your silk, boys." Yatzekk tugs at a rope tied to a muzzled bonecrusher pup.

The pup growls and tries to pull away from his master. Yatzekk jerks the rope taut and follows behind his daughter.

Jupp punches me in the arm.

"I didn't get her name." I let out a disappointed sigh.

"Her name is Miann," the last young woman shouts before she steps down the stairs outside the temple.

"You were almost killed by the great Yatzekk," Jupp teases.

"And you would've died as well, brother." I punch him back.

"Eh. I could've taken him," Jupp says.

Part of me believes he could defeat the warrior of Dul-Tonn.

"What about the bonecrusher tethered to him?" I say.

"Minor details. It's time for training." Jupp pats me on the shoulder as we leave the temple.

The next day, we all gather in the stadium between the temples. The walls are high and windowless. The open roof is covered in canvas for the event. Today thousands of people inhabit Sol-Boski. Many are inside the stadium, feasting on the great surplus of longtusk brought by Dul-Tonn. They are proud and boastful about their hunts. The other clans are all grateful for their generosity.

Yatzekk drinks more than his fill of fermented berries as he recounts his adventures. His sons surround him and chime in with their own adaptations of the hunts. Meanwhile, I trade flirtatious smiles with his daughter from across the room.

"What are you doing?" Hellahh smacks me on the back of my head to break me free of my trance.

We are near the front, with the other Erowkahnn. King Lakk sits at the center, elevated above everyone.

"We need to focus on our training. There are many great fighters we can learn from here. I need you with me." Hellahh takes a deep swig of her drink.

"You're right. I'm with you," I say with my focus return-ing.

"Damn you." Hellahh takes another swig.

As I'm taking a drink of my own, a hand rips me out of my seat. My inner fire ignites. I swing blindly as I scramble to my feet. Jupp slides in, pulling me free from Yatzekk's grasp. I re-claim control of my breath and begin to calm my senses. Yatzekk and his five sons face us.

Hellahh kicks at one of the sons. Jupp catches her, taking the bite from her kick. One of the sons swipes at her in response. He misses, and Jupp shoves him back. It's only a warning, but he curses as he stumbles back into his brothers.

The feasting area grows silent as eyes fall on us. Yatzekk glares. His good eye is filled with rage, while his scarred eye is strangely cloudier than before. Our respective clans gather behind us.

"You entitled worm shit," Yatzekk spits.

I clench my fists, ready to fight.

"Shorttusk." Hellahh returns a crude gesture.

King Lakk is sitting calmly, watching us.

He hasn't moved in the slightest during the commotion.

"The king's son thinks he can lay claim to my daughter." Yatzekk spins around to the crowd.

His lies fill my belly with embers of rage. Jupp and I are moments away from engaging with the sons of Yatzekk. Luckily, our weapons are outside. The laws of the city prevent events from escalating, but most men can fall by hands alone.

"Yatzekk," King Lakk says evenly.

His calm presence fills the stadium. Though not loud, his voice commands respect.

"Your son steals from me," Yatzekk says.

The Dul-Tonn crowd roars behind him. Sifting through their faces, I'm unable to find Miann.

"What has he taken?" King Lakk says.

"He is trying to steal my daughter, with no respect given to me." Yatzekk takes a swig of his drink and spits chunks of berries at our feet.

I want to break one of his bones, but my respect for our father holds an obedient grip on my will.

"Enough," King Lakk interrupts. "You do not own your daughter. When I defeated your clan in the war that united us, I didn't kill you. Instead, I killed your rules of slavery and ownership. In our Illitaww, the one we have rebuilt together, no person owns another. Your children are as free as mine, not any more or any less."

"Your son has no"—King Lakk takes a step down—"right," Yatzekk says.

"You are right. If she is of age, no one has a claim on her person, not even you. I will not repeat myself on this," King Lakk says.

They exchange glares. Enough time passes for me to go back and forth between each man twice. Finally Yatzekk breaks the contest.

"If that is all, my king." Yatzekk flips his heavy coat around to leave.

"No, Yatzekk. That is not all," King Lakk says.

Yatzekk stops but doesn't turn around. He sighs and drops his head.

"You have made a false claim of theft against another Illitaww person. This is a punishable offense," King Lakk says.

The Dul-Tonn clan shouts in revolt. Yatzekk waves around to quiet everyone.

"You will spill my blood here, on the Sol-Boski flat?" he says.

"No, I will not stain this sanctuary with your blood. Since you cling to the old ways, I will decide your fate in combat," King Lakk says.

It feels like the air is sucked from the stadium. Not even babies dare to cry.

"I'm sorry, my king. I drank too much, and I have grown tired from the long season of hunting." Yatzekk cowers back and kneels.

"Marr will be my fighter to deliver the law," King Lakk says.

I jolt my attention back to my father. He sends me the slightest glance, and I nod in agreement. Anything to quell my building rage is welcome.

"To the death?" Yatzekk says.

"No. Not in Sol-Boski during summons. This tournament will be for the honor and the foolish pride of two old wolves." The crowd roars with laughter. "Pick your champion, and we will have a contest to see who has properly trained their children." Lakk smirks.

"Yes. Finally we have something to enjoy with these rocks. My son versus yours? That's a contest worth watching." Yatzekk chugs the rest of his drink and smashes the cup.

Sol-Boski empties. The crowd gathers around the pit, which is dropped to the depth of a man's height.

"Marr," my father calls.

I search for his place outside the pit.

"Two swords." He chops imaginary weapons.

I grab two and pass my shield to Jupp.

A great deal of arguing occurred before they decided who would fight. First, Dul-Tonn wanted me to fight Yatzekk's eldest son, Yatzarr. Our father disagreed. Yatzarr is twice my age and a veteran of the tournaments. Yet our father argued he was soft and too worn to fight his son. Then Yatzekk wanted me to fight his twin sons, Yatzymm and Miekk. The argument led to Jupp entering the contest alongside me. Yet instead of his twins, Yatzekk wanted us to battle Yatzarr and his youngest son, Gillekk. Gillekk is from the same brood as Miann.

"It's only fair your eldest and youngest fight my eldest and youngest," Yatzekk said.

Jupp is my elder by a half-day, while Yatzarr is Gillekk's elder by years. It was a maneuver of words to get his best son back in the contest. All his sons are older than us, but Yatzarr is by far the largest. Our father agreed and winked at Jupp and me when he crossed forearms with Yatzekk. With Jupp beside me, I'm unstoppable. I can't imagine him being defeated by anyone, which gives me strength.

Yatzekk's sons are ready across the pit. Their arms are thickly muscled, while mine are long and lean. Covered in scars from bonecrusher bites and longtusk gouges, they look the part of ruthless hunters.

"This will be fun," Jupp says.

"Fun? These ones are going to try to kill us." I slash my blades back and forth, mimicking our father.

King Lakk stands and walks to the edge of the arena. The crowd exchanges hushes.

"Today these sons of Illitaww compete for glory, honor,

and fathers, for their fathers are too old to fight." He grins.

The crowd laughs. Even Yatzekk's belly jumps up with laughter. Yet his sons remain serious, unwavering in their stance.

I scan the crowd for Miann. Hellahh is shadow fighting when my eyes meet hers.

"Hack 'em up. *Wrekk!*" She aggressively jabs at the air.

I smile and continue searching. Yet Miann is out of sight. Jupp taps his shield with his sword, drawing my attention back to the pit. Yatzekk's sons step forward. Both are larger than me, but neither are as tall as their father or Jupp. Each is burly and more masculine than most, with large bellies and thick beards. The eldest, Yatzarr, carries a two-handed sword, while Gillekk carries the traditional set.

"Dul-Tonn!" Yatzekk swings his arms from his chest to his sides. The clan roars at the sound of their name.

"Erowkahnn! Illitaww!" King Lakk raises his arms wide. Our clan roars to match Dul-Tonn.

The crowd quiets and waits for the signal. The king throws a fist of dirt into the pit to initiate the contest. Everyone cheers as it begins.

"*Drah! Drahkua! Drah, drah, drahkua!*" Jupp chants.

Clan Erowkahnn echoes his chant in a chorus above us. The crowd shouts warnings as Yatzarr and Gillekk interrupt the chants with a charge. Jupp steadies his feet into a stable stance, while I loosen and readjust my grip. Yatzarr slices the gap between us. His blade sticks in the ground as we both spin away. Jupp's shield is perfectly positioned for another attack by Gillekk. I slip a sideswipe from Yatzarr's heavy blade.

With their maneuver, they control the center of the pit. Jupp works on one edge, while I prepare myself for another assault. Before I can plan, Yatzarr rips his blade through the air. This time, I try to block his attack. It's a mistake. His powerful swing is barely impeded. My wrist twists over and gives way to his blade. My sword is vibrating my hand numb while I spin away and step all the way back against the pit wall. He closes in to swing an arcing slice down on me. I weave to the left, as the tip of his blade sticks into the wooden rim of the pit. As he tries to rip it free, I jump up and off the wall behind me. In the air, I stab down into his shoulder, disarming him.

Clan Erowkahnn cheers louder. Before I can deliver an-other blow, Yatzarr grabs my blade and rips it out of my hand. It is a risky move, and he would not have attempted it if our blades were sharpened. With another fist, he uppercuts into my stomach, knocking the air out of all Erowkahnn. In this close proximity, I can smell the musk of longtusk fat wafting from his armpits. Yatzarr tosses my sword near the center of the pit and works to detach his two-hander while I recover.

Jupp is pushing back on his end, yet I'm outmatched in strength on mine. The crowd is shouting insults, strategy, and blurred combinations of both. When I gaze up, our father is scis-soring imaginary swords.

"Marr! Together!" Jupp shouts as he bashes Gillekk off his feet.

I dive to dodge a low slash at my feet, grab up my blade, and flip over to arrive beside my brother. Yatzarr and Gillekk meet as well. Yatzarr is breathing heavily, but Gillekk is poised. Yatzarr raises his hands to ignite the crowd, and to extend the break.

"What happened over there?" Jupp grins from the side of his mouth.

"This one is strong," I say.

"Strong?" Jupp laughs, shakes his shoulders loose, and steps forward.

My words are like a challenge for him. Jupp is strong but not fully grown.

"As one!" Our father shouts his first words since the dirt left his hands.

"Jupp. As one," I say.

"As one." Jupp steps back, nodding.

I step to the right of Jupp. Our shoulders almost touch. Our father nods his approval as Yatzekk's sons rush us.

We exchange blunted blocks for attacks. After a while, they are slowing, while we maintain our pace. We will outlast them. Yet I'm unable to deliver any true damage, because of our positioning.

Jupp is absorbing most of their attacks on his shield. In each sequence, he blocks and returns an attack. I follow in with a swift assault of my own, but I can't get a clean slice in before we are out of position. We jump back to avoid the heave of a great sword. We repeat, chipping away at the others' stamina until Gillekk makes a mistake. He overswings an attack at Jupp. The blow glances over the side of Jupp's shield, creating an uneven screech. By fatigue or laziness, Gillekk leaves his shield arm down. Jupp capitalizes by knocking Gillekk's shield completely loose. Yatzarr is a step behind and breathing heavily, while Jupp tackles Gillekk to the ground.

Before Yatzarr can recover to aid his brother, Jupp slams his shield edge into Gillekk. I can almost hear the bones cracking underneath his skin. Gillekk falls unconscious.

Yatzarr yells as rage ignites him. His face is blood red, and his arms are swollen as he swings down. Jupp rolls out, losing his sword in the roll.

Yatzarr's sword swats the ground, sending a plume of sand out of the pit.

"Jupp! Block!" I flank Yatzarr with a jab and a side slice at his thigh.

Jupp jumps up to meet an attack with his shield. The unstoppable swing is deflected, and Jupp is back at my side.

"You have the strike." Jupp nods.

Yatzarr swings high. Jupp deflects the attack over us as we duck. Before we rise, I jab two sharp strikes into his gut. He grunts and tries to punch me, but Jupp comes back around with his shield. The block breaks bones when it meets Yatzarr's hand.

Yatzarr tries to grip his sword, but it is no use. He yells out, and his limp hand falls to his side. I step around him with both blunted points of my blades at his neck.

The crowd, which fell silent in the last few seconds, erupts in cheers from both sides. Gillekk stumbles to get up, and Jupp catches him before he falls. I lower my blades and look up at the crowd and our king. King Lakk is calm, as always. Yet a hint of satisfaction rests on the end of his half grin.

Yatzarr grabs my arm with his good hand and raises it in the air. The sudden jerk almost sends me into another attack, until I realize he is congratulating me. I bow my head as another uproar from the crowd sounds in response. Yatzekk steps forward to the edge of the pit. From here, he is larger than ever and appears as wide as he is tall.

"Your sons are as much Illitaww as mine. They have proved themselves to be as clever as you," Yatzarr says.

"And yours are tougher than any others," King Lakk says.

They exchange a nod, and Yatzarr steps away.

The crowd of the Erowkahnn clan swarms the pit to congratulate us. During the commotion, my eyes remain fixed on my father, our king.

☾

The next day, I find Miann walking alone between the temples. The sun and I have barely risen, but I knew I would find her here. Gillekk told me she comes here every morning.

"Miann." I run up and reach for her hand.

Her hair is loose, flowing down in front of her. She wears tight purple silks with furred shoes. She smells of flowers and sweet oil. Her elegance is rare and in direct opposition to my coarse attire. My worn leather pants and twice-knitted shirt display my warrior style.

"Marr." She glances over and continues to walk.

"Miann, did you hear of the fight?" I say.

"Yes," she says.

Her words are cold and stiff. My eagerness deflates. I step in front of her, stopping.

"There is no conflict. Our clans drank together afterward," I say.

"I know, Marr. My brothers told me you are a much better fighter than you are a drinker." She smiles.

"That is true. They are much better in that arena." I laugh.

"You are like my brothers, my father, and all Illitaww people. You'll always be searching for the next hunt or the next fight." She studies me, waiting for my response.

"It is our way," I say.

"Yes, it is our way, but I'm not like everyone else. I want to build something that will last. Something like this city. When winter ends, I'm going to stay here with a few of the elders. We are going to look after the city," Miann says.

"What will you eat?" I say.

"There are many fish. Pela's grandmother says holes can be broken in the ice to fish through. There are ways to live in one place," she says.

"I don't mean any offense. I love the city, the temples, and everything here. I'm glad you are staying here to help," I offer.

"You don't think it's a sign of weakness?" she says.

"Weakness? No. On the contrary, it's brave," I say.

"You could stay too, you know. You could stay if you are brave enough." She nudges me and smiles.

"Ow." I rub my shoulder to feign a wound.

She rolls her eyes as she begins to stroll on.

We reach the corner of Kwatteh's temple and begin to

ascend the stairs. Kwatteh is the god of discipline. He is a dangerous god who demands devotion. Whoever prays often to Kwatteh is greatly rewarded. Yet those who pray to him inconsistently are worse off than those who never pray at all.

"I can't stay. After winter ends, we will begin the trials. Jupp and I have been waiting our entire lives," I say.

"Yes. You're Wrekk-Taww. Is that your path or your father's?" she says.

"Mine." I stop on the stairs, confused by her question.

To be Wrekk-Taww is to exist. She's right, I'm a warrior like our fathers. Becoming Wrekk-Taww will prove I'm worthy to be my father's son. It will prove to everyone that I'm as strong as my brother. Most importantly, it will prove I am who I believe I am.

She turns back to me. Facing the sunrise, her eyes reflect the beautiful yellow light. Wind ripples through her silk dress.

"Goodbye, Marr. I hope that I will see you during a future summons." She smiles, twirls around, and strides up the temple steps.

I swallow imaginary morale. The trials will be long and arduous, and we won't finish by the next summons. I watch her walk away, appreciating her unique Illitaww beauty, and knowing we will soon be parted.

CHAPTER SEVEN

The Bastard

Nok

AUTUMN K12, 48 AE

The Rock Hollow castle is more colorful than ever. The walls are painted with the banners of nations near and far. Below the great mesa, travelers gather. Each visitor brings a new potential escape from my mundane life. I release the stirring paddle and let it sink into the gravy as my eyes wander to the single window above the furnace.

"Keep stirring. We have another batch to make before morning." Tif slaps a wad of raw dough onto the counter beside me.

Tifania Homin is the ruler of the kitchen, and my adopted mother. I pick up the paddle and continue to stir as I roll my eyes at Margo. She is one of the younger kitchen servants, and the easiest to talk to. It also helps that she always laughs at my jokes. Today the kitchen is crowded with extra servants for the festivities.

Tomorrow the tournament officially begins. Our job is to prepare the foods for the tournament and the victor's feast, which follows. The food is simple to make. Bread filled with bits of meat is our most popular treat. Some of the wealthier lords request fresh fruit among an endless stream of wine. We spent last season stocking the cellar with wine, and Tif is confident we have enough. I'm not sure if I agree. I have never witnessed this many people gathered in one place. There are bound to be some surprises.

Dregadins from each nation will compete for a purse and the title of Tournament Lord.

"I think I will have a look at the tournament tomorrow," I say.

"Mother, I think I'll take tomorrow off as well." Margo smiles as she passes by on her way to chop some felroot.

Tif scrunches up her freckled face. She is a hardy middle-aged woman. She always keeps her curly red hair in a tight entanglement because she is almost always working. Many servants refer to Tif as their mother out of respect. They all love her, but I'm the only one she raised from birth. She has the important job of teaching all the servants their roles. Without Tif, we would all be lost.

"After I finish the gravy, of course," I say.

"Come on, Nok. I really need you here helping us. There is so much more work to do beyond the gravy. Besides, you won't be able to see anything at the tournament. The tournament grounds will be packed with lords and ladies." Tif tosses a handful of salt onto the dough.

She has always been wary of my interactions with those in power. I'm the bastard son of King Donak, the beloved king of all Magnavoz. Before I was born, Tif and my mother were servants together. When my mother was removed from the castle, she made Tif promise to keep me safe. Under Tif's watchful eyes, I've lived a boring but safe life. Now, when my world has been filled with as much color as I've ever seen, she won't let me risk being noticed.

"There will be other tournaments in the future." Tif squeezes the muscle on my shoulder like she is kneading the dough.

I keep my mouth sealed while my mind schemes for a way to reach the tournament grounds. Margo sneaks a sly glance. I hope she doesn't think she is stopping me. I flick a bit of gravy off my spoon, onto her cheek. She scoffs and throws a slice of felroot. It lands on my neck, and the food fight blooms across the kitchen.

The next morning, we load a cart of wine, sausages, and cheese.

"That's the last of the cheese we can spare. We need to save the rest for the feast," Tif says.

I grab hold of the cart handles and wink at her as I step out into the grand hall.

"I need you back here as soon as you deliver the cart to Ron. He's on the west side of the field with the other merchants." She slips back into the kitchen before I respond.

I pass three handmaidens heading toward the prayer hall. Their dresses are each freshly dyed in the most pungent pink a man could create. All servants add one distinguishing feature or another to their attire. The handmaidens all wear pink dresses and veils that cover most of their faces. The veil has religious meaning, but not all handmaidens worship the Trinity. Some handmaidens simply wear their veils for fashion.

For the followers of the Trinity, the veils represent the innocence of the child. Unmarried women almost always wear these veils, while married women usually only wear the veils for special occasions. For the wealthy, veils covered in gems can reflect both power and social status.

The Trinity is the most common religion in Elybion. The religion focuses on three figures who serve different aspects of a person's life. The Mother is the first piece of the Trinity. She represents sacrifice and selflessness. Next to her, the Father stands for justice and obedience. Finally, the Child completes the Trinity with faith and emphasis on the frailty of human life. The faithful believe all three are required to balance a righteous life.

Every step I take brings me closer to freedom. The guards draw back their crossed lances, allowing me to pass. My chef headpiece tilts forward as I nod to the guards. It's a patchwork of several different chef headdresses, but I wear it well.

As I walk toward the field, the crowds are cheering with so much excitement that I forget my task. I release the cart handles. Temporary tents constructed from large, draping canvases of varying colors and textures dot the field. Each nation, besides Fangour, is represented. Fangourians were always in low attendance at the tournaments. Their people thought the tournaments were an extravagant waste of resources, which they are. The Fangourian Empire is blamed for many things, but they were mostly guilty of being boring.

I grab the handles and guide the cart to the tents.

On my right side, there are gray tents outlined in bright blue thread. The thread wraps around the trim and up the crown

of the tent in wavy lines. On the face of each of the eight sides
is a dolphin emblem stitched in blue and gold threads. These are
the markings of Delphinus, a wealthy nation known for ship-
building and the great white city of the North.

To my left, green-and-orange banners stand over tan canvases. These banners hail, along with their people, from South
Aptoria. Their relatively plain emblem represents their nation,
which is not known for its extravagance. Aptorians of the South
are more likely to be seen covered in mud than fine silks.

Ahead of me, a tall man steps out of a quaint tent. Outside
the tent, banners stand tall with the feathered hand of North
Aptoria pressed into a midnight-blue background. A nation
keener on the luxuries of life than their southern brothers and
sisters.

Three figures in white follow behind him. He slides out of
their path, and they fade between the tents toward the tournament. I don't recognize them, but they are easily the most attractive people here. Their faces are youthful and polished. None of
them look like they are from the same region, apart from their
matching attire. Each has a different skin tone. Their eyes are
as colorful as flowers. Greens, violets, and yellows. They stroll
away stiffly with perfect posture.

The tall man is Lord Davon Mercah, lord of North Aptoria. He is freckled, with thin hair. For a lord, he is underdressed.
He takes a double glance at me as I approach. King Donak and
Lord Mercah were friends in a younger life. People have said
the king and I share faces, but many people have forgotten due
to his thick beard. Perhaps Lord Mercah has not.

As I roll the cart around a foot-sized stone, four of his
guards encircle him and begin to lead him to the tournament
field. The field is in the center, which is where the jousting and
single combat take place. Along with archery, jousting and single combat are the most anticipated and highly regarded events
of the tournament. I would happily trade everything in this cart

to get a glimpse of either.

Finally I roll the cart to a stop near the western border of the tents. Back east, Swedas banners speckle the opposite edge of the camp. Their banners are the most intricate of all. Black stitching forms broken swords crossing on a yellow and purple background. It would've been honey-sweet to have been born in a place like Swedas. They love art more than life, and indulgence is commonplace.

"Nok?"

I spin around to find who has called my name. Elise Samon and her herd of gossiping fawns. Elise is the eldest daughter of Lord Sanak Samon, and the niece of Queen Tyra Nagidah. Lord Samon and the queen are close siblings who share the gift of youthful faces even as they age. Elise shares more features with her mother, who is of Aptorian descent.

"Lady Elise." I bow quaintly.

"It's so good to see you, cousin," she says.

Good to see me? The last time I saw her was at Vega's funeral, and we didn't speak. Before the funeral, I hadn't seen her since we were children.

"It's good to see you as well," I say.

"Yes, and what a wonderful tournament this year." She smiles.

"The brightest one I've seen." I touch the back of my head.

"What is that on top of your head?" She laughs, and a chorus of fawns echoes her from behind.

"This?" I rip the chef hat off my head. "I'm helping in the kitchen for the tournament."

"That's very...humble of you." She looks back at one of her fawns, who struggles to contain her laughter.

"Well, I better finish my task. As always, it was pleasant to see you, Lady Elise." I heave the cart to initiate its roll out of the mud.

"No, you don't need to go. Others can service the crowds.

Please join us." She reaches out to me.

I hesitantly release the handgrips. Elise seems sincere, but her friends are less interested. I do want to explore the tourna‑ ment, but the kitchen needs me. She can sense my indecision. She twists her hand over to offer her empty palm.

"Yes, my ladies. I have some time to spare if you'll have me." I grasp her hand and enter her herd.

We steadily roam through the grounds as Elise clings to my right arm. Her friends follow behind us, whispering and pointing people out to each other. Clashes of metal quake in the distance.

"Many of the best dregadins are here," Elise says.

"Yes, that's what I've heard. Each country has brought its best this time." I smile.

"Oh, really? Is that what you have heard?" She grips tight‑ er around my arm.

I don't remember her being this kind when we were chil‑ dren. She was always the quiet one, playing alone when we were all together. I was the one who always wanted to play and be the center of attention. Yet I could never be in the center for long before someone brought up my bastard roots. It was always one of the older children or the servants. Usually the younger children would forget my roots and play with me as if I was their own. This is not the case for Elise. She is playing some political game, which I will learn to play better than her.

"How is everything here in the capital? You must get to see many tournaments," she says.

"Yes. I see my fair share," I lie. "There haven't been many lately... This is the first tournament held since Vega's death."

"Oh, I see. It's horrible that Vega was taken from us. He would have done so well at the tournament. Many say he re‑ sembles my father riding a horse and holding a sword," she says.

"Yes, I have heard the same compliments being given." I nod.

"Did they ever find the Fangourian daughter?" She pulls

me a little tighter.

"No. I would have heard something if anyone had. Every-one has been pretty quiet lately," I say.

"Yes. I'm sure the king and queen are still grieving over their loss. And how are you? You and Vega always loved each other." She gently shakes my arm between her two hands.

Loved each other? What distorted painting does she see of my life? We barely spoke to each other. I'm his closest sibling in age, but being a bastard separated us by more than years. He was never foul, nor did he show great kindness either. He toler-ated me as well as anyone else.

"Yes. I'm grieving as well. Vega would've made a fine king," I say.

The horns sound, and people begin to shift behind us. Peo-ple part as South Aptorian soldiers make way for one of their dregadins. A stout man in freshly molded armor leads the ram-bunctious group of young dregadins from the jousting area. His armor is shiny, causing me to squint in defense against the sun's reflection.

"Do you know who that is?" Elise releases my arm. "Ky-ber Lofelaborn. He's the prince of South Aptoria. The hunk of Moorquarry."

House Lofelaborn resides in Moorquarry. The fawns swoon behind us as the soldiers continue to open a path for the dregadins. Yet my eyes are fixed on Kyber. He flips his long, curly blond hair out of his new helmet before he passes us. His hair pulls me into his best features, which are his large brown eyes. They are as deadly as they are stunning. Though he isn't a tall man, he walks as if he has conquered the realm. His legs are as thick as tree trunks, and his shoulders are broad. Where most dregadins are rugged, something is refined about the primness of this man.

"Your Royal Highness." Elise waves at him when he meets us.

"My lady." Kyber nods to Elise and continues to walk.

When he passes, our eyes meet for a moment, and we see each other.

"By the Trinity, did you see him? Absolutely gorgeous." Elise reattaches herself to my arm. "We must go and see him in the archery competition," she says giddily.

I should finish my task and get back to the kitchen, but Kyber has caught my attention. The cart can wait. "Yes, of course. Where else would we go? We must see how he fares." I lean into her.

"I knew I liked you." She laughs.

The sun breaks into its last phase as everyone crowds around the archery ring to watch the conclusion of the competition. It began with a dozen dregadins. Each was outmatched by Kyber, besides Freden Mercah. Freden, son of Lord Davon Mercah, is a wide dregadin. Other dregadins call him the Bull of Dalveri. He doesn't compete in most of the events, because of the movement required, but he is exceptional with a bow.

Elise and I are sitting in the front row thanks to her clout as the niece of the queen. Her friends sit a few rows behind us. The crowd is divided between the North and the South. The Delphinish cheer for the Bull when he lands, while Arilandic people shout each time Kyber delivers a perfect target.

"He is absolutely spectacular," Elise says.

His sleeves are rolled up, and light sweat glistens on the back of his choksilk shirt. Kyber releases an arrow from his gilded bow. The arrow soars downrange at the target. He knows his arrow has landed before anyone else, so he pumps his bow in the air to inform the crowd.

As the Bull prepares for his turn at the long-range target, commotion stirs. Princess Velvia, my half sister and the eldest daughter of King Donak, makes her way through the crowd. She is led by a battalion of Magnavozian guards and followed by a horde of handmaidens.

"Make way for the princess." Yellers push commoners from their pathway.

"It's wonderful for the princess to join us, finally." Elise perks up. "I'll get her to come sit with us."

My eyes skip around, searching for the most convenient exit. I don't want to ruin this fine day by including Velvia in it.

"I'm not sure Velvia would enjoy my company. I should get back to the kitchen..." My words trail off as Elise stands and waves fervently at the princess.

Velvia and I have never gotten along. Unlike my relationship with Vega, Velvia and I have often opposed each other. Velvia has adamantly made my life more difficult. She never accepted me as her brother and often reminded me I was a bastard. Elise catches her attention, and Velvia strolls to us. She is dressed in light clothing, and flowers are woven through her dark brown hair. She must have spent the entire day preparing her hair and gown for this entrance. Velvia looks and moves like her mother, Queen Tyra. With her sunset afterglow, she could pass for an Arilandic prime. I can't deny her beauty. Yet unlike most of the people gawking at her as she enters, I'm familiar with her dormant ugliness.

"It's pleasing to see you, cousin." Velvia sits on the other side of Elise, with her gaze fixed forward.

"Velvia, you are so beautiful. You must tell me the name of the tailor who made your dress." Elise clings to Velvia's arm like she did mine before.

"She's a tailor from Swedas. She doesn't make many dresses, and they are quite expensive," Velvia says coldly.

I let a sigh escape in response to her rude reply. She responds with a glare from the side of her eyes.

"You're right. The dress is more suited to a princess." Elise rolls her eyes to me. "Nok and I have been watching the archery competition since it began. Prince Kyber has performed exquisitely."

"Yes, I have heard the prince is an excellent bowman," Velvia says.

Velvia and Elise continue to exchange pleasantries while I try not to react to each of Velvia's ridiculous statements. When there is a pause in conversation, Kyber notices her and walks over to us.

"Princess, thank you for joining us today." Kyber bows.

Velvia responds with a slight nod of her head. Kyber looks at Elise and me.

"I shall slay the Bull and bring his horns to you, my princess." Kyber pumps his bow up and turns away.

The crowd ignites in a chorus of applauds and a few boos from the supporters of the Bull. Kyber looks back once more, but not at the princess. This time, he is looking at me. There is something new in the prince's expressions. He sees something that I don't. His sight is unblemished, and it has found me. I look down with embarrassment. He sees me for who I am and who I want to be.

Elise is red when I turn back to them. Her perpetual smile is being overtaken by a gruesome frown. Before she turns to speak to Velvia, she tightens her smile back up.

"Prince Kyber seems to have found your beauty as well, Your Highness," Elise says.

"No. His father did though. He sought out mine, and they planned our union." Velvia flicks her dress and smooths out the ends. "At least they did not set me up with the Bull. His father is still upset with mine, but he can't really believe his son a good match for me."

"That's wonderful. When will the wedding be?" Elise grinds her teeth.

"Soon if King Kassin has any say. He is afraid Lord Mercah will try to steal me away if it doesn't happen soon." Velvia straightens her posture.

Elise forces a giggle while I search the crowd for Lord Mercah. He's watching his son, the Bull and the pride of Dalveri and North Aptoria as a whole. I find him sitting across the ring, next to one of the people dressed in white. The man in white has dark hair and violet eyes, yet his attire is the whitest I have ever seen. It is smooth, without flaw, and it covers his entire body up to his neck. He is perfectly groomed and among the handsomest men in the realm. Yet his appearance is so clean and striking it makes me uncomfortable.

"Who is the man with Lord Mercah?" I say.

"What? Oh, I'm not familiar with him. An Arilandic highborn?" Elise says.

"That's Vzar Musa," Velvia says.

"Vzar?" I say.

"Sincerely? We should go introduce ourselves." Elise tugs at Velvia lightly.

The crowd interrupts with applause. Kyber must have landed his arrows, because he is bowing and waving to the masses. The Bull throws his bow to the ground in frustration. The string snaps, and the wooden part of the bow ricochets off the ground and flies back up to snap him in the arm. The crowd laughs at his frustration, and the Bull stomps off in defeat. Velvia's handmaidens help her up as she begins to walk toward the ring.

Vzar? The title is rarely spoken, and never in the present tense. It's reserved for members of the Venith, a mysterious group of outlanders who disappeared from the realm hundreds of years ago. Before, they were advisers to kings and queens. They are said to have brought knowledge about city building

from waters beyond Elybion. The stories depict them as powerful magic users and capable of unfathomable displays of the
unnatural. Yet magic hasn't flowed in the realm since the Fangourian Empire rose. Why would they return now?

"Nok." Elise pulls my hand to follow Velvia with her.

Kyber meets us at the edge of the ring. He is holding a
massive bouquet of local wildflowers.

"Princess." Kyber hands the bouquet to Velvia.

She reluctantly takes the bundle and quickly hands it to
one of her accompanying handmaidens.

"What an elegant gesture." Elise steps up to Kyber.

There is a moment of awkward silence. Kyber looks over to
me and smiles. His teeth are white and framed by his thick lips.

"Thank you, my princess, my lady, and..." Kyber stumbles
on a title for me.

"Nok, Your Royal Highness," I say.

"Nok, it was nice to meet you." Kyber offers me his hand
to shake.

Velvia's glare pierces through me. If eyes could harm, hers
would conquer the realm.

"Thank you, Your Highness. Great aim today. I must be
returning to my duties. Thank you, Elise, for the wonderful
company today. Your Highness." I bow and quickly begin my
retreat.

"Oh, goodbye, Nok." Elise waves me away.

●

When I reach the cart, it has been toppled over, and one
of the wheels is detached. A hooded stranger bumps into me as
I approach. Nothing is left within the cart, and there are only a

few meat pies left, trampled into the mud. I sigh and stomp the meat pies deeper into the ground. Was it worth it?

"Yes. It was."

I reattach the wheel in a crooked fashion and begin the long journey back to the kitchens for my punishment.

CHAPTER EIGHT

The Investigator

Kai

AUTUMN K16, 48 AE

I'm thumbing through the worn pages of a book older than Summer's Light.

"We shouldn't be here, Kai." Phan paces at the entryway to the hidden library.

She's right. Only the masters are allowed in here. Here, in the Cache, they keep the minted scrolls, the originals, the records of the realm. I'm here to uncover the truth about the glowing eyes that haunt me. Now that I have access, I can't give up easily.

"I know there is more information here. I need to find it."
I slam the book shut and pull the next from the shelf.

"Fine. Let me have the book. I can read much faster than
you." Phan takes it from me.

"Thank you," I say.

She flicks through the pages so rapidly that I'm afraid she
is going to tear them. The single candle that illuminates the pages dwindles down to its last flickering gleam. I've read so many
books, and all have fallen short of providing the information I
need.

"This section is written in Old Nevian. It says, 'They came
from lands above, carrying light in their eyes,'" Phan says.

The Nevites were ancient rulers. Legends say the Nevites
rode on great owls rivaling the size of Aptorian eagles. Before
Fangour was an infant kingdom, the Nevites ruled Elybion.
There are no texts explaining their downfall, unless they lie hidden here in the Cache.

"What else does it say?" I step behind Phan.

"Here. 'For they can see through the veils of time. Their
power is only limited by their connection to the origin. We will
follow them through the gateways so that we can feel true power.'" Phan fingers through more pages and closes the book.

"What about the rest? Is there nothing more to learn?" I
grab the closed book as she skims in search of another.

"The following pages are filled with a registry of family
names," Phan says.

"Are there more books?" I say.

"That is the latest Nevite book, but I've read of the gateways before, in the scrolls of Revan's war. They talk about the
Xyji, who helped him escape the Battle of the Crossing."

I flip to the back of the Nevite book to find the ledger completely filled with Nevite names.

"You've seen the scrolls from Revan's war?" I gently close
the Nevite book and place it back on the shelf.

"Yes. It was an assignment the grandmaster selected San-ya and me for a season ago." Phan grabs the candle and rushes down to the end of the Cache.

Phan has become one of the most trusted apprentices of Summer's Light. Soon she'll become one of the youngest masters in the temple's history. Her risk to aid me is one greater than I deserve.

"We were to find and report any text that spoke about the Venith." Phan hands me the candle and pulls a large wound scroll from the shelf.

"Here. This is the one." Phan unfurls the scroll and points to a section of text.

The passage explains how the Venith used powerful mag-ic to oppose Revan's rule. They were succeeding until Revan called on the Xyji and their ancient divination.

"The Battle of the Crossing was lost, and Revan narrowly escaped through a gateway," Phan says.

"Do you think it's the same gateway in the Nevite book?" I say.

"No. This gateway took Revan back to the Skyfort, where he was able to rebuild his army and fight to reclaim control of the realm. The Nevite gateway traveled to somewhere much farther away. However, I do think the gateways are linked to the magic of the Xyji, the Venith, and the glowing eyes you obsess about," Phan says.

She's right. I'm obsessed. In between each lecture and scribbled duplication of tedious fact, I'm drawn back to the vi-olet eyes. For years, I've searched the libraries for information about the supernatural. Now that Phan has joined my pursuit, I'm finally drawing nearer to the answers I seek. I feel a thump on my chest, where the leather-bound stone resides. My reach for the stone is interrupted by rattling keys echoing down the hallway. Phan delivers a distressed expression before she blows out the candle.

"We need to read more. There must be more answers here." I grab her wrist to stop her in the dark.

It's forbidden to touch another apprentice of Summer's Light, and I immediately regret my grasp. I release my grip and apologize.

"Kai. We have to go," she says.

"Yes," I whisper.

We sneak to the entrance of the Cache as Master NcTully rounds the shelves outside. I can tell it's him by the way he scoots his feet without lifting them. We close the gates and snap the lock back into place before he reaches the end of the row.

Right as we step into the row parallel to the one NcTully travels, Phan drops the bronze candleholder. I hold my breath as it tumbles onto the floor, creating an obnoxious clatter.

"Who's there?" NcTully increases his shuffling pace.

Normally, I would panic and run, but a sense of courage to protect Phan overcomes me.

"Go." I push Phan away from the candleholder.

There's no time to take any chances. Phan has risked too much for me to let her be caught breaking into the Cache. She scurries away in silence. I break away in the opposite direction, toward the end of the row. I meet it before NcTully rounds his row, so he can't see Phan fleeing. I close my eyes as I turn the corner.

"Foyd?" Master NcTully yells as I nearly collide with him.

CHAPTER NINE

The Coveter

Nok

WINTER 05, 49 AE

A season has passed since the tournament, but tattered banners of defeated dregadins still litter the fields outside the castle. Our regular duties have been postponed to advance the union between Velvia and Kyber. More importantly, the union between Magnavoz and South Aptoria. Tonight lords and la-dies gather from all around the realm to witness the impending wedding. The ceremony is tomorrow, but the celebration begins tonight.

I'm perched between the great hall and the kitchen. From

here I have a perfect view of everything happening inside. I have my job, but I can't help thinking about seeing Kyber again. The way he looked at me at the tournament made me feel important. For the first time, I wasn't a bastard.

"Nok. They're coming." Margo rushes toward the kitchen.

"Grab the basket of bread," I snap.

The serving hands standing behind me awake from their daze and scurry after Margo. I flatten the upturned chest pocket of my vest, right as the bards begin to pluck on their instruments to usher in the guests.

Governor Andros Palenor, the appointed ruler of Delphinus and the North Isles, is the first notable person to arrive. He's quiet and mild mannered. Palenor's son, who is older than me, follows next behind his father. The Delphinish way of rule is odd. The governor holds power until he dies, but his children are not guaranteed the same privileges. Instead, they elect another governor to take his place. Their new form of rule has only seen two governors since the Fangourian fall. I'm curious to see if their way of ruling will last.

Lord Mercah and Lord Samon follow close behind Palenor's entourage. They refuse to call themselves kings. They maintain the lower title of Lord, while Prime Raylia Tiraban considers her title equal to or greater than a queen's. She follows a parade of servants to her table near the back.

King Ginnis Kil'Maalot and King Kassin Lofelaborn have no problem calling themselves kings. Their parties gather in conversation for a while before sitting.

There has never been a room denser with royalty. The ladies wear extravagant gowns, while the men play heroes in their polished armor—none of which has ever met combat beyond the courts of politics.

"Margo. Take this basket to the little lords and ladies. We need to keep them occupied. Otherwise, they will sour the evening." I toss her a heavy basket full of sweet bread.

"Yes. Right away, Lord Nok." Margo flashes a fake smile.

While Tif is busy tending to her responsibilities in the kitchen, I'm in charge of coordinating the services, a task that is as embarrassing as it is exciting. It was difficult to persuade Tif after my experience with the cart. Luckily, she has a weakness for my charm.

As more people enter, we go around the room, serving drinks and the first delicacies of the night.

The young lords and ladies are playing with their sweet bread while the elders sip on their wine. The real players this evening are the young adults. Some of them are newly married, while others are wealthy bachelors. Governor Andros Palenor's son, the young Lord Yondal Palenor, recently married to a beautiful islander who is the most interesting person I've ever seen. Many ladies flock around her, including Elise Samon, who is squeezed tightly next to her. She is expressionless and relaxed. Her eyes are a deep blue like the ocean, while her skin is dark, dotted with intricate tattoos, and kissed by the sun.

I would love to be right in the middle, helping them make fun of their parents and trading embarrassing stories about Velvia. No one knows her better than me.

Clinging to her new best friend, Elise is neither married nor boasting any real prospects. Love is different for people of her status. Unfortunately, her father is the notorious Sanak Samon. Lord Samon is a great warrior and longtime champion of the tournaments. He is known for his serious demeanor and being unbending in negotiations. Has anyone offered him a fair proposal, or does he demand the realm in return?

The large entrance doors creak, echoing across the hall. Hushed whispers sprout all around. Shuffling chairs followed by light applause invite Velvia into the hall. She ambles to the front and into my view from the kitchen passageway. She is wearing a traditional Trinity veil that is heavily coated in rubies and thin bars of gold. Each of the bars is no larger than a needle.

The stark whiteness of her dress makes me pause. A gift from the Venith?

Everyone's attention is focused on the princess—everyone's attention besides mine, which belongs to the prince. He is dressed in the finest silver armor. It has been polished and etched with an intricate river pattern on the chest of the armor.

Margo approaches me with another delivery of appetizers.

"Where do these go?" she says.

"Wait for the princess to be seated. Then take them to her handmaidens." I block her with my outstretched hand.

Kyber waits for the princess to sit, then gently follows her into his own seat. They are the painting-perfect rulers, with no limits to their power or decadence.

"Here. And you." I organize a pack of servers, following behind Margo. "I need you to gather more wine. The lords of Ariland haven't had their glasses filled since I've been watching. They will be offended if they aren't well taken care of."

"We don't have much to spare. The lords of Swedas drink faster than we can retrieve it from the cellars," one servant says.

"Forget about King Ginnis and his men. Besides, they prefer mead. Send all the wine to the Arilandic lords," I say.

Margo laughs as she returns to the kitchen.

"What is it?" I say.

"You. It's like you were born for this. Lord Nok, deliverer of wines and commander of all things savory." She bows and spins around before narrowly escaping a collision with another servant.

With Velvia in her seat, we serve the next course and begin preparing the hall for the gift giving.

"Who do you think will win the gift giving?" Margo whispers.

I jerk away, surprised by her closeness to me. "Velvia, I'm sure." Margo giggles behind me. "Go out and make sure their cups aren't at risk of being spilled while the gifts are presented."

I point without looking at Margo.

She's not wrong. It will be a bit of a competition. In modern times, it's considered an insult if the gift is available to commoners without clout.

First, Prime Raylia presents her gift to the young couple. She unfolds a thick hide of foreign animal on their table, spilling a glass of wine along the way. Margo releases a look of stress from across the hall. She isn't sure what to do about the spill of wine. I flick her away with my wrist to stop her from getting involved. Inside the unfurled hide lie two spearheads and a gown of choksilk. The silk is a rare commodity acquired from their southern neighbors. Illitaww trades sparingly with the rest of us, but the items they trade are some of the most valuable in Elybion. Their impenetrable silk is among the most desired commodities, but only the wealthiest can afford it. It is an excellent gift, and Prime Raylia has made it difficult for the next presenter.

"Thank you, Prime Raylia." Kyber grips the hands of the Arilandic prime. "There is a lot of material here. Is there enough for a few shirts?"

The crowd laughs as Velvia yanks away her gown and hands it to her nearest handmaiden. Kyber throws up his hand, and people laugh. Their game is entertaining because Kyber plays the crowd, where Velvia is greedy. She has everything a person could ever want, but she is still gnashing at others for more. Even her husband isn't safe from her wrath. If anyone deserves more, it is Prince Kyber.

The Swedans are next to present. King Ginnis Kil'Maalot of Swedas offers the gift. He brings a small box and sits it down in front of the princess. Velvia looks at the box and then at King Ginnis. The crowd is quiet.

"Well, don't look at me, Princess. Open the box." King Ginnis points.

Velvia is stunned by the gesture. Kyber pulls the string

on top of the box. The sides fall, and the top of the container collapses and slides off the table. Underneath, there is a small figurine carved in white rock.

"Yes. Thank you, Your Majesty. It is intricately carved. I shall add it to my collection for our future children." Kyber holds it to the light for further examination.

"Are you serious? A toy for our future children?" Velvia says.

The crowd laughs, yet the king of Swedas is laughing the loudest of them all.

"You may keep the figurine if you desire." The king's belly shakes.

A man dressed in extravagant clothes and a jeweled hat shuffles forward.

"This is Atymus Grogonvolantus. He is a master sculptor and the greatest in all the realm. I have commissioned a sculpture of the new couple to be chiseled out of the white rock of Delphinus." King Ginnis bows.

Lords clap in response to King Ginnis Kil'Maalot's gesture.

"Thank you, sir. What an amazing gift. One my princess will truly appreciate." Kyber turns to Velvia.

"Yes. Thank you, Your Majesty." Velvia nods.

Many others present their extravagant gifts to the couple. Each giver attempts to surpass the last with a grander demonstration.

King Donak and Queen Tyra watch every presentation. Their personalities are as different as Delphinus is from Illitaww. The king is charismatic. He is always the first to laugh, and the loudest. People are drawn to him. As the gifts are presented, the room looks to the king. He cheers and comments about his favorite details. The room echoes his sentiments. He is the warm side to the queen's cold. She holds bitterness as a hard shell. She loathes the presence of other people.

"One last gift shall complete the ceremony and conclude

tonight's events." King Donak steps out of the center of the room.

The Venith rise, ready to present. The three of them, dressed in white, walk side by side. Their steps are in sequence, and they move like a marching army.

Whispers chirp throughout the hall. I extend my arm to block an eager group of servants.

"Wait," I whisper.

The Venith leader lays down the polished silver box between Velvia and Kyber, who are standing to meet them. Velvia stares down at the box. Anticipation grows from the corner of her mouth in the shape of a grin.

"Vzars Nyla, Musa, and Jaina, your very presence at our wedding is an honor and a gift alone," Kyber says.

"The gift is small. Yet it may help you greatly." Vzar Nyla turns to the crowd.

Her eyes glow bright green.

"This is a gift for you all." Vzar Nyla directs her words to King Donak and Queen Tyra. "Your prosperity is our only desire."

"Vzar Nyla, we thank you for your gift." The king raises his glass. "To a new beginning and prosperity for all nations."

"To a new beginning," people echo.

Everyone takes a drink from their glass except the Venith. Vzar Nyla leads the other two out of the center of the room, where I can no longer see them. Lords and ladies applaud as they walk away. The lords and ladies revere the Venith outsiders like they are equal or higher than kings. What power do they hold?

"Go. And make sure everyone has a drink this time, especially the Venith." I release my arm holding back the legion of servants.

"I'll take that." I remove one of the serving platters from a servant and send them back to the kitchen.

Now is my chance to see the prince up close one last time.

I walk to the front with my head down. Out of the corner of my eye, I catch Elise. The glimpse causes my stomach to churn, and I twist the platter in between my face and her view of it. The drinks swish to the edge of the cups and nearly spill. My hands loosen on the platter as sweat pools in my palms. Elise turns back toward the island princess as I let out a sigh of relief.

I place the drinks on Kyber's side of the table. I pause for a moment, hoping to catch his gaze, but he doesn't look my way. My hands are shaking, and my confidence leaks out with the sweat trickling down my brow. The crowd of lords and ladies trade new gab with each other.

What am I doing here? This is stupid.

As I step backward, I trip on the pile of gifts. In the last moment, I catch myself, with one hand slapping a column and a foot stomping on the floor. I slowly rise, with Velvia's eyes cutting through the back of my neck. I'm waiting with my eyes on the floor for her to say something cruel, but nothing comes. Velvia hasn't noticed me. She is preoccupied with the Venith's gift box. I'm invisible. Everyone is enjoying conversations with their tablemates, and no one notices me. Then I see King Donak, who is ignoring the lord of Swedas and staring directly at me. Shame is all I feel. His expression is clear. I want to close my eyes and disappear. King Donak has the most to lose from his bastard causing a scene. I can't embarrass the king—nothing would be worse.

I lower my head and step down from the platform where Kyber and Velvia are sitting. A finger pokes me in the lower back. Another servant? No. Kyber's thick palm gently touches my back. He grins, yet his eyes are on a target in the distance. He knows it's me. My body tenses, and I force myself to look away from Kyber.

Get out! a voice screams inside my head.

I dart off toward the kitchen in such a rush that I stumble into one of the servants. Her platter of turkey shavings crashes behind me. I continue without remorse. I travel through the kitchen, ignoring words from Tif and other servants. Slamming the door of the servants' quarters behind me. I slide my back down the door until I'm crouched, sitting on my heels.

Did anyone see me? The king noticed me a moment before Kyber's hand found my back, but he didn't see. Did he? It was nothing, an accident. Kyber thought I was someone else. No, he knew it was me.

"Nok, what are you doing?" Tif pounds on the other side of the door. "We need you out there. I'm sending the final cours-es."

"Yes," I shout.

"What?" Another series of knocks pound the door.

"Yes. I hear you." I swing open the door.

Everyone in the kitchen pauses their chores.

"Are you well, Nok?" Margo steps forward.

"Even if he is not well, he is." Tif waves at a group of servers. "Nok. Go make sure they don't give the felroot fried in avashew nut oil to the lady from Tyfu. The rumor is avashew will swell her face."

Margo chimes in with a snorting laugh. Tif returns an ex-pression of seriousness.

"Yes. Yes, I'm going. Thank you, Margo. I'm fine. I'll ex-plain later," I say.

She whips a wet towel behind me as I walk away.

The lords and ladies enjoy their meals, leaving little scraps to share with the commoners. One by one, they retire for the evening, taking the children away with them. Handmaidens and the dregadins' attendants gather the gifts and take them out while I help the servers clean, avoiding eye contact with the royals. Eventually, only the young lords and ladies remain to gossip and celebrate the evening.

Prince Kyber is slumped down in his chair, while Velvia re-mains stiff. The young future rulers have gathered closer to the head table to trade whispers and drink. I watch them all from the edge of the hall, seemingly out of sight.

"Nok. Get in here." Elise stands on her stool and waves to me.

My cover has eroded, and my fears are realized. I take a step backward into the shadows. I'm afraid of what she will say next.

"Nok. I see you in the hall. Don't play shy. Come out here and join us. We are playing the turnover game," she says.

I slowly step out from behind the corner and walk toward them.

"Well, hello, Nok. Where have you been?" Elise slips off her stool as she tries to step down.

A young Delphinish lord catches her.

"I apologize. I was just...performing my duties in the kitch-en," I say.

Velvia is surprisingly gentle with her dagger eyes.

"You did a wonderful job. We are all bloated and popping out of our dresses." Elise lets go of the hand holding her up and slides back into her seat.

"Thank you, my lady. It has been our pleasure. Is there anything else I can get you from the kitchen?" I bow and take a step backward.

"No, you mustn't leave me here with all these people." She tries to whisper from the side of her mouth while covering her lips from the others, yet they can hear her. The Swedas princess rolls her eyes.

"Who is this servant?" the young Delphinish lord asks abruptly.

"This is Nok, the king's bastard and Velvia's brother," Elise says.

Everyone stops their whispers to look up at me.

"Is that true? It is. I can see the king in his face now," a young Arilandic lord says.

The Arilandic man resembles his mother, Prime Raylia Tiraban, though his face is more feminine.

"Please. Sit with us and play this ridiculous game." He
slams his fist on the table.

"I wouldn't dare stay without the princess's permission,"
I say.

My words cause Velvia's glare to surface.

"We have a wedding in the morning. If they want to get
drunk and embarrass themselves with a bastard, that is their
choice." She shoves herself away from the table. "Until tomorrow, Prince Kyber."

"Uh, yes. Princess." Kyber stands and kisses her outstretched hand.

Her handmaidens guide her through the great-hall doors,
which slam behind them.

"Have a seat." Elise pats the empty chair and makes pouty
lips.

"Very well. It will be your pleasure to have me." I bow
and wink.

The Arilandic lord chuckles. The Delphinish lord scoffs,
then smiles.

"See? You are all going to love him," Elise says.

There are a few more than half a dozen young lords and ladies present. Magnavozian guards stand by each doorway, while
handmaidens creep against the walls until they are summoned.

Kyber, Elise, Governor Andros Palenor's son, and the islander bride surround the main table. The Arilandic lord, his
two younger brothers, and the quiet daughter of King Ginnis sit
to the right of the main table.

Kyber slams a mug down in front of me when I sit.

"So, the point of the game is to drink all your drink—as
fast as you can. I mean all of it, because when you finish, you
have to turn your cup over and prove there isn't a drop left."
Kyber brings a cup to his lips. His cheeks pull a smile around

the edges.

"Wait. The first one who has a drop fall from their cup must drink another drink. So you don't always want to be the first person to tip your cup over, unless you are certain every drop is gone." Elise holds her hand in front of my cup.

"Well, you are no fun." Kyber relaxes the drink away from his lips.

Elise giggles and removes her hand. I take up the cup, and I mimic Kyber's hold on his. He winks, and we both chug. I finish mine with only a few dribbles of liquid dripping down my chin. Kyber is waiting for me to finish while holding his cup outstretched in his hand. I push my cup out to meet his, and the edges clank together. We both nod and turn our cups over. A few droplets dribble out from his cup, and the room erupts with laughter.

"Damn. You have me on that." He pours himself another cupful and throws it back, slapping the table with his free hand.

We watch the others take their turns, and I play a few more rounds as well. Each time someone drinks, Kyber smiles and looks at me with his big brown eyes. The other servants finish their duties while I sit and play. I find Margo stepping close to the head table, trying to get my attention. She nods her head to the side, beckoning me to come with her. I should go with her, but I can't. I may never have another night like this. I ignore her attempts. Margo lets out an audible sigh and quickly walks away. As she leaves, my eyes catch the white ribbon of the Venith's gift.

"Are those people really the Venith?" I say.

The words fall out, and I want to put them back in, but I can't. The question has been on my mind since I first saw them at the tournament a season ago. Everyone is staring at me.

"I don't know. I thought the Venith were legends, like dragons, and Xyji." I take a gulp of my drink.

"We are so lucky to have them. They arrived before Vega's

funeral and have been gracious guests here. I'm surprised you haven't seen them," Elise says.

I was at the back of the temple, where I could not hear a word the priest said nor view anyone of importance.

"Yes. Vzar Nyla is truly wise. She discussed an irrigation plan with my father that will help us during the dry seasons," King Ginnis Kil'Maalot's daughter says.

The Venith have returned? I can't believe it. I can't believe any of this—serving in the kitchen and scrubbing cobblestone to gossiping with lords and ladies about mythical beings from faraway lands.

"That's amazing. Vzar Musa is the handsomest man I have ever seen. I wonder if they marry." Elise laughs and shakes the Tyfuan island princess by her arm.

"What is the young one's name? The one with yellow eyes? I would make her my wife," Prime Raylia's son says.

Kyber chuckles. He has been quiet since he lost the game. Yet he isn't angry. A smile remains as his eyes follow each person when they speak.

The Venith are as different from the lords as they are from the commoners. The Venith are another step above. Their attractive features are not the only thing separating them from others. They move differently as well. When they walk, it is in perfect synchrony, like a dance or a military march. Their gaze is deliberate, like they are memorizing every detail of their environment.

"I'll be glad when they go back to where they came from." The island princess leans forward.

"Dear." Palenor's son, Lord Yondal, tries to hush her.

"I mean, where in the outland did they come from? There is nothing beyond the Isles to the north, and nothing beyond the Illitaww and the islands to the south."

All valid points. She raises many of my own concerns.

"Their people have always helped those of Elybion, and

they must live far away, because they visit us so rarely," Elise says.

The island princess crosses her arms and sits back.

"What's your opinion on the Venith, Nok?" Kyber says.

"Well... I don't understand why there are only three of them and why they have come now and not earlier. However, they seem to be doing good things for the realm. Has anyone read the texts that refer to the Venith?" I say.

"Whoa, Nok. We don't have time to go to the library and read all the old texts. That would make for a dull night," Elise jokes, and leans back in her seat, folding her arms like the island princess.

The Delphinish lord and his princess are trading expressions with each other. The Arilandic lord is carving into the table with his knife. Tif would cringe if she saw it. The young Swedas princess hangs her arms limply, and she is looking up at the ceiling.

"I don't want to bore you all. How about one more cupful before we close the kitchen?" I say.

"I think I'll pass. Thank you all for the company. I shall see you all for the wedding tomorrow." Kyber stands and pushes his chair in with a screech.

"I'll have one more," the island princess says.

He stumbles to the giant doors that lead to the rest of the castle. Before he steps out, his eyes find mine, and he nods his head to the side. Does he mean for me to follow him? I can't follow him. It should never have gone this far, and I won't let it go any further. I should be in the kitchen, piling the scraps for the castle dogs. Yet I remain seated, nodding my head in agreement to the gossip Elise spews. Kyber disappears into the hallway, as does my interest in this table.

PART II

JOURNEYS OF THE JUST

CHAPTER TEN

The Castaway

Kai

SUMMER L37, 50 AE

Master NcTully jabs me with his pointed finger as he lectures me one last time in the empty hall outside his chamber.

"Your common lack of understanding, your tardiness, not to mention your incident in the forbidden Cache. Each are reasons enough. Now go." NcTully pushes me out of his way as he enters his chamber.

The heavy temple door fills my nostrils with the scent of dusty scrolls as it slams shut. Master NcTully has no choice. The council and grandmaster already decided before we met.

My leg quivers. I never thought my life could turn out this way. For the last four years, I've devoted my life to the temple and its teachings, and now it's over. As my stomach twists, I think about my life path winding away from what I know, what I have always known, to something unfamiliar.

As I turn and begin the long walk down the halls, I ponder my life's journey. My thoughts and memories carry me back to a whelpling on the North Isles. I recall spending every day studying inside when there was so much to see and feel outside. I remember the scent of the sea wafting in through the window of my family's shack. I would stay up late at night, by the light of a candle, attempting to memorize all the available texts. My hands ached from practicing my script-hand every day.

I squeeze my fists in and out, flexing tired muscles, which seem to belong to an older man. As I reflect on all my effort to this point, I begin to see flashes of red. My vision is blurring from the water swelling over the cusp. Blood rushes to my head. My knees weaken, and my stomach turns. Forgetting to breathe, I become light-headed and press my palm against the high walls of the temple's halls. This is failure, an ever-consuming monster. I'm frozen.

I feel surreal. The walls around me feel like they are falling in. Nothing seems real. How did this happen? Unfortunately, I was complacent with the repetition of the daily routine. I have duplicated entire books several times. At first I loved to read the great books. It was pure joy and pleasure to read the words of the great masters. All their wisdom and knowledge is organized into each paragraph. Eventually, the words blurred together, and I wasn't reading them anymore. My mind would travel somewhere else while my hands continued their work.

I thought it wouldn't be noticed if I took a few days away from my work and roamed the city. Did one of the other apprentices notice? In their place, I might have been jealous to see someone else escape the monotony for a day, but I would never expose them. Regardless of how it started, the masters began to watch me. They found several mistakes in my duplications of the texts. The masters expect high quantities, but purity is of the greatest importance. The simple mistake of writing a t in place of a k was enough to infuriate the masters. They believe misinterpretation of the texts will create chaos in the realm for generations. Was I the only one who ever made these mistakes?

I vomit. The release of vomit onto the otherwise pristine temple floor improves my cloudy vision. I walk out with a fresh-er conscience. It's odd how losing everything can free you from caring about anything.

"Kai?" Sanya yells as she runs down the hall to catch me before I step out into the garden.

"Hi, Sanya," I say.

"What happened? Is it true? You are leaving?" Sanya's voice sounds like she is talking about someone who has died.

I try not to vomit again as I tell her what happened. I explain the major details, avoiding the bit about the forbidden Cache.

"Go see Phan. She'll want to see you before you leave. Oh no. I need to make a trip to the Foyer of Letters before Master Hans's lecture. Bye." Sanya pulls the end of her robe above her ankles and runs off.

"Bye, Sanya." I turn away and step out into the gardens.

Each step delivers me from the darkness of my failure and into the light of my future. I can't take the time to dwell on the pain. Controlled by other teachings or by a stronger nature, I walk through the sorrow attempting to grab hold of me. I must decide my next course of action. What path can I take? Part of me wants to give up and join the old man Mesea, begging for coin outside the city. Is there anything else for me? My hope is enigmatic, and it dies slowly.

Walking out of the temple, onto the white bricks covering the city's roads, I raise my chin up to the large constructs overshadowing the streets outside. Pillars block out the sun and shade my path. Seagulls fly above the pillars toward the ocean, creating their own tiny shadows on the white bricks. The Temple of Summer's Light is made up of three large towers with nested spires. The towers are surrounded by circular halls cased in the same white bricks that most of the city is crafted from. The entire city is a white obstruction in the nation, and the occupants take exceptional care to keep it clean and glossy.

"Well, how do you believe life was first created, Master Gwen?"

One of the masters argues an opinion on the Plat as I exit the inner walls of the temple. People of the city are gathered around below the stage to hear the philosophies of the masters. A year ago I would have been hanging on every word. Today I continue to walk through the garden, disinterested in their babble.

I'm on another path, and my options are limited. I don't have any valuable tools, nor skills in any tradecraft.

Guards suited in full armor line the entrance to the temple. I send a shy wave as I walk by. None of the guards react to my gesture. I hang my head. It's like I'm already a ghost here. I could join the Royal Guard of Delphinus. I would guard the temples and noble houses of the great city or other strongholds in the North. I wouldn't be expected to join in any war. The nation of Delphinus has been peaceful for many years. Yet peace may be coming to an end, so I might not be so lucky. The grandmaster frequently warned us of the cadences of harmony and war. I don't want to die fighting a war for selfish rulers.

I pass by a pod of apprentices. They are carrying a long pole of hanging fish gathered from the fish market in Phys. Each apprentice has a part of the pole resting on their shoulder while large fish swing behind them. There are redfish, pop-eyed fish, and tuna with orange tails spread along the pole. Maybe there is another option for me. I could find a captain willing to take on a sailor for his fishing boat. Yellers are always shouting about fortunes a new sailor could find at sea. I would begin as a deckhand and work my way up. One day, I would pilot a grand vessel of my own. I remember the smell of the ocean breeze, and sailorhood clings to me. However, I'm not ready to sail into the vast sea in search of fish and fortune. First I need to sail back to the North Isles to confess my failures to my mother. I grab the stone through the leather where it hangs under my robe. I haven't been home since I first arrived at Summer's Light. The shame of failure swells again as I imagine telling my mother. I dread the pain it will bring her. Still, it's time.

●

I await a transport for my voyage home to the North Isles.

The air is warm. Dockworkers shoo away the squawking seagulls while I wait for my transport to finish loading. Growing restless, I take my coin pouch and shake it. The few coins jingle against each other, with plenty of space between them. This amount won't last me very long.

"Kai." Phan waves to me from the end of the dock.

"Phan?" I shove the pouch of coins back into my satchel.

I raise my hands to welcome her over. After we exchange greetings, we sit down together on the stone bench. Phan scrunches her nose. I assume it is an attempt to wall off the aroma of salted fish that covers the area.

"I'm sorry, Phan. I tried to see you before I left, but I couldn't find you," I say.

"Yes. It's not your fault the grandmaster has me working another job in the Cache. I've slept a few nights in there, if you can believe it. It's starting to become a home for me." She smiles.

"Anything useful?" I say.

"Maybe. I came across a section describing the magic of the Venith. The grandmaster thought it was important enough for me to copy, so I made a copy for you as well." She discreetly slips me a small rolled parchment.

"Thank you, Phan. You didn't have to do this for me. I don't want you to lose your mastership, especially when you are so close," I say.

Phan shrugs her shoulders like she isn't worried about it. I would be less worried if I were her too.

"The grandmaster gave a speech about how each one of us has to prove dedication to knowledge, or we will meet a similar fate." She laughs, struggling to get out the end of her sentence.

I fidget with the edges of the stone bench, but I'm too embarrassed to respond.

"A similar fate," she repeats mockingly.

She notices my silence and changes her tone to a more serious one.

"You are going to be fine. You would have made a great steward or master, but I have a feeling you will find something else. Something to fulfill you even more," she says.

Her calming presence brings me ease and helps lessen the sting of my dismissal. She is the most knowledgeable apprentice in our rank, and I'm lucky to have her for a friend.

"Art will guide you on your path, and you will find another way to gain necessary knowledge pleasing to her," she says.

Phan remains a devout Artian, while my faith wavers. Unlike most Artians, I'm not sure the pursuit of knowledge is as important to me as I must portray.

"Thank you, Phan. Art blesses us with your wisdom." I recite the common phrase.

We are staring at each other. Sad twitches at the corners of our mouths express many words of a friendship, but neither of us speaks them. A few seagulls waddle closer to us in hopes of crumbs.

"You must return to your studies," I say.

She looks at me with swelling eyes. The eyes tell me she is both concerned and happy to see me one last time.

"Goodbye, Kai." She throws her arms around me.

The embrace catches me off guard, until I realize I'm no longer tied to the forbidden affection laws of the temple, and I graciously return the embrace. A pounding bell marks midday at the temple. My heart sinks, knowing the embrace is coming to an end.

She pulls back, smiles, and begins to retreat toward the temple. I stand to watch her leave. She turns around once more to smile and mouth a goodbye.

"Farewell, Kai," she says.

CHAPTER ELEVEN

The Islander

Kai

SUMMER L41, 50 AE

The second moon falls toward the horizon. Her delicate strength has faded, and she no longer possesses the will to remain in the heavens. The goddess flashes with intensity equal to the sun, and light turns the night into day. Giant waves swell in the north and swallow every sea vessel until the ocean is cleansed. The swollen waves pull themselves apart to reach the moon before she crashes into them. The fear of being swallowed by the waves consumes me. I turn my back to the sea.

When I turn away, my mother is right in front of me.

"Don't be afraid, my son. Art has returned, and our struggle is over."

She places her gentle hands on my shoulders and forces me
back toward the sea. Dark water flows around my ankles. For
a moment, we are safe. Then the waves surge more powerfully
than ever to drag me down into the deepest part of the ocean.

⦿

The spraying sound of a whale blowing ocean water right
beside the ferry wakes me from the vivid dream. Somehow the
dream seemed more real than my current circumstances. I'm on
the calm waters between the North Isles and Delphinus. Our
transport is a large sailboat, and not something typically used to
transport passengers to the Isles. We travel accompanied only by
the creatures of the sea.

The ocean is breathtaking this time of the year. Sunlight
shines over the beautiful blue ahead of our ship as we glide between the whales on either side of us.

A spout of water sprays up from the ocean. The mist rains
back down on us. The whales are migrating north for their annual mating. I have seen them many times in dense pods around
the North Isles. By the end of summer, the whales will leave
and travel in their large pods southward. The men who travel
with me are the usual inspired workers with dreams of gaining fortunes from the sea. One peculiar old woman is sitting
across from me on the deck. I keep catching her gaze, aimed at
me. Maybe she is someone that recognizes me from my village,
Watertree. No, her skin is far too pale to be that of an islander.
Maybe she travels on a religious journey.

In the *Great Text*, it says, "Art bore us at the edge of the land so that we may grow and flourish throughout all lands."

It's widely accepted that the edge of the land is considered to be the shores of Delphinus. For that reason, the masters built the Temple of Summer's Light there. However, there are some who believe the true birth of men occurred on the North Isles. Does this woman share those beliefs? I catch her staring at me once more.

"How are you doing this evening, Mother?" I say.

The woman looks at me with new eyes and smiles. Her mouth is missing many teeth, and she is happy that I have acknowledged her, but she does not answer.

My mother is one who believes the North Isles are the birthplace of man. Her belief was so strong that she traveled to the North Isles when I was young just to get closer to Art. Her homeland of Ariland is an arid country between Magnavoz and the northernmost lands of Illitaww.

I remember when I was a whelpling and used to complain about how cold I was.

"One day in the North has more warmth than a whole year in the South," my mother scoffed.

It's a common saying among southern people, though now that I have studied the geography of Ariland, a mostly desert land, I question my mother's experience with truly frigid weather.

One of the pestering whales bumps into the ferry, sending a tremor through the entire vessel. A worker standing near the starboard edge stumbles, and before he can regain balance, another whale bumps the ship. The worker trips over a sack of grain and falls into the sea. I jump up, shifting my vision up and down the deck to see if anyone has witnessed this.

"Man overboard!" a sailor shouts.

The shout shifts the crew into motion. A sailor swings down from one of the sails, and one shipmate runs to the edge of the ferry the worker fell from to grab a long boat hook.

Simultaneously two more sailors run to the side nearest the overboard passenger while tying ropes around their waists.

The old woman looks blatantly at me this time. Her eyes are sharply violet, which I didn't notice before. She is communicating her fear to me. I should do something, but I'm unsure how I can help. Deciding my nervous disposition is not going to hold me back today, I rise and make my way toward the old woman. The vessel maintains slight, residual tremors, shaking the entire structure. With more than an arm's length between us, I reach out toward the woman as if to say, "I have you."

Before I reach the woman's seat, another substantial mass hits the ferry. The collision knocks me off-balance, and I tumble several feet and over the edge into the blue. I see the bright sky for a moment before I splash into the dark water. I'm under the water, swirling around in the wake of the ship. My limbs flail without purpose. The fear tells me to kick and pull, but my efforts aren't coordinated. I'm afraid I won't reach the surface again. Then the waves knock me against the side of the vessel, and I forget everything else. With a rapid transition of the mighty water, I'm pulled underneath the stream of the ferry. Smacking against the hull, I begin to lose track of the surface. All I can see is a faint refraction of the sunlight through the surface of the water. I set that as my target and kick with all my strength. I just want to breathe, one last time.

A whale spouts as I come to the surface, and the water sprays down on me like rain. The whale hovers below the surface with its eye peering out of the water directly at me. It's like he has something to tell me, but our language barrier is too vast to try. He blinks before submerging down to the deep. I wipe the salty water from my eyes and locate the ship.

The ferry is drifting farther and farther away. I try to swim toward it. I can't keep up. Panic flourishes inside me like an infectious weed in an otherwise healthy garden. Flailing with dread, I thrash in the water until an arm finds me. It's one of the sailors. She is connected to a harness and rope, and she commits to rescuing me. Finally she grabs me. The harness gives a sharp tug as it becomes taut, skimming the ocean surface. There is an exuberant strain on both the rope and our arms as we grasp each other and struggle to stay above the surface. She's my only hope. I want to cling to her like she is the last person I'll ever meet. She wraps a band of line around me, and we painfully make our way back to the ferry.

Pulling myself onto the ship, I fall forward onto the deck's wooden surface. Spitting up water, I roll over onto my back, then back onto my stomach, choking on my water expulsion. Finally I catch a breath and get a full glance at my rescuer. She has a stern expression, as if she wants to scold me for misbehaving, but she says nothing. With her dark hair and narrow features, she is of Fangourian descent. The Fangourians I studied with at Summer's Light were known for their shrewd prowess at the practical studies, like construction. Her eyes are emerald green, and her hair is the moonless black of a starless night. She is of average height and build, and her strength is not apparent. Something about her is different from any other Fangourians I have encountered. Noticing myself staring at her for too long, I look away to my surroundings and all the other passengers staring at me.

The other victim of the whales' attack is sitting up on board as well. Everyone is settling down, except for one man: the captain. He is hanging over the edge of the ship, belting curses out toward the whales. He thinks the whales intentionally knocked his passengers overboard. As he yells, the whale pod drifts away northeast of the ferry.

The captain approaches me.

"Don't quite have your sea legs, do you, soldier?" he says with giddy delight.

"I'm not a soldier, sir. I just lost my balance when that whale bumped us the second time." I rub the back of my head.

"Everyone is a soldier. You might not know what war you are fighting in yet, but you are still a soldier," he says.

He pats me hard with two slaps on my shoulder and welcomes me back aboard.

"What are you doing heading to the North Isles? You aren't one of those Artians, are you? I mean, I wouldn't have a problem if you were. I don't see many of you anymore." He wobbles and sways with the ship.

"No. I'm journeying to Watertree. I left the Temple of Summer's Light. Now...I'm heading home." I fumble to get my words out, but he understands me enough.

"Oh? An island native? He is an islander!" he yells.

I realize he is heckling me, so I laugh off his comments. He walks away with another hard slap on the back and reminds me to stay on board.

"And what happened to you?" The captain points at his sailor who was knocked off.

I see the old woman who I tried to comfort.

"I'm sorry, Mother. I wish I could have been of more use." I squat down to level our faces.

"I don't know what all the hollering is about, but I wish you would leave me alone." She clutches her belongings tightly around her.

She isn't looking at me. She is blind, and her eyes are gray and weathered, not violet like I thought.

"I'm sorry. I won't bother you. Art's blessing on you," I say.

●

Several days later we arrive at the Port of Tyfu.

The port is known for its crime and pestilence. It is regarded as a nasty wart on what is otherwise a beautiful island. Laws are loose, and criminals roam freely. There is more wood, from the mainland, covering the city than the natural white sands. From the white beach, pathways lead up to the city that are covered in wooden planks from retired ships. Each path leads into the tight alleyways of the town. There are no extravagant buildings or structures in the city, but the city as a whole is unique. It is one cohesive piece connected by wooden paths to each house. If the island sank below the ocean, the city would remain floating above.

It has been a few years since I left from this same port to voyage to the temple. Yet the same fishy smell lingers from the clam shuckers nearby. A stench to welcome me home.

"Come speak to me if you want some work. We'll leave port on Repaday," Captain Davinor says.

The last several days of my laughing off his continuous heckling has apparently appealed to the captain.

"Yes, Captain." I awkwardly give a Magnavozian soldier salute.

The captain shakes his head, as the joke failed to result in humor. It's not a bad proposition, but first I need to get to Watertree.

The young Fangourian sailor hurries past me, bumping me with her shoulder. She looks back to see who was in her way, and continues stomping the wooden planks leading into the Wart.

The Port of Tyfu is a maze of tightly knit wooden planks. Losing your direction is expected in the city. I believe the pirates that built the city intended the maze-like pathways to create a business of mugging. Waiting like predators around every lane, the locals pour into the streets around us as we dive deeper into the city. I'm careful to move my satchel in front of my chest instead of behind me.

Down my path, I notice two men following the woman who rescued me. Does she not know how dangerous Tyfuan streets can be? I check my satchel again with my sweaty palms as I follow them from a distance. Eventually, one of the men bumps her while the other reaches for her bag. She glides out of the way like a water snake, tripping the assailant. Then she cinches the thug to the wooden ground with two of her throwing blades through his shirt collar. Everyone backs away from her. Now they recognize her rash nature. She is as dangerous, if not more, as they are.

"Wait." I run after her as she escapes down another narrow corridor.

Turning around the corner in pursuit of her, I'm slammed against the partial hull of a retired warship.

"Why are you following me?" she says.

Her voice is calm and monotonous.

"I wanted to thank you for saving me from the ocean... when I was knocked off," I reply with a faint voice as she pushes the air out of my chest.

She loosens her restraint and looks around us. "I was doing a job. I don't need any thanks," she says.

Her emerald eyes are piercing through me as if I'm an animal or something less. I want to apologize, but I don't think she will respond well to it. She fakes a smile and turns to walk away.

"Well, thanks anyway."

She disappears into the maze before I can finish.

I wander around the city in search of a meal until I find a man peddling coconut shavings. The shavings aren't substantial, but they are enough to abate my appetite. I trade one of my last coins for a half shell. It's an overpurchase, but I'm starved and sick of salted fish. As I turn to head east, I hear someone call from behind me.

"Kai Foyd?" he says.

"Oh, hi." I stare with reluctance at the familiar face.

"It's me, Cody. How have you been, friend?" he says.

"Cody?" I struggle to find words to interact with my old friend.

He has a much larger build, and he has grown a monstrous beard. Vague memories of a scrawny, shaved-headed boy come back to me. His tan covers once pale arms. He was always wild and liked to get into fights when we were kids. Like most kids from the island, his father was a sailor who was rarely on land. My mother often invited him and his mother over for dinner.

"How long have you been on Tyfu?" He gives me an excit-ed shake.

"I just got off the ferry from Delphinus. I'm headed back to Watertree," I say.

"I'm sorry, my friend," he says.

His eyes are full of so much pity that I feel the urge to console him. Does he know about my dismissal from the temple? It's surprising, because he never thought temple work was sig-nificant before.

"It's fine. We make the best of what Art gives us, right?" I shrug. "Well, how have you been, Cody?"

"Very well, mate. I've been sailing with the highest bid-ders for the last couple of years. Now I'm catching up with the maidens of Tyfu." He laughs hysterically. "So, I guess you're headed to the Oasis Tavern to see Kara. Or have you already been there?" he says.

"Kara is working at a tavern? I thought she was serving at the temple in Watertree," I say.

Kara is my sister. However, she wasn't born of my mother. She has always lived on the islands, and she was orphaned long before our mother arrived here with me. Our mother helped many children on the island, but Kara is different. Kara is as much a daughter to Joleen as I am a son. Naturally, she was content with the island life, never pursuing knowledge, like me. I was bathed in the idea of education being the only pursuit worth having.

"You haven't been around for a while, have you, brother? She has been working at the tavern for several years. She took over the place once the captain and his wife disappeared. She owns the whole damn place." He pauses.

Is he expecting me to gasp in disbelief?

"Oh...well, that's great. I haven't heard from Kara, and I didn't know," I say.

"Aye, maybe I'll see you there, brother. The Oasis has the finest lasses on the Isles," he says.

Cody gives me an island nod and struts away with a drunken stride to a group of women disembarking another ferry. I eat the rest of my coconut shavings while he proceeds to kiss each hand as if he were a nobleman. Then I turn away to find the tavern before he sees me laugh. The encounter with an old acquaintance was amusing, and it lightens the feeling of being an outsider in my homeland.

●͛

The tavern is raised on pillars over the shallow waters near the edge of the beach. There is a narrow walkway leading up from the shore. Small openings in the floor give sight to the clear waters below. A few smaller ships anchored below the tavern gently bump up against the stabilizing pillars as the ocean waves come in. The location is perfect for someone with a home in Watertree, which is just east, across the narrow waters.

Watertree might be the smallest village in the North Isles and all of Elybion. There are a few fishermen and divers living there, but nothing of note, and no reason to visit.

The music is exciting as I enter. A group of bards pluck

various sizes of stringed instruments. Taking a seat at the bar, I gaze around at the tacky decorations that cover the walls. Differing bits of glass and seashells are patterned into images of a mermaid. The glass makes her tail, while the seashells form her skin. When Kara and I were whelplings, we collected seashells from the ocean every morning before mother conducted our instruction. There's no doubt that Kara has contributed in some part to the hundreds of seashells covering her tavern.

Finally, from across the room, I watch Kara sweep in and issue commands to her legion of dancers, tenders, and musicians. Even from a distance, I can see she has changed. She is beautiful, like many island women, but bolder and less withered than most. She wears a visible cutlass at her waist. She was always an advocate for peace and freedoms. Has the harsh city warped her?

Her tenders and dancers disperse, while the bards jump into another tune.

"She's coming, across the desert, to meet a man you know. Her dresses...are lovely, though her skin is old. She's a prime example of a story untold..." A bard plucks a melody along with his song.

Lost in memories of the past, I lose track of my surroundings. Sharp objects poke into my back.

"Are you lost, baby whale?" a voice, made to be deeper than natural, says.

I jump away from the bar and twist around to the person issuing the threat.

"Quick reaction, for a whale," she says.

"You can't hold a weapon to a man's back." My voice cracks.

My ego is damaged by embarrassment, but I'm intrigued by her presence. She conceals her blade and raises her hands to further poke at me.

"May I buy you a drink? For helping me get back on board

the ferry," I say.

"Sure, baby whale, if you must ease your own conscience," she says.

"My name is Foyd, Kaison Foyd. Since I owe my life to you now, you may call me whatever you please."

She stares at me with her deep-emerald eyes. Her face is softer up close. She stops as if she is trying to decide if she trusts me enough to stay.

"My name is E-Agta, Shiva E-Agta. You may not call me another name besides my own," she says.

She puts her hand on the hilt of her dagger and settles in the seat beside me. We sit in awkward silence as she drinks her drink and I go back to admiring my sister's work.

I catch a movement out of the corner of my eye.

"Did you see that?" I point to a creature waddling around the corner of the bar.

"Yes." Shiva leans back.

An otter jumps onto the bar in front of us. Shiva catches herself from falling backward by the tip of her toe pressing into the bar. Another otter jumps up beside the first. I turn to Shiva and laugh. She lets free a quaint smile. The otters are jumping up and down, clapping their hands together. It's a beg for treats.

"These are not wild critters," Shiva says.

Kara notices the commotion and gives me a second glance to confirm her recognition.

"Brother?" Kara exclaims in disbelief.

The two otters jump off the bar and scurry into one of the openings in the floor.

"Kara." I return the greeting with a mirrored enthusiasm.

She makes her way across the tavern with her arms already forming a hug. "When did you get here?" She embraces me warmly.

"Today. I've come to visit you," I explain.

Kara takes a step back from me, and she has a distraught expression.

"I'm sorry, Kai." She takes a shaky breath. "It's Mother... She's very ill. Has been for a while." Her eyes fill with tears as her voice becomes shakier. "She hasn't led ceremonies at the temple for a year. I fear..." Kara shakes her head, looks directly into my eyes, and scrunches her face. "I fear she is nearing the twilight." She hides her sorrow in my shoulder.

I pull her in to hide my own tears forming. "We should go see her." I squeeze her tightly.

"Yes. She will love that. Tomorrow. We'll go tomorrow. I'm so happy you are here. We've missed you so much," she says.

Her words tighten up my throat like the taste of a stiff drink would, but I'm not surprised. Somehow I suspected our mother wasn't right.

"I'm here now, sister. I'm proud of you and what you've done with this place." I point at the mermaid mural.

I try to comfort her by patting her on her back and wiping her tears away.

"Oh, this place? It's nothing. We serve drinks to drunk pirates," she says. She laughs and begins to regain composure. "What about you? How's Summer's Light? Is it as grand as they say?" she asks.

"True, it is marvelous. The three crown towers at the center of the temple extend high into the sky, as they say. It is beautiful, but I'm no longer an apprentice of the temple. I left. Well, I was asked to leave," I confess.

"Oh, Kai, I don't understand. Why would they ask you to leave? You have always been the most disciplined. You're the model Artian." Her eyes wander. I think she is trying to construct a way in her head to get me back to Summer's Light. Her eyes continue working back and forth as she waits for me to respond. She has always been a problem-solver. I admire her for those qualities.

"No, Kara. It's fine. In truth, I've begun to get lazy with the philosophies, and I've been less interested in ceremonies.

The truth is I did not belong in the temple anymore," I say.

"I don't quite understand, Kai. I thought becoming the grandmaster was your dream. Well, it doesn't matter. I'm happy you are here. You can have whatever you want from the tavern. I'll catch up with you after I speak to the bards and the cook to make sure we are ready for tonight. I hear there is a large crowd gathering in the Port of Tyfu," she says.

She hugs me once more as she kicks into action with her duties. Whistles sound out with pointed fingers as she orders her staff into action. She has changed a lot since I last spoke to her. She has become a leader, in contrast to the lonely free spirit she was as a child.

The perfect cool breeze blows in with each customer until the place is completely full and our drinks are finished. Shiva stands and raises her glass as if to gesture a respectful farewell. I raise my glass to her to match.

CHAPTER TWELVE

The Opportunist

Shiva

SUMMER L44, 50 AE

Captain Davinor, Mitch, and a few others slip by me as I trail down the bridge leading from the tavern to the beach. Each of them holds a grin larger than they can afford with as few teeth as they all share. Davinor looks back when he realizes I'm not following them.

"There you are." Davinor opens his arms. "Where are you going? I've just arrived."

"I'll be on the ship." I turn and keep walking.

"I found our next squeeze. It's a big one, dear." He

measures a distance with his hands. "You're going to want to hear this. It's Fangourian gold."

He smiles and nods his head toward the tavern, where he likes to announce his heists. He knows he has me with the mention of Fangourian gold, but I won't give him the satisfaction of following them now.

"Whatever it is, I'll be waiting on the ship until we leave," I say.

"Suit yourself, then. Come on, chaps." The captain leads them into the tavern.

I wait awhile at the end of the walkway, watching questionable men enter the tavern. What does he mean by "Fangourian gold"? Curiosity grows until I can't help but peek back inside.

All eyes are facing across the room when I enter. Kai's sister swats would-be sailors with the end of her broom to get them off her tables.

"It's the Golden Gulf, I tell you. You think it's by chance they call it that?" Captain Davinor gives a speech with one foot planted on a chair.

I lean against the support beam near the entrance. The floor creaks as an imbalance of patrons gather near Davinor.

"You all know the goods transported through the gulf. You know about the fish and the cheap art of Swedas. But..." Davinor wags his finger. "You don't know the secret export... Don't worry, I'm going to tell you. Treasure and gold beyond your imagination."

"That's enough. There have always been rumors of gold in the gulf," a burly man says from his seat in the corner.

"Yes. Yes. You're right, but no one has ever known how they transport the Fangourian treasury. No one has until now," Davinor says.

The burly man dismisses Davinor with a wave. Kai walks in front of the man and takes a seat at the table closest to

Davinor. A drizzle of mead spills down Kai's shirt as he takes a long gulp. The ends of his messily quaffed hairs drip with sweat as he finishes. Everyone is hot; I can smell my own odors in their full ripeness from days of sailing. I take a step away from the men standing beside me to make certain no one smells my stench. They won't notice it over their own foul combinations of sweat and mead breath, but I do.

"How do you make these claims?" I step up behind the crowd.

Their heads all turn back to me at once. Screeching chair legs follow.

"Ah, yes. I'm glad you asked. Borus, come here." Davinor brings up a thin young man. "Borus here has sailed on the vessels carrying the treasure. He's told me how to find them." Davinor shakes the boy.

"It's true. I've been on several ships carrying the treasure. There is more on one ship than would fit in this tavern," Borus says.

His accent is thick with the Magnavozian plains. It's a clear indication of his culture, but does he really know about the treasure galleons?

"They only transport it twice a year—"

"That's enough. They'll have to sign up if they want a piece of the prize." Davinor interrupts Borus with a hard slap on his back.

I look around the room, and a few patrons are convinced enough to whisper among themselves, but none are ready to leap on board.

"I've heard enough, and I've heard it before. The marked ships with the treasure of an empire." The burly man slides his chair in and starts to walk toward the door.

I step away to allow him to pass.

"He's right. It's not the first time we've heard these sto-ries, Captain." I fold my arms.

Kai steps onto the table that he has been leaning against.

"I'll join. You all should. Let's go." Kai pumps his fist in the air.

My head falls. The captain laughs and catches Kai. Other foolish young men follow with a pledge to join. It's probably another empty pursuit, but if he's right...the Fangourian treasure belongs to me as much as anyone.

CHAPTER THIRTEEN

The Son

Kai

SUMMER L45, 50 AE

Drenched in sweat and sticky from the morning spray, I rise from my slumber and find myself alone in one of the guest rooms of the tavern. With a light headache and a swollen stomach, I begin to make my way around, gathering my belongings and searching for people. I pass Cody coming out of the adjacent room.

"Kai, my friend. Fun night. I guess we'll be crewmates. No more maidens for me."

He rambles on about his experience with an Aptorian

maiden the night before.

"Great, Cody," I answer.

I walk past him in discontent. His vigor is too great for me, and I'm confused by his statements because I don't remember the night before.

Finally I find my sister issuing orders to her staff as they are making final cleanups.

"Kara, good morning, my fair sister. I didn't drink too much last night, did I?" I chuckle.

"That's an understatement. You drank enough for the whole week. You are not healthy, brother. That whole thing with the expedition—what were you thinking? You need to go back to Summer's Light and continue your studies," Kara says.

Then she softens her gaze and grabs my hand. "Today we are taking my raft to Watertree to visit our mother," she says.

"Yes, we need to visit Mother. What expedition are you talking about?" I say.

"You won't be drinking any more from my tavern, brother. You really don't remember?"

She proceeds to explain the events of the previous night as we walk down the stairs leading to the waters below the inn. "Captain Davinor and his men came in last night and threw out some gold coins like a bunch of monkeys. He exclaimed to everyone that he knows where more gold can be found. He intends to go claim the sum of it," she recounts.

She looks at me to see if I recall anything. It's starting to come back, but my head aches each time I try to remember.

"You were the first arsehole to stand up and proclaim that you'll sign up for the expedition to go to parts unknown with Captain Davinor. Then every sailor in the tavern followed, and you all drank more. More coin for me and less sense for you all," she says.

She wants to be angry at me, but I can tell it's difficult for her. She laughs as she begins to direct me to her raft. We are walking along a waterlogged dock partially sunken below the tavern.

"My apologies, sister. I was having a rough day. No, a rough week," I say.

She ignores me and continues to walk down the soggy planks below the tavern. She may never honestly be bothered by anything I do.

The two otters from yesterday swim up from underneath the planks. They rush in front of us and jump into the well-crafted raft

"Wadie. Luelue." Kara claps her hands twice.

The otters jump up with their paws on the edge of the raft, waiting attentively.

"Out." Kara points at her feet.

The otters look up to her, then at each other, before diving off the raft.

"This is yours?" I say.

"You can swim if you prefer." She points at the waters between us and Watertree.

"This is good. I like it." I step into the raft without another word.

The Oasis Tavern is much grittier in the light of the sun this warm morning.

"It really is amazing that you are doing so well, sister," I say.

She smiles and squeezes my hand. Unlike me, she seems to have an idea of what her life is supposed to be like.

●

The room is gray with a swirling emptiness of air. Our

mother lies in her bed, warm and happy. She is not asleep, sitting there smiling at us when we enter. The breeze seeps underneath the door when I shut it behind us.

Usually she would be greeting us and making sure we had water and food when we entered. She was always the best host, going out of her way to make everyone comfortable.

"Mother," Kara says. "I told you, you need to have the windows open to let some sunshine and fresh air blow in."

Her words aren't out of anger, rather out of care and love. I'm speechless. Finally I bring myself to make eye contact with our mother. She is quietly staring at me. My throat is cinched by the pain of longing and the fear of losing her. Kara grabs my hand to make me follow her.

"My children. My children are here. How Art has blessed me to have you both. My life is fulfilled having you live out all the dreams I wished for you," Mother says.

"I'm sorry I didn't know... I would've come sooner," I whisper.

Our mother seems fragile, and it hurts to witness it, because she was always so strong. I reach to hold her hand as I speak. Her hands are soft.

"Kaison, my little boy, why has Art blessed me with such a son?" She coughs as she praises me.

I feel like I need to cry, but my eyes are too dry.

"Mother, I've failed you. I can't go back to Summer's Light." I confess the words blockading the openness we once held with each other.

"My Kaison, Art has another plan for you," she says.

I stare in disbelief. Has the fever wholly taken her mind? She spent her entire life saving coin to send me to Summer's Light.

"Mother..." I stop myself before I say anything to dishonor her faith.

"Don't worry, my son. Art will open the gateways for you.

I promise," she says.

"All right, Mother. Let's feed you and get you some rest," Kara says.

Kara shuffles over to the kettle on the other side of the room. I try to step back, but Mother doesn't let go of my hand. With a loving gaze shining from her, she tugs me. I move in closer to listen.

"You still have it, don't you? Take the Art Stone to the Cradle of Man before the moon falls. Once you're there, you'll understand." Her hand falls limp as she drifts away.

"Kara," I say.

"It's fine. She needs a lot of rest these days." Kara wipes our mother's brow.

I take a step back and pull the object out from its pouch. It's a beautiful glass stone, with a slight blue hue. What has she bestowed on me? I step back and sit in the chair beside her. I forgot how seriously she takes her religion. Tears form at the cusps of my eyelids when I look back to our mother. She is taking slow, labored breaths. I want to help her. I want to heal her. But I can't.

●

Later Kara and I catch up with each other. She informs me how hard she worked to improve the tavern. I believe her. Once, it was a grimy pirate nest.

"Well, as distinguished as a resident of the Isles can be. You give me that look, but it's true. I've hosted the princess of Tyfu," she says.

"Tyfu has a princess? Who's that?"

"Princess Galisia NcLetti. Where have you been? She had

so many servants, and they rented out the entire Oasis last year."

"The NcLettis are calling themselves kings now? It has been a long time." We laugh together.

Kara shrugs her shoulders, and we try not to wake our mother with our laughter. I look over at her, on the other side of the small shack we grew up in.

"Do you remember when we were caught playing with jellyfish?" I show a massive smirk.

"Yes. Oh my..." Kara says.

"Yeah, the shore was covered in them!" I interrupt.

"Which one of us had the idea to dig a pool for them?" she says.

She is referring to the sand pool we spent the whole day digging for them. The pool was meant to be a new home for all the jellies. Unfortunately, they perished before we finished the pool.

"That was you." I point.

"You both had me swimming," our mother speaks up from across the room.

We both laugh as the impish memories return and we are caught again. I start to drag my chair across the room and Kara follows.

"If I hadn't found you two there on that beach, I would've had a pit full of jellyfish." She smiles as her voice cracks.

"How are you?" I grab my mother's hand.

"I'm happy. Having you both here fills my heart," she says.

She hides her pain well. Kara gets up to make some more tea. I pat my mother's arm softly and try not to cry again.

"When did the illness come?" My question is crude, and I begin to regret asking it immediately.

She is quiet for a moment, and I expect she won't answer, nor do I really want her to answer.

"I've always had the illness. It has always been here, even when I was a little girl in the desert," she says.

"How is that possible? Is it something that comes and goes?" I say.

"No, son. It has always been a part of me, but Art protected me from the pain. Art gave me purpose to live and raise you both," she says.

I smile, and Kara brings us both a cup of tea. We spend the rest of the night telling our mother about our mischievous memories. She laughs at every story, and loudest at the ones we thought she would never forgive us for.

●

The next day, our mother passes away quietly. We prepare the customary Artian ceremony for death. We complete the ritual by sending her body in a small raft north toward the open ocean.

"Praise Art," we say in unison as the raft vanishes.

We sit together with our feet pressing into the sand. Tears roll down my cheek. My body feels more fragile than it ever has. I wasn't ready for her to leave. Kara seems more accepting, like she knew it was coming. She squeezes my arm and hugs my side.

"Thank you for coming back, Kai. She must've been waiting to see you," Kara says.

"Thank you for staying and being her caretaker." I kiss my sister on her forehead as we stare into the distance with the warm winds blowing across us.

"What are you doing next, brother? The temple here in Watertree could use a caretaker," she says.

"Eventually. But not now. I must see where the north winds take me," I say.

Kara plays with sand while I look down at the stone, which

I've been fiddling with.

"Did she ever speak of this to you?" I say.

I drop the stone into her hand. She holds it, examining it closely.

"Yes. Many times. Don't you remember?" she says.

I remember her talking about a stone that protected her, but I never saw it out of the leather pouch.

"This stone is your father's. It is the gift he gave our mother when they met," she says.

I remember our mother speaking about a precious gift our father gave to her, but I have never seen it. Stupidly I thought the gift was me.

"Do you want it?" I say.

"No. She specifically told me to make sure you always have it." Kara drops the stone back into my palm and rubs her sandy hand through my hair.

"It's yours if you want it," I say.

I want her to take it. Kara loved our mother and deserves all the heirlooms left behind.

"It's not for me, brother," she says.

"She told me to take it to the Cradle of Man. Do you know what she meant?" I say.

"She meant for you to take it to the Cradle of Man, and not to try to give it to me." Kara laughs. "It must be in Ariland, no?"

"In Ariland?" I clean the sand flakes she left from my hair. "Maybe I can journey with Davinor to the gulf and travel inland from there."

Part of me is afraid to travel so far. I've never been south of Delphinus. I only know the other nations by descriptions I've read.

"Don't give it away, Kai. It's important to her," Kara says.

"I won't. Why are you always right?" I put my arm around her.

CHAPTER FOURTEEN

The Leader

Jupp

SUMMER L50, 50 AE

The bonfire roars as the celebration cracks off. Today my brother, Marr, is to be honored with a new title. Akkimon is the title; the Twin Blades are the pillars of the power that the title carries.

Nestled in the Jarko Forest, below the Scalar Mountains, we gather. Summer winds blow down the mountains and through the forest, bringing in a transition. All chokworms have slowed their production. Some of the worms have already begun their hibernation, and the ones that haven't will soon encase

themselves in silk cocoons, making them indestructible. Annual-
ly our people follow the worms to Ruthatt's Glade. In the fall,
the worms will make another migration through the ice lands to
their breeding nests near the southern seas, and we will follow
them again. Yet those days are long ahead of us, and the warm
days, here in the forest, are not taken for granted. After the celebration, we'll take in all the warmth we can while the worms
rest.

"Does this mean you are too good to wrestle with me?"
Hellahh says.

Marr looks back as Hellahh jumps up, grabbing him around
both bare shoulders. Marr is darker than most in our clan but
lighter than Hellahh. Hellahh of Unthapp is stout. Her hair is
thick and dreadlocked. Yet her most distinguishing feature is her
plump lips, which tighten and shrink as her temper rises. She is
a formidable warrior, especially in hand-to-hand combat. Marr
outmatches her in cleverness and obsessively practiced skill. He
flings her over the side of his hip while dragging her chest over
his shoulder. His knotted hair unravels and falls down below his
chin. In another twist, he slaps her down into a pile of melting
snow.

"I'll never be too good to return you to the snow." Marr
loosens his grip as he gazes down at Hellahh.

My approach is announced by my boots splatting in the
melting snow.

"Jupp." Marr pulls Hellahh up as he rises himself to meet
me.

"My brother, the Akkimon." I grab him behind his neck
and pull him close to me.

Our foreheads almost touch before we break apart, and I
find a place to settle in and watch the events. The clan ignites
into further celebration as the bonfire continues to burn.

As I settle into a carved wooden stump, others whisper
across the pit, farther into the glade.

"Is Jupp jealous that his brother has the honor?" one elder clansman says.

"Jupp will be our leader. He can't be both leader and Akkimon," a den-mother says.

"I'm not sure he has it in him," the elder clansman says.

I don't mean to be eavesdropping. I look around myself. I'm not hiding, and there isn't any reason I can't be seen.

"I don't see why Marr can't be Akkimon and leader." I step closer to the elder.

"And what do you know, boy? You wouldn't know a good a leader if—" The den-mother pats him on his forearm.

Noticing who I am, they cower and disperse. I give them a nod and chuckle as they flee. The chatter of the clan grows as more fill into the glade.

"What was that?" Hellahh slaps a tusk full of mead into my hand.

"Oh? You weren't supposed to see that...our secret meeting. Yes, it was a gathering of great minds." I take a sip of my drink.

A group of children splits us apart, chasing each other with a bakett. Two snow-white foxes follow. The foxes are common pets for the youth of our clan, but these ones are especially light. Their fur is whiter than the snow, and their ears stick out wide on each side. The bakett is a stone wrapped in several layers of silk and covered in a final layer of animal skin. It's a toy for children, but many adults play a dangerous game with the bakett. An equal number of warriors from each clan will fight from the base of a post until the bakett is delivered to the top or the sun falls. Clans hold annual events for the game, among other competitions. Marr and Hellahh are both experts at the game.

Silence falls over the crowd as a large man covered in furs enters the glade. The largest of his furs is formed from a giant tiger pelt, which he acquired in a war against northern invaders. His tiger cloak drags along the ground behind him, while the head of the beast rests on his shoulder. His path is partially covered in snow and somewhat overgrown with wild grasses. No one stands on the pathway, but everyone takes an exaggerated step back and lowers their head as he passes.

Marr stands alone next to the carved boulder, watching the man make his way through the crowd. The Twin Blades lie across the rock altar.

The man's back turns away from me as he reaches the boulder. I can't see his face, but his expression must be friendly, because Marr returns a grin in response.

"Erowkahnn. Today we name our next protector." The man shakes off his furred cloak.

For our people, he is our king, Lakk the Blunt. For Marr and me, he is our unbreakable father, undefeated hero, and undeniable king.

Without his cloak, his bare arms break free. They are thick and carry many hard-earned scars. I reach down with my left hand to squeeze my right bicep. My arms are thick and durable, but they don't seem as large nor as hard as his. In his seventies, he has the gray hair of an elder, and the body of a man in his prime.

Lakk reaches for War first and then Harmony. He pulls them off the altar, causing a subtle screech. Like a swordsmith judging his work, he peers down the blade edge of War. Everyone waits in silence while he admires the blade.

"Akkimon, you are summoned." The king flips the blades around in his palms and drives them into the ground.

The blades break through the soil and submerge several inches, displacing dirt and rock along the way. On one knee, he releases the hilts. Then he rises and motions for Marr to stand across from him.

"If you choose, claim these blades and all the responsibilities owed with them." The king shows his empty palms to Marr.

The clan tightens as the king releases the words. Marr

steps up to the blades and examines them. He has spoken about the blades every day since we were first told the heroic den stories. There is nothing he reveres more. Marr wraps one hand around War and the other around Harmony. He pauses to look up at our father. Our father nods his approval. With this reassurance, Marr rips the blades loose, throwing clumps of soil and rock into the air. The clan roars, and the bonfire flames crackle. I nod my respects toward my brother.

A few of the older children wrestle over each other to get a glimpse at their new hero as I work my way through the crowd. What legends will this Akkimon forge? A thin man with a northern hood slides by me and disappears deeper into the crowd. I follow him until my eyes catch the king's. I respectfully nod as I approach. The king breaks eye contact with me first as he backs away. I grasp Marr's forearm and raise it toward the sky.

"The Akkimon has returned." I squeeze tighter around his forearm and gaze around the glade.

The people are thick, but the forest behind them is more abundant. I'm worried Marr will never reach the heights many Akkimon have before him. That is the consequence of peace. I watch our king, who is already settling himself into one of the carved seats on the other side of the altar. Whispers of an idea grow in my mind. It's almost as if the ideas aren't my own. They are the will of something greater than me.

"The Akkimon have always led the front lines for our people," I say.

Marr nods his head in agreement. He is still holding on to the hilts of the Twin Blades.

"Who will join our new Akkimon and me to complete the trials?" I say.

Questioning voices call out throughout the crowd. Marr's eyes trace away from his new tools and up to me. His expressions are severe. He knows my words are leading us somewhere dangerous, but he nods in agreement.

"You both have completed the trials. Neither of you have anything to sacrifice as Wrekk-Taww." The king adjusts himself in his carved seat without looking our way.

What he says is true. We have completed all the tasks and requirements to be initiated into the warrior class. These tasks began with physical challenges, like climbing the Path of the Forgotten. The challenges grew into mentally straining obstacles like solving the Elders' Riddle. For the climb, we reached the summit of Yauyconshel, the highest peak among the Scalar Mountains. We were praised for completing the climb faster than any others before, but still, our father was not impressed. Once we reached the top, we raced down on bare shields. Our mistake was enjoying the challenge, because it was meant to be grueling.

The riddle was another beast.

"Hot when it flows and cool when it is still. A man cannot live without it, but his family requires it. The living are greedy for more, while the dead freely give it away."

Each among us could only make one attempt before we would have to climb Yauyconshel again to earn another attempt. Fortunately, our will was thick enough to solve it.

Other challenges were placed between us, but in the end, we accomplished enough to join the Wrekk-Taww. Still, there is one trial left to be attempted.

"Together we will complete the final trial, Kall um Shacc," I say.

Whispers follow my utterance of the trial. King Lakk glares at me.

"I follow you." Marr points Harmony into the canopy of the glade.

"Who else will claim glory on this day? Who else will follow the Akkimon north to seek and challenge their best?" My fists tighten by my sides.

Hellahh and a few others begin to step up out of the crowd. "Enough." Our king glides over to meet me face-to-face.

His fierce eyes lock with mine, and I can't escape. I only have two options: to hold my place or cower away. At this moment, I'm not his son. I'm an up-and-coming challenger to his rule as king. Yet at this moment, he is still my father. I would never challenge him for his rule. I bow my head and step away.

"Many clansmen died for our peace, those who gave their lives in the battles against the North, and they will not be disrespected on this day. This is a day of celebration and honoring our traditions, new and old. We will not forget the trials that make us strong. And we will not forget the people who fought for our ways," the king says.

The crowd praises our king, a great, accomplished man, as my attempt at claiming my own glory is forgotten and buried in the snow.

·

Smoke and incense billow out of the tent as I pull back the animal-skin cover. A few days have passed since we celebrated our new Akkimon. I have traveled farther into the forest, beyond the glade and near the base of the mountains. Alone, in the hollow space between the mountains and the forest, lies the home of Elder Tal Gashh. It's common for Illitaww elders to venture off in solitude before they become burdensome on others. This is another common practice our father will soon end. Yet Elder Tal Gashh is different. She is a wise hermit, hoarding knowledge of all things of the earth and heavens, and she has always lived alone.

The warmth draws me farther in. Fragrant smoke

challenges my sight. Inside, the smell of damp earth is overpow-
ered by the scent of burning herbs blended into animal fats. The
fire cracks when the cool breeze follows me in.

"Come in, Jupp. I have many words." Tal Gashh appears
behind me, near the entrance.

She walks deeper into the tent, waving a woven bundle of
herbs. Her hair is gray and filled with twigs and earthy trinkets.
Stained silk is draped across her body, and the hem of her gown
drags on the floor. Her sweeping scoot brings twigs and other
natural things along with every step.

How did she know I was coming? I left alone, the morning
after the celebration, to meet her. It isn't likely someone reached
her before me. The gods have shared my coming with her. Tal
Gashh is well-known for her wisdom and spiritual guidance, but
some people doubt her connection with the gods. Those people
have never met her.

"I need guidance." I release the opening of the tent.

A flame ignites on the cinders, which I assumed were all
burned to coals.

"You don't need anything." The skirt of her gown sweeps
back and forth on the ground as she brushes off a woven stool.

I take a step farther and duck my head to the side in avoid-
ance of a hanging idol. When I look back, she is motioning me
to sit. So I sit.

I stare at her, trying to understand her ways. She looks all
around her tent, but she doesn't make eye contact with me. She
saunters around her domain, grabbing herbs from one side and
bringing them back to the other. Everything she does is tedious
and lacks organization.

"Please, Mother..." I slump down, pointing at the seat
across the fire from me.

"Yes, Jupp?" She pulls off a bowl of boiling water from the
coals.

Tal Gashh steeps a braided silk pouch filled with herbs and

dried leaves in the water.

"Jupp, son of Lakk, why have you come to visit me on this day?" She pours the water into two carved cups and hands me one.

"I need your guidance." I grip the cup tighter.

"It can be difficult seeing so many futures, but I think you said that only moments ago." She cocks her head to the side and winks at me.

"Marr has been named"—Tal Gashh waves her hands in front of me—"Akkimon," I say.

"Yes, he is Akkimon in most futures. Are you here to talk about your brother? I thought you were here for your own guidance," she says.

I stand. Maybe it was a mistake coming here.

"You are large. Yes, larger than most, but size won't be enough. Sit and drink. I will give you the answers to the questions you must hear." She jerks her head back to finish her drink. I sip the herbal tea and slouch back down.

"The first answer is yes. If you travel north, you will encounter the most powerful among them, but they will not oppose you." She smacks her gummy mouth as she chews on herbs.

I didn't ask the question, but somehow she knew what I wanted to know.

"Will we bring honor to our clan?" I say.

"The second answer is yes. You will seize honor along the way, but it will cost you something greater."

My stomach warms with an inner fire as I swallow the last gulp of tea. She is telling me the words I want to hear, but I fear the riddles in between.

"What will it cost me?" I say.

"That is not one of the questions. You know this, Jupp. You can't ask a question about an answer. The gods won't allow me to speak the words." She squeezes my knee with her soft hands.

"Is this what you told my father when he came to you?" I say.

"Asking more questions about answers I have given in the past—that will work, huh?" Tal Gashh shakes her head in disagreement. "I gave your father the same thing I have given all the great men and women who have sought me out. I gave them the words."

"Thicker than a worm. What else am I supposed to ask?" I cross my arms over my chest.

"You know what you want to ask. It has been waiting at the back of your throat since you left the glade." She gazes directly at me for the first time.

"Will it be worth it?" we say in unison.

"The third answer is yes." She points at me and stomps her feet up and down in rapid repetition.

I allow myself half a smile and rub my hands together.

Idols jingle loosely above us. Tal Gashh raises her hands.

"If you and the Akkimon venture north, you will know a king, an empress, and a god. They will all love you, but you will never return to Illitaww. That is the trade." She abruptly stands and brushes the ground with her gown as she glides to the opening of the tent.

"Marr and I alone?" I say.

"The best answers are given in threes." Tal Gashh disappears through the opening.

I run out to follow her, but she is gone, and I'm alone at the base of the Scalar Mountains.

CHAPTER FIFTEEN

The Sailor

Kai

SUMMER V9, 50 AE

The elegant sails of the warship ripple as the crosswinds flare from the south. *Jasmine* is a mighty sea vessel rivaled by none. Her hull is sealed without fault, and her sails are thick and without tatter. We sail around the eastern edge of the realm, far north of the northern shores of Swedas. The wind brings a salty and ever-so-sweet fragrance as its passenger.

Each day begins the same. Captain Davinor, sitting proudly at the helm of his ship, barks out orders to his crew. Everyone is squirmier while the captain is watching. Some of the crew leaders echo the captain's orders with repulsive shouts.

"Grab the rope!" Mitch Black yells.

He's an ugly man with many missing teeth and foul breath. With rope already in hand, I clutch the line tighter in both fists and pull it across the deck.

"That's it! Pull!" he yells.

I'm pulling the rope before he has a chance to command it. Perhaps he fears that if he quits yelling, he may have to do the work himself. He doesn't realize shouting mindless orders is the worst role on the ship. When I'm not performing mindless tasks, I'm learning the craft of navigation and general ship up-keep from Captain Davinor. On some of my more prestigious tasks, I give slight course adjustments to the crew. Navigating the open ocean is more complicated than I anticipated. The in-tricacies of maintaining course are vast, and the experience of other seasoned sailors is vital.

Cody stumbles out from below deck. His tardiness goes unnoticed except by me.

"Brother... You look worse than I feel." He walks past me and slinks to his duties.

Last night was full of drink to celebrate our nearness to the Endaes. The islands are mysterious, but everyone seems to have a story about them. The crew calls them the Love Islands. They say people travel there from all around Elybion, seeking love and pleasure. One of the sailors claims that he met his lady there.

"I swear she is from the Love Islands. I took her away with me," he says.

"I've met your woman. She is the same barmaid that served us drinks when we were too young to drink on Tyfu. She is no Endaen, and she is twice your age," another sailor says.

The entire crew laughs and gathers around as other sailors tell of their experiences on the islands. I'm not sure if any of them are true.

"Are those the islands?" Cody runs down the deck shouting.

Everyone halts their work except me. Even Mitch stops yelling for a moment.

"We don't have the time to stop. Please don't beg me, lads," the captain says the moment he spots the islands.

Now he is hanging off the back of the ship as the islands pass out of sight. I'm cleaning the upper deck while the rest of the crew cracks open another barrel of spiced drink. It's the only means Captain Davinor can provide to prevent a mutiny.

"I assure you, we will stop here on the way back, soldier. Besides, we will be wealthy, and the Endaes are much kinder to a wealthy man." The captain cackles as he performs his monologue for his audience of one.

"I've never laid eyes on the fertile lands of Swedas or met a Swedan, but I've seen and heard marvelous things from the country," I say.

The captain ignores me, with his sights still focused on the vanished islands. People say Swedans have the intellect of the Delphinish without any of the arrogance. They use their minds to create paintings, sculpt statues, and build beautiful gardens. The best art decorating the Temple of Summer's Light came from these unique lands. Swedans assign rank in their society based on influence and creative ability. Their decor and extravagance are their most potent trade commodities, and they thoroughly abuse them.

Everyone is thrilled and equally disappointed to be this close to the islands and not visit. Regardless of how everyone feels, the islands give us reassurance of our position relative to the realm, confirming our route. For me, the islands are evidence that I've traveled my farthest south. Well, my farthest south since my mother journeyed with me in her arms from Ariland. She often expressed the difficulties of her journey to me. She described the specific geographies of the land that she traveled. She was from the southern span of Ariland's barren desert, the Torish Desert.

I cling to the leather-pouched stone hanging loosely around my sunburned neck. My mother once carried it, and now it is my only possession. I don't trust anyone on the ship enough to show them, so I keep it covered in its leather pouch. After this season of sailing, I will return it to Ariland and find the cradle my mother spoke of.

Monotony begins to seep in with the afternoon as I continue to swab. Fog and the occasional ocean mist surrounds the ship. It brings a pleasant coolness to my face, and it isn't heavy enough to slow my work. Yet the boredom is. Gazing around the ship, I catch Shiva looking back. With foolish instinct, I attempt to spin the mop around my hand. I lose control of the handle and send it flying. It smacks against the railing, ricochets around, and falls to the deck surface in a dribble. Many of the crew stop drinking and shake their heads in disapproval of my clumsiness. Jests and crude remarks follow. The ship seems to shrink as my vision narrows. Refusing to raise my head, I grab the mop and continue to swab the deck.

"Having trouble staying on board, baby whale? I can push you back into the ocean if you please," Shiva says.

Her words hold some sincerity as she sneaks up behind me. Without a good answer to her comment, I remain silent and send a half smile in her direction.

"Would you like to learn something, baby whale?" Shiva says.

I search for an incentive in her deep-emerald eyes.

"What are you offering to teach me?" I say.

She looks me up and down slowly. "I'm going to teach you everything you haven't learned from books and scrolls," she says.

I take a step on the wooden planks to get closer to her. She piques my interest, but I attempt to remain neutral. What does she know that can't be read?

"You've learned many things from your temple. None of them are useful out here on a ship. None of them are useful in a battle. Most of all, none of them are useful to a woman," she says.

She spins around and kicks the mop out of my hand. It flies into a mast and rebounds perfectly into her hand. She secures it without losing eye contact with me. I look back and forth between her and the mast several times, contemplating the difficulty. How did she do that?

"Things will not remain as pleasant as they are this day. I do not want a weak baby whale getting me killed with his clumsiness. That is why I'm going to teach you how to stay alive first."

She breaks the tasseled rag head off the mop and hands me what remains of the handle.

"This is a staff," she insists.

"It's a broken mop handle," I say.

"Some people believe the staff is the most versatile weapon. A balanced staff is better than a shield for defending. A strong staff is deadlier than a sword. Unfortunately, your staff is neither...but it will do for today," she says.

I don't understand what she means, and I'm stunned by her attention to me. She hasn't said more than a few words to me since we boarded *Jasmine*.

"Well..." I shrug my shoulders.

I concede to whatever point she is attempting to make and submit to her instruction. Shiva is a complicated person and very hard to ignore.

"Use your staff to keep me at a distance so that you have the advantage." Shiva brings her fists up like a brawler.

She swings her fist in a looping throw, which cracks me in the cheek. Like a baby animal, foreign to violence, I do nothing to impede her strike. The smack thrusts me into an awakened reality. It's a swift, fleeting pain. I grab the side of my face and wipe away the moisture along with the sting.

"Are you serious?" I say.

She is serious. I'm foolish to have just realized it. Some of the nearby crew members pause their songs about the Endaes to watch. The sun sinks behind a cloud, teasing a potential for rain.

"Not good. You may need more training than I thought." She brings her hands up again.

More crew members gather around, like flies to rotten meat. I drop my hands, attempting to give in and avoid any more embarrassment.

"Come on," Shiva taunts.

I poke at her, unsure if I really want to continue. She slaps the mop handle to the side in one move. In the next, she backhands my cheek. As more sailors gather, my embarrassment grows. I tighten my grip on the mop handle until I feel a slight vibration on my chest.

"Ah, there you are, baby whale. You might have some fight in you yet," Shiva says.

Before Shiva can land another assault, the ship rattles, and I lose my balance, tripping to my knee. Shiva stumbles back as well, but she remains standing.

"Rogue wave." Mitch scurries across the deck.

A wave slams into the hull. The water explodes from the side of the ship, spraying into the air as ocean water sweeps across the deck. Shiva's normally calm expressions shift to show slight concern. The water pulls me down, and I slide a few feet before it washes back into the ocean. The entire ship shakes and sways as we recover. Shiva pulls me up by my shoulder.

"I'm proud of you," Shiva says.

"Proud? For what?" I allow a naive smile to form.

"I know you wanted to slide back into the ocean again with the other baby whales. But you were strong. That's a good thing, because I won't rescue you again." Shiva tosses the mop handle back to me.

"Really?" I say.

"Again," Shiva says.

Rolling over on my hammock, I dodge each wound Shiva inflicted. While the bruises soak in, the intended lesson was not absorbed. The constant swaying of the ship is especially irritating this night, but the discomfort from sailing on a warship for weeks has worn on my body more than my wounds have.

Men from the second shift lie around me, in their own raised pallets and hammocks, but I'm alone in my thoughts. I flinch reflecting on Shiva's assault on me. Soon the second shift will replace the first, and I'll be out there again. What did she mean when she said nothing I learned from the temple was useful? Unlike Shiva, most Fangourians value the knowledge spread from the temple. The Fangourian Empire valued education more than anyone. They spat on traditions like religion, but the temples were of supreme value to them. Like the Fangourians of old, my mother thought differently from Shiva. I begin to grieve over her loss and turn my attention toward the clear sky. Has Art accepted her?

My mother passed on Femday, and we left on the next Companday, the forty-eighth day of Lebonor 50 AE. It was a darker night. Tonight both moons are visible. The symbol of a goddess, the smaller moon shines with full brightness while her guardian, Huma, wanes. When I first began to doubt the Artian faith, I often questioned why the faithful chose Art as their mother god and neglected the larger moon. The moon representing Art is a smooth, flawless orb, while Huma is imperfect and bumpy, like a youthful face. Though I worship neither, Huma is my favorite.

"You got your arse whipped today, brother." Cody sits up and looks out of the porthole in search of my view.

"Did I? I thought I was letting her off easy," I say.

"I have seen her do much worse to men, brother. She is going easy on you." He lowers his voice. "Be careful with her, my friend. Don't get any ideas. I sailed with her on an expedition last season. A couple of men were getting lonely at sea and decided to get attention from her," he whispers.

"I'm not looking for that type of attention from her." I lie down on my pallet.

"Good, because the two men that overstepped her boundaries last season disappeared," Cody says.

He stares at me, but I'm too tired to give him the reaction I think he wants. I look up toward the foremast, where Shiva sleeps, claiming her own nest in the top castle. Although I'm exhausted and beaten, I'm content with my new life at this moment.

A pack of wolves chases me. Their feet stomp on the ground like a legion of raiders. Massive mountains grow up from the ground behind me, and the wolves are lost. A vast expanse of water stretches out ahead of me. Wolves howl in unison, but they are lost far behind.

"Joleen. Let's go."

A man calls for me from a small boat balancing on the water. The man's face is covered with desert cloth, and he reaches out for me with both arms. A woman stands up behind the man. Her eyes match the deep green in her burning sword. I try to yell out a warning, but my voice is empty and powerless.

The woman shoves the burning sword through his neck and out of his throat. The cut spills blood into the expanse of water as the sword disintegrates. The woman's glowing green eyes linger until she closes them and fades away. The water turns to crimson sand, and it sucks the boat down into the earth. An urge to save the man crashes into me with a pulse as I dive into the cool sand to follow.

A bite pinches my side.

My side is vibrating where the pouched stone rests. The dream was not my own. It belonged to my mother. My heart sinks back down to the bottom of the well of my grief for her. I imagine her soft hands touching me like they did when we last spoke. She hasn't been gone for long, and I feel like she isn't far along her path in the heavens. How did her dreams become mine?

A gentle poke interrupts my thoughts.

"Still fighting me in your dreams, baby whale?" Shiva reveals herself.

My mind is weak from the lack of adequate sleep. I turn my body away from her, hoping she will leave, yet she does not disappear. Instead, Shiva jabs me harder.

"We train every day. You are behind, and you must train harder to catch up," she says.

Giving a long exhalation, I stand and grab the mop handle from her in silence.

"This morning I want you to do one simple thing with the staff." Shiva leads me out to the deck. "I want you to hold it above your head."

I grab the end of the handle in my left hand and extend my arm above my head. "Like this?" I say.

"Widen your stance," she says.

She kicks my thighs apart and straightens my feet both toward the starboard edge.

"Hold the staff straight and even with the deck. When you get tired, switch hands, but do not move your feet," Shiva says.

Something inside me desperately wants to succeed. While holding the pose, my mind wanders onto other things. The first thing I notice is the stench of myself swelling as the sun rises. I haven't appropriately bathed in weeks. On the ship, we use the ocean water to wash and rinse off with, but there is no clay or sand aboard the vessel for deep cleansing. The salt water sticks to us, and we have all begun to carry a moist, musky scent of the ocean.

"Straighten your staff. Widen your stance," Shiva says.

She walks away to begin her work on the port side. I switch hands and reposition my feet in the stance she forced me into before. Will this stance allow me to be as swift and exquisite as she is? Regardless, I've already decided to try anything she requests.

"What are you doing, idiot?" Mitch stomps onto the deck.

I loosen my grip and put the mop handle down. Shiva walks up.

"I moved the baby whale to my crew. He is blocking out the sun with his staff," she says.

Mitch grunts and mumbles under his breath. Like most people on the ship, he is afraid to confront her.

"Continue," Shiva says.

I take a step away from Mitch to fulfill her request. Sweating in the light of the sunrise, I stand like a statue of a greater man. My hands are shaking when I release my grip. I shake my arm loose.

"That won't do, baby whale." Shiva returns. "Why are you here?"

Why *am* I here? For her entertainment?

"I'm here to sail," I say.

"Raise the staff up." She grabs my hands and forces them up.

"You belong in a temple with scrolls containing stories about sailors, not sailing yourself. Why did you leave Summer's Light?"

Her words hurt, but I have nothing to say in defense. Sailing is harsher than I imagined. It's more arduous work than romantic exploration. I'm already shaking because my arm is heavy on its own. Adding the mop is over-encumbering.

"I was forced to leave." My grip breaks, and the handle falls again.

"Don't stop. Switch your hands if you must. Why were you forced to leave?" she says. Her voice is less harsh.

"I wasn't good enough. I failed. I made many mistakes, which are unacceptable to the masters," I say. The strain on my body is like a truth potion.

"Well, there are plenty of mistakes to make here on the ship. Yet unlike the temple mistakes, these ones will cost you a life," she says.

She looks around the ship. "What's your plan after this? When we complete the journey, Davinor will berth his ship at Tyfu for a while."

"After this, I'll travel inland to Ariland. My mother is from the Torish Lands, and I promised I would return something there for her," I say.

Shiva paces around and repositions my hips, shoulders, and elbow.

"And you?" I say.

The breeze parts loose pieces of her hair.

"Me?" She frowns.

"Do you have somewhere to go?" I say.

"No," she says.

"Another captain to sail for? Back home?" I say.

"No. I only sail with Davinor." She stops pacing and looks off the port side. "I haven't been home in a long time."

"Where in Fangour are you from?" I say.

"Fangour? How...?" She looks away.

"You are Fangourian, no? Am I mistaken?" I say.

"No," she says.

"You should visit again." I lower the mop handle and switch back to my right hand. "I've read extensively about Fangour, if you want to hear some of the histories. Since the empress was executed, Fangour has been occupied by the Magnavozian army, but your people weren't always slaves to Magnavoz."

"Slaves? Fangour has no slaves," Shiva says.

"I'm sorry. I meant no offense." I raise my sinking shoulder before Shiva notices.

Shiva is looking far beyond the horizon. I try to find what she is looking at, but I don't see anything.

"Yes, it's time to return." She sighs. "Continue to hold this position, and I'll grab you before we break fast. You have a long journey ahead of you, baby whale."

◖

The island of Stenhas, known for grapes and wine, lies ahead of us. It's the midway point between Fangour and Swedas.

"Who among you has ever been spat on by a highborn? Who among you has worked hard for a bag of coins to share with your wife and children, only to have a thieving highborn come along and take half of what you earned? Now we take back what was taken from us. There's gold out there, and it belongs to you, and you, and me, and us all." Captain Davinor points toward the crew.

Cody shakes the back of my shoulders. Every word Davinor utters causes another excited quake to rumble from Cody.

"Do you hear that, my friend?" Cody says.

"Yes, I hear it, brother," I say.

"We are taking back everything the empire stole from us," he says.

Shiva stands with her arms crossed at the right side of the captain. This is a rallying call for every sailor on board.

"Take it back," the sailors chant.

I quietly mouth the chant to go along with the crowd. Shiva steps away onto the quarterdeck, while Cody is shouting the loudest of us all.

"Take it back!" everyone screams.

CHAPTER SIXTEEN

The Pirate

Kai

SUMMER V25, 50 AE

Cliffs bulge around us, forming Shelby Cove. The water is dark and still, and the bottom is far below us as we swim around the jagged rocks. The rocks are like guards, reaching out of the water to protect the shoreline.

"Move as I move," Shiva says.

Shiva is calm and unwavering as we begin our mission. I try to remain silent, but my heart is racing, and my breath is irregular. The cove is a beautiful section of the island. With a small, narrow channel to the inlet, we are forced to embark on a long swim into the heart of the cove. The guardian cliffs block any view to an escape route.

The first treasure galleon was intercepted last night. The take was flawless, and the first team slipped away quietly into the dark with an empress's ransom. Why isn't it enough? After this last ship, we will be rich enough to buy the island of Tyfu.

Do your job. The last words of the captain echo in my mind as I watch Shiva swim ahead of me.

My only job is to get to the helm of the ship and pre-pare the wheel for departure. Shiva's role is to deliver me there silently before she heads to her next mission. I mimic Shiva's every move, at least what I can see, as we swim toward the treasure ship. Art is not shining tonight, and Huma is at his slimmest crescent. This is one of the darkest nights of the year, and for that we are lucky.

Nearing the docks, I see Cody and his team making their way to the boarding platform. They are moving in stealthily, stopping to hide behind each crate as they go. Shiva, many body lengths ahead of me, is within her arm's length from the hull next to the rudder. She begins to ascend by stabbing into the rudder with her short daggers. Shiva balances atop the rudder as she takes her beautiful dark wooden bow off her back and wipes the water off. The solid flick causes a series of light sprin-kles in the water. I place my hands on the bottom of the rudder as Shiva nocks an arrow attached to a thin rope. She pauses and motions me to stop. I attempt my best dead-man impression and float on my back.

The wind is slightly blowing, and the crescent moon is re-flecting off the waters of the cove.

Focusing in full draw and leaning back in an awkward po-sition, she aims for the perfect place on the railing of the quar-terdeck. The arrow snaps into the wood above as the slack rope unravels. She tugs hard on the line twice and nods her head in confirmation. She motions for me to climb onto the rudder as she begins her ascent up the rope. Hanging from the railing of the quarterdeck, she pulls herself over. She's an expert at this, reading the ship like I would a scroll. Her shadow, standing on the rail, waves signals to the second group. Then she makes a smooth whip, which causes the rope to slither like a snake into my hands. I grab hold of the line right before I fall.

Reaching the top, I pull myself over the rough wood. My muscles ache from the climb, and even more from the training Shiva has imposed on me.

The second team boards the ship. My chest beats with excitement. Then I notice my palms are dry. How is this possible?

Shiva bursts out of the captain's cabin door.

"Something is wrong." She draws her bow.

She is as serious as I have ever seen her. Her head is shifting all around as she looks up and down the galleon, toward the dock, and back onto shore. She spits an arrow over my head and back toward the docks. The wild arrow hits an armored man in the chest, ricochets off his breastplate, and knocks him into the water. A battalion of Magnavozian soldiers marches behind him. I stand stunned in the moment, with no plan made for this circumstance.

The Magnavozian soldiers march up the docks like a flood. They are led by a soldier with a large spear, spiked shoulder plates, and an iron-covered head. He's a head taller than the soldiers marching behind him. His arms are sleeveless and hulking, and his chest is bare and scarred.

Our second team retreats to regain ground against them. One sailor dives off the dock in frantic desperation, but an arrow finds him as he reemerges. Unfortunately, our men are outclassed in skill, equipment, and armor. The hulking soldier leads up the ramp with thunderous stomps. Reverberating tremors begin to shake the vessel as they board in their heavy armor. Shiva takes her bow in hand and walks forward, only pausing to release a carefully aimed shot at one of the invaders. Cody holds his ground against them. He swings his cutlass in large, sweeping arcs, yet he is quick enough to outpace the overly armored attacker.

I'm afraid, and I can't act. Our men are falling to the soldiers while Shiva steadily eliminates an equal amount in return. Finally something inside me gives way to a hint of courage. I become overwhelmed with urgency and start to run at the oncoming assault.

"No!" Shiva shouts, stopping me in my tracks. "At my back. I need your help if anyone gets too close," she says.

The hulking soldier bursts through the line of our men and heaves his spear straight through one of them. The wailing scream makes me stumble even farther behind Shiva.

Then the soldier sees me cowering behind Shiva. With his large shield raised, he charges toward us. Shiva manages to land a few arrows in the creases of his legs, unprotected by the armor, but he still charges.

Shiva abandons her bow for her daggers. I take a step forward, swinging hard against his shield with my staff. My staff slams into his wall and shakes my hands numb. His spearhead jolts in front of my eyes as I stumble backward.

"Come here," he says.

His voice is creepy. It sounds like he is speaking gently, but his will is insidious. He knows he almost had me, and next time, he's going to catch me. Shiva jumps in front of me, spins around, and ducks a robust jab from the giant spear as she slices the man's ankles. As if the world has frozen, the hulking beast of a man stops his attack.

"You?" he yells.

The giant is stunned by the sight of her. She is stunning in a simple kind of way, but he freezes as if she is a nightmare. Shiva pushes me back as she backs away too.

"On me, Kai," she says.

I glance back and forth between the two, trying to

understand what's happening.

"Out the way we came." She nods her head toward the edge of the ship.

The mind of the man flickers back to life. In the next moment, he's rushing me again. His shield bashes into my shoulder, knocking me to the ground. The skin scrapes off my right cheek and forehead as I slide against the wooden deck of the ship. Blunted pains in my shoulder are outscreamed by the multitude of tiny stings on my face. The wood cracks with my ear pressed against the deck. He's coming to finish me. Shiva jumps onto his back, digging one of her daggers into his neck as I roll away. He reaches behind his back to rip her off his shoulders. She fights well against him, but now the other Magnavozian soldiers are encircling us. Our opportunity to escape is vanishing.

"As we came." She releases her hold to point toward the mouth of the cove.

As she releases it, the soldier grabs her hair and throws her off. I reach the edge of the rails and look back at all the slaughtered men I came here with. Only Shiva and I remain. She fights up to her knees and rolls away before he can stomp her back down.

"Go!" Shiva rolls into a sprint.

She waves me off from a few staff lengths away. I dive right before she meets me. I splash lightly into the water and wait a moment, expecting another splash behind me. Yet no one follows.

I'm losing my breath. The water stings at the scrapes on my face. Remembering the sailor who was shot with an arrow as he reemerged near the dock, I make myself stay under. Quick, flashing splashes followed by swishes of water begin to dribble behind me. I kick vigorously because I'm afraid an arrow will find its way through the water to me.

A blue radiance illuminates the water below my chin. The light is seeping out of the corners of the pouch that holds the

Art Stone. It rattles inside the pouch like a bird caught in a box. The water seems to draw around me, propelling me forward. I'm expecting to run out of breath, but it never happens. With full breath, a glowing blue light, and growing confusion, I surge through the water like I belong in it.

•͑

"What do you mean, trap?" Captain Davinor paces down the deck.

"It was a trap," I say.

The captain issues commands for departure.

"They knew we were coming. The ship was completely empty... I thought Shiva was right behind me when I dived into the water, but then she wasn't. We need to go back," I say.

"Open the sails!" Davinor yells.

"What are you doing?" I say.

"If what you say is correct, there will be a fleet of Magnavozian ships pouring out of that cove before your piss hits your ankles." The captain comes face-to-face with me. "You led them right to us."

His breath is hot. I want to beg, or fight, or scream at him, to make him go back. My heart sinks as he looks away from me. I realize there is nothing I can do to stop him.

"Please, Captain." I reach for him.

My hands slide off his coattail as he walks away.

CHAPTER SEVENTEEN

The Fighter

Shiva

SUMMER V25, 50 AE

Rolling away from the burly giant, I search for an escape. Beyond the beakhead dances a sliver of hope. Kai is the only resistance in my path.

"Go!" I turn my roll into a dash.

With my bowstring over my shoulder, I'm running like a tigress in a chase. Yet Kai remains stuck to the ship. He will either move, or I will tackle him into the bay.

Before I reach him, Kai comes alive out of his trance. He jerks left, jolts forward, and stops at the edge. If he were in reach, I would push him off. I want to yell at him, but I don't waste the breath.

Finally Kai dives. I sigh in relief as I'm preparing to follow. I jump.

A hand slips around my hair and yanks me back. In the fall, my bow overextends, and the string gives way with a hard snap. My head is spinning in disarray, and my balance fades. One sol-dier kicks the bow and the splintered string across the deck. In a groggy haze, I try to reach for my dagger, but a massive boot stomps into my head. I drift into darkness.

●

Heavy footsteps descend wooden steps to the cargo hold. Stillness returns, and I'm wondering where the footsteps have gone until the woven net is yanked away. Sunlight flashes from the portholes. I squint to mitigate the harshness of the light. It's the first light I've seen in days.

"I believe we have found a stowaway," the man says in a low, scratchy voice.

The man stands over me like an obedient hound sniffing out a treasure. His teeth clash against each other for room in his small mouth. The only less appealing feature of the man is a horrid stench leaking from his body. He's the same man who was asleep the night I sneaked out of Fangour. Now the Skyfort slips away with the breeze as this fool peers down at me.

"I found her," he calls out to another man climbing down the ladder.

The other man climbs down the stairs, pauses with his hands on his hips, and slowly approaches us. He ducks to dodge the low ceiling and takes another moment before he speaks. He is contemplating something serious.

"Hello. My name is Davinor. I'm the captain of this fine ship." He bows in a quaint tilt forward.

The captain is dressed in all black leather, and his large hat has been reworked many times. I stand slowly as I size up the captain and his mate.

"Answer the captain when he speaks to you." The sailor pokes at me.

I stand in silence as I try to plan my escape. I can evade them both and climb up the ladder. Yet out to what? An open sea is the only escape waiting for me above. Before I can decide, the mate grabs me with his blistered hands. His sudden grasp propels me into violent retaliation. I push his arms up and to the right of me, causing him to shift his balance forward. I reach for the cutlass at his left side and disarm him with a fluid swipe. Before he knows what's happening, I kick down into his bare left knee. The blow lands, his knee snaps, and he falls to his other knee. The captain watches calmly as I bring the cutlass up to his mate's neck.

"Kill this wicked siren." The mate spits at me.

I push the cutlass deeper into his neck, which silences his complaints. The captain applauds.

"Good. Very good," he says.

Laughing, he steps back and falls against a crate. He continues to laugh and point while his mate curses me between his wails of agony. I remain silent, with a plain face, so I won't confuse them about my threat.

"Very good, you can let Mitch back up, and please remove the blade from his neck, dear." He reduces his laughter.

I loosen my wrist with the cutlass as I back away from both.

"You are hired. I can use some more muscle on this ship. Mitch doesn't look like he will be able to work for a couple of days, so you can take over his duties," the captain says.

Mitch curses at me, and the captain hushes him. I don't trust him, but what choice do I have? His other men are climb- ing down the ladder in response to the commotion. I turn over the blade to the captain such that he can grab the handle. Yet he refuses it.

"Keep it. I like my people armed. Welcome aboard my gal- lant ship. Jasmine is the fairest ship on the waters today. It is a pleasure to have you aboard." He smirks and raises his hands to the air in proud admiration of his vessel.

"Thank you. I'm honored to be here," I say. I decide to play along.

"We are honored to have such an ally as you. And what will we call our new crew member?" He narrows his glance.

"Shiva E...Agta is my name, sir," I lie.

●

I try to suck in a deep breath but choke on mucus and blood. I've shifted in and out of consciousness for several days. The soldiers have tightened shackles around my ankles and hands, which are bruising the skin on my wrists.

Where am I? Iron bars encase me in a small room, while two double-sized cages mock mine across the way. There are barred doors to my cell, one beside me, and one slotted into a double across the room. The other's door is unhinged and lying upon the ground, which is dirt. Crickets and roaches scurry in the corners, welcoming me to their home. The neighboring cells share inner bars, while the outer walls are made of stone. There is a single table with a single lit candle, and a single empty chair at the bottom of the stairs. The empty seat belongs to a guard whose tether is not too far stretched.

The darkened stairs begin at the end of the path and flow up with an extra-long climb. Only a giant man would step up them in comfort. Up to what? I surmise I'm in a local holding cell, not too far from our failed heist. My head aches. Faint memories return as splintering thorns. I collapse back onto the ground. My head feels oversize, and my left eye is swollen shut, but I can see out of my right. Was it a nightmare? Were Lord Pikon Gravesmon and his beast on the ship?

Slowly the pain in my head dwindles to a throb. With the throbs, I feel aches over the rest of my body.

"Shiva," a voice whispers.

I look around to the other cells. A figure crawling into the light from the adjacent cell reveals himself.

"Cody?" I say.

I recognize the island accent before the light illuminates the man.

"Hi, sister. How are you faring?" he says.

"Cody. I thought I was alone. Where are we?" I say.

"We haven't traveled far from the cove. We're still on Stenhas. Is your head healing? You were bleeding quite a lot, sister. I wasn't sure you would make it," Cody says.

Before I answer, a door swings open with a resonating clash against the wall. Sunlight and soldiers bleed down the stairs. Cody retreats to the corner of his cell as five Magnavozian soldiers flood the small dungeon. Following the soldiers, a caped man with a hooked-blade hand takes a few steps down the stairs.

"Gravesmon," I say.

"I found you. You thought you got away from me, didn't you?" Gravesmon spreads his arms out as he steps down another step.

His name sticks to the roof of my mouth. I want to spit him out of existence. Gravesmon is the reason for everything missing in my life. His polished boots and pompous cape, stitched with fine thread winding up and down his shoulders, only feeds the fire growing in my chest. What cost did my people pay for his finery? My vision narrows like a hawk's, searching for the soft spots on his head to attack first.

"Shackle her properly. She will take advantage of any loose restraint," Gravesmon says.

He is less of a fool than I remember. One of the soldiers begins to unlock the door to my cell. I stand and raise my fists to the sides of my head, readying myself for a brawl.

"She doesn't know when she has lost," Gravesmon says.

They enter the cage, and I manage to land a few fists, knocking teeth and blood free. Inevitably, they overwhelm me. I'm trying to memorize their features for my future vengeance, yet none of them have any remarkable attributes. They're all average height and covered head to toe in Magnavozian armor. I'm captured, but I'm still jerking every chance I get. If they don't kill me, I'll do everything in my power to eliminate them all.

"That's enough. You've lost. It's over. You will crumble with the rest of your empire as we wash it away from this world." Gravesmon enters my cell and meets my face with his. "Nothing you do will stop us."

"I only need to stop *you*," I say.

"Me?" Gravesmon forces a fake laugh. "The Venith charged me with cleaning out the rotting wounds of your Fangourian Empire. They knew you wouldn't accept the marriage. It was only by the kind heart of a potentially great king that you ever had a chance."

The Venith? I haven't heard the word since my mother explained the history of the early empire. The Venith used magic to oppose the infant empire.

"I can see your little head spinning tiny Fangourian ideas." Gravesmon whips his cape to the side. "If only Prince Vega could witness what we have planned for you."

If the Venith have returned in support of Magnavoz, the realm is in danger.

With shackles locked around my neck, wrists, and ankles, they carry me up the stairs into the blinding light. Before I lose sight of the prison bars below, Cody sticks his head out. He is helpless, but he hasn't lost hope. He extends a farewell, raising his fingers. A soldier knocks my head against the doorframe as we exit. My head drops, and my body goes limp.

●

"It's time to return to your shackles," Frenton Jaspermon says.

He's the young Magnavozian guard charged with watching and feeding me during the voyage. He is rugged, but he is kinder than his superiors. He acts much harsher when he is in their presence. When we're alone, he loosens my restraints. Yet now he helps me back into them, and I comply so he can save face.

When he first loosened my restraints, I was tempted to end him. It would've been quick and easy, but I would've regretted it. I wouldn't have gotten far from the ship. I'm unsure what awaits me on the gloomy shores of Simb's Point. Would drowning at sea be a better fate?

"Do you have her ready?" A handsome soldier bursts in.

"Yes, she's ready," Frenton says.

Moments later the skinny soldier drags me up onto the deck as the ship is docking. The shoreline is covered in a long white sand beach. Beyond the beach is a wall of cliffs extending as far as I can see. The cliffs grow higher than castle walls. At the top of the cliffs, pelicans peer over the beach, waiting for fishermen to slip up. Paths are carved from where the pelicans rest to the white shores. People fill the trails like an army of ants. Some, carrying oversize containers, are traders, while others, marching in groups of eight, are more soldiers.

Six soldiers, including Frenton, are assigned to transporting me to another dungeon. I'm wrapped in several ropes around my upper body, which form a restraint coat. A cloth rag, meant to keep me from speaking, cuts the edges of my mouth. There isn't anyone for me to talk to, but still, they fear my words. Everyone here is Magnavozian, and everyone believes I'm the enemy.

The escorts drag me up the beach, never allowing me to gain my own footing. Fishermen wind their nets up while they try to fight off their curiosity. Most of them don't know who I am or what I've done.

"Mind your work." The skinny escort stomps toward one of the elderly fishermen. The man must've looked at me for too long.

I nod at the elder fisherman. It's my only way to give partial thanks.

"What has this woman done that you need to wrap her in so many ropes?" The fisherman untangles a line.

"She is a traitor to the king. I should have your head for the question." The skinny escort unsheathes his sword.

"Soldier. We have a job to finish," Frenton says.

Two muscular fishermen step up behind the elder. Their bodies are covered in tattoos. Within their grips lie meat cleavers that are meant for larger fish. The bustling docks have grown quiet in the last few seconds. A dog barks and comes running up to break the silence. He jumps up to lick the fishy guts off the pant legs of one of the fishermen.

"Mind your work. I have more important tasks than taking your head." The skinny escort slides his sword back into its casing.

Finally we reach one of the pathways up to the city. My face has healed enough for me to see, but my body aches from the chains hanging on my limbs. The docks smelled of foul fish and rot, but those are all smells I'm familiar with. The city is foreign. The architecture is unlike anything I've seen in Fangour or the islands. The buildings are cobbled together from hard-ened clay and straw. Each is a different shade of brown, but it is difficult to see where one building ends and another begins.

As we travel deeper into the city, the stench subsides, and it's replaced by smoke and iron dust. One of the guards releases my arm, dropping me into a puddle of stagnant water.

"Damn you." He kicks me for splashing him.

I struggle back to my feet, ignoring the pain in my hip from his metal-ornamented boots. Frenton grabs my arm again, pull-ing me the rest of the way up. Then he catches me from falling all the way forward.

"What makes her so special that she gets to keep her head?" the clumsy one says.

"Lord Gravesmon said she is to await a trial before any justice can be done to her." The escort with the gapped teeth grins his broken smile.

Frenton remains silent, relaxing his grip on me and allow-ing me to walk upright on my own. Their leaders need to make my execution public so they can blame me for everything wrong with their nation. To them, I represent an evil that they must vanquish.

"I say we take her behind the shop here and take turns with her," the nasty one with a limp says.

"Are you crazed? Or do you simply wish to die? Lord Gravesmon said, 'Do not stop. Do not harm her. If you do ei-ther, I will have each of your heads,'" Frenton says.

They shake their heads without answering. If I could get them alone, I could kill them one by one, choking them with my legs. Then where would I go?

Everyone in the city is Magnavozian, and everyone is a potential enemy. Frenton urges me forward and pats me on the back. He means to say he will protect me from the others, doesn't he? He may be the only decent Magnavozian man I've met.

The escorts remain silent until we meander up to a large wall. This wall is made of the same clay and straw that is plastered throughout the city. However, there was much more required to build it. In each direction, the wall stacks like a downed tree in the Okiari. No buildings outside are within arm's reach.

"Is this it?" the skinny one says.

"Of course it is. What else would it be?" the handsome one says.

Frenton releases his grip on me and walks ahead.

"Come on. We don't have time for this," he says.

The skinny one reaches back and yanks me forward. The pain is a pestering sort. He wants me to scream, but I won't give him the satisfaction. I remain calm and silent. Breathing only through my nose, I walk forward in front of my escorts. Frenton begins to pound on the gate. He stops and shrugs. They obviously have no further instructions on how to transport a prisoner to this hold.

The soldiers take turns pounding on the gate. I'm leaning against the wall. My head is throbbing again, and my throat is dry from thirst.

Finally we hear a muffled voice from the other side. Clunky footsteps approach the entrance.

"Who sits outside the gates of Roknamar?" a deep voice says.

Everyone looks at each other awkwardly for a moment. Frenton puts his hands up to stop the others from speaking.

"We have a prisoner to hold in the dungeon." Frenton seems unsure about whether anyone is listening. "Lord Gravesmon commanded us to deliver this prisoner to the cells, to be held until she can be put on trial."

With a screeching sound, a metal window slides open in the gate, and a helmeted soldier peers through the slit.

"Yes, fine." He grunts and slams the window.

The same unnerving screech echoes as the metal window

slides back against the door. Moments later the massive gate
begins to push against the ground and behind the wall. It opens
enough for us to walk through in a single line.

Pushing in my bruised shoulder, my escort guides me
through the gate. The walls reach several people high and are at
least my arm's length thick.

"This way." The guard is muffled by his iron helmet.

No. I can't go any further. Once I'm in, I'll never leave. I
halt in my tracks. A sudden fever of anxious sweat comes over
me. Why have I not tried to escape? Have I missed my oppor-
tunities? Thoughts race through my mind as sweat beads on my
forehead.

"What do you think you are doing?" The skinny one grabs
me and pushes me up ahead of everyone else.

I nearly stumble into the armored back of the guard before
I catch my footing. The ground is soft and squishy with the
moisture of a recently fallen rain. It reminds me of the Okiari
Forest after a downpour. The woods were always sensational,
but trampling forest growth in a chase behind Bulba was more
beautiful than anything else.

No. They can't hold me here forever. Greater men have
tried to defeat Fangour, and they have all failed. I think back to
the fire my mother carried. The fire she unleashed on Gravesmon and the prince was just. She knew that men would try to
take everything. I turn my back to the skinny one to give him
a smile through the rag. He will be the first one I kill when I
escape.

"We haven't received any prisoners this season," the guard
says.

Where's the dungeon? There isn't much inside the gates.
A large oval boulder swells through the ground in the middle of
the enclosure. A tower rests in each corner, and two at the sides
of the gate. Two guards occupy each tower, but the prison is
desolate. The guard leading us takes a cautious step up the oval

boulder. My escorts look at each other with puzzled grimaces.

"Watch your footing. Keep to the dimples. She is more slippery than she appears," the guard says.

I follow the guard, making sure to step in the same eroded footholds. Behind me, my escorts struggle to climb the sloped bunker. Ahead of me, the guard disappears into the oval.

Peering over, I witness the beginning of a large circular carved staircase. It's etched into the middle of the boulder. Dim torchlight glows from somewhere beyond my vantage point. Frenton comes up behind me, followed by the others.

"Walk." The handsome one tries to reach around the others to push me.

He loses his footing and steps back onto the smooth surface of the boulder. His legs split apart, and fear glows on his pale face. In the next moment, he is sliding down the boulder. His leather pants catch on the stone for a brief stop. Ultimately, it causes him to lose control, and he tumbles the rest of the way down to the yard. The other escorts' voices combine into a chorus of laughter and mocking jabs. Their enjoyment matches mine, and for a moment, I'm not a bound captive.

"Go make sure he survived." Frenton points to the quiet one.

The handsome one yells curses from the ground. Although I had nothing to do with his clumsiness, his fall makes me happy. The quiet soldier slides off the side with nimble ease.

"Let's go." Frenton gestures me to walk down the staircase.

I peer into his eyes, begging him to not make me walk down the steps. He looks away but remains insistent, with his hand gesturing me to walk. I can't blame him. He has a duty to fulfill. I walk down the carved staircase toward the dim, flickering torchlight. The light from the sun fades as we dance down the stairs into the dungeon.

CHAPTER EIGHTEEN

The Prisoner

Nok

5 0 AE

Heavy rains begin to pound as moisture bleeds in from the cracks in the ceiling and the walls. Murky water with flakes of rust and stale rock fill my chamber. I'm underground, but my hole has a small barred window at the ceiling, which faces the gulf. The window is high and too small to see any of the ocean. Only rogue rays of light gleam through. Occasionally the breeze will blow perfectly, and my cell fills with new air. Today is not one of those occasions.

The repugnant dungeon of Roknamar is my home. It

wasn't always a gloomy prison. It was built thousands of years ago as a resting place for some of the first settlers of Elybion. People say the dungeon was utterly underground until parts of it broke off and crashed into the ocean. The breaking exposed Roknamar on its eastern side. I push my hand against the wall. The bricks and window on the east wall are newer additions to the dungeon. The masonry is less precise compared to the rest of Roknamar. Whatever skills or tools the first builders had were forgotten when they repaired the walls.

I'll be the last occupant here. The mixture of my lineage and crime is rare enough to land me in such a place. Soon I'll be forgotten along with everything else.

"Roknamar. The last resting place of Nok the bastard," I say.

What day is it? I rub the scrapings on the walls, which depict a crude calendar. The markings are my only connection with the outside world. A world I once knew. I imagine myself back in the castle. Tif is baking me rolls of sweet bread, which I consume until I burst. Margo has a bottle of wine she stole from the cellar. We drink until we are silly. Salivating, I rub my sunken stomach. I would do anything for sweet bread. Back then it was so abundant. Now bread seems like a divine treat of the gods. I would take back everything for one piece of the hallowed delicacy.

◦

Princess Velvia screams. The castle of Rock Hollow quakes in the wake of her tendrils reaching out through sound. The night before her wedding has transformed into an undeniable nightmare. Kyber grabs his gear and throws his shirt on before her yelp ends in a screech.

I can't move. I'm stuck in the sinking sands of disbelief. Only hours ago we were celebrating their impending wedding. Now our deceit is visible for all.

"Bastard!" Velvia screams.

Her handmaidens appear behind her while Kyber slips to the door. Kyber stops to look at Velvia. His expression is full of grief, but Velvia ignores him. Her rage is focused on me.

Kyber disappears into the castle as guards shuffle into the room around Velvia and her handmaidens. Unsure of what has transpired, the guards stop and linger.

"Kill him!" She points at me. "Kill the bastard!"

Kill me? She's almost frothing at the mouth. If we were alone, I'd be afraid she would scratch my eyes away. The guards look at each other and then grab me. I'm not fighting them. I won't. As they are dragging me past Velvia, she steps out to block our path.

"I said, kill him. Do it now," Velvia says.

"Your Royal Highness, we can't kill him for this. We must take him to the holding cells. The king will decide what to do with him in the morning," the elder guard says.

I can't bring myself to look up at Velvia. I'm ashamed. She is right, and I am wrong. I tried to take something from her, something I had no right to have. Velvia reaches for the guard and rips his sword from its sheath.

"Your Highness!" her handmaidens scream.

She takes a wild swing at me, and the guards jerk me away from the tip of the blade.

"Your Highness, stop!" The elder guard releases my arm and holds his hands in front of her. He catches the next swipe of her blade as it cuts into his palm. "Your Highness, please release the sword," the elder guard says.

Tears are filling Velvia's eyes as she loosens her grip. The tip hits the ground first. Her handmaidens circle around her as she falls into a bawling rage. The guards grab up the sword and drag me out. Our eyes meet as I pass the threshold. If her eyes could speak, they would say I was nothing.

●

I often recall the night as I waste away in the dungeon.

Before I came to Roknamar, I waited several days in Rock Hollow while my fate was decided. Meanwhile, Kyber fled back to South Aptoria. He isn't as noble as I thought. No one ever said Aptorians from the South were brave, but I thought Kyber would be a man to break that mold.

I wish I had stayed in the kitchen, or at least entertained other young lords and ladies that night. There were so many wrong turns.

The following nights were worse. Sitting alone in the dungeons of Rock Hollow, contemplating my choices, and meeting with the king were torture.

"Go back to your quarters! Sleep!" I scream at my memories.

●

A rare torchlight startles me from my sleepless night in the Rock Hollow dungeon. It's King Donak, and he's alone.

"My king." I fall to both knees.

I hang my head as low as I can. I can't look at his face. Three days have passed since Velvia discovered me with

Kyber, and every breath has been met with sorrow since. Now my throat seals completely.

The king remains silent. I don't raise my head, but I know he is still there with the torch.

"Look at me, Nok," the king says.

His expression is full of sorrow, agony, and defeat. The creases around his eyes, shadowed by the torchlight, are moist with lingering tears.

"I've lost too many children. One to a fallen empire, and now another to a broken heart. I can't lose any more," he says.

Another to a broken heart? It's the first time he has acknowledged me as his own. Seeing his tears destroys me. I want to crawl up to his feet and beg for forgiveness, but the iron bars separate us.

The king explains Velvia's tragic ending. She took the only life she could: her own life.

"I won't let them execute you." The king's bottom lip shakes. "For now, we must keep away from everyone else. I'll release you when people have forgotten."

"Who...would ever...forgive me?" I'm bawling between the words.

"They may never forgive, but they will forget to blame you," he says.

•

The king's last words ring through my memories.

They will forget to blame me? Those were his words, but I'm afraid the queen will never forget. She will blame me forever.

When Velvia took the guard's sword, she wasn't telling

him to kill me. She was giving an ultimatum. She didn't want to live in the same world as her foolish bastard brother. Unfortunately, no one understood what she meant until it was too late.

When the king walked away, I howled in pain. Velvia hated me and deserved retribution, not death. If our roles were reversed, would she have shed a tear? I loved her even though she never accepted me. She had everything I wanted. Velvia was a pure-blooded princess pledged to the finest prince. I would have done almost anything to have her life, but not at the cost of both of our lives.

When the rains seep into my dungeon and my eyes are wet enough, I cry a few tears for her. In a different life, where she wasn't a princess, she could have been my friend.

A series of clanking irons echo on the other side of my dungeon door. The screeching metal breaks me away from my recollections. Is it time already? No, the guards brought me rotting mash yesterday, and they never feed me more than twice per week. It's too late in the afternoon for a meal. This isn't a meal. Many heavy feet stomp down the hall. Have they finally come to kill me? My back is pressed against the wall farthest away from the door. Only silence arrives.

"No!" The silence is broken. "Please, you can't!" a woman screams.

Another door is slammed. My eyes are racing back and forth between the sounds on the other side of my northern wall. A few moments later, my ear is pressed to the wall. A series of closing doors tells me the guards are leaving. But who have they left behind? I rub my hand along the inner wall separating my chamber from the one next to me. Another soul has been placed beside me, but who?

A few hours pass in silence. Finally I snap. I scurry to the shared wall and tap on the bricks until I run out of space. Nothing. I turn around and start tapping the other way again. No response follows. Is my mind playing tricks on me? The guards never come here in the evenings. They have no reason to bring another prisoner this deep into the crevasses of Roknamar. No. They are playing tricks on me. They want me to believe there is another prisoner here, but there are guards on the other side, laughing at me as I pace in my dungeon. I try to scream, and my voice cracks. My throat is too dry to yell. My foot splashes in one of the puddles, and I bend down to take a sip. The water is disgusting, so I spit it out. The flavor is of piss and rat. Or is that flavor mine? There are no rats in here.

My mind wanders until I come back to the stacked bricks in front of me. Someone is on the other side. I didn't imagine it. I run up to the wall and tap until my hands are numb. Then I tap again.

"Stop!" the woman yells.

●

Weeks have passed since I met the woman on the other side. The dungeon seems brighter, the air smells a little fresher, and my mind feels more complete every day. She knocks on the part of the wall closest to the window, to signify she wants to talk.

"Hello, Your Imperial Majesty. How can I be of service?" I knock back on the wall. "Hello? Are you still there?"

"Nardok, how long have you been here?" she says.

"I've lost count and started over many times." I spit out of the window hole. "About sixteen days since I was graced with your presence, Your Imperial Majesty."

We take turns telling stories. Most of the tales, I make up, and some are true. Lifia likes the ones about King Braydenwolf, but she goes through long spurts of silence while I'm speaking.

The stories she tells are mundane and obviously true. No one would make up stories so dull. She talks about how she trained to be an empress from a young age. There is a lot expected of the empress of Fangour. Most things aren't expected of rulers from other lands. In Fangour they practice fighting with staves daily. When they finish with staves, they rehearse histories of their empire and spend extended periods holding expressions. Their idea of ruling sounds painful, and I can't imagine why anyone would want to rule that way. If I were the emperor, there would be many more celebrations, and no one would be expected to hold a frown.

The most interesting thing she speaks about is the Skyfort and all its majesty. The way she describes it is romantic. The elegant bridges that connect the towers are a sight I long to see. In Magnavoz, non-Fangourians describe the Skyfort as dark and evil.

"It's an abomination," the king once said.

Lifia sees the Skyfort through fresher eyes. To her, nothing is more elegant than the walls of the Skyfort. She is the first person to make it seem appealing enough to visit. When I asked her where she has been, she said she found a way to remain out of sight. I've tried to ask about the night she escaped, but she is adamant about avoiding the topic. I'm curious about whether she knows more about what happened to Vega.

"Yes, that seems right. I thought they would have come for me by now. They will come, soon. They want to end my bloodline," Lifia says.

Her words hearken to my own desires. Since Lifia arrived, my existence has felt more meaningful. She is right. Her life is a threat to everything the Magnavozian leaders want. Yet she isn't the cruel, passionless warlord they want the realm to believe she is. I fear her time is fleeting, and I desperately want to find a way to keep her alive. For now, we play our storytelling game.

"What about men? An empress must have lines of men to choose from," I say.

"No. I'm not experienced with men," Lifia says.

"None?"

"Well, no. Besides, partnership is different for my people. The history of our empire has many empresses, none of whom were married. Mates are important, but they have no role in ruling. Until Vega proposed, I assumed I would never marry and possibly never have a mate," Lifia says.

"Never? Don't you like men?" I say.

"Yes, I like men. That's not the reason. Our traditions were crumbling before I was born. I thought I would be the last empress. There was no reason to have children, and few reasons to have a mate," Lifia says.

"Well, what about Vega? It would be rare for a woman to see him and not like what she saw," I say.

"Vega? I barely knew him. He was painfully handsome. It's true." Lifia snorts a dry laugh. "The marriage was decided for us. It was never going to work without my mother's consent."

"Why did she react so violently to the proposal?" I say.

"It wasn't like that. She was protecting me from a life of servitude to Magnavoz or the Venith...or whoever is in power." Lifia pounds the wall between us.

I retreat far away from the wall. There is fire in her, and I can feel its heat through the bricks.

"What do you know about the Venith?" I say.

"Nothing, really. Is it true? Have the Venith returned?" Lifia says.

"Yes," I say.

"Are they the Venith from legends? I mean...have you seen them use magic?" she says.

She questions all the things I've pondered, yet I have no proof of their rumored powers. Long ago the Venith were said to have brought the magic with them when they traveled from distant lands. Elybion was impregnated with their magic, and it grew until the Fangourian Empire wiped it away.

"I've never witnessed their magic." I pace farther away from the shared wall.

"What are they like?" Lifia says.

"Beautiful. Undeniably above others. Yet awkward in their bodies. Vzar Nyla is their leader. She has the face of a goddess and the most eloquent voice I've ever heard," I say.

"And the others? How many have you seen?" Her voice draws back and forth like it's floating on harp strings.

"There were two others who were equally beautiful, one man and a younger woman. They only wore white on both occasions," I say.

Her silence tells me she is thinking. She only sees them through a tainted vision of Fangour. The Venith were the first to threaten the Fangourian Empire, and their failure bolstered the empire for years to follow. Yet not all nations despise the Venith as they do. Magnavoz welcomes them with open arms.

"I'm sorry the marriage was forced upon you. I wish it hadn't been. In another life, you could've met Vega under natural circumstances. You would've loved him if you'd had the chance to know him. Maybe then, neither of us would be in this dungeon." I pat the inner wall gently.

CHAPTER NINETEEN

The Damsel

Lifia

SUMMER V38, 50 AE

This is Roknamar? I always thought the legendary dungeon of Simb's Point would be more grandiose. What it lacks in beauty, it makes up for in sheer size. From what I can tell, the massive boulder is the primary entrance. However, the bulk of the dungeon seems to extend all over the city. There could be other forgotten entrances scattered around. Since the sun shines in during the early part of the day, my cell must be located somewhere near the beach.

"Four strides down, two strides right, a trek toward the

ocean, and..." I tap my finger. Each digit represents one of the turns we made. Yet the memorized path fades the longer I wait.

Fortunately, I'm not alone. Rubbing the wall, I try to imagine the troubled soul living on the other side. The cool stone sends an army of mercenary-ant bites up my spine. I want to retreat to the leather pallet in the corner, but I'm drawn to the light. I reach up to the edge of the window and pull myself up to peer outside. I'm hoping to see something new. Is there a sign of the world changing? The balance of keeping my right side pushed against the inner wall while my hands grip the stone corner is a constant struggle. I can't distinguish anything of significance outside, but the sun shining on my forehead gives me hope. No one knows where I am, except Cody. He knows I'm alive, but he must have met the gallows by now. I slip and fall from my perch. Another bruise is added to my collection. Instead of trying to climb back up, I lay my back on the uneven stones of the floor.

My food hatch screeches open. A piece of bread falls in with a pat on the ground, followed by a piece of fruit splatting in half beside the bread. As the fruit bursts open, juice squirts onto my ankle. Two rapid knocks followed by three slow, measured beats echo through the shared wall. The signal tells me my neighbor is trying to communicate with me. I have little will to rise and do anything. I should be hungry, but the food does nothing to entice my appetite. Again two rapid knocks followed by three slow, measured beats sound through the wall.

"Morning, Nardok." I pull myself back up to the sun glaring through the crack in the wall.

My eyes squint closed in the light, and I keep them closed as I hang on the sliver of a window.

"Good morning, Your Imperial Majesty," Nok says.

"I'm not your empress. I told you to call me Lifia," I say.

When he asked who I was, I didn't consider telling him my borrowed name. I've been found, and there is no more escaping who I really am.

He laughs. I let go, readjust, and pull myself up to the window again. He is the type of person who enjoys hearing his own voice. I can't decide whether he believes I lied about my identity or whether he merely finds it amusing that an empress is locked up with him.

"If we are friends and you are not my empress, you may call me Nok," he says.

"Good. Nok it is. How are your mushrooms?"

"They are growing. I could use a little less moisture. Did they bring you more food?" he says.

"Yes. Rotten fruit and moldy bread," I say. The bread is fine, but I don't want him to feel any worse.

"They've been more generous since you arrived, though I haven't felt any of their generosity," Nok says.

"If there was any way to share, I would," I say.

"I know. I know. Don't mind my begging. A conversation is more filling," Nok says.

My belly tightens. I'm starving, but I can't imagine how much worse it has been for him. My fingers are beginning to fatigue as I struggle to keep my grasp on the bricks.

"Where were we? Have I told you about Elise?" Nok says.

"No," I say.

Nok wants to play a game where we describe acquaintances to pass the time. He's always searching for a way to keep me at the window, and I can't blame him for wanting to talk to someone. The more we speak, the easier it is for him to make sense of his own words. At first he mumbled to himself between his comments to me. Sometimes he shouts quirky phrases. The shouts scared me at first. Now I kind of like them. The shouts let me know I'm not completely alone.

"Well...she wasn't perfect," Nok says.

I let out a snicker at his abrupt introduction while he continues to describe the young lady.

"Oh, was this your sister?" I say.

"More like a cousin," he says.

"The name sounds familiar, but I can't place where I've heard it," I say.

"Oh, is that so? Have you heard of the Lady Elise of Moonfall?" Nok pounds the inner wall while laughing hysterically. "Could there be a more pompous name to give a daughter?"

I drop down to adjust one side of my back more firmly against the inner wall between us. He finishes his story before I reposition myself up at the window. I missed parts of his recollection, but I understand Elise is a cunning politician.

"She sounds...boring. I have a low tolerance for chumminess," I say.

"I have plenty more to say about her, but my stories are filled with her fake smiles. You should tell me about someone worthy of a better conversation," he says.

I want to tell him about Bulba, but I want to save my sweet giant for a later time.

"Anyone? For the sake of hearing something beyond my own voice?" Nok says.

"How about Kai?" I say.

"I've never heard a person with that name. Kai. It sounds like a pretentious name, if you question me about it," he says.

"Actually, quite the contrary. Kai has no connection to a ruling bloodline or any measurable wealth. He is a young man from the North Isles. He's never owned anything, as far as I am aware, but he has a good soul. His mother died from sickness before he became a sailor. He isn't really a good sailor, but he never stops trying to improve. He isn't particularly proud, yet he draws you in when you speak to him. He is smart, but he never boasts his wit. He's timid, but you can tell he wants to be brave," I say. I go on to explain how I met Kai.

"He seems like a good enough kit," Nok says.

His voice fades away from the window. I let go of my side

and slide my back down the wall to the ground. I'm weak and I should eat, but the mashed fruit is no more appetizing during starvation. Flexing my hands in and out in a stretch, I begin to drift off into a daydream.

The next day, my dungeon door screeches open, and a dark shadow of a man crawls in front of the torch.

Lord Pikon Gravesmon coughs and reveals his face. One side is lit by the torch, while the other is dark and hidden. Is it time? I expected I would meet him again, and I assumed it might be when he was delivering my sentence. He's standing with one hand on his hip, while his knobbed wrist, attached to a crimson hook, hangs by his side. His dark red cape with black lining drags along the ground as he steps through the gap.

Behind Gravesmon, Frenton stands attentively. Has he been there the whole time? Has it been Frenton sneaking me extra scraps?

Gravesmon runs his hook down my cheek as he steps up to me. He underestimates me still. I could disarm him, cut off his only hand, and slice his throat before his cape folds to the floor. Unfortunately, I would have to kill Frenton as well.

"Soon you will answer for what you did to the prince and his men." Gravesmon reeks of a fishy odor.

The words fall out of his crooked face hole. He hates me, and the hatred is mutual. One day, I will take the hand that my mother spared. Every time I think back to the night they came to the Skyfort, I think of Gravesmon and his role in ruining my life. He has no idea what happened to the prince. He fled like a coward when his men were defeated.

"Vzar Musa is on his way to bring the queen's justice," Gravesmon says.

What justice does the Venith need to deliver? Fury flows through my veins like a raging river after the rain, but I keep my chin tucked. He's a low man who doesn't deserve my gaze.

"Has she begged to be let free yet?" he says.

When there are no replies, he turns toward Frenton and a guard standing behind them both. Neither one answers his rhetorical question.

"She will," he says.

Ten dances trot through my mind, tempting me to attack him. He seems disappointed. My reactions aren't the ones he's searching for. Does he want me to attack him? There isn't a scenario that he survives if I do. Why isn't he afraid? My confidence wavers slightly.

"Unfortunately, the disobedient rodents of South Aptoria want to be heard. I won't get to see Musa burn you. Oh, what a sight it will be." Gravesmon grinds his teeth.

Why are they waiting to kill me? Gravesmon wants to do it now. That's why he is tempting me. I can smell his lust for violence, but he isn't in control. Someone moves him around a map, without him understanding his role.

Keep your back straight, and use only the necessary words, Empress Dianame's words echo in my mind.

No words are necessary here.

Lord Gravesmon whips his cape around and steps over the threshold. Frenton pauses with an expression of empathy before he closes the door. The key turns, and the gears twist the lock closed. Metal clanks are the last sounds before they disappear down the hall.

What would my mother do? She never would've allowed herself to be taken. I'm reaching into the nether for answers from her spirit. Straightening my legs and stretching my bare calves on the smooth floor, I lift my chin to look up into the dark void of a ceiling above me.

"She would tell me to remember my dances," I say to the quiet darkness.

CHAPTER TWENTY

The Vagabond

Kai

AUTUMN K8, 50 AE

Light flickering through heavy dust causes me to twist into the depths of my feather-filled pillow. Yet my throbbing head keeps me awake. Once light penetrates my eyelids, the dreamless sleep has vanished.

Rising from my rented bed, I sit upright. With legs hanging over the edge, I stretch and give out a long yawn. A shake of the leather satchel lets me estimate my remaining silver. The coin represents my share of the loot. Captain Davinor kept his end of the bargain before dropping me off. Compared to the total, my plunder of gems and silver was only a slice of a slice. Still, it has been enough to eat and drink like a king for a few weeks. I toss the half-full satchel against the wall as my self-loathing surfaces. I left my allies behind when I dived off the ship. For what? The guilt plagues me as Shiva returns to my thoughts. She would never have left me there. We're running and she's diving right behind me in my memories. I hit my stiff palm against my head.

"Argh." I pull my face down as I run my fingernails through my thick, overgrown beard hairs.

For a moment, I sit, holding the leather-swathed stone hanging around my neck. I think of my mother and the last time I felt her grace.

"Art has another plan for you," she said.

To become a coward? I was unable to act when I was needed the most. Art doesn't see me. She never has. With my hands firmly gripping the stone, I think back to the night. Somehow I swam faster than any man should be capable of as I held my breath longer than any man has. I could've died by an arrow or drowning that night. Yet I lived.

I pick up the coins, place them back in the satchel, and sling the satchel over my shoulder.

"Kaison Foyd." Bo Kil'Flanning slams his hand on the bar as I step down the stairs.

"A good morning." I keep walking.

"A drink to start your day?" Bo says.

"No. I..." I slow my stride.

The bar is uncharacteristically crowded this morning. I chose the inn because of the quaintness and proximity to the ocean. Something has changed.

"Who captains these men?" I step back to the bar.

Bo Kil'Flanning, the barkeeper, owns several shops. He's a friendly, balding man who never allows a dry cup.

"These men aren't sailors." He leans toward me.

His body smells of mint and clove.

"No?" I lean in closer.

"No. These men are here for the tournament." He widens his eyes and presses both hands onto the counter.

"Oh, Rotho City hosts tournaments? I suppose...the city is much more accessible than Lothbrooke," I say. The Golden Gulf is accessible to most of Elybion, but Lothbrooke is a fortress locked in the eye of Swedas.

He seems frustrated, and he slaps his rag down on the bar. "No, they aren't here to watch dregadins play with swords. They are here for the real fights—the underground fights," he whispers.

Bo pours a cup of mead and slides it to me.

"Save this for me. I have an errand to finish," I say.

Bo laughs and chugs the cup as I walk out with a smirk.

Outside the inn, one direction leads to the marketplace, and the other points toward the docks. Rotho City is a coastal civilization that hugs the gulf. During the wet season, the waters between the great lake and the Golden Gulf seep into each other. The fishermen trade from the gulf to Lake Oga during the wet season because the channels are filled and transportation is more reliable. The town is made up of many streets trickling from the gulf. Most of the buildings near the water are raised on wooden stilts. Dockworkers curse each other in one direction, while bards pick at their instruments and beg for coin in the other.

There are many rich sounds and smells. Some are pure, while others are foul. I smell a sweet fragrance of flowers. Two young whelplings plead with onlookers as they pass.

"Please, sir, don't you love her?" one boy makes pouty lips.

"If I had a lady." I nod as I step around the boy.

My interest is redirected by the clang of metal originating from the blacksmith's shop. Three fast hammerings followed by a fourth hard smash repeats. The smell of the forge billows out in a cloud of smoke from the shop.

Waving the smoke out of my face, I lose sight of what's ahead. I bump into a large man, but I manage to catch my balance before ultimately stumbling over. For a moment, I'm terrified. He has the same build as the beastly man I ran from in the cove. Yet he's not the same man. This man is younger. He carries a large shield on his back while armored in leather shorts and vestments. At his waist, he carries a shield attached to each hip. He must be a sort of Arilandic shield salesman. I've never seen a man so large. I rise without losing eye contact with the man. His eyes are mahogany brown with shades of red intertwined. His hair is shaved close to his scalp except for two-finger-broad streaks of hair stretching from his forehead back to his neck.

"I'm sorry, my friend," I say.

He looks at me, raising his thick eyebrows crookedly.

The stone seems to pulse, and I feel like I'm going to vomit. Then my ears start to hum. I close my eyes and hold my belly. A moment passes. When I open my eyes again, the man is gone, my ears stop humming, and the sickness fades.

I arrive at a parchment shop in the center of the city. Commoners frequent the shop to exchange letters or hire couriers. I'm searching for neither service. I require a map.

"The Torish Lands, southern Ariland." I push my hands low to emphasize the "southern" description.

"Oh, yes." The woman with thick black curls bounces them with a nod.

"You have a map of this region?" I say.

"No, but we have couriers who travel in the caravans to Enix twice a year," she says.

"Enix is in northern Ariland, but that's close enough. When do the caravans leave next?" I say.

The locals of Enix will know the terrain better than any trader here in Swedas. Once I'm there, I can find a guide to take me to the Torish Lands.

"I'm afraid they left only a few weeks ago," the woman says.

"And the next is in half a year?" I say.

"After the wet season. If you need to get there sooner, Magnavoz will have more trade routes. Take a ship into Simb's Point," she says.

"Thank you for your help." I drop a silver coin on the cluttered table.

"Whoa." She examines the coin. "Can I pass on anything else for you? We have couriers traveling to Delphinus and northern Magnavoz every few weeks."

"Sure. I'll stop in again tomorrow." I grab a few sheets of parchment. "How much for these?"

"Your silver will pay for the whole shelf." She twirls her curls in her fingers.

"Tomorrow, then." I grab a few pieces as I exit.

A few nights later, I follow some of the bar-goers to the tournaments. The crowd consists of diverse people from beyond Swedas. Swedans are commonly lighter of skin with wispy hair. Yet many here have dark skin, thick hair, or combinations of all. Wealthy landowners are gambling for coin, land, and servants. Bakers are auctioning whatever is left from their shops today. Maids dressed in minimal clothes hand out mugs of mead. The rest are various groups of spectators squeezed in tightly for a glimpse of the brutality.

I stand alone near the stairs, sniffing in the familiar aroma of the arena. It's cold, damp, and musky, like the island caverns. Unlike the caverns near Watertree, the arena is lit up by hundreds of torches, one placed every few feet on the walls and supporting beams. Eight wooden beams grow up from the bottom level and mature to the ceiling. The ceiling is high and spacious, leaving only a few feet between the arena and the market above.

The first level, which is the highest, is set at the average level you would find a storage basement at. It forms a sizable wooden walkway encircling the pit below. The whole arena must've begun in a basement, which grew and evolved into a concealed field. The entrances are found below several marketplace shops. I can't be sure, but the arena seems to be directly under the center of the market square. It was a remarkable feat to construct everything, especially in secrecy.

The second floor mimics the first. It's a wooden balcony encircling the pit, with several seats included. A man dressed in elegant clothing sits surrounded by others with more fine clothing. They all drink and laugh until the combatants enter the ring.

The third and final deck is low and near the sand cavity. Only combatants and their trainers occupy these steps.

"Ladies and lords." The announcer raises his hands and twirls around.

The announcer is a lively Swedan man with a square bronze beard. He announces each fighter as they jump into the pit.

"Here we have last night's champion, Rash Gulban, hailing from unknown parts of Ariland." He points at the man on one side of the arena.

The announcer's voice fills the space, exciting the crowd and forcing them into another roar.

Rash is a stout, aggressive man who defeated the previous

challenger by gouging one of his eyes out. He paces back and forth on his side of the pit. The brutality of this man makes me question whether I should continue my quest to Ariland.

While the announcer pauses to soak in the crowd's admiration and excitement, two large men stand up at the opposite end of the pit. I haven't watched either of these men in the fights, but I recognize the larger of the two men. He is the same man I bumped into in the market the other day. He smacks the other against the back and shoulder. The second man stands dead-eyed and focusing on nothing other than Rash. The second man is like the first. They are similar in their body types, which consist of thick muscles, hard facial features, and unique reddish-brown eyes. They differ in stature, hair, and attire.

The smaller one will be the combatant tonight. His rugged hair is mangled into a knot on top of his head. It whips loose as he jumps into the pit with a thud. The crowd cheers and hollers. Some of the men in front of me break into whispers. Others join in as the crowd mumbles in swarms.

"And here we have Ma-a-a-a-arr!" the announcer screams.

The crowd is a mix of wild cheering, booing, and stunned amazement.

"Hailing from the barbaric lands of Illitaww," the announcer says.

A few people gasp as the rest of us realize who these men are. They aren't ordinary men. These men are the fabled Illitaww warriors, and one of them is about to perform hand-to-hand combat with an Arilandic killer. What are they doing here? The Illitaww haven't traveled north in my lifetime.

Since the first scrolls were written, the Illitaww have been depicted as outsiders. Their language is full of hand signs and double consonants, and their religion is vastly complex. I have no way of knowing their values, but they could be as different from ours as trees are from seaweed.

"Fight!" I draw in closer with the rest of the crowd and jab my fist into the air.

The battle is over before it begins. Rash is stumbling around in the sand as he attempts to regain consciousness. For a lengthy buildup, the contest ended too quickly. Nonetheless, people are amused, and they begin chanting the victor's name.

"Marr!" I join in the chant. "Ma-a-a-a-arr!"

The guards shuffle us out for the night.

As I reach the blacksmith's basement, a brutish man pushes past me, slamming me into the side of the staircase. My satchel falls, and all my coins bounce out in a cascade of silver and copper. Men clamber to retrieve the shiny treasures. One scrawny man with a balding head and a toothless gap grabs one of the few gold pieces. He pauses as he contemplates whether to give it back to me. Then he dashes past me in a mad escape. I'm stuck holding out my hand as he disappears into the marketplace above. I crack a slight chuckle in response to his daring thievery. Surely, he needs the coin more than me.

"Art guide you." I smile.

Following the trail of rolling coins, I manage to recover a few more at the feet of the moving crowd. One young woman slides a few pieces of silver into her boot. She tries to ignore me until a man in front of her turns back.

"Give the man back his coinage." The man blocks her on the steps. "Have you no decency?"

She bends down, takes the coins out from between her ankle and her boot, and slaps them into my hand. Then she pushes me out of her way.

"I'm sorry," I say.

Finally I reach the bottom of the stairs, and one of the florist boys is picking up the last coin.

"Is this yours?" he says.

"Yes."

"Here you are, sir." He hands me the coin without hesitation and continues on his way.

"Wait," I say.

He looks up with a fearful expression.

"Keep it. I will pick up some flowers from your shop later, and this will be my payment," I say.

"This is far too much for a bouquet." He stares down at the gold shining in his hand.

"You're a good salesman and honest. Good things find good, honest people," I say.

He holds the golden coin tightly in his hands as he runs to catch up with his brother.

I drop the recovered coins back into my satchel, counting them. Rising, my vision is filled with two engulfing figures. The Illitaww men stand before me. In their rough native language, the large one says something, and they both laugh.

"Pardon me," I say.

I respectfully move out of their path. They remain standing in front of me for a moment before they walk past me. I grab at my necklace, underneath my shirt in its leather pouch. They are judging me as I judge them. I see men, large men, but men nonetheless. What do they see?

Stepping into the empty darkness of the market square, I watch the last townsfolk disappear. Every shop is closed and locked up tight. With nothing else to do, I begin to walk south down the road, toward the gulf and my rented room. The wind blows a chilling breeze through the streets and up the back of my shirt. The coolness awakens a deep-rooted paranoia.

I sense a presence behind me, and I feel a quick jabbing throb hit my chest. I glance back to find a shadowy figure a few paces back. The person makes no attempt to correct their awkward proximity to me, so I lengthen my stride toward the inn. I'm picking up my pace, and the following footsteps are pounding more rapidly to match. Did someone see my coins drop? Have they followed me to take the rest? My breathing mimics the rapid pace of my feet.

Three dogs dart out in front of me as they cross from one alley to another. They're stray beggars in search of leftovers. Led by their noses, they sway close to me with the pitter-patter of sniffs. Disappointed by my wares, they dash off into the dark alley, out of my sight. With a newfound vigor, brought on by the threat of desperate strays, I run toward the inn. I can't look back. I know someone is right behind me.

Finally I reach the weathered, warped wooden door of my inn. I turn and push my back into the door. To my relief, there are no followers or misplaced townsfolk around. Warmth billows out from under the door, welcoming me inside. I've escaped thievery for the night.

A few guests are sitting at the bar, while others lie sleeping on benches. I step up to the bar and slide a silver coin toward the barman. Bo sighs and continues to wash mugs with a heavily soiled rag. I press the coin of silver into the uneven placemat until it slides off the edge. The coin falls and bounces off the ground on the barman's side of the bar. Then I push another bit of silver his way. His eyes flick up at me, but he doesn't stop washing his cup.

"And what is this? Your debts are paid for the rest of the week." He stops, pushes the coin back to me, and begins to stack the mugs.

"Drinks for everyone," I say.

The remaining two men seated at the bar lift their heads and gesture their mugs at me.

"You have already paid for many drinks still full. Yet if you are going to leave your fortunes lying around..." Bo turns around to hide the coin somewhere safe as I climb the stairs.

My room's door is open, with a finger's width between the frame and the door. Once a week, Bo's wife straightens up my room and washes my clothes, but she has always done this on Estaday. I slowly push the door open from the gap.

A mild breeze blows in from my open window. Noticing

nothing else in the dark, empty room, my body relaxes, and I close the door behind me. I take a few steps toward my bed, and I toss my bag in the corner, where a waiting chair sits. The bag doesn't make the expected hard jingle. Instead, a muffled light shake reignites my paranoia.

"Hello, my friend." A figure rises from the waiting chair.

"What...what are you doing in my room?" I leap back and position myself against the wall.

While the figure steps to the center, I reach for my staff, blended into the crease of the wall, until a face is illuminated by the light of the moons.

"Cody?" My hand falls away from my staff and back to my side as I step up closer.

I can't find the words to greet him. Last we spoke, we were preparing to commandeer the treasure ship. When I dived off the back of the ship, I never thought I would see him again. Eventually, relief overcomes my surprise.

"Is it truly you? I thought...on the ship...we were overwhelmed," I say.

"I'm fine, brother. You know me, always getting in and out of trouble," he says.

He has a way of speaking that makes me relax in the most threatening of circumstances. My back loosens, and my eyes blink.

"I...I don't understand how you are here," I say.

"That's because you jumped off the boat like a fish out of water and swam away," he says.

I pace a few steps away from him, toward the window. The night has been a nightmare, and somehow the ordeal has turned into a reality with Cody's return.

"I'm only joking, friend." He laughs the silence away with his childish laughter. "Well, you did abandon us, but you would've been killed or captured if you'd stayed. So I don't blame you."

He slumps down on my bed. I stare down at him, still puz-zled by his presence.

"You were captured? Was anyone else?" I say.

"They executed most of us right on the spot. But I know what you are asking, brother. Did they kill Shiva?" he says.

I can picture a sarcastic grin, though I can't see his face in the shadows of the room. Cody leans up. He's shaking his head, causing shadows of his curly locks to bounce on the wall oppo-site the window.

"I told you to stay away from her. And no, they didn't kill her," he says.

"She's alive? Where is she?" I say.

"That was the odd part. The Magnavozian soldiers thought she was someone else. They thought she was some prin-cess, brother. Shiva, a princess?" He chuckles under his breath.

"What are you talking about? If they thought she was a princess, what did they do? Did they let her go?" I drag the waiting chair closer to him and sit down in the center of the room.

"Well, no. It gets wilder. They say she is the princess who killed some important prince. Prince Vega Nagidah. He was the oldest one, who was supposed to be the king. Anyhow, the sol-diers argued about it for a long time before deciding what to do with her," he says.

"What do you mean? I heard the Fangourians killed the prince." I lean to the edge of my seat. Cody has never held my attention like he does now, and he is taking his time to keep it.

"Well...while their commander, Pikehand, was issuing or-ders and arguing with his largest soldier, I was held down with a long sword against my neck." Cody sits up and pulls the neck of his shirt down, yet I can't make out his display in the darkness.

"I'm sorry, my friend. I wanted to go back, but I had no sway with the others." I'm searching for an expression that proves he believes me. "How are you here?"

The guilt returns in the form of warm sweat. The brisk wind continues to blow in through the open window, giving me some relief, yet what I need the most is some semblance of forgiveness.

"Ah, brother, you forget. I can't be held down, by man or woman," he says.

"Well, I'm glad you're alive," I say.

"Yes... Shiva is also alive. The guards said something about Simb's Point when they dragged her off," he says.

Simb's Point is a port city and gateway into eastern Magnavoz. It's their main naval base, and well occupied by Magnavozian soldiers.

"Why would they take her there?" I say.

"Well, before I drank the guard under the table and threw him in my cell, I overheard the guards talking about Shiva. They are taking her to... Ah, what is the name of the famous dungeons?"

"Roknamar." I walk over to pick up my staff.

"Yes. She is there until she faces judgment," he says.

The news is overwhelming. I blamed myself for her death. Yet she's alive, and redemption whispers in my thoughts.

"There is one more thing, brother." Cody throws his feet up. "They said something about the Venith returning. You haven't heard anything about them, have you?"

"The Venith?" I say.

"Pikehand said that the Venith told him to find Shiva. Whoever they are, they want her gone," Cody says.

The Venith? The mystery of their people seems bottomless.

"Why would the Venith want her?" I say.

"They think she's a princess, brother. I'm telling you, she's important to someone," Cody says.

"Even if they claim to have magic, it doesn't mean they are the Venith," I say.

There were others rumored to have control of magic, who were called the Xyji. Their magic was more natural to the realm. Yet none of the wielders were said to be as powerful as the Venith.

"I'm only telling you what I heard, friend," he says.

"At least she's alive. How did you find me here?" I say.

"I saw you at the tournament, and I tried to wave at you from the other side of the arena, but you were focused on the fights. Those warriors are something, you know?" he says.

"You were there?" I say.

"I was going to talk to you there. Then...I ran into a few beautiful ladies, and I lost track of you," he says.

I can picture his enormous grin in the darkness. I've seen no attractive women at the tournaments, and I assume he is lying.

"The Illitaww fighter pummeled the desert warrior. It was amazing, wasn't it? I followed you here afterward," he says.

Cody shifts around in my bed to get comfortable. His muddy boots scrape the feather-filled pillow.

"What are you doing here? Any plans?" Cody says.

"I was planning to leave soon. Tomorrow, maybe," I say.

"Where are you going? Back to Watertree?" he says.

"No. Ariland. It's where my mother was from," I say.

"I see. Well, before you go, I have a plan. I know a way we can get our treasure back and rescue Shiva." He chuckles himself to sleep.

I exit the room and carefully close the door to within a few fingers' width. I want to believe Cody has a viable plan and that Shiva is still alive, but I also have a journey of my own. I reach down to the stone. Return it to the Cradle of Man? I'm still not sure where the cradle lies, but I'm obligated to search. Perhaps there is a way to help Shiva along the way.

What's the point of this? I'm squeezing the stone in the dark hallway. Down below, people trade their currency of whispers.

"Why did she give me this task?" My thoughts spill into words.

The stone throbs like it did before. A gleam of blue radiance peeks through the folds of the leather casing. Blue light illuminates the backdrop of the wall like an anomalous torchlight. My shaking hands release the object, and it hits the floor with a thud. When I reach down to retrieve it, the world is pulled away from me. The sky opens above me, and the stars wink a greeting. I'm alone in the wilderness.

"Kai." The stars twinkle along with my spoken name.

"Who's there?" I say.

"There is great power in the stone. It will protect him when you cannot." The stars shine brighter in half of the sky, along with the man's voice.

"How do I summon its power?" My mother's voice arranges a sparkle in the other half of the sky.

"The stone will provide," the man says.

"Mother?" I say.

The stars burn out as the voices fade. The sky is pulled into the stone in a whirlpool of air and light until I'm back in Rotho City. The Art Stone lies unwrapped in my hand, and I'm left with a strange sensation tingling throughout my body. The feeling is the same as what I felt on my swim to Captain Davinor's ship and in the dream before. In the dream, I saw the world through my mother's eyes. It was a distorted world, pieces were missing, and like the vision of the stars communicating, there was an overwhelming feeling that someone was with me.

"Kai?" Bo is standing at the edge of the hallway. "Is something wrong?"

"No. I'm fine," I lie, hide the stone, and step back into the room.

CHAPTER TWENTY-ONE

The Warrior

Marr

AUTUMN K10, 50 AE

He paces opposite me. The floor of the arena has a layer of sand foreign to the area. Left, right, left are his steps. He brings his right foot even with his left before he opens his hips to switch directions. He kicks sand up as he twists. All the while, his head seems to hover atop his shoulders.

He is of warrior breed, and his movement is like my brother's when he is preparing to use the Aktarr form. The form is wild, violent, and predictable. Warriors adopt this form of combat when they believe they have a strength advantage.

Sometimes they are too blinded by rage to use one of the more balanced forms.

"Show him respect, and give him your best fight," Jupp says.

Jupp and I stand together outside the pit. I'm the combatant, while he is the trainer. He always won the fights growing up due to his size advantage over me, and anyone else brave enough to fight him. Time has passed, and we've each grown stronger in different ways. Now I'm the superior unarmed warrior between us, though he will never admit it.

The bearded native man enters the center of the pit to make an announcement for the fight. He begins to shout something in the common language. I don't understand much of the language, but Jupp's fluency is adequate for us both. I'm told the fight is to be nonlethal. The way this man paces across from me, I don't believe him to be one to soften the killing blow.

I'm focused, and my mind settles. I will use the Holohh form against my opponent. This form will allow me to knock my overaggressive adversary off-balance and take the fight to the sand.

"Ma-a-a-a-arr!" The bearded man distorts my name with his foreign tongue.

Jupp slaps his paws down on both of my shoulders, and he steps back out of the arena. I take one step into the pit and exhale. My muscles are twitching in anticipation of my opponent's movements, but I'm in complete control.

The Arilandic man charges and swings massive looping fists. I move right out of his range and return a few straight punches to clip his nose. I'm already disappointed because he is much slower than I anticipated. Pushing his left shoulder down and away, I slide out of range of a tackle. His miss lands him in the sand. He gathers himself and punches the pit ground, which causes a plume of sand to puff out like smoke.

I duck a hard looping punch from his right arm, and he

loses balance. He swings too far, extending his body. Bringing my knee to my chest, I turn my hips over and return a swift shin to the back of his head. The kick knocks the light from his eyes, and he falls into the sand before the light returns. Silence falls over the crowd, followed by thundering applause and cheering erupting throughout. Jupp shrugs his shoulders and nods his head in approval.

The bearded yeller rushes to my side and grabs my hand, yet I pull away and retreat toward my brother. The yeller wants to celebrate me by raising my hand. It's something I saw him do with the last victor, but I don't wish to take part in the act. The fight was unsatisfying and beneath my skills. I will need more significant battles to satisfy my growing hunger.

I follow behind Jupp to the man who is to pay us for the fight. His name is Goldteeth, and he says something exciting to us in the language of the North. He's smiling at me and mimicking my actions, but he loses balance when he tries to kick. I stand to the right of Jupp, bored and embarrassed. My brother says a few words in reply to him. I'm sure he's asking for our part of the bounty in the bluntest way possible. It's a noble virtue for an Illitaww man to be direct, and Jupp embodies that virtue completely.

The man shakes his head and says many words I can't comprehend. Even if I understood the language, this man speaks it so quickly that I still couldn't keep up. Jupp, towering over the man, holds out his hand, palm flat, straight to the man's face to stop his rambling. Jupp turns his head back over his right shoulder.

"He says you have to win more fights before we receive any portion of the prize. Do you want to kill this man?" Jupp says.

I draw the Twin Blades from my back and wait in anticipation. The exchange won't grow into any skirmish, but I'm happy to participate in the threat. Yet I'll always desire a real fight, and I quietly hope for it to evolve into one. The crowd is shuffling up the stairs and out into the streets. A few armed peacekeepers notice me drawing my swords. Jupp holds me back with his hand. I relax. He's making a mild threat to our debtor, but he doesn't want it to go any further. The man surrenders by dropping two dirty coins into a small pouch and handing them to Jupp. My brother nods in approval, and he turns to walk away. I'm facing the man and his guardsmen as I back away several steps before turning and sheathing my blades. After I turn, the man shouts a plea.

"He's begging us to come back tomorrow. He says he'll pay double." Jupp shrugs.

As we walk up the stairs, a clumsy young man with short, feathered hair is picking up coins off the staircase. The man is at the age when it is hard to tell if he is a man or a boy. His skin is naturally lighter with silver undertones, but the sun has warmed it with a tan. He seems distracted, but when he finally notices us, his eyes open wide. He's an average or better size for a northerner, but smaller than any Illitaww man.

"A shame we are not thieves. This one seems desperate for someone to take his coin," Jupp says.

His joke causes me to produce a light chuckle. The clumsy young man says something soft and removes himself from our path. As we pass, he is stunned, like many others we have met. We are as rare a vision for them as they are for us. Jupp and I reach the top of the stairs and turn out to the market of the city.

"There was no honor in the pit," I say.

"No, there was not," Jupp says.

Later in the night, Jupp wakes thrashing on the ground.

"The gods spoke to me," Jupp says.

We're on a ship that is permanently docked. It sways throughout the night, making me sick. Nonetheless, I'm grateful for cover over our heads. There are hanging silks meant for sleeping, but Jupp and I are too large to lie in them, so we lie underneath.

"Tal Gashh was wrong. They said we were lost," Jupp says.

"Tal Gashh? We are far from home, true," I say.

"They said the only way for us to complete the trials is to follow the boy," he says.

"What boy?" I sit up.

"The gods will show us the way. Trust them." Jupp rolls over.

It seems like he never awoke. Was he sleep talking? Either way, I don't see how a boy could help us. I lay my head back down on one of the many woven sacks of grain that fill the vessel.

☾

Several days pass, and we return to our paymaster for the last payment. We've made him over-encumbered with coins from our victories, and he has become jollier each time we meet. He opens his arms high to the sky, saying something exciting as we approach.

"Thank you, Marr." He grabs my limp hand and forces me to look in his eyes.

I understand. His gold teeth shine through his grin. He goes on with more words beyond my understanding. He's sincere, except for his extravagance. With good intent, he hands us each two square coins. I toss mine back to my brother. I have no use for the bits of metal. Goldteeth frowns, and he waves his hands halfway up his side.

"Where...?" Jupp says.

He's asking about a location for something, but I don't understand the rest of his question. Not speaking the language has been more frustrating than I expected. Jupp spent every night talking with the elders and learning many things about the North, including the language. Unlike my brother, I was never interested in foreign languages or culture. I was more interested in our people, especially the women warriors who fought well when we skirmished.

Illitaww women are very different compared to northern women. Our women are much harder in appearance, personality, and leadership. They are often the leaders of their clan. Women from the North are docile and usually not expected to work like men. They almost always birth one baby at a time, whereas our women rarely birth one child. It's far more common for our women to birth two or three children once and continue performing all the same duties as men. We call them out-mothers after they give birth. Yet a few women in our society have a gentler touch. Those women are den-mothers, and they watch over and care for the entire clan's children. The den-mothers and children remain sheltered, while out-mothers and men hunt and farm. Every woman I've seen in the North would pass for a scrawny den-mother back home. Even our den-mother, Pamahh, who was softer and smaller than most Illitaww women, was larger than any woman I've seen in the North.

"Let's go," Jupp says.

I follow behind him. Goldteeth bids us a farewell and begs us to come back next season for more fighting. Neither of us returns the farewell.

We reach the surface and pass through one of the buildings, where they sell cheap weapons. Outside the building, we weave our way through some of the crowd. One man shouts something and points toward us. Jupp continues to push his way through, and I follow. Some of the barmaids cling to us with their small, clammy hands. I cringe at their unwarranted groping. They laugh in a chorus as I gently pry them off.

Finally the crowd begins to part, and hushed whispers fall over them as we pass through separate groups of people. One small man, skinny and dry of skin, steps out in front of us with his two young boys. Jupp halts in front of the man. The man speaks something in a begging tone as he pushes his children forward.

"He wants us to take his sons and train them to fight." Jupp shows his crooked eyebrows.

He bends down and says something to the smaller of the two boys. The boy flexes his arm muscles, turning his fists toward his head. Jupp grabs his skinny arms, and he mimics the crowd and their gawking as he congratulates both boys. After the crowd calms a bit, he rises and continues forward as the man and his two boys step backward out of our pathway.

The father puts his head down and pats his children on their chests as we pass. The boys will never be warriors, but Jupp chose to encourage them rather than tell them the truth.

The northern people were not bred for war, as we were. They would rather talk, and they belong in this soft world they have created for themselves. Their world has men raising flowers, boys studying the markings on the skins of trees, and old men pretending to be warriors for a time. Those old men will settle down to make cheap swords for younger pretenders. They only admire us in their games because we offer a glimpse into the harshness of our world. It's a world created especially for us. A world none of them could ever belong to.

Our people choose to be warriors for life or never at all. We are Wrekk-Taww, like our father before us and his out-mother before him. Joining the Wrekk-Taww elite is an easy decision, but it is not one to take without thought. The commitment requires ten years of training and an absence of childhood. We left the warmth and love of our den the day after our eighth life day. I can't imagine a northerner with the toughness to do the same.

We could take this man's children and train them to be like us, but he doesn't understand what that would mean. He would lose his children, and they would still be the first to die in a battle no matter how well we trained them. We honor battleground deaths, and we would show gratitude during their passing. Yet in their culture, living remains supreme.

Nearing the edge of the crowd, I fight the urge to look back at them. I don't want to glorify the practice fighting I performed in the pit, but another notion sits at the edge of my mind. What if I can inspire one young man to achieve feats greater than his destiny promises? I raise a fist into the air as we vanish into the darkening streets of the sophisticated city. The crowd cheers, and we travel onward to the real battles ahead.

●

The city grows high above us. The deeper we penetrate it, the larger the homes and buildings grow.

Three dogs linger a few paces behind us. They are starved, stray, and have short, mangy fur.

At least a soft world affords them permanence. Through permanence, they have long-lasting structures to shelter in. In Illitaww, there are large moving cities following the longtusk. The northern people have smaller, softer cousins of the longtusk, which they keep in fenced lands until they are plump enough to butcher. They call them pigs, cows, or some other strange name.

The few permanent cities of our homeland are near the

chokworm farms. Sol-Boski has the greatest potential to rival a city in the North. It was once a great city, but Miann and the others who remained have a lot to do before it reaches these heights.

Jupp stops. "Arm," he says.

The strays dart off down one of the narrow walkways intersecting the main road.

Reaching behind my head and pulling my swords up and over, I unsheathe the Twin Blades in one clean motion. I crouch down and position the blades across each other in front of my neck. Through my peripheral vision, I gaze around at the empty streets. Jupp arms himself with his dual shields, covering his fists.

Silence grows all around us until two men step out from around the corner. Each has a single dirk. On the path behind where we were walking, another man reveals himself. He's the Arilandic man I defeated in the pit. He carries a double-bladed sword staff, and he is twirling it around as he approaches. It glints with the light of the moons every time it reaches a point in the twirl. The blades make a high-pitched howl as the wind breaks in response. The weapon is elegant, but its beauty won't be enough.

"We have one to the death, it would appear," Jupp says.

I try to measure his thoughts. He bashes his shields together, confirming my suspicions. I stand from my crouched position and whip my blades to each of my sides. Jupp sidesteps to his right and positions his back against mine.

"We have not spent the life of a man since we arrived in this city, but tonight we are made to," Jupp says.

The Arilandic man begins to spit a powerful speech. Jupp turns his ear over his left shoulder, and my right, to listen to the words.

"He says you cheated in your fight with him. You should not have done that, brother," Jupp says.

I smirk. Three enemies lie in range, and another archer is hiding on the other side of the building. I notice his silhouette hanging out, with his short bow shadowed on the ground. He doesn't realize he is found, which may give us an upper hand if we react accordingly.

"Bide, kill, range." Jupp issues the sequence of our actions.

The sequence always changes in a fight, but we were trained to issue a focus to save energy in wartime. As Wrekk-Taww, it's imperative for us to trust and understand each other completely.

I swing both swords overhead in an arcing cross motion down onto the Arilandic man's blade-staff as he approaches. I hear slams and the crumbling of stone behind me as Jupp engages. I block shot after twirling shot. The man is dexterous with his choice of weapon. His attacks are swift and powerful, but he loses no balance in his effort. He shows signs that he is a master of the weapon, while I perform simple, fundamental blocks and conserve as much energy as I can. He is becoming more anxious with each block. I can end him now, but I maintain the directive as Jupp commanded. A snapping bowstring releases an arrow behind me. I spin around, extending my off-hand blade. I peek to see the condition of my brother. He slams one of them against the wall.

"Range!" Jupp yells.

I'm spinning away from the blade-staff as Jupp takes my place with a running leap. The familiar sounds of his shields clashing iron break behind me. My spin turns into a dash as one man rises. I sweep my blade high, slicing the top of his head off before he completely stands. His body crumples as the bowl I created from his skull flies forward toward the archer peeking around the corner.

The archer releases his arrow before it is completely notched as I come to a full sprint. I dodge the miscued arrow and drag my blade across the ground. The archer sinks back behind the building.

When I step around, he tries to jab me with a dagger. I drop my off-hand blade to catch the oncoming dagger. With one hand catching his looming blade, I drive my main-hand sword straight through his stomach. Allowing the body to crumple, I withdraw my blade and retrieve my discarded off-hand sword. The warrior who I fought in the arena is holding well against my brother and his thunderous pounding shields. Maybe he senses his allies are down, because he makes his first mistake, overextending himself in a greedy swipe. As I approach, Jupp disarms him with a hard bash to the wrist. Rash falls, clutching his broken hand. The bone was no match for the hardwood sheathed in black iron.

Jupp stands over the Arilandic warrior for a moment as I step to his side. The man yells something vulgar at us both, kicking at our shins as he squirms on the ground. Jupp jumps into the air and slams his massive boot through the man, shattering chest bones. He gasps for breath and goes silent.

"What did he say?" I grab the back of Jupp's shoulder.

"He believed we are something less than men. Like many others, we are only animals to them," Jupp says.

Jupp turns down the path as if nothing happened. I can't yet follow him. Jupp's dispirited signs sadden me enough to close my eyes. I try to remember the prayers.

"Marr?" Jupp doesn't stop or turn back.

"Once, life was given."

He halts his step as I speak the battle prayer, but he doesn't turn back.

"Life was taken and replaced by an honorable death. May my enemies and allies rest freely."

The words are meant to release hatred toward my enemies and grief for my allies. They are essential words taught in the tenets of the Wrekk-Taww. Jupp honors the tenets better than me, but the words of our enemy have robbed him of his clarity.

Jupp enters the building ahead of me. The walls are saturated with moisture from a week's rain. Every place in the city needs fresh air and a break from the muggy drizzle. This one represents the muggiest in the city. Today we are meeting with a man, a man who the gods favor.

Women giggle in the corner as the door swings. The place is filled with wily men. They are the type who fight for scraps their entire lives. Many of the faces are from the crowds down below, in the pits. In the center, surrounded by the unreliable sort, is a young man. He's the same one who lost track of his coins down the stairs the night after my first pit fight. I can't discern anything special about him, but Jupp believes he's blessed by the gods. If so, we'll need him to complete our great task.

We patiently move to the bar. Though we have nothing to fear, the other patrons could easily lose more than they bargained for. Taking lives absent the field of battle is a bitter task, and we want to avoid it.

"Two." Jupp holds up two fingers to the hoarder of drinks.

The hoarder quickly fills two cups and hands one to each of us. Jupp lays a few coins on the bar. The man says something slippery in the common tongue and pushes the coins back to us.

"It's better if we are direct." Jupp leans back to me.

I disagree with him. The northerners haven't given me a reason to believe they prefer bluntness over cunning babble. Still, there is no use explaining that to someone as stubborn as my brother. We take our drinks and walk up to their tables. One man scoots back, and his chair screeches against the floor. The man between the boy-man and the women sends us a sly glance. He has light, curly hair and a cocky expression stuck to his face. He might be the one to test us.

Jupp looks back at me. "Who do you think their leader is?" he says.

I stop drinking the bitter ale, which tastes dry and void of flavor. It's nothing like our mead or fermented berries.

"The woman looks like she's the best fighter." I nod my head in her direction, and I wipe my chin.

She smiles at me like she understands, though I know she doesn't. Cups slide on cypress tables while men stare with bitter expressions. Seven throwaway daggers are strapped around my waist. I count the throats of the men who might receive one of my stingers if they push us into conflict.

"I'm the captain of the ship." The boy-man stands and waves the others out of his path.

His Illitaww words draw my attention away from everything else in the room. Jupp looks at me and grins. To Jupp, it's further proof that this boy is our answer. I'm not convinced.

"I'm Jupp, and this is my brother, Marr. We are warriors from Clan Erowkahnn. We've traveled here in search of passage." Jupp slams his fist into his chest.

I mimic Jupp with a hard pounding on my own chest.

The curly-haired one stands in his chair and points his sword. My finger tickles the edge of a dagger. One blink could occur, and we will be in a bloody mess. Jupp raises his hand and slaps his palm into my abdomen.

"This isn't a fight," Jupp says.

The captain calms his ally with a melody of Northern words. His eyes remain fixated on Jupp and me as his partner settles back into his seat. The women retreat away from the table, smiling out of the door.

"Jupp." The captain bows his head. "Marr. I'm Kai, the captain of the ship."

"We aren't looking for passengers to ferry...but we can make an exception to bring you along," Kai says.

"We are warriors, not passengers, and we don't need a

ferry." I nod toward the door.

I've seen enough, and Kai isn't the answer we seek. Yet Jupp remains fixated on the man. I don't know what he sees, but I trust my brother enough to stay a little longer.

"Yes, you're Illitaww warriors, and Illitaww warriors need battles. Where we are going is dangerous, and we could use your talents," Kai says.

"We aren't here to fight your battles. What do you know of war?" I say.

Jupp lingers in patient silence.

"Nothing. Absolutely nothing. But I know you know of war. I know Illitaww has the greatest warriors the realm has ever known." Kai pounds his chest like we did before. "I'm not a warrior, but I see you. I watched you fight in the pits. I saw you refuse to celebrate your empty victories. You want something more. You want a real battle, because you are real warriors. I want to show you where the real battles lie."

Jupp looks back to me. It seems this man has said correct words. This man, Kai, knows more about our culture than our language.

I nod my submissive agreement.

"We will fight alongside you until our paths part," Jupp says.

We push our fists toward Kai's drink on the table. Kai shakes free of his surprise and grabs his drink while we pull ours back to finish. In three gulps, my drink is gone. Light expressions grow on the faces of the surrounding men, and their bodies loos-en as the tension subsides in the room.

PART III

HOWLS OF THE HUNT

CHAPTER TWENTY-TWO

The Whale

Kai

AUTUMN K26, 50 AE

With waves crashing against the hull, I open the last sail. The ship is gaining speed, and she is ready to fulfill her ultimate purpose.

"Are you ready, my friend?" Cody paces down the deck.

He jumps, stomping on the planks. We're running out of time as dawn approaches from the horizon. Soon the sun will rise out of the gulf, and we will be exposed. The preparation for the night dragged on longer than I anticipated, and we need the cover of darkness for what comes next.

"Keep her tight to starboard." I'm trotting down the deck to meet him.

There's a wave swelling from my right. It smashes into our starboard hull. The water sweeps over my ankles. I lock my elbows around the mast before the rush sucks me down. The water seeps back overboard as the ship rebounds. I stand and survey my ship as she concludes her maiden voyage. I've only had her for a few weeks, but her glorious moment has come.

"Cody." I wave him off the ship.

I've placed ample trust in Cody for this adventure. His information has proved useful, by luck or real insight.

He releases control as I climb the two steps to meet him. When I take the helm, Cody dives off her back. Alone on my crewless vessel, for the first and the last time, I examine her weathered features. She's old, abused, and longing for greater use. Nerves rattle me alert again as I measure the docks within an arrow's release. I go over everything in my mind one last time before I take my exit. The sails are open, the ship is empty, and I'm terrified to jump. The stone vibrates as if to reassure me.

"Yes. I can do this," I say.

I take one moment to gaze at the thin beach, covered in the veil of early dawn. The beach is surrounded by massive cliffs climbing several feet into the sky. Torches decorate the shores and the walls of the cliff behind it.

"Now!" I yell as my opportunity flees, and the stone vibrates more intensely.

Crushing the festering doubt, I shove a rusted short sword into the helm control. It locks into position, and I take one leaping step, which turns into a twirling dive over the edge. With the high dive into the water, time allows my legs to go up behind my head. The flip disorients me in the dark waters.

I reemerge from my dive and notice several things. First, I notice my fatigue and how laboring it is to swim in the ocean water. Second, I see a man running up the docks, waving his hands and yelling at the ghost ship heading straight for him. I turn my head, spit out a mouthful of salty water, and watch Cody drag himself onto shore with the brothers.

Finally the ship smashes into the docks. The man running up the docks jumps off the northern side of the pier to escape the collision. As he splashes in, the wood of the docks collides with my ship. Planks snap off and spray into the air until they all sprinkle into the water with a patter of timber.

The last line of waves lifts me out of the water. Jupp draws in the sand to explain something to Marr. Cody is standing on a boulder to get a better view of the destruction at the docks. The sail is sinking through the heap of dock and ship while waves swirl broken pieces around. Several workers dash out of their garrison in response to the commotion. One small ship floats off to the gulf, dragging dismantled dock pieces with it as it flees.

"Onward," Jupp says.

His confident command breaks our attention from the crumbling site. Marr runs ahead, up the secret paths carved in the cliffs that separate the beach from the city. His long limbs stretch his stride, so that he moves like a charging horse. Cody tosses my staff, and I catch it with one hand and sling it into a rope and over my back. The staff is an upgrade from my mop handle. I play through the words I'll tell Shiva next time I see her—how my mop-handle skills are improved since we last spoke. My only hope is to uncover her rare smile when she sees my improvements.

"See you on the other side, brother." Cody and I slam our forearms together.

He will ensure we have an escape and our portion of the loot is kept safe.

"Do your job," I say. Captain Davinor's frequent words crawl back into my mind from somewhere in the past.

"They will be keeping her in Roknamar," Cody says.

Roknamar is a rare creation. Legends tell of a vast ancient

city deep below the entrance here in Simb's Point. When I learned of this repurposed prison, I hoped to visit it when I became a traveling master. I'm grateful to witness some of these inspiring structures earlier than I anticipated. However, I never imagined I would visit under such extreme circumstances.

Cody shakes seagrass off the covered raft as I sprint after the brothers and the painted view of Simb's Point.

The hike up the loose stone and fish bones consumes the last part of night, but we reach the flat cliff tops without being seen. We find the first dwellings as we enter the edge of the town.

I trace the shoreline in search of Cody and the shore boat, but I find nothing. Instead, a small ship holding several soldiers captures my attention. They are in pursuit of the stray ship. The sight of the chase brings a joyful snort as I fight laughter away.

"Captain." Marr waves me on.

Candlelight flicks on in the windows of the dwellings. Men and women of the city wake and prepare for their daily duties. One door swings open in front of us, and a mother pushes her three whelplings out in a rush. They stride past us without hesitation. One of the girls looks up, and her eyes follow us until her head twists to its extent. The mother urges them all forward without looking back. The young girl reminds me of the lack of subtlety I have with these Illitaww men. There were other recruits who would've been more suited to sneaking through a city. However, none exist who are more suited to being caught sneaking through a city. After we secured the treasure galleon, the other recruits had no reason to help me with this task. I don't blame them. The braveness of Jupp and Marr is as rare as my stupidity for trying this.

Cody should be boarding our stolen treasure galleon turned escape ship by now. It is the ship we were trapped on the night we lost Shiva. I recognized it as soon as we boarded. Flashbacks from the failed attempt stick in my confidence like barbs in bare feet.

My nerves rattle me back to the task at hand as more people exit their homes. Most of the residents glide past us, toward the docks. Some give us questioning looks, but no one tries to stop us.

Our pace brings us to the structure sooner than I expected. The plastered stone walls surrounding the entrance raised above the buildings outside. From our position on the ground, the walls extend several stories and seem to fall over. There is an intentional space between the walls of the prison and the surrounding structures of the city. Nothing is within a fisherman's rope to the walls. We peer around the corner of the nearest building as we make our final plans. The sun rises on the horizon, illuminating us and our treacherous path to the prison gates. Everyone and everything around the walls is silent.

"The guards will be inside," I say.

"Then we will go inside." Jupp adjusts his shield.

"We should wait until a guard arrives for his shift. Then we can follow him in," I say.

"We won't wait. It's best to move while the guards are half-asleep," Marr says.

"How will we enter?" I say.

"We will go through. If it doesn't open, we will go over," Jupp says.

"If you can get in, I'll follow. They won't be able to strike us with arrows once we are against the wall. Are you ready?" I say.

My breath is short, and I can't make myself breathe

normally. I try to measure their doubts, but they aren't afraid. Looking deep into their muddy red eyes, I see no fear besides my own reflecting back. Jupp and Marr are either extremely confident in the success of the mission, or they are happy to die during the attempt. Either way, their confidence lifts me enough to continue.

"Remember the commands," Jupp says.

I nod. On the ship, he explained the importance of him leading, should any combat arise. I'm wise enough to trust him in his expertise of battle.

"Will you stay behind me?" Marr questions in his native language as he grabs my shoulder firmly.

I'm not sure if I'm in his way or if he means to protect me. While I'm inexperienced and out of place, these men are calm and ready for battle. Jupp steps out from around the corner and charges at the gate. Marr follows, drawing his massive twin blades. I grip my staff in my hand, twisting the wood with a nervous clench. The brothers never intended to follow the guileful approach I suggested. Running through the city, avoiding confrontation along the way, and arriving at this moment was as much stealth as I could have hoped for from the two. I struggle to keep up with them as we approach the walls of Roknamar.

When we reach the gate, Jupp bashes it with both shields simultaneously. Then he takes a step back. Does he believe his arms should've gone straight through? He gives one more serious smash with his main-hand shield, busting out a small slit in the gate for a guard's view.

"Over." Jupp points to the top of the wall with his shield-covered hand.

Marr nods. Without any delay, he sheathes his blades and sprints straight for Jupp. Before they collide, Jupp bends down to one knee and points his shields at a favorable angle toward his brother. Marr leaps up from the shields as Jupp stands and throws him. The timing could not have been more accurate.

Marr flies up the front of the wall and reaches the top before his weight brings him back down. As he lands softly on the top of the wall, my staff loosens, and I try to measure the distance from the ground. The feat is astonishing but also impressively flaw-less. How many times have they practiced similar maneuvers?

"Prey?" Jupp says.

Marr shakes his head to indicate a no. Why aren't we being attacked? I'm relieved guards haven't impaled us with arrows or spears, but something is wrong. A ghostly feeling grows as a tingling vibration originates from the leather pouch containing the stone. When I grab the stone, the vibration fades.

Marr drops down inside the fortified prison walls, which brings me back to the world. Jupp paces in front of the gate, readying himself to charge in. I draw myself closer to him, with my staff firmly in both hands. I scan our surroundings. Some-thing isn't right, and I'm afraid that I've fallen into another trap. This time, I don't have Shiva here to help me get out.

With a screeching jerk, the gate opens to Marr and the in-side. Jupp bursts through the opening to the inner fort. I follow blindly, awkwardly adjusting my grip to get my staff through the narrow opening of the breached gate.

An unusual emptiness welcomes us in. Nothing. Open space surrounded by more space makes up the inner fort. Now inside, I understand the straightforward design. There are sev-eral towers at key structural and defense points around the pris-on. The walls are thick, and the stone is flat without perceptible notches. At the center of the courtyard rests a large boulder. Jupp releases an angry expression along with a grunt. Marr con-tinues to study the area. He spots something of interest and runs toward a corner tower.

"This is the place, but I..." I shrug my shoulders. "Wait."

Jupp turns back toward me instead of following Marr.

"The hold is said to be mostly comprised of underground structures. We have to find the way underground. Over here."

I run toward the tower. Through the portcullis and around a corner, I find a staircase leading up, but nothing down. I search around, throwing a chair out of my way. I want to confirm the edge of the tower. Nothing.

I run back out. Jupp is standing in the center of the fort. Marr is making a bird call from the top of the corner tower. My back beads with sweat as I spin around. Marr shouts something indiscernible in Illitawwe as he disappears back into the tower. Jupp is calm, and he tightens the leather straps of his shields.

"Marr says there is a slain guard atop the tower," Jupp says.

I start to respond, but my words lie dormant. Marr runs toward us, and we all meet next to the gigantic boulder in the middle of the fort. The brothers converse as Marr describes the guard he found. I remain vigilant, scanning for signs of danger. This spider's web was designed by someone dangerous.

"Poison," Jupp says.

"The men in the tower have been poisoned." Marr imitates choking. "They've choked on their own breath. We have a root in Illitaww that causes this, but I'm not sure if you have the same plant here."

Fear lowers my confidence. Part of me, my weakest pieces, wants to abandon hope and run before we get caught. The brothers don't seem to have the same fears. They would be happy to fight out of a trap, and they might succeed.

A familiar voice claps from atop the boulder, beyond our vision. I take a cautious step back to find the origin of the sweet sound. Appearing from somewhere inside the white stone are several shrunken figures. One bears the crimson armor of a Magnavozian soldier, while the other two are dressed in combinations of undergarments and rags. Of the two dressed in rags, one is a sunken man with smooth black skin, no shirt, and dreadlocked hair growing into his beard. The other ragged person is Shiva. I want to climb the boulder to hug her.

"Baby whale?" Shiva shouts.

A lump forms in my throat when she speaks. She steps to the edge of the boulder above us. The soldier pulls her back from the brink, and she stares with a confused expression seared into her face by sunlight, which she has lost her acclimation to.

"Shiva," I say.

The brothers step back to gain my view to the top of the boulder. My curiosity about the rock and the hidden entrance to Roknamar grows. Unfortunately, I don't have time to explore the marvels inside.

"Are there enemies?" Jupp says.

"No," I say.

I don't recognize the other two, but Shiva is the opposite of an enemy.

"Who is with you?" I say.

"This is Frenton. He has helped me escape from the dark hold," she says.

The soldier doesn't look at me. He nudges Shiva to continue walking. She says he's an ally, but he doesn't treat her like one.

"How...how are you here?" she says.

"Cody...he explained that you were—"

"Cody? He's alive? That guy..." Shiva smiles and quickens her pace down the winding steps."Are you ready?" she says.

"Yes, of course," I say.

"Then follow us. We don't have time for a reunion." Her voice carries her as they swing around to the other side.

Shiva and the other two are stepping on specific pieces of the boulder as they descend. They circle down and disappear around the other side before reemerging on our side again. When they circle back, they are much closer to the ground. Finally the three touch feet to the ground beside me, and I see the dimpled trail in the boulder. Shiva embraces me as they meet us. Her clutch is tight as she brings me in. Her head lowers at my neck. Before I can commit to the hug, she releases me, sliding her hand down my arm.

"Come." She waves us on.

Her face turns away, leading us out of the walls of Rok-namar.

After a long stare, our new acquaintances all dash for the gate. Jupp and Marr are following right behind them. I run but stop when the straggler slows down. The unnamed stranger bends down to his knees and rubs the grass through his fingers. His eyes meet mine. For the first moment, he is delighted and smiling at me, unaware of anything else. Embarrassment and fear ripen in him, and his smile fades. He stands and follows the others out.

Shouts break out on the other side of the wall. My abdo-men flexes as my heart begins to beat harder. What am I running towards?

Screeching clashes of steel greet me as I exit the gate. Marr slays a soldier while four more lie lifeless at his feet. They are covered in blood and the same crimson armor as our new ally. Yet our ally seems unaffected. He presses forward, urging every-one to run.

Jupp bashes his way through a line of soldiers by himself. Shiva makes sure I'm behind her with a glance. Jupp shouts to his brother right before an arrow flies over my shoulder, break-ing into the wall behind me. The other three continue down the northwest road. Jupp runs up beside me to block another arrow. With a sizable sweeping heave, he removes his great shield from his back and holds it above us. Bolts split off the buffer above us as we run.

"Marr!" I shout.

Marr finishes the soldier fighting in front of him and re-turns to us. Once he reaches our position, we run. Jupp heaves the massive wall of a shield onto his back.

Several streets later we find ourselves running out of

breath and city space. We lose the pursuit by what was left of the guards, leaving us with a temporary break. The Illitaww brothers pace back and forth. On the other shoulder, the starved stranger leans against the wall of the building. He is more drained than any of us. Shiva is looking back and forth between the Magnavozian soldier and me. The soldier is the first one to break the silence.

"This is the northwestern edge of the city. That road leads to Rock Hollow." He points westward.

Shiva nods her head and thanks him. The stranger rises from the ground and speaks his first words.

"Wait. We aren't going to the castle, are we?" he says.

His voice is musical, sturdy, and opposite to the body it comes from.

"No, of course not," Shiva says. "What's your plan, Kai? You did come for me, right? What's next?" Her eyes are saying something else, but I can't read them.

"I...just..." I forget the words I have been rehearsing for this moment.

"Are you going farther inland?" Shiva says.

I step closer and try to pull her away from her Magnavozian companion. I explain to her how Cody and I developed a plan to reclaim the treasure, rescue her, and escape to the gulf.

"He's waiting just offshore," I say.

"Frenton can be trusted. I would still be locked away if not for his bravery," she says.

Her words are an insult, though they aren't meant to be. Am I not brave?

"Cody will return once tonight with a signal. If we don't meet him, he'll go on to Rotho City for a day or two, and then back to Tyfu to berth," I say.

I release our plan to them, trusting Shiva enough to vouch for her new companions.

"Will that work?" she says.

Cody is my source of confidence in this ridiculous plan. Without him here, I'm at a loss for words.

"We protect," Marr says.

Both the Illitaww brothers slam their fists together. Shiva scowls until she bursts into a laugh.

"And who are these men?" she says.

"These two...Jupp and Marr. They are Illitaww warriors," I say.

She nods but says nothing more as she studies them. Marr turns away to scout around the corner of the alley.

"This is Frenton, and this is Nok." She gestures to the other man.

Nok is skinny, above average height, and as dark as twilight, like the depictions of the legendary Dregak Magnavoz.

"It's a pleasure for you all to meet me." Nok pushes himself off the wall and bows.

CHAPTER TWENTY-THREE

The Thief

Nok

AUTUMN K26, 50 AE

The sun is shining through our thinning skin as we step down from the great white rock. The grass sticking between my toes is sensational, causing bumps to grow up my legs. Before, I would never have risked stepping with bare feet on soil. Yet on this day, I find myself on my knees, soaking up the sunshine. I want to kiss the ground at my knees. My eyes meet the whale-boy, and his curious expression brings me back to reality.

"You are not free yet." I urge my broken body to get up and run.

The soft part of my foot slices open on a jagged rock as soon as I exit the gates. I wince and continue to follow Lifia.

"Can you manage?" She looks at me over her shoulder.

Lifia doesn't move like an empress. She is sure-footed and as graceful as I imagined a Fangourian tiger would be. A clash of swords and stone rumbles behind us. She slows her stride and turns back to watch. When I've almost caught up to her again, her face relaxes, and she starts sprinting again.

"We are not free yet," I say.

"Are you sure it won't kill them?" Frenton crouches on the other side of my cell.

"It wouldn't kill a hound," I say.

The poison, which took many days to brew, consists mostly of my mushrooms, but there are a few ingredients Frenton provided. Museweed, when milled and heated, creates a drowsy effect, but the purple prairie petals are the most harmful ingredient. If the guards survive the shakes, they'll remain paralyzed until sundown.

"Pour it in their porridge so you can save the empress." I pass the concoction through the feeding slit.

At first I didn't think he had found enough to sedate the guards. In the end, it was plenty.

We are at the far western edge of the city. This side of the fort is protected by an enormous four-story wall that encircles half of the city. The other half of the city is cliffs and the rocky beach below. There are many guards near the gate a few blocks beyond our position. Frenton paces back and forth down the alley to peer around each side. Lifia and the whale-boy stare at each other without speaking. The hardy warriors stand firm yet relaxed. I inhale deeply to regain my breath. Their faces are much kinder and younger than I expected. Before, they were too far away to notice. The larger of the two giants smiles at me, but his smile is forced and creepy. I turn away from them and meander toward Lifia.

"We should wait here until the evening," the boy says.

"No. We should leave." Frenton paces by. "The longer we wait, the more likely we are to be found."

His point is valid. My mind begins to wander to thoughts of food. When I was locked away in the dark cell, I often dreamed of the food I would have if I ever escaped, although I began to believe the dream would never become a reality.

They continue to argue about what course would provide the best chance of success. All I can think about is spices and fresh vegetables. Water gushes under my tongue as memories of sweet melon seared and sprinkled with sea salt return to me. Next, bread comes to mind. The faint smell of freshly baked bread wafts into my memories. Kneading dough in preparation is enough to let my lips spill out what little water they hold.

"How far can we get on foot?" Lifia's stern voice brings me back to reality.

"We will go farther on foot...a lot farther than if we head toward the gulf," Frenton says.

Lifia shrugs. Frenton throws his hands to his sides and turns away.

"We already have a plan in motion," the boy says.

"Explain your plan, Kai," Lifia says.

"Cody waits for us offshore. We'll wait until nightfall for the signal. With the signal, we can take the hidden raft out to meet him," Kai says.

"And what signal is that? A blowhorn? One that will signal to everyone that your escape is coming?" Frenton says.

Frenton and Kai exchange glances, and Frenton steps up to meet him. His hand is on the hilt of his sword at his waist. Lifia steps in front of them to moderate the growing disdain. The larger of the two barbarians steps up behind Kai. Frenton wisely holds his words.

The thought of warm, fresh bread returns to me. I can't focus on the conversation. I'm tired from hunger, thirst, and running.

"Wait," I say.

The thoughts of bread coming to me aren't of my own creation. They spawn from the slight scent of bread blowing down the alleyway from one of the buildings nearby. My words startle the others. The slightly less gigantic man reaches for his swords, slung behind his back.

Lifia carries a puzzled expression. She is quite Fangourian, has a straight back and black hair, with green eyes, and this is the first time we really look at each other. She really is the lost empress of Fangour.

"What is it?" she says.

"Uh, well, whatever we decide to do, we need to eat and rest. Our bodies need to be strong, should anything go awry," I say.

Everyone is staring at me. They are confused.

"Leave it to me," I say.

They exchange questioning glances with each other.

I'll locate the origin of the bread fragrance myself. Maybe I'll share it with them. They fall back into their argument over which way to go, and I discreetly back away to follow my own desires.

The scent of dough rising over a flame grows as I follow the lovely heated smell to its source. I approach the brown stone premises by the city's northwest corner. I peer around each side. On the front entrance, a worker loads a cart for a delivery of some sort. Around the other side of the corner, there are a pair of windows spaced out on the wall. Above the farthest window from me, a deep brown, almost black, burn stain scorches up the stone.

My mouth continues to fill with saliva as I peer back and forth from the corner of the building. At the front, where a cart full of bread is being overfilled with fresh assortments, the young man returns to the shop.

"That's it. I'm claiming a piece," I say.

Right when I take my first desperate step around the corner and toward the cart, the young man hustles out of the door. Someone inside is yelling at him as he exits. He grabs his cart and heads down the street without turning back. If he did, he would find me.

Smoke billows out of the farthest window. A fresh batch of balled dough? With hope, I glide over to the open window. Waves of heat and smoke hit me when I peek through. The heat pushes me back and leaves a singe on my forehead. There's no use trying to get in through this window.

I make my way back to the first window. Before I arrive, a couple of ladies dressed in gowns and veils stroll by, giggling in conversation. I lean up against the wall, hoping they don't notice me. My dark skin contrasts with the light-brown stones that form most of the buildings. I close my eyes. When I open them, they have passed. Their happy chatter echoes down the street in the same direction the bread cart rolled off in.

When I turn back to the window, I see mounds of bread stacked on tables on the other side of the glass.

"Please be unlatched." I run my hand down the window-pane. "It will be unlatched," I say.

With a little hand strength, I jiggle the window, and it opens. Again the scent of bread swarms me, but this time, there is no scorching. I poke my head in. It's warm inside, and the smell of food is all I ever wanted. I stop to listen. The only sound is the roar of the flame inside the bread oven. Sliding in through the window feet first, I duck and twist to the side to get my face in. My tender foot presses onto stone floor. I catch myself from falling over and hobble back on my good foot. Then I realize my hand is pressed into a fresh roll of bread.

Instinctively I squeeze it. The warm roll mushes between my fingers. The moist bread, crumbling in my hands, is almost as pleasurable as it is when it touches my tongue. Some of the loaves of bread have twists of spice rolled into them. I eat sever-al bites out of each type and quickly reach my capacity. Then I stuff more into my mouth for the pleasure.

Quickly I realize how dry my mouth has become from gorg-ing on the bread. Searching around the room, I find a few bottles of seawater and one bottle of mead. There isn't any fresh water, which I crave the most. I take a large swig of the mead, which is delightfully mild and refreshing.

"Pete, are you back already?" a voice calls out from the other room.

I can't be sure if the voice originates from a man or a wom-an. Before they have the chance to swing open the door to find me here, I stuff one piece of bread in my mouth, grab the most substantial loaf on the table, and dive out of the window.

I'm running for my freedom and for my bread. After a time, when I realize I'm not being chased, I slow my pace and begin to make my way at a stroll. The cut on my foot bleeds, leaving a trail behind me. The pain of the wound is minor compared to the aches within my body. My legs haven't been used in these ways for a long time.

I pass a few people on the street. One person turns her nose away and pinches it closed. How long would she survive in my reeking cell?

"Not long at all," I say.

The horrors I've survived are not for the average person.

"Who is the drunk?" the woman says.

I scurry off and avoid further contact as I go.

●

Lifia is the first to notice me. She checks behind herself as I approach.

"Where did you go?" she says.

"I found something to break our fast." I hand her the bread and take another swig of the mead.

The drink has a refreshing citrus taste. It tastes better than anything I've ever drunk, and I'm reluctant to share. The others notice me, and fumbled words break their conversation.

"Did anyone see you? Anyone in the city could be looking for us," Lifia says.

"No, of course not. I'm barely noticeable. No one saw me. The bread fell off a passing cart, and I rescued it," I say.

She examines the loaf. Her hunger interrupts her anger, and she squeezes off a piece before passing it to Kai. One of the barbarians rips the bottle from my grasp. He takes a swig and gives it back, nodding his head in approval.

"And what about the bottle?" Lifia says.

"Uh... I found the bottle lying in the middle of an alley on my way back. I'm not sure it's worth drinking. I'm afraid it might be a bottle full of piss," I say.

My naughty attempt to discourage the others is met with raised eyebrows all around. Kai laughs.

"I'm beginning to like this one. Have a drink." I motion the bottle toward Kai.

"I'm not thirsty, thank you," he says.

The barbarians exchange words in their native language.

"Marr does not drink piss," one says.

He rises and addresses me with disdain in his thick accent. Then he grabs the bottle from me, just like the other one did before him. After a gulp, he tosses the diminished bottle back to me before he swishes the last juices.

"Not piss. Good." He smacks his lips and says something sassy in their language. They both laugh.

"Marr...and...?" I point at one barbarian, then to the other.

"Jupp." He pounds his fist into his chest.

Lifia shakes her head and returns to her conversation with Frenton and the whale-boy.

"If you have a way out, I'll follow you, Kai," Lifia says.

Frenton's face turns red, and he stomps his foot on the ground, rattling his metal armor.

"You are welcome to come," Kai says.

Frenton ignores the invitation.

"What about you, Nok?" Lifia sets her sights on me again.

"Me?" I have yet to listen to either version of their escape plan. "I'll be pursuing the most logical plan," I say.

"And which one is that?"

"North to Delphinus, of course. The North Isles will do." I drink down the last swig of the mead.

Kai sits down with his back leaning against the wall. I think I catch him grinning, but I'm not certain. I'm not sure whose plan it was to go to the North Isles or what part of the plan it would be, but I heard someone say something about it.

"We'll wait until the evening and then sneak to the docks,"

Lifia says.

"Wait? We need to leave now. There's a battalion of soldiers searching the city for us as we speak," I say.

"That's why we should go southeast, out of those gates, and toward the Aptorias. The longer we wait, the less likely we are to get away," Frenton says.

"What if your friend doesn't show? Then you'll be stuck, with fewer places to hide." I toss the bottle into a mound of rotting hay.

"If you must go, then leave with Frenton." Lifia exhales a labored breath.

"Uh...yes. Then...we shall be off as soon as we can." I take a step toward Frenton.

Frenton readjusts his bracers while staring down at the ground. Lifia sits between the barbarians with her head hanging. No one is looking at anyone else, and the decisionmaking has concluded.

"Yes. We leave now." Frenton stops adjusting is equipment.

For a moment, I find myself drowning in indecision. I would rather be moving toward somewhere else than waiting to be captured here. I'm happy to be out of the cell. The dusty air of this alleyway is fresh compared to the stagnant air I'm accustomed to. Yet fresher air lies ahead.

"Wait." Lifia slides her back up the wall.

She glides up to Frenton and embraces him.

"How will you get past the guards at the gate?" Lifia releases Frenton and hugs me.

She's the first person I've felt in so long. My first instinct is to back away, but I easily give in. Her back is riddled with hard muscles. I catch a closeup glimpse of her face as we release each other. It's smudged with mud and grime, but perfectly proportioned and full of Fangourian features, from her cool undertones to her thin black hair.

"We will manage," Frenton says.

"Will we?" I say.

Lifia raises her hand in an invitation to the others.

"We can help you. We owe you at least that much," Kai says.

The sealed gate is our only exit, besides the ocean. Ten guards argue with tradesmen and farmers who are attempting to enter the city. They must have orders to keep anyone from going in or out.

"We fight. There is no difficulty," Jupp says.

"I'm sure you would have no problem with these city guards, but they'll call many more soldiers, and if we get away, we won't get far," Lifia says.

"There'll be many more chances to fight," Kai says.

"Frenton, what do you think?" Lifia says.

"I wear the same armor as those guards. I can get past them, but they'll be cautious of others," he says.

He wears the same armor, but he's not the same. His plains-man accent gives him away.

"What if we could do something to draw the attention of the guards? Take Nok and tell them he's a vagrant... Sorry." Kai frowns.

I smirk to show him I'm not offended. Vagrancy is a nice promotion.

"It may turn the key." Frenton nods his head in agreement.

We begin our walk up to the gate. The walls seem larger than when I was first brought through them. Frenton's hand is steady as he pushes me forward. His shove is practiced, and it helps sell the trick. One of the guards laughs as we draw nearer.

"What do we have?" The guard's voice is muffled inside his helmet.

"This begging shit has jumped the wall, and I'm throwing him out," Frenton says.

I'm impressed. His act is beyond believable for such a simple man. He flings his hands up to gesture his disgust as he shoves me again. His hands hang in the air to give the signal. Windows shatter down the block.

"Thieves again? We'll take both their hands this time. You. With me." The higher-ranking guard directs four of the lower guards.

They run off toward the crashing, including the first who addressed us. Frenton continues to usher me forward. We stop in front of the last few remaining. None of them are wearing helmets. They all appear young and naive.

"Let me dispose of this garbage before he shits in the streets again," Frenton says.

The guards look at each other. None of them are sure who should make the decision or what the decision should be.

"We aren't supposed to let anyone leave, sir," the youngest among them finally responds.

"You are damn right. Captain Yeston to you. Open this gate, or I'm going to have you clean up him and the stains he's trailed through the city," Frenton says.

I curl my neck back to him. Where has he kept this part of himself hidden? I chuckle, remembering my own secrets. The guard stammers, takes a few steps, and frantically turns. Finally he stops.

"Yes, sir...Captain Yeston. I don't know how the gate opens," he says.

"Open the side gate, boy." Frenton points at the smaller metal gate beside the large entrance.

The young guard finds his way to the gate and manages,

with the help of the other guards, to raise the portcullis. Frenton and I stride out as quickly as we can without running. Our feet hit the graveled path outside the gate, and we're off.

Several paces down the road, we pass a convoy of eight soldiers galloping toward the city. One of the soldiers turns his head to look at us, but they don't slow their pace. Frenton lowers his thick head. Is he afraid?

"Frenton...Jaspermon? Where are you from?" I say.

His name suggests the middle caste of a time long ago. Before Dregak Magnavoz united the former kingdoms into modern-day Magnavoz, before the first Nagidah king claimed Rock Hollow, and long before the Fangourian Empire rose and spread throughout the realm, people in the middle realm were divided into three castes. The high-caste people were given -voz in their names to signify their godliness. Those with the gods' blessings, like Omavoz, Clinuvoz, and the illustrious Magnavoz, owned land and people. The middle caste, with -mon in their names, could own land, but their people belonged to one of the nearby high-caste families. The low caste, with names ending in -min, could not own land or businesses without the sponsorship of a higher name. Still, there were those in lower castes who had no names, or their names were outside the castes, which usually meant they were slaves.

"Be quiet. Did you not see them? They'll be turning back around any moment," Frenton says.

"Who? The soldiers? They didn't seem to mind us at all." I grab my swollen belly. "I just wanted to know if you know where you are going."

"Yes, I know these parts well. My family sows the north plains," Frenton says.

"Ah, yes. A farm boy. You bear resemblance to a farmer, yet you're dressed in soldiers' attire." I wave my hand at his Magnavozian armor.

"We need to get off the road." Frenton grunts and

continues to stomp ahead. He doesn't want to speak to me or anyone else.

"Why does a farmer's boy join the Magnavozian army, capture an empress, and then release her? I can see how you fell for her. I saw her beauty when we stopped in the alley," I say.

"What?" Frenton stops.

Have I stepped on a nerve?

"It was your choice to make. It was the right choice, if you ask me," I say.

Frenton places his hand on the hilt of his blade.

"You don't seem like a soldier. But there must be a reason you joined."

"I didn't need a reason, because I didn't have a choice. I'm the only son of Tullen Jaspermon. Do you know what that means? To be the son of a landowner? There are responsibilities involved. If I hadn't joined the army, they would've called my family traitors and taken our land."

He doesn't know my heritage or the name of my father. So he doesn't understand I know everything about upholding a high name, even though I can never wear it.

"We all do what we must to survive. You haven't done anything wrong," I say.

His tight expression says he's deciding whether he wants to say something else or continue in silence. I've spoken too much. Regret swells in my bread-filled gut.

"No. You're right. Why do I need to escape? Empress Lifia is who they're searching for. No one knows that I helped," he says.

Someone will know his place in our escape, but I don't respond.

"I could say I was poisoned as well, and I awoke and chased after you all," Frenton says.

"Well, you did poison the guards' porridge, did you not? I think they will consider that someone helped us escape," I say.

I continue to walk forward, trying not to make eye contact. His rambling reminds me of other arrogant lords who I've heard speak the same way.

"They don't have to know how I helped," he says.

"I don't see how else we could've removed ourselves," I say.

"The warriors from the South and the sailor could've helped you escape." His pace slows.

I realize what he is pushing toward. I turn around, and his eyes are fixed on me.

"I must take you back." He draws his sword.

I would rather be cut in half by his blade than return to a dungeon.

"Whoa..."

He points the end of his sword at me.

"Fine, I'll return with you. It's no problem. I grow tired of walking. It's fine. I've experienced enough adventure for one life. I hope the others are enjoying the beach more than we are our little stroll." I raise my hands.

I turn back around and begin to walk back toward the city. Surprised by my obedient actions, his sword hand falls limp, and he turns around with me. When I hear his metal blade sliding back into its sheath, I bend down to pick up two fistfuls of sand.

"What are you doing?" he says.

I grit my teeth, jumping up with my fists of gravel. I fling the cloud of sand and pebbles into his face. Before I can see the effect, I'm running again.

I zig in different directions. Then I zag around a tree and over a hill. Frenton yells curses at me as I increase the gap between us. I run down the valley, away from the road, until I get to a sparse tree line and another valley beyond the range. I keep pushing forward. Pain begins to grow in the arches of my feet, which haven't moved like this in some time. The pain doesn't halt me. In fact, the pain propels me onward. The pain, fear, and agony of being locked in the dungeon again move me beyond what my withered body should be capable of.

Eventually, I come to a stream. One leap gets me across the watery gap. I look back across the creek to measure the distance between us, yet he is out of sight. My throat betrays me, and I begin to cough. Saliva and mucus form large knots in my throat. The taste of blood and iron find a place on the back of my tongue. My chest aches, and my body fights against fresh air. Worst of all, my head is spinning. I've pushed myself to my limits, but capture is not an option. I will not return to Roknamar. I sink into the grass and cover myself in foliage.

CHAPTER TWENTY·FOUR

The Visitor

Kai

AUTUMN K26, 50 AE

My mother brushes her fingers through my hair as we swing together outside our provisional shack. The waves roll up the beach until they disappear under our raised porch. She hums an old song that has no words.

When I try to speak, seawater squirts out.

"Wait...just wait here, my son. Art will guide you," my mother says.

When I look up, her face is hazy from light shining around her. I try to rise, but again my body fails me. This time, my back is stiff, filled with sand, and too heavy to lift.

"No, son. Rest," she says.

Calming waves swish under the porch as the tide pulls a calmness around us.

I follow the leather string down to the covered stone. When I grasp it, the pouch gives way, and it crumples in my palms.

"Yes, son. Art is here."

I open my hand, and the stone reappears. The stone is like a starless sky during new moons, and it absorbs the light around us. *Wait. This isn't happening.* It's like a dream and memory combined, but the memory isn't mine. In one moment, my mother fades away with the tide. In the next, I'm alone in complete darkness.

The heaviness of my body returns to the earth, but my mind remains in flight.

"Oh, what is this?" A voice echoes.

"Who's there?" I say.

I can't see them, but I feel their warmth.

"The guardians show us to another. This one carries a stone, and he's not alone...no," the voice says.

Mild light gleams into my eyes, and I squint to protect them.

"This one shines brightly. Agonok. Come." The voice shakes.

"What is this?" says a deeper voice.

A man with a long, drawn face and thick, dark eyebrows appears in front of me. Light glows from behind the man, creating a distinct outline of his figure wrapped in robes. The second man is bald with a thick gray beard. He holds a stern gaze behind the first man. The discontented look reminds me of the disappointed expressions I received during my dismissal from Summer's Light.

Beyond the first two men, several faces fill the dark,

moonlit room. They trade whispers while the first two men study me. A large opening cuts into the ceiling, forming the stadium. The stars flicker through the opening.

I try to open my mouth, but it won't oblige. I bring my hand to my throat to coax the sound free, but nothing comes.

"He can't speak," one says.

The thick-eyebrowed man bends down to examine my feet, which causes me to jump back. The stern, bearded man circles me.

"Not in the way we have learned to speak," he says.

Tiny glowing shapes float around them, but they don't seem to notice. I follow the faces behind the two men in search of anyone I recognize, but none are familiar.

"Raise your hand if you can hear me," the bearded man says.

His interruption rushes my wandering eyes back to him. I can hear him plainly, but my mouth will not produce the sounds required to communicate. I slowly raise my hand and drop it back down to my side.

"Good. Good. How have you come to be...? Well, no, that won't work. Let's see. If you are Arilandic, please raise your hand," he says.

I remain still. Although I hold Arilandic ties from my mother's family, I don't believe he's questioning my bloodline.

"No. You don't have the look of a sandman," he says.

"If you are a son of the forest and of the old ways, raise your hand." The first man places his hand on the second man's shoulder.

No. I'm not what he suggests. Their questions turn into muddled clumps. Their words sound like jumbled mumbles spoken underwater.

"Do you carry a stone of the tribes? Is that what has brought you to us? Raise your hand for yes," he says.

Could he mean the Art Stone? He must. I raise my hand.

"Yes? Yes, that is the only way. Where are you from? Who are you?" He slams his fist on a stone altar. The light fades around me.

"He's fading," a voice shouts from the crowd.

"Wait. Please, come back to us. You can't wield the stone alone. The gateways... Use the gateways. The stone will show you how," the thick-eyebrowed man says.

The ground rumbles. I feel the world rip away from me. It's like I'm trying to hold on to a wet fishing pole during a storm, and now a giant fish has taken hold of the other end. I'm yanked into a whirlpool, along with the light, faces, and floating geometric patterns.

Images flash through the ripples in the vortex. First, a cave is buried in a barren desert. A garden grows outside a dark tower. A canyon falls below a great bridge. Other images swirl around, but none are discernible. Finally, a river flows from the peak of a mountain.

"Raten" is the last word I hear before the light completely fades, and I'm alone in darkness once more.

I inhale, and the cold air cuts at my throat. I'm suffocating as I rise from the dream. Was it a dream? No. It was something more. As my eyes focus, a towering figure stands over me. It's Jupp, and Marr is behind him. I lean away from them and scoot my back upright from the ground while maintaining eye contact.

"The gods speak to you?" Jupp says.

"The gods?" I say.

They were somewhat divine, but they weren't gods.

"What did the gods whisper to you?" His accent is thicker than usual.

"I don't know... I...I don't think the gods spoke to me. It was someone else," I say.

Jupp takes a step back.

"Hey, baby whale. Were you fighting someone in your dream?" Shiva pokes me with the end of my staff.

I reach for the staff, but she teases it away. The sun is setting, which marks our cue to leave.

"It wasn't a dream, but I'll explain later. Is everyone
ready?" I jump up and meet the others.

We sneak through the city, toward the beach. Shiva leads.
I mimic her movements, like I did the night she was captured in
Shelby Cove. This night will be different. It must. Even Jupp
and Marr are treading more carefully than before.

We reach the edge of the beach cliff. I peer over into the
gulf, hoping to see signs of Cody. "This is where you came up?"
Shiva says.

"This is it." I take the first step down the path.

Jupp, Shiva, and Marr follow behind me. The beach is still,
allowing only small waves to come onto the shore. There are no
torches, candles, or lamps down below. In fact, the garrison and
docks are spookily quiet.

"You crashed your ship into those docks?" Shiva says.

"Yes. I suppose they did straighten things up well." One of
my steps turns into a slide.

Gravel pours beneath me like a powerful river. Fortunately, I stop before I slide over the edge. My breath is rapid. Jupp
slows his climb, grabs my shoulder, and pulls himself in front of
me, taking the lead. Shiva touches the back of my shoulder to
communicate something wordlessly as well. I take my next step
carefully.

Reaching the bottom, I extend out my hand to help Shiva
off the path, and we walk toward the same beach that I crawled
from earlier this morning.

As we approach, remnants of the dock collide as they twist up in the tide. We all meet at the bottom of the hidden trail leading up the cliff. The beach opens to the north and extends for miles. The only cover between where we crouch and the ocean is speckles of larger rocks, which dwindle in size the closer they are to the waves.

A single torch hung on a fisherman's hook illuminates half of the dock. I chuckle when I realize the small ship knocked off to sea on our arrival is not among the ships docked. Shiva glances at me when I laugh.

"We should wait here until the sun goes down a little lower." I point to the rocks where we hid the other seagrass-covered raft.

The brothers nod, but Shiva seems distracted. I go to her to make sure she understands, but her eyes are searching past me, toward the docks. I follow her gaze until it jolts away from the docks to me.

"What is it?" I say.

Breaking from a trance, she shakes her head and vision free.

"It's my bow...the Evoni Bow." She points above the docks to a series of large shark hangers.

I gaze for a time before understanding what she means. Finally I spot it. Tangled in the fishing rope, her beautiful black bow hangs from the farthest shark hanger. The Evoni family were the sovereigns of the Fangourian Empire. Finally I realize the significance of the bow strung on the hanger.

"The Evoni Bow... Shiva, who are you?" I say.

She withdraws, sliding her back against the rock until her bottom touches her heels. Jupp and Marr begin down the path, hidden from the docks by boulders, to the beach.

"Kai... I'm not...Shiva." She puts her head in her hands.

I take a step closer, searching for words to say.

"My name is Lifia of the Evoni dynasty, the daughter of the last empress, Dianame. The bow is the Evoni family's treasure, valued beyond any other, and the legends it helped twine are all sacred to me. That is why I was taken as a prisoner and not executed that night on the treasure galleon. That is why they baited me here. I'm sorry I lied to you," she says.

Are those tears? I slide down to her level. It's difficult to witness someone so strong being so vulnerable. If she is the lost empress of Fangour, we are in greater danger than I could've imagined. Our escape means more than rescuing a friend. I'm more afraid, and more empowered to protect her.

"I understand. You don't need to apologize to me." I grab her hand.

She pulls it away. "Is it that easy for you to forgive me, when I've gotten you into this?" Lifia says.

It does not matter. She is still the same person. The same risks are still worth it. I cough to dissolve the lump forming in my throat.

"I don't care what your name is. You saved my life. Let me return the favor. Let's get out of here." I grab her hand again.

Her shoulders seem to soften. Together we sneak down the beach to meet the brothers.

"Cody will show the signal there." I point into the gulf.

We settle into anxious squats. I count a hundred waves washing in and out, but no signal arrives with them.

"I could take it," Lifia says.

I refuse to acknowledge her words. I stand nearest to the water, leaning my right shoulder against a warm boulder. It's night, but the sunbaked rock still holds warmth. I haven't looked away from the gulf. I'm afraid if I look away for even a moment, I'll miss the sign.

"I'll help you," Jupp says.

"The numbers won't be on our side." I shake my head as a mutiny forms behind me.

"*Wrekk*," Marr grunts.

Their eyes grow heavy on my neck, but I won't look back

at them. Something inside me knows Cody isn't far away.

"The sign will come soon. We can take the raft out to meet him halfway," I say.

The wind intensifies as I sneak to the place where we hid the raft. Moist, compacted sand squelch under my feet as I go. I find the raft in wet seagrass behind the rock we used to mark its location. The tide is high, which will only make it easier to get the raft into the water. I squat low and give a labored heave. My feet dig in, and my bottom slips into the sand while the raft rolls over with a thud.

"Help me get this in the water." I wave to the ghosts of my companions. Their dancing shadows are gone. "Shi...Lifia," I whisper.

I rush back to where I left them. I search around the rock. My eyes tingle with pain as I strain to shift them over the dark docks. Sweat trickles down my side as anger climbs inside. When did the brothers acquire such guile?

The bow is still tangled in the fisherman's rope and strung on the shark hanger. A small relief comes over me, and I release a deep exhalation.

A cry sounds from the docks, destroying the small relief I felt. Torches light up the docks, and more than twenty soldiers flood down from the barracks. Rising from their crouch, Jupp and Marr equip their weapons. Lifia swings from her knees, upside down on the hanger, as she frantically cuts her bow free.

I stand at a distance with one hand on the boulder and the other on the vibrating Art Stone.

CHAPTER TWENTY-FIVE

The Rider

Nok

AUTUMN K26, 50 AE

The fragrance of manure climbs into my nostrils. When it arrives, vomit forms in the back of my throat and falls back into my stomach to warn me of the disgusting composition.

Moments after the scent finds me, I locate a group of rancher dwellings. I'm somewhere southwest of the city gate. My wounded foot is raw, and I need to find a safe place to rest. All my cunning and all my stamina were drained to get away from Frenton. If not for his heavy armor, he would've caught me. Why did he change his mind so abruptly? I'm not sure if he wanted to betray me or if he was caught up in a fear-fed tantrum.

The house seems abandoned at first. However, the tidy porch and a glow of light flickering from somewhere deeper inside suggests quaint occupants. West of the house lies the stable. Sneaking from tree to tree, I separate myself from the line of sight to the house and make my way to the stable.

A goat cries out from inside. Free to roam, it passes in front of me as I enter. The stable smells of mold and manure. There's a single open stable door at the end. A resting spot?

"Better than the dungeon." I walk toward the end of the building.

A neighboring beast emits a snorted neigh as I walk by. The closer I get, the more a horse stomps on the other side of the closed stable. I peek over the stall to see what it is. On the other side, an old dust-gray stallion snorts air up at me.

"Hello, you." I pat his matted coat.

Tangles and dirt span the length of both his mane and tail. His stomach is sunken beyond starvation.

"A bit underfed, you old cat?" I brush the dirt off his back.

In the corner of the stable lies a sack of dry grass.

"Here you are, old boy." My hands cup grass for him.

He jerks away from the moldy hay. I drop the rest at his feet.

"Not hungry? Well, I wouldn't eat it either. I'll try to find you something...else."

I walk outside the stable. Gazing northward, I locate a fruit-bearing tree. The tree has a short, stubby trunk, and the branches expand as wide as any tree I've ever seen. Some of the branches on one side of the tree are overweight and drag along the ground as they sway in the breeze. The leaves are green and decorated with bright red bulbs throughout. Walking closer to the tree, I recognize large, ripe pieces of fruit.

"Rose crisps," I say.

Some are overripe, and those ones lie at the base of the tree, but most pieces are perfectly aged. I reach and pluck out a medium-sized piece. I press it against my nostrils in search of any scent the fruit might carry. There's a slight tart smell, along with the earthy aroma of the tree. As I take a bite, sweet juice squirts onto my chin. I can't remember the last time I ate a fresher bite of fruit. The taste is intoxicating, and the pleasurable flavor invigorates me. I finish the fruit core with a crispy crunch and gather a few more of the ripened yield. With hands and forearms overfilled with wads of fruit, I waddle back toward the stable.

The faint sound of a woman's voice echoes from the house, eliminating any winnowing hope for an abandoned farmhouse. I hurry to the stable, dropping fruit along the way, to get out of the view of anyone peering from the house. A thin adolescent girl in a prairie gown steps out. She rounds the corner of the stable and heads back toward the house. My breath, which is held, releases itself, and another piece of fruit falls to the ground.

"Where's the hen?" the woman yells.

The girl shouts something incomprehensible as she starts to run, and I enter the stable before she notices me.

The seasoned horse snaps his huge, gnarled teeth through my gifts. His ears are perky, and he is snorting out through his nostrils with quick whiffs of air to express his pleasure. His body doesn't tremble and lean away from me like it did when I first patted him.

"Now you need some fresh air," I whisper to him.

The shadow at the stable door begins to shift due to the sun setting. The reflection of my own needs is obvious. Settling down into a seated position in the corner, I realize the comparable size of the stable to my cell. The stable is better. Despite the horse manure, it is an improved station. Staying and feasting on the fleshy, sweet fruit bits will be a nice enough life. I'm a lazy cat, enjoying his new freedom.

"This will do...for now." I close my eyes.

○

Muffled voices startle me. My eyes peel open, expecting me to be surrounded by Magnavozian soldiers or Frenton holding his blade to my neck. Neither is true. The horse begins to bump into the inner wall that separates our stalls. My fantasies of feasting in solitude fade along with my short rest.

"Quiet, beast." A raspy voice breaks right outside the stable. "Don't make me come in there, ya worthless—" The horse neighs.

The steed becomes more anxious and more spooked with every curse the man pours from his foul mouth. I peek under the stalls to find the man's knee-high boots standing in the opening of the stable. The last light of the day squeezes through behind him.

"That's it. It's time I make use of this beast. Leon, go to the house and grab my carving knives." The man turns back to someone outside the stable.

A juvenile boy lets out a horrific laugh and kicks up pebbles as he dashes off in obedience. The man is lighting torches around the stable. His foot stomps into a rose crisp.

"I told you all not to waste good crisps on this damn horse," he spits out with vile intention.

Silence falls over the building. My heart is bursting through my chest with a throbbing beat.

"Is someone in here? Show yourself."

Fear grasps me around my neck, keeping my breath in as the man paces toward my stall door.

Without uttering another word, the man kicks the stall

door open right after I roll underneath to the horse-occupied stall. The combination of my entrance to the stall and the abrupt flinging of the stall door sends the horse into a panic.

"Here, Father." The juvenile voice interrupts the man from further investigation.

"Well, don't stand there. Bring me my long carver," the man says.

Shuffling noises are made as the boy rustles through the hay.

"Go get a rope and a milk bucket," the man says.

"What is the milk bucket for?" the boy says.

The smacking sound of a slap echoes through the stable, followed by a thud as the boy falls to the ground. I'm expecting tears or a cry from the boy, yet there is only silence.

"Get up and do what I said," the man says.

The man paces back to the stall door. Sounds of metal sliding across stone scream as he sharpens a blade.

"Tonight...is your last night." The man slowly opens the door.

I'm already mounted, and I give a swift kick to the ribs of my friend. Bursting through the stall door before the man has sight of us, we knock him over into a heap of tools and hay. Curses scream behind us as we flee. His son steps into our path as we exit the stable. He jumps back and trips over his dropped bucket. I grasp the mangy mane of my friend, and we run into the night.

I pat the horse on the side of his neck as I lean in to inform him of his name. The wind blows across us as we rush up the valley.

"You are Braydenwolf!" I yell.

My words invigorate the steed. His hooves continue to pound harder and faster than any horse I've ever known.

"King Braydenwolf became a great warrior and king after his sons died in battle. He was old, childless, and withered, until one day he decided he wouldn't accept such a fate," I say. "To-night, Braydenwolf, we deny you the same fate."

I ride off into the night.

CHAPTER TWENTY·SIX

The Companion

Marr

AUTUMN K27, 50 AE

When Kai leaves, the woman stands and turns to us.

"Where...?" Jupp says.

I lose the rest of the question, spoken in slippery Northern words. The woman utters nothing in response. Instead, she steps away from us and begins to make her way up the beach. Waves rush up behind her to hide any small sound she makes. I look back at my brother for permission to follow her.

"She means to reclaim her weapon," Jupp says.

"The trap will mean warriors, and that means the potential

for glory." I grind my teeth, waiting for his response.

He makes himself more comfortable by sitting his bottom in the sand and spreading his legs out wider. The decision is uncharacteristic of him.

"We should help her." I stand.

His silhouette is there in the darkness, but his facial expressions are hidden from me.

"No, we don't need to help her. We've aligned ourselves with Kai's quest, and we don't know this one," he says.

"She is of his clan, and thus, she is of our clan," I say.

Jupp leans his right side against the boulder between us and the waters. I try to get his attention by tossing a fist of sand at his side. He grunts back at me, denying any further communication.

"Kai is a good man, but we seek glory for our clan. Waiting here in the sand is not honorable." I search down the beach, toward the direction Kai went in.

"Are you sure glory is what you seek?" Jupp says.

It's the sort of question that he knows the answer to.

"Yes. That's why we traveled north. That is our way. And she only desires to reclaim her heirloom...a relic of her clan." I'm pacing back and forth, watching her disappear from the last reaches of my sight. "Look. The gods have told you to follow Kai, but maybe we were meant to follow him here to this choice."

Jupp chuckles. "Admit you would have this northern woman, Lifia, as your battle maiden if you could, and we can go," he says.

He stings me with the revelation of his real thoughts. Did he witness my glance in her direction?

"No. That's not true. I only seek glory through battle," I say.

Jupp yanks my foot out from under me. I twist around in my fall, catching myself with my hands in the sand. I jump up with fists clenched and rage growing in my chest.

"You are as thick as a worm. Naturally, we are going with her, bakett-boy." Jupp rises without another word and begins to stomp down the beach after her.

Swallowing my anger like a thick lump in my throat, I follow his obnoxious splats in the wet sand. As I run to catch up, the thud of Kai flipping the raft flops behind us.

The woman is at the edge of the docks, where they slaughter the fish. With her long, slender limbs, she propels herself up the hanger where her bow lies entangled.

As we approach, I sense eyes upon me, and I sense the trap falling around us. She senses it too. She slashes at the tangle of a fishing line more frantically.

"Arm," Jupp says.

A weak battle cry reaches from the barracks as torches begin to burst alive with flame. The Twin Blades are drawn and placed gracefully in my grips. Jupp stands in a wide stance with a shield equipped on each forearm.

Jupp adopts the Turakk form. A form I rarely use, Turakk is defensive and traditionally utilized in hand-to-hand combat. However, with Jupp's dual shields, the form becomes impenetrable to melee attacks. The growing torchlight catches the edge of my vision, and I spin around with my blades outstretched and even, parallel to the ground. There are more than twenty soldiers circling around us. They encroach from mainland, north, south, and west of us. The only gap in their line is where the beach and the water meet.

"*Wrekk!*" Jupp shouts the battle cry with the full force of his lungs.

It's my favorite sound, and I can't wait to howl in response. "*Wrekk!*" I yell.

"Tonight there will be good deaths." Jupp bashes his shields together.

The woman cuts free her bow, releases herself from the

shredded tangles of fishing line in an acrobatic flip, and lands on the wooden deck with a nimble thump. Meanwhile, the soldiers march toward us with their spears and swords pointed. The woman begins to back away from the dock, but she stops, realizing we stand our ground. She shouts something in the common language, urging us to follow her. She doesn't realize we've already begun the battle.

I raise my swords up to the sky and howl my loudest call to the heavens.

"We are greatly outnumbered, brother. Today we fight for the exiles," Jupp says.

With our refusal to flee, the woman equips her dagger and steps into a crouch between us.

Swarming around us like a legion of bees, the enemy offers us a great battle. My heart beats wildly with excitement.

"Sweep," Jupp says.

I eagerly cut down the first line of soldiers with a massive sweep below their knees. I rise, and the next line of enemies is stepping up, over, and around their allies. Jupp jumps ahead of me, smashing through a wall of men like a war ram. Their bodies break and crumble as they collide with the ground. Again the fallen wall of enemies is filled by the next. A skinny soldier slips by Jupp and reaches the woman.

"Empress!" the skinny one yells.

The soldier recognizes her, and she shares a stout disdain for him. Before he can finish his ramble, she slips his grasp, slices through his groin, and pricks him through his cheeks. While the skinny one bleeds out, Lifia slips under a great-ax, which crashes through the planks. She is quicker than any soldier, and she delivers stings with perfect accuracy. Her movements mimic the artful form of Ugayah. The attacks overwhelm and disorient an untrained fighter. The form utilizes swift flurries, absent power.

After I cut down another encircling wall of soldiers, Lifia shouts and points up to the barracks. Her meaning is

understood, though her words are not. She challenges us to attack the head of the chokworm.

"Head." Jupp points in the same direction.

I nod, and we converge our attacks toward the center. In
a flurry of shield and sword, we hit the line. Spinning around,
we cut through one soldier after another, littering our pathway.
We maintain a balanced attack as I slash through one with my
main hand, spinning with my blade as it slashes. Jupp follows behind me to block any counter. Coming back around in my spin,
my off hand jabs through the next. Before my blades are pulled
back out, Jupp smashes his shield into a chest to help release my
blades from the flesh. We repeat variations of our assault until
we have sawed a line through the encircling legion. For every
fighter we cut down, two step up in their place behind us.

We reach the barracks and the caped leader standing in
the doorway. Candlelight shines onto the back of his neck, but
his face is dark. His sword for a hand is a menacing feature,
and there are seven between him and us. Without warning, our
brave ally darts for the man. Her ferocious presence inspires me
to fight harder.

"*Wrekk!*" I yell.

She slides underneath the first soldier, splitting him below
with her dagger. As the first soldier screams in anguish, she
jumps up on top of the next and shoves both blades into each
side of his neck. Jupp and I chase after her to fight soldiers pursuing at her back. The smell of blood quickly fills the air. Before
we can reach her, several soldiers bring her down to the ground
right in front of their leader. Each one has a limb, and although
she struggles with lethal intent, they have her subdued.

Meanwhile, more soldiers continue to march at our backs,
pushing us into the walls of the barracks. Jupp fights off men in
a mad assault toward the leader. He notices my pause. When he
does, he raises his arms and points behind me. Light flashes in
my eyes, and darkness follows.

With a spinning head, ringing ears, and a swollen eye, I peel myself up off the sand. Jupp is standing over me, shouting something, but my ears are deafened, and I can't distinguish his words. He spins around over the top of me, knocking attackers away. Between his shield bashes, he is urging me up. Before I can rise, a stinging pain in the back of my head disorients me, and I fall to my knees. One soldier jabs his spear down at me. I roll away from the spearhead, but it glances off my shoulder, spilling my blood onto the sand.

Rage overcomes me. The cut on my shoulder is enough pain to rear me back to the battle. I fight through the sand to rise up. I find my off-hand sword, Harmony, and I stab it into the ground to finish my ascent. Despite my blurred vision, I swing a mad flurry toward the sea. With cloudy vision and a throbbing head, I have only one desire: the desire to fight beside my brother.

CHAPTER TWENTY-SEVEN

The Revenger

Lifia

AUTUMN K27, 50 AE

I slice toward the seven unfortunate men who separate me from Lord Gravesmon. The Illitaww brothers fight through the sandstorm of soldiers with gallant ferocity at my back. I've never felt more empowered than I do now. Their twirling dance of sword and shield vanquishes multiple enemies with one spin. It's one of the most beautiful dances I've ever seen.

"Gravesmon!" I pull my blade out of one soldier's throat.

He stands with his one hand resting on his hip while his sword hand points at us. His pompous stance won't be possible after I cleave his hamstring from his leg.

The next soldier comes straight for me while two others flank me, one on each side. I stab the one in front of me, but before I can pull my blade free, the other two swarm at my hands. One grabs my arm and drags me into the sand. The other punches me in my lips. With my free legs, I jab my heel into his neck. The soldier stumbles back, but another takes his place by holding down my legs. I'm fighting with all my will to shake free, but there is a soldier for each of my limbs. I would remove an arm for a chance to strike them all down. I bare my teeth and scream at them.

Gravesmon steps forward and looks down at me. "That's not empress-like of you, though you were never worthy of the title by my account." He spits on me. "Kill the barbarians before they cause any more damage."

I relax to bide my time while the brothers fight up the path to help me. Jupp fights over Marr as Marr regains his footing.

"Where did you find them? Were you that desperate?" Gravesmon says.

"You are desperate!" I scream.

"I'm glad it happened this way. I wanted to be the one to drive the knife through the space in your chest where a heart should be." He looks away from me, toward the beach. "What is that?"

Beyond the brothers and the wall of soldiers, a glowing blue light bursts through the darkness. Men scream as their metal armor smashes together.

Jupp pulls Marr up by the waist while his gaze is fixated on the light. Marr grabs his twin blades, one in each hand, as he rises.

A wave of air breaks in front of us, and several soldiers are swept off their feet. They fall back, crashing into each other until another powerful gust blows through. It knocks them off their feet and back against more soldiers.

"The gods!" Jupp shouts.

Standing where the soldiers were before, a thin man with a foggy mist surrounding him steps forward. The light shines from the chest of the figure, illuminating the sea of fallen warriors.

Gravesmon shouts orders to the soldiers in front of us. He wants them to attack the glowing man. Reluctance fills their footsteps until Gravesmon threatens to take their heads if they remain still. The reinvigorated soldiers march toward the glowing man. Standing back to back, Jupp and Marr brace themselves for another assault. Yet the soldiers run around them, toward the mysterious figure.

The four soldiers detaining each of my limbs are the only men who remain near.

"Head!" Jupp shouts.

"One hundred Fangourian farms for the man who kills these beasts." Gravesmon points at the two men holding each of my ankles.

They release me, grab up their weapons, and step toward Jupp and Marr.

The remaining two men pull me up to my feet. Their hands hold firmly the back of my arms and neck.

Before Jupp and Marr meet the two men who held my ankles, metal crashes again. Soldiers hurtle through the air. The sight is unbelievable and terrifying. It's as if an invisible titan is grabbing and tossing them aside before they can reach the glowing figure.

"*Wrekk!*" Marr shouts.

His boom breaks the confidence of the soldiers, and they drop their swords. Before Marr can cut them down, they race off behind the barracks.

I laugh as they scatter. Gravesmon screams in response to my joy. Then he takes his own grip on my neck and places his blade into my back. The remaining two soldiers release my arms and step away to meet Jupp and Marr in combat. Wasting no time, Jupp charges up, grabs them by their throats, and slams them into the ground. They squirm for a moment, but they can't escape.

"I will have your life before I leave this world," Gravesmon whispers.

Marr sprints to me, but he won't reach me soon enough. Right before the blade penetrates my back, another flash of light shines in front of me. A wave of air twists around me. As it passes, it intensifies and flings Lord Gravesmon into the bar-racks.

Marr pulls me up with him as he rises. The figure stands a few steps away. The light emitting from his chest fades, and the fog around him subsides.

"Kai?" I say.

"Lifia?" Kai raises his hands to peer at his palms. Then he releases a screech as he faints and falls to the ground with the twisted heap of soldiers.

I push the dead soldiers away and bring Kai's head into my chest.

"Brother. Your vision," Marr says.

"The gods didn't want our good deaths this night," Jupp says.

"Help him," I say.

We are running at the fastest pace Jupp can manage while carrying Kai. My gaze is fixated on our wounded friend, slung over the man's back. Kai is flopping loosely and nearly lifelessly.

As we continue to run through alleyways, I keep replaying what happened at the docks. What Kai did was not possible for a man to do without magic. In the stillness of the night, the dull clapping of hooves echoes on the wet stone. The sound grows as we draw into the market of the city. The brothers come to a sliding stop ahead of me.

Galloping hooves smack against the cobblestones as the rider winds around the building. Jupp turns to run, grunting with each movement. After he takes a few steps, he realizes we won't escape. He lays Kai down against the side of the building and dons his shields. Marr follows by drawing twin blades. The moonlights shine on the rider when he exits from a narrow alleyway.

"Wait. It's Nok." I jump in front of the Illitaww men, showing my palms to stop their attacks.

"Nok. What happened? Where's Frenton?" I say.

Nok shrugs his shoulders without an answer. We are in a large, open plaza. I hear a groan from behind me. Nok begins to explain what happened to him, but he stops abruptly when Kai releases a heavy moan.

Kai pushes himself up from against the side of the building. The others fall silent while his body rises against the wall.

"Kai?" I step to him with my outstretched hands.

"Lifia." He wobbles and takes a feeble step to me.

I catch him before he knocks his head on the plaza.

"I didn't do it. I mean...I saw it happen." Kai's voice is dry and vague.

"Another time, Nok." I guide Kai to Nok's horse. "We need to go. Our pursuers won't give up easily."

The city is silent. If there are any people near, they are hiding inside their dwellings. Noticing my struggle to push Kai onto the back of the horse, Jupp walks over, picks him up, and sets him on the horse. The anxious emotions are palpable in the night air. Everyone seems to be uncertain of what to do next.

"Where to, Your Imperial Majesty?" Nok bows.

Leaning over in a crumpled heap, Kai mutters, "The Cradle..."

CHAPTER TWENTY-EIGHT

The Host

Kai

AUTUMN K29, 50 AE

The stone calls to me with its ancient language of prismatic shapes, which are either foreign or forgotten. It knows my name, but it communicates in a language beyond words. It's a silent language that flows through space on waves of light. Yet there is another voice. It's reaching out through the stone like a beacon well lit. It's like the voices that I visited in the alleyway, but different, because this one has come to visit me this time.

"Ah, there you are." Violet eyes ignite with the words as a dark figure appears.

I can still feel my hand on the sandy boulder, yet my surroundings have faded away in a hazy fog. The figure is at the forefront of my vision. Their face is dark, while their attire is as white as the sands of Watertree.

"Who are you?" I say.

"I've been searching for you for so long. I've come close before, but never this close." The figure steps out from the other side of the boulder.

I recognize the glowing violet eyes that haunted me at Summer's Light. There's sulking darkness flowing from him, and my instincts scream not to trust him.

"It's you. I've seen you before. Who are you? What do you want?" I clutch the Art Stone, which is vibrating wildly in my hand.

"Yes, I'm the one who watches the watcher. The stone calls to its maker." The violet eyes flicker as the figure looks to the faded docks and back at me. "Who are these people to you? A broken builder dynasty and forgotten protectors? What use are they to you?"

On the docks, beyond the hazy barrier, torches ignite as soldiers draw in.

"I'm not who you think I am," I say.

The man flashes to my side and sniffs across my shoulder and up to my neck.

"That's it." The man bursts into maniacal laughter, which screeches in my ears. "You don't know the powers, and you can't understand the language of the stone."

The man lingers creepily. I'm holding the stone against my chest because I'm afraid he'll try to take it.

"Stop. I did not invite you here." I try to push the man away, but my hands float through, breaking him into a cloud of mist.

"No. You left an open invitation, and I retrieved it. You're a child who doesn't understand the powers you meddle with."

The man appears behind me and whispers at the back of my ear. "I'm so close to you now. After I sterilize the rotting dynasty, I'll come for you."

"No!" I try to push the man off my back, and again my hands fall through a foggy reflection.

More maniacal laughter reverberates from every direction. I'm shifting back and forth on the beach in search of the man. Then he appears right in front of me.

"Let me show you the powers." He grabs my wrists and steps inside me.

☽

The light swallowed me like a bloated wave. Its vibrancy was not from the sun, nor from a torch, nor from a flame of any known source. It wasn't hot. Yet there was a tingle on my skin like a fire had kissed it and left a lingering sear. The brighter the light grew, the blurrier my vision became.

When the sensation left me, I hungered for rest. The exhaustion was more of the mind than of the body. It was a similar weight to diving for shells on the North Isles. Until the moment on the beach of Simb's Point, I have never felt as heavy. What did the man with glowing violet eyes unlock?

We are traveling southwest from Simb's Point, onto the Plains of Leon, which spread across most of Eastern Magnavoz. The plains are filled with tall yellow grasses, sparse trees, and a wide variety of creatures. A herd of mixed gazelle grazes in the distance, unaware of our existence. Marr is intrigued by them, and he wanders closer as our path crosses theirs.

"Their hair is short, no?" Marr says.

I nod. Most of the creatures Marr is familiar with must

have thick hides, with long hair to protect them from freezing.

Before I finish my nod, a cat growl initiates a rout. The gazelles scatter. Most gazelles skip north, but a few are separated from the group and flee southeast toward us. As the stone vibrates, a connection to the earth grows inside me. My senses seem to enhance, and I see the pursuit in more detail. Chasing behind the gazelles are three plains cats. They have large black tails, which flick as they run. Patches of dark spots cover the rest of their light coats.

Clinging to the stone as if it is a precious inheritance, I question its purpose. Did my mother know it contained this power?

Two of the cats converge on either side of the weaker gazelle, while the third closes in on its rear. The gazelle makes one last effort to weave around and escape. When the gazelle leaps, the rear cat catches a back leg, tripping it. The gazelle tumbles and crashes into the grass as all three cats swarm onto their meal.

Marr raises his hand in excitement and looks back at us. I release my grasp on the stone and exhale.

"Will they attack us?" Jupp says.

"Not with their meal already crunching in their teeth." Nok calms Braydenwolf.

We redirect our path out of the way of the cats' feast and continue our pace westward.

The yellow grasses sway in waves as the wind ripples across, bringing the scents of grass and dirt to us. Lifia releases eye bolts at me, interrupting my thoughts. What does she want to say?

The presence of the stone lingers on the tips of my fingers, and I resist its calling. I don't know how to explain the man with glowing violet eyes or how he moved my hands on the beach. We travel off-road, avoiding eyes of all sorts.

"How does one become an Illitaww warrior?" Nok

questions bluntly, which seems to be the preferred mode of communication with the two brothers.

"Why do you think we are warriors?" Jupp says.

Marr walks up closer to include himself in the conversation.

"Obviously you are. I can see you are more than simple warriors." Nok laughs off the awkwardness and questioning glances from both brothers.

"What I mean to ask is, are all Illitaww people as big and formidable as you two?" Nok says.

Jupp exhales a labored breath as if he does not wish to continue in the explanation.

"We are Wrekk-Taww," Marr interjects, and punches his fists together firmly.

His knuckles smash into each other. With an exaggerated pause, he holds them together firmly as he slowly raises them.

"All Illitaww people are warriors. All men, women, and children old enough to grip a weapon are taught to hunt and to protect. Marr and I have passed the trials only a few complete, making us Wrekk-Taww. Now we are upon the final trial," Jupp explains.

"I knew you two were more than the average Illitaww." Nok smiles. "*Wrekk*... I've heard you speak this word before. What does it mean?" Nok prods.

"It does not translate," Jupp says.

"Well, is there a word it is like?" Nok says.

Jupp takes a moment before he answers. Interest has drawn us all closer.

"'For honor. Glory to. Protect...' Something like those words, but something more. It's a sacred word to us." Jupp looks over his shoulder at me. "An Illitaww leader from long ago formed a band of warriors from the greatest of those loyal to her. They became the first Wrekk-Taww, and it has been the greatest honor for our people ever since."

"We have a similar word for high-status warriors. We call them dregadins, though their trials are much less intense, and most waste their talents in tournaments." Nok laughs.

The group falls into silence.

"What trial are you on?" Lifia says.

"Kall um Shacc." Marr shines a broad grin as he turns back to her. "It's the final trial. One that is no longer required...but... our father, the greatest of Illitaww men, completed the trial. As his sons, we owe our lives to the Kall um Shacc."

Jupp glances at his brother, turns away, and strides ahead. Their father must be a great man for these men to revere him so much.

We travel in silence until we find a subtle camp and settle in for a chilly night without the warmth of a fire.

"What happened to Frenton?" Lifia pats Braydenwolf.

"Frenton. Sir Frenton Jaspermon of farmlands unknown." Nok brushes the ground with a mesquite branch while he mockingly repeats the name. "No. The man flipped. I'm surprised he wasn't holding hands with Lord Gravesmon on the beach. Still, the man was a traitor, and a traitor he remained."

"What did he say?" Lifia says.

"He didn't say much. It was difficult to get the man to speak at all. He just changed his mind. Perhaps a soiled man wasn't as appealing a trophy as an empress," Nok says.

"He was brave, and he protected me from lesser men." Lifia takes the branch from Nok and brushes her own little space clear.

Lifia seems different. She's more talkative and less closed off. Whatever happened to her in the dungeon has adjusted her perspective.

Jupp and Marr return from a patrol.

"There are soldiers in pursuit, but they have made camp. Plumes of smoke stain the sky, which reveals their location east of us. There are many of them, and they aren't equipped to travel discreetly." Jupp leans in. "Battle will be upon us as we rise in the morning."

"No. We can't fight them," I say.

The brothers long for battle and another chance to prove their worth, but we all have desires, most of which involve survival.

"Mal Eonn is with you. Mal Eonn is with us." Jupp pounds his chest like a rhythmic drum.

"Mal Eonn?" Lifia says.

"He shows Kai the magic." Jupp points at me with both hands.

"Why do they march with an army this large?" Lifia says.

"The empress has wisdom. Why would they use so many resources to hunt us when twenty men would suffice?" Nok says.

"They fear the gods." Jupp presses his shields into the rocky soil.

"There are no gods here with us, only feeble men," Nok says.

"You know nothing about my gods!" Jupp's voice rumbles like a thunderclap. "You weren't on the beach, and you didn't witness the power."

Jupp's rumbling voice brings me to the tips of my toes. Soon I'll need to speak.

"What am I missing?" Nok raises his hands, with each palm facing up.

The seagulls have spotted a crumb on the beach, and they circle around me.

"No. It's true. We wouldn't have survived the beach without Kai's magic, though that doesn't explain the bulk of soldiers," Lifia says.

All eyes are fixated on me, but all I can think of is another set of eyes. The unnatural eyes that claimed control of me on the beach.

"This." I unwrap the Art Stone and hand it to Lifia. "This is the source of the magic, not me. It shakes whenever the magic is near."

"It shakes?" Lifia tumbles the stone in her hand, holds it up to the sun, floating on the horizon, and studies it.

"Yes. My mother gave me the stone. She told me to take it to the Cradle of Man, but I didn't know what she was talking about. I'd never heard of the place until she spoke of it on that day. Reluctantly I took the stone. I thought the Cradle of Man might be somewhere near the Torish Lands, which were her homelands. I was planning to go there before I heard Lifia survived the attack on the ship."

Jupp listens inattentively, while Marr seems confused. Lifia fastidiously studies the stone. Nok is harder to read. He seems to be waiting for more information before he releases an expression.

"At first I thought the stone was a benign religious relic. Islanders call them luck charms or protection trinkets. I was wrong. The stone was invasive with its power. I began to see visions both while I was asleep and sometimes while I was awake. The visions seemed random and indistinct, like a vivid dream at first. Then I realized the visions weren't random. The visions are placed in my mind by the stone as a form of communication. The stone is alive," I say.

"What do you mean?" Lifia stops evaluating the stone and returns it to me.

"It's alive in a different way than we are. It communicates, but its language is inhuman. The visions were terrifying from the beginning. The colors were vivid, while the smells and sounds seemed more intoxicating than anything I've experienced in the natural world. I thought I was safe, until the visions began to speak back to me. In the alleyway, where we hid from the guards, the stone connected me with others. The others were in the Cradle of Man. They understand the stone, and I think they can help me," I say.

"Let me see." Jupp reaches for the stone.

The stone shakes with subtle vibrations, and I tighten my grasp in response. The residual trembles subside, and I release my hold on the stone. Jupp takes it and squeezes it tightly into his fist. Jupp's touch is gentle as he caresses the stone. I relax back into the heels of my boots.

I reach to reclaim it, but Jupp releases it and tosses it to Marr, who turns it over quickly and hands it back.

"I'm not sure what Mal Eonn would need a pebble for. His power is beyond the chains of our world," Jupp says.

Nok laughs. We each turn to him for an explanation, but he keeps laughing more hysterically. Eventually, he composes himself and places one hand between his abdomen and chest while he stretches the other hand out. "May I see the stone?" he says.

Jupp slides the stone into Nok's skinny fingers.

"You have a magical stone that sends you guardians for guidance? What's stopping us from defeating the entire Magnavozian army?" Nok says.

"I didn't say we should do that. We need to take it to the Cradle of Man. That's what my mother wanted, and that's where we will find answers," I say.

"It's just a stone. I'm locked away in a dungeon for a couple of years, and everyone has lost their minds when I get out?" Nok's expression is equal to pure horror when he drops the stone.

"What is it, Nok?" Lifia says.

"I felt... I thought it was a bug wriggling in place of the stone, but there was nothing," Nok says.

"Yes. That is the stone. It is trying to speak to us," I say.

"If this isn't a cheap islander trick, and the magic you witnessed on the beach is real, then there are higher stakes for the entire realm," Nok says.

CHAPTER TWENTY-NINE

The Advocate

Lifia

AUTUMN K29, 50 AE

Each of us nestled in the savanna nook represents a unique threat to Magnavoz. Jupp's and Marr's fighting skills have exceeded my expectations. The prowess of their people is not overstated in the legends. Nok is the most capable man I've ever met, and his instincts to survive rival mine. Kai was only a baby whale when I first pulled him out of the salty wake, but now he is something more. Yet the magic isn't what makes him great. His experiences are transforming him into someone worth following.

Cats howl in the distance as Nok finishes his sentence.

Fangour and my past reach for me, while my present owes gratitude to these men. Our combined enemies surround us as we kneel in the tall grass. Soon they will send their hunters.

"What are the limits to your magic, Kai?" I grab the stone out of the grass, where Nok dropped it.

"I don't know." He turns away from me.

Kai seems taller and better looking than he was on Davinor's ship. He was brave to come to Roknamar.

"Can we use it to fight them again?" I say.

"I'm still not sure how to control the powers," Kai says.

"On the beach? It couldn't have been by chance," I say.

"It wasn't me." Kai is pacing. "It was a visitor. There was a man who found me through a connection with the stone. He was vile and dressed in bleached whites. His eyes glowed with a wonderful violet radiance."

Kai's voice is trembling. Any bravery he carried when he stormed the beach is gone.

"Violet eyes?" Nok steps between Kai and me.

"Yes. His eyes were something out of a dream, but it wasn't a dream. He was there. More than any other vision before, he was there. And...somehow he took control of me. I watched as the soldiers flew across my path, but I had no handle. It was like someone's firm hand lay around mine as we wrote a passage together. Neither of us had complete control, but his hand was the more practiced between us."

"I've only known one man matching that description: Vzar Musa," Nok says.

"Vzar Musa is the name Lord Gravesmon used when he threatened that Musa would be the one to carry out my sentence," I say.

"Vzar? Of the Venith..." Kai says.

"If Musa met you in a vision, then their magic is real as well." Nok bounces lightly.

"You've seen the Venith?" Kai says.

"Yes. Before, when I was in the castle, I witnessed three at a wedding. They were treated like royalty. Kings and queens bowed graciously upon their arrival. If the magic you witnessed on the beach came from Vzar Musa, the Venith should be added to our list of enemies," Nok says.

"A person should have a fair number of enemies," Jupp says.

Jupp's adamant nature reminds me of my mother, who reminds me of Fangour. I long to be in the Okiari Forest, with Bulba. I don't want to be here, surrounded by magic and Magnavozian threats.

"If the Venith are real...what is their place in all of this?" Kai reaches his hand out, and I release the stone back into his palm.

"If those legends are true, what about the Xyji? The Xyji fought the Venith alongside your ancestors." Kai points to me. "They were magic wielders."

Kai releases words that reflect my thoughts. In Fangour, the Xyji were protectors of the people, while the Venith used their powers to conquer the weak. In Magnavoz and Delphinus, perspectives would be contradictory. Each of us has a different understanding of history. Yet any history of magic involves either the Xyji or the Venith. Illitaww is the exception. Their people have more complex magic, which is derived from their many gods.

"How can the Xyji help us? What makes you think they still exist?" Nok says.

"They can't help us, but their legends might." Kai holds his pressed fingertips up to his lips. "Do you remember how the Xyji banished the Venith?"

They had Emperor Revan, who was the greatest strategist the realm has ever known. He had a legion of giant tigers. What more did he need?

"They had a secret weapon. They could move across the land in flashes of lightning. When the Crossing was lost to the Venith and their followers, the Xyji escaped using the gateways. If we can find the gateways, we can travel back to the Skyfort," Kai says.

"Yes, I've heard the stories, but the gateways you speak of are not real. I know every structure within the Skyfort, and there are no magical gateways," I say.

"Your people moved away from magic after the Venith were banished. Perhaps the gateway was destroyed. Still, there could be other gateways. The people who I met in my visions told me to use the gateways. I didn't know what they meant at the time, but now I understand," Kai says.

The sun is giving in to the darkness, and our faces are less visible. Kai has a firm conviction to return the stone and complete his mother's task, and I can't deny him his quest.

"Please, trust me," Kai says.

"I'll help you return the stone, Kai. But..." I step into the middle of the group. "Fangour will be my final destination."

The high branches of the forest sway in the wind of my memories as I walk down the black marble skybridge. Soon I'll return home.

They all remain silent until I turn back to Kai.

"Thank you," Kai says.

"We'll head west to the Crossing. You said the Xyji escaped from there. If we can find your gateway, we'll take it. If not, we'll travel farther west until we reach the Aptorias," I say.

Kai agrees.

"Nok, are you with us?" I say.

"What choice do I have? All I want is food in my belly and the promise of a feather bed at the end of this," Nok says.

"Will you fight alongside us?" Kai gestures to Jupp and Marr.

"Kall um Shacc is not complete, but Mal Eonn is with you, and we will follow him to see your trial through." Jupp pounds his chest, and Marr follows. "*Wrekk!*"

"Get some rest. We have a few hours before we need to leave. Use it how you need." I put my hand on Kai's shoulder.

We gather together in the small, dusty corner of earth carved out by the wind. Jupp and Marr sit back to back, each leaning one shoulder against the other. They occupy the ground closest to the opening. Nok buries himself in the corner, leaning his back against the same mesquite tree that tethers Brayden-wolf. Kai sits alone on the other side of the horse, with his head down. Dust blows in with the wind, and I cover my face to stop the earth from going into my eyes.

"How are you feeling, Kai?" I resist calling him baby whale.

His eyes are the same kind eyes of the man I pulled from the ocean, but the face housing them is more worn.

"I'm fine," he says.

"Are you feeling different since the magic?" I kneel beside him.

The brothers glance over at us and exchange hushed words in Illitawwe.

"I feel the earth and the moisture in the air. I feel the warmth of the sun fading as it sets. I feel everything I've always felt, but it feels like more." His head hangs while his eyes follow the stone in his lap like a bee does a flower.

"What did Musa do to you?" I say.

"Honestly, it's becoming more of a blur. I'm not sure what part was my hands and what part was his," Kai says.

"You should get some sleep." I lean against him, and his hand slides against mine. Eventually, his hand brushes away as he lifts it to turn over onto his side. I release my held breath and roll until my back is to him.

The next evening, I wake to a delicious smell of fresh flesh cooking over a flame. The savory aroma drags me from my slumber. The juicy carvings of a prairie chicken rest over a bed of coals. One bead of oil rolls down the breast and falls into the embers, causing a sizzle. At the same time, a drip of saliva leaks from my mouth, disappearing into the earth.

"Meat is good, yes?" Marr says.

I didn't notice him in the shade of a mesquite tree behind me.

"Yes." I maintain sight of the juicy chicken.

I wipe the drool from the corner of my mouth before he notices.

"Is this yours?" I turn to look over my shoulder.

Yet my nose pulls me back toward the chicken.

"No. Not Marr's. Nok stick have." He grunts in frustration. Then he says the Illitawwe word for "trap."

"Nok set up a trap made of sticks?"

"Yes." Marr nods and pushes his lips together. "Trap," he says.

I nod and smile back at him.

"Bow is broken?" Marr points to the Evoni Bow.

I lift it up and examine it. The bow is the sturdiest weapon I've ever known.

"It's scratched but still intact," I say.

"I fix. Here." Marr reaches with his open palm.

"The string... It's no use." I shrug.

I'm not sure if he understands, but his hand remains outstretched.

"Yes. String. I fix," Marr says.

Reluctantly I hand him the bow. He takes it and eyes it up and down on each side. Then he flexes both ends like the bow is in full draw.

"Please." I almost jump to grab it.

"Not broke," Marr says.

He takes choksilk string from his pouch and ties it around one bow tip. He does the same to the other tip and hands it to me. I draw the bow back. It's much tighter than before, but it works.

"Marr, it works." I lift the bow and show him. "Thank you."

He grins, and his gaze shifts to focus behind me. When I turn, it's Jupp and Kai with hands full of leafy greens and mushrooms. Jupp says something in Illitawwe and holds up a giant mushroom. He throws it at Marr. Marr laughs and knocks the mushroom to the ground.

"Skin of my tribe," Marr says in Illitawwe.

Jupp and Marr both laugh and throw mushrooms back and forth. I don't understand the joke, but it's nice to see them both relaxed. Kai raises one of the mushrooms. Jupp falls back into Marr in a fit of heavy laughter. Noticing the chatter, Nok turns away from where he is tending to Braydenwolf. For the first time, we are all smiling at the same moment.

●

Several quiet nights pass as we travel southwest to avoid the coast until we enter the Plains of Leon. Open fields expand as far as I can see. There is no feature of the flat land that could provide cover. So we travel down overgrown wagon trails during the night. The lands will be flat until we reach the canyons of A'Laure.

"This will be the last thing they expect from us. I'll agree with that." Nok leans into Kai.

Kai laughs off the comment. A few moments of silence pass by. The silence reminds me to stay vigilant. I practice removing an arrow from my quiver and slotting the nock around my new string in silence.

Jupp leads with a watchful gaze into the darkness. Absent from his usual position at the tail of the group, Marr walks beside his brother. They have a detailed strategy for every circumstance, including sneaking through enemy territories. They trust me to guard the rear.

"Your arrows can travel faster than my knives," Marr said.

It's a great honor to guard their backs.

"Nok, may I ask you a question?" Kai says.

Nok looks over the back of his horse.

"What was your crime?" Kai says.

"What is anyone's crime...for living a life laid out before them?" Nok says.

Kai goes up on his toes to see over Braydenwolf. I close the distance between myself and them to listen in.

"Were you the only one there? Besides the guards," Kai says.

"Truthfully, I don't know if there were ever any other prisoners. I thought I heard voices at times, but it was only the creaks of the crumbling structure," Nok says.

"I'm thankful Nok was there. It took a unique strength to survive alone in the dark for so long." I step up beside Kai.

My sweet, mad neighbor made all the difference while I was stuck there. I don't know how he survived so long, but there is something special about him. Below his sarcastic comments, constant jokes, and crude mannerisms exists something powerful. There is something thicker than those stone walls that held him.

"Sunrise," I say.

Marr paces from the lead to meet me.

"The sun is rising." I point to the horizon. I translate the words to Illitawwe and repeat.

He stops for a moment, stunned by my poorly spoken

Illitawwe words.

"Yes...the sun is rising." He goes back to the front of our group to meet Jupp.

Of all the languages I was forced to learn, Illitawwe was always the most difficult. My tongue resists the subtle vibrations of the speech, and the hard cracks in the words require time to master. The time I should have set aside for learning languages was spent mastering my favorite dances instead.

Despite his overwhelming physique, Marr is endearing. He would be a great dancing partner, because his strength and eagerness to learn form the foundation of a dancer. I look forward to Jupp, leading the pack, and shake free of friendlier thoughts. The two of them embody the legends of their people. They each have long limbs, wide shoulders, browned skin, thick hair, and red eyes.

My teacher once said, "The barbarians from the frozen waste carry fire in their eyes to keep them warm during the winter."

I've seen a glimpse of red in Marr's eyes, and I would like to study them more. As I walk behind the foreign warriors, I remember my people.

"An interesting dance you have chosen," my mother might say.

Kai crosses in front of my sight. He's patting the side of Nok's horse. The others are content with leaving him alone, but I'm curious. His unknowing and lack of control with the powers concern me.

As the sun rises, we search for an enclosed place to make camp for the day. To the west, the rolling hills of the Tatum Prairie offer the best cover. The lands to the north and east are flat grasslands.

"There." Jupp points to a rare part of the hills wrapping together.

As the coolness of winter grows around us, we draw in

closer to each other. Nok shares many stories as we attempt to sleep. Some are true, and some seem to be dreamed up from the recesses of his mind.

He tells a story of a king who once starved all his people to survive a famine. That king became the first with the name of Nagidah.

"Those are not the same stories I've read in the scrolls," Kai says.

"No? And you believe everything you've read in the scrolls?" Nok says.

"Well, yes... Of course, there are missing tales. There is a fair bit of mystery surrounding the family. That is true. Other tales say the family landed in the gulf on their great ships from faraway lands to the east. The scrolls record their rise from farmers to lords sometime during the early Fangourian Empire." Kai speaks like a man on a stage.

"There are always more stories than actual events," Nok says.

"That we can agree on." I sit cross-legged and begin to sharpen my daggers.

"Have I recited the story about the returned sailor?" Nok says.

"Jupp and Marr, Nok and Kai, and then me," I say. Issuing the order of watches eases my mind, but not enough to sleep.

"Well, Her Imperial Majesty must have already heard the story." Nok rustles around in the grass. "The returned sailor was a crew member for the legendary ship *The Queen's Wish*. The ship was the first to sail around the entire realm. One day, the ship departed from its mother port in Delphinus, heading south along the lifeful shores of North Aptoria. Next, it passed the Vulture's Beak, a narrow strait that separates the great western lands of Aptoria, continuing farther south down the coast of South Aptoria."

He hesitates on the words of South Aptoria, but I resist

turning back to see him.

"Finally, it swung down to the most majestic land in all Elybion: Illitaww. These were difficult waters to navigate for northern islanders, and many did not survive," Nok says.

The brothers heave measured laughs.

"Barely surviving the swing around the frozen shores of Illitaww, the crew finally began its adventure northward. Their first stop northward was at the small, barren island Neva, off the coast of Ariland."

I rub my hands together for warmth. Kai must have noticed, because he rubs my shoulder. I shrug his hand off, and he doesn't seem to care. I don't want him to think I'm weakened by the cold.

"The barren island has a few old tales in its own right, but I will tell those another time. At this point, almost half of the crew had perished from either disease or freezing. The crew members remaining were some of the grittiest and toughest men to ever sail, including the returned sailor. The second half of their trip should've been a quick and peaceful journey up the east coast of the realm. The journey was peaceful, for the most part. *The Queen's Wish* sailed northeast around the jungle land of Fangour. Redirecting the sails west toward the Gulf of Swedas, the crew sailed into the heart of Elybion. Modern navigators choose the quicker option of sailing around the eastern side of the Swedas island Stenhas. *The Queen's Wish* stopped once in Magnavozian territory at Simb's Point, the modern port of the Magnavozian warships. You are all aware of Simb's Point, are you not?" Nok laughs.

The brothers' hands clap in the crisp air.

"You know the land far better than we do," Kai says.

My abdomen shakes as I fight back laughing at Kai's poke.

"My good sir...if I may continue. From Simb's Point, the ship carrying the returned sailor began its last leg around Swedas and back up toward Delphinus. In the very last part of

The Queen's Wish's voyage, the captain made a fatal mistake. Unfortunately, the journey around Elybion took much longer than anticipated. The crew arrived in the North during the most dangerous weather season, and to avoid a large storm heading east along the Northern coast, the captain decided to adjust the sails northward in hopes of sailing in a large loop around the storm. The last anyone saw of *The Queen's Wish* was at the sister city of Phys."

"Where did sailor ship go?" Marr's broken common language causes Jupp to chuckle.

"I thought you might ask. Well, some believe the lone survivor of *The Queen's Wish* was stranded on one of the smaller islands of the North until he was able to fasten together a small boat for his return. Others believe the crew continued sailing northwest, avoiding the North Isles, toward the ends of the ocean before returning to Delphinus. For this belief, you must assume the ship and its crew discovered new lands. Still, there are others who believe Art saved the returned sailor. They believe Art was pleased with the returned sailor, also the navigator of the ship, because of his devotion to knowledge. No matter what you believe, the facts are undeniable. After ten years missing at sea, the returned sailor finally came back with a mission. Within the first year, he constructed the first iteration of the Temple of Summer's Light and became the first grandmaster, Master Artum."

"I thought you would be more of a worshipper of the Trinity rather than Art," Kai says.

"Like I said, there are always more stories than actual events. This is especially true with the gods," Nok says.

When I awake, I find the camp abandoned. The horse re-mains attached to the limb of a mesquite tree, giving me some relief. I wipe the crust out of my eyes and sit up.

A clashing of swords over the hill alerts me. I spring into movement as fear for the worst overwhelms me. To my dismay, Nok is swinging a sword against Marr. Marr spins and slashes his blades across the open air so fast that it causes a screech. When Marr notices my approach, he stops and steps back from Nok's last clumsy backhand swing. Marr drops his hands down to his sides. Jupp is crouched a few feet away from them. Nok turns around to see Marr's view.

"Good morning, Your Imperial Majesty," he says.

"Stop," I say.

"My apologies." He winks and bows to me.

"What are you doing, slamming your swords in the middle of Magnavozian territory?" I say.

"I thought I would teach them a lesson about elegant swordplay, but...they are slow learners." Nok smiles.

Marr looks at Nok and then at me. It's clear he doesn't understand much of what we are saying, but he senses my anger.

"Very well." Nok bows again and turns to hand the sword back to Marr.

Marr returns an awkward expression, sheathes both swords, and nods to me.

"We should continue." Jupp brushes his shield with a cloth.

"Yes. Yes, we should," I say.

We walk back to camp. I look around the plains in front of me. Grasshoppers make their chirps. The earth is warm from the sun, and the bugs of the weeds are livelier as the dirt cools.

"Kai? Where is he?" I say.

"On the other side. He's over there." Nok lazily points to a hill in the distance.

"Over where?" I say.

"The Illitaww men found a stream before I woke. We've

all visited, and Kai remains." Nok throws up his arms.

"I am Marr." Marr brings a closed fist to his chest to re-mind Nok of his name.

"Yes...Marr located the stream earlier." Nok tends to his horse. "No one is perfect, Your Imperial Majesty."

"What did you say?" I stop and turn back.

"Nothing," Nok says under his breath as I leave.

Kai stands in silence at the edge of the narrow stream when I arrive. Underneath his shirt, his back is riddled with lean muscles. Kai looks back, hearing my feet scrape against the gravel bed. A leather pouch containing the stone swings across his firm chest as he turns to me. His smile is genuine for the first time since we escaped Roknamar.

"Hello, Shiva." He grins widely.

I fight off a smile.

"I'm sorry...Lifia, I mean. Hello, Lifia," he says.

I didn't notice his mistake. I've gone by Shiva for so long, and I've forgotten what it was like to be addressed by my own name.

"There is no problem. You knew me first as Shiva. You may call me either," I say.

"No. A person should be called by their true name," he says.

His argument is appreciated, and I release the smile.

"We should leave soon."

"Yes. The farther we travel from Simb's Point, the better we will all be." Kai slides his shirt on, covering himself.

"Have you learned any more about the magic?" I say.

He looks me in the eye, searching for my motives. Grass-hoppers continue to chirp from the grasses behind me, filling the momentary silence.

Kai slips his cured leather boots back onto his feet and takes a step toward me.

"The stone is trying to show me how to use the power, but I can't understand it." He trails off, holding up the leather pouch hanging around his neck.

I take a step closer, studying the object held in his hands.

"My mother said it protected her and that it will protect me." Kai laughs.

Islanders are well-known for their superstitions and luck charms. Many sailors carry rocks or braided tree stems to protect them and bring them home from the sea.

"I know it sounds...hard to believe, but this stone has something inside it. Something powerful, and it wants to be un-locked." Kai studies the pouch in his hands.

I nod to show my understanding. Kai pauses for a long time. He's more careful than when we sailed together.

"Kai?" I tilt my head to the side.

I want him to succeed, and I want to be there when he does. I simply want him, which I didn't realize until now. He doesn't care who I am, what I'm supposed to be, or what I've done. He accepts me, regardless of my name. Kai leans to the side.

"She told me to take the stone to the Cradle of Man, but I couldn't. I...couldn't do it until you were free from Roknamar. I owe you my life," he says.

"You are in no debt to me, Kai. I will help you take this to wherever we need to take it." I grab his hand holding the Art Stone.

"*Wrekk*!" Jupp shouts from beyond the apex of the hill.

An expression of fear flashes over Kai's face.

No. Not again. My mother's instincts in me take over.

"The Magnavoz?" I sprint to the top of the hill, and Kai follows.

More than ten Magnavozian riders charge Jupp. I release an arrow into the group of charging riders. The arrowhead sticks into the leg of one of the men, but his mount is unaffected.

Jupp and Marr cross my line of sight as they rush toward the riders. I lower my bow and release the tension in the string as I run alongside the hill to draw a better angle. I release one more arrow into the neck of the closest scout, right before Jupp and Marr meet them.

Jupp leaps up and tackles one of the men from his horse. Marr slides underneath one of the horses right when it reaches him. The animal runs past him, abruptly falls to its knees, and topples over in a flip. The flip hurls the mounted soldier forward and through the air until he crumples into the dirt below. Jupp continues to wrestle the man he took to the ground while a dust cloud from the toppled horse spouts up.

Idling my bow around my back, I dash to aid them on the field. Once I reach the bottom of the hill, Nok gallops past me on Braydenwolf with his blunted blade drawn. He points it ahead of himself like an experienced lancer. As I take another advancing step, Kai runs up beside me.

"Lifia." He reaches me and continues to run.

I pull on his hand and chase after Nok. He glides over the short grass with little effort. Kai has much better control over his body than when I first began to teach him the dances. By the time we reach the field, Jupp is blocking spear thrusts with each hand from three riders encircling him. Farther down the field, Nok is locked in a mounted duel. His sword clangs off the shield of one of the more armored riders, but he manages well enough. Marr sprints forward toward the rest of their troops entering the pasture.

"Kai, see if you can help him dismount the riders." I point at Jupp.

Kai runs right for them without hesitation. While in stride,

I draw an arrow the same way I practice every day. Sliding my string into the nock initiates my dance. I pull up and draw the string back while tracing a line with my arrow from the ground to the six riders assaulting Marr.

The moment my sights align with the neck of one, I release the arrow. The arrow zips through the air like an agitated viper in a strike. It pings off the breastplate of one of the riders. Yet it's enough to take his balance, and he slides off the side of his mount. Marr raises his blade hilts to the sky, and drives the edges through the dismounted rider. Another rider charges behind him. Marr ducks and rolls as the rider swings a slash over him. I release another arrow, and the rider catches it in his shield.

With a gaze fixed upon me, he shouts something to the other Magnavozian riders. His beautiful black steed kicks up dust behind itself as it charges at me. Whistles and different sounds follow. The remaining riders disengage and begin to charge at me as well.

"The empress!" The man on the beautiful black steed points at me.

The riders are charging, but my sight focuses on my allies. I'm stuck. Marr chases after the riders and grabs onto the tail of one horse. As he grabs it, the horse kicks backward and knocks Marr to the ground. The others are too far away. Kai is the nearest. Once I make eye contact with him, my senses return, and I take a quick step back toward the hill. I stumble on the rocks at the bottom, and some of the stones slide away. The more I fight, the more the gravelly ground slides out from under me until I lose step and fall.

CHAPTER THIRTY

The Seeker

Kai

WINTER So1, 51 AE

There are only a few moments before the riders reach Lifia. I unwrap the stone, hoping the removal of the barrier will grant me access.

"Please," I beg.

Yet the stone remains silent.

Twirling blades fly over my head and plunge into the closest riders. They tumble off their horses as the rider with the black steed pulls the reins of his horse. He watches the other riders disappear in the high grass. Now I'm running to Lifia. I won't reach her before the rider, but I must try. Jupp is closing the distance behind me, but he's too far behind to help.

The last remaining rider, on the black horse, is mounted a hundred feet from Lifia as she struggles to climb the hill. He looks to me running, and he turns his horse to the north. With one swift kick, the rider is off. I fall to the ground as relief flows over me, wind rippling across a new sail.

After gathering supplies from the battleground, we meet underneath an unusually large tree for the area.

"Now they have more reason to pursue us. The one who fled will be back with the entire Magnavozian army." Nok is pacing and holding his shoulder.

A gash across his neck trickles blood down his back. It's proof of his tussle with one of the riders. He's tougher and sturdier than his lanky physique would hint.

"We are few, but we are strong," Jupp says.

Marr, also injured in his fall, stands beside Jupp.

"We are strong." I allow one end of my staff to fall to the ground. "We are. But we cannot fight the entire army in open battle. We are lucky to have survived against the riders."

My ankle is swollen from a twist while running down the hill. The others appear sunken from weeks of surviving on plants and vermin of the prairies. Only Nok's health has improved during the journey.

"We should travel north to another city. The Crossing is out of reach," Lifia says.

"There's nowhere else to go. We have to stick to the plan. The Crossing is our only way to the west without traveling for days to the north," I say.

"The Crossing. It's west of those mesas in the distance there." Nok points beyond me to two distant mountains with their tops cut off.

"Well, yes, of course, the Crossing is west of us, and so is the rider that fled, and so will be the Magnavozian army." Lifia stretches her bow.

The Crossing, also known as the Bridge City, is a wealthy Magnavozian trading center. The marvelous city was built around a bridge that crosses the great canyon Palon Dur. The city is the only natural means of travel west without going weeks north or south for a lower crossing point. The ruling family who controls the fortress controls commerce in Magnavoz.

"Nok is right. I believe the Crossing is our natural destination. Besides, the city may hold a gateway, which could be our only real escape," I say.

"Sometimes the most obvious path is the least guarded," Jupp says.

"We will carve a path if one is not available." Marr looks up from his neck stretches and extends his arms.

"Kai, we are with you. If the Crossing is the only escape, then we will follow you," Lifia says.

There is a danger traveling west. Yet I'm excited to peer into the great canyon of Palon Dur. The view that it rips through the earth is said to be one of the most amazing in the realm.

The next day, I walk alone with Lifia on a hunt for prairie fowl. Nok remains at camp with the brothers.

Lifia's figure is thin and healthy. I'm more drawn to her than the hunt. She hasn't spoken to me much since our skirmish with the Magnavozian scouts.

"Lifia, I...tried to use the stone when the riders came. Yet I couldn't summon its power. It's silent for me." Feeling her cold shoulder, I try to crack the icy wall between us.

Yet she remains silent.

"The brothers seem unsurprised by the magic, and Nok seems doubtful." I jump over a fallen tree as I struggle to keep up. "What do the Fangourians believe about magic?"

Lifia draws her bow like she is going to release an arrow, but backs off on her pull and lets the arrow fall limp.

"It's true what you said. There was a time in our history when magic was important to my people, but that faded as our empire grew." Lifia looks back at me. "What do the temple scrolls say?"

"There were conflicting beliefs at the temple, and only a few scrolls support any existence of magic. Most of the legends are not written in the scrolls, at least not the ones I've read," I say.

"What do the masters believe?" Lifia says.

"Some of the masters indulged our interests in miracles of magic, while others insisted on natural causes for all things. Master Vivamin told us the canyon was formed after many years of a mighty river rushing through the land." I step beside Lifia. "I remember arriving in her hall when she poured a tanker of water onto a mound of dirt for a demonstration. It was one of my first weeks at Summer's Light, and in that moment of joyous humor and wonder, she convinced me to search the world for all things magnificent. She left me wondering if the natural and the magical could exist in harmony. The rainwater that formed the river and carved the great canyon could have been poured by powerful magic pressed upon the perfect places in the sky."

"That is an interesting idea." Lifia rests perched on a mound of fallen leaves.

"Lifia. Thank you for coming with me and for trusting me," I say.

She looks at me like she did when we didn't know each other. Her face is void of emotion and impossible to read. Neither of us is hunting for signs of prairie animals.

"It was brave of you to come for me at Roknamar. Many

brave men wouldn't have risked it." Lifia dances her fingers along her bowstring. "It was also foolish."

"You would've done the same for me," I say.

"No. I would not." Lifia stops dancing her fingers. "You are a kinder person than I."

"You are kind. I believe you are one of the kindest people in the realm, but the realm hasn't allowed you to be yourself," I say.

She studies me for truth and would find any lie I tried to keep. I step close to her, and she bows her head.

"I wanted to protect you," I whisper.

I want to protect her like she has protected me many times before. My admiration of her is evident, but what does she want from me?

"I don't need your protection," she says.

"No, you don't," I say.

Her lips separate, but no words follow. Her dark hair is beautiful as it falls down her neck to her chest, but her eyes finish me. I lean in to press my lips against hers. Our lips hover next to each other, both desiring to meet yet quivering until we can't resist each other a moment longer. Finally she is the one to complete the kiss by bringing her lips around mine. The uncertainty fades away, and I feel alone in Elybion with her.

The kiss innocently fades, and she pulls back before it expires. I follow behind her, smiling to myself as we continue the hunt in optimistic silence.

PART IV

FIRES OF THE
FIVE

CHAPTER THIRTY·ONE

The Brooder

Lifia

WINTER S14, 51 AE

We arrive outside the Crossing before dawn.

"Does everyone understand?" I say.

"Find the gateway and travel through. In the likely event that we can't find the mythical passage that Kai has dreamed of, we pass through the Crossing and head west to the Aptorias." Nok rolls his eyes.

Marr releases the forearm of his brother and begins to trek northward without us.

"Marr is a great climber, and he'll be on the other side

before we can cross the bridge," Jupp says.

"I fly with the wind at my back," Marr says.

While we enter the city, his mission is to climb down to the canyon floor and up the other side. He'll scout ahead for any signs of the Magnavozian army.

"Travel well," I whisper to Marr as he disappears into the tall grass.

With our weapons well concealed, we trek forward to the city gates. Kai's staff passes for a walking stick, and my unstrung bow fits well on Braydenwolf's back. Unfortunately, one of our greatest weapons, Jupp, is impossible to hide. At least with only one of the brothers, we won't appear as menacing.

Most of the city guards are preoccupied with women and drink at the taverns just beyond the entryway. The guards at the gate wave us in behind a butcher and his cart. The cart reeks of unclean meats, yet we are all hungry enough to be enticed by the odor. The butcher pays the toll for his meats, and the guards usher us in behind him. The butcher glances back to see who we are, but his looks don't linger. Instead, other curious eyes find and follow us as we walk.

"Hello, handsome. Another stout man in this city. Oh my, a genuine man," a tavern maid calls out to Jupp.

Beyond the first buildings and city folk hugging the main road, a copper dome juts into the sky. The copper span seems foreign to the rest of the city.

"Is he the same one that wore the helmet the other day?" Another maid studies Jupp, looking him up and down.

Nok turns to Kai. His humor-filled smile is contagious, and Kai can't help but to send one back in return. With better manners, Jupp takes half a glance and continues to scan, not recognizing her as a threat.

We make our way to the other side of the bridge that nests the city. Braydenwolf claps the stone behind us.

"Wait." Kai grabs his chest as we approach the gates. "The

stone is trying to tell me something."

"What is it?" I say.

"A vision. My mother was speaking to a man about the gateway. She was afraid, but the man was helping her. We are close, I'm sure." Kai nods.

"The gate is just ahead." Nok points his hand leading Braydenwolf.

The entire city is set up on a distinguishable grid, where each building is of a similar shape and size. The organized network reminds me of the market outside the Skyfort. Did the Fangourian builders have their hands on the Crossing? There are two major roads large enough for horses and armies to march through in lines of eight men wide. They meet in the center of the city, creating a cross. One of the major roads goes from gate to gate, while the other crosses the width of the town from the Airwalk to the Climber.

The Airwalk is a simple solution for their executions. They send their criminals off to the canyon below. The Climber is a large wooden box attached to ropes. It's a complex system that allows travel to the canyon floor. For the rest of the city, there are narrow walkways wide enough for two men to walk shoulder to shoulder. The town is extraordinarily clean because their waste slides into the canyon.

We slow our pace and turn off the main roadway. I look around the corner building to view the gate. Several more guards occupy this side of the city compared to the east side, where we came in. At the threshold of the gateway, a man waits as the guards ransack his single mule-led cart. Behind the man, a line of traders wait to have their belongings searched.

"We should wait and check back here later, give Kai a chance to find his magic gateway," Nok says.

"It may be easier to leave in the night either way," Kai says.

"Jupp, what do you say?" I step back.

"I counted eleven guards at the gate. Four rest on top of the gate with arrows. Then there are"—I peek around to get a glimpse of who he describes—"three guards sitting at the table, while two guards search through the people's things. Those two are claiming valuables. Finally, there are two guards who are leaning against the wall of the building next to the gate. These two are weak from the night before and will be easy to drop. One of the archers above holds his bow with real purpose, and I believe he may have a true release," Jupp says.

He explains all without looking.

"No, there is only one leaning against the wall," I say.

One of the men leaning against the wall sits up off the wall, while the other guard remains. I look back around the corner to everyone. Jupp gives me a nod. Clearly, he has already considered going through the guards, but he hasn't bashed his shields together and begun shouting his war chants. Has he weighed the odds and found them unfavorable for once? If *he* doesn't like the odds, none of us will.

"Fine. We can leave tonight. Where do you expect us to go until then? This city is much busier than Simb's Point. We can't hide in the alleyway and expect to remain unnoticed," I say.

"We should go to the temple." Kai peers around the corner to check again. "The man my mother spoke to was a priest of the Trinity. I think."

I'm not convinced there's a gateway here, and even less that we'll find it still. Something in my expression betrays my thoughts, because Kai removes the leather necklace and hands it to me.

"Here. Take it. Maybe it'll communicate more clearly with you." Kai turns away.

I squeeze the leather around the stone. I want to trust him, but I don't know if he understands what magic he dabbles in.

"A tavern would suit me better." Nok pats his lips.

"We don't have time to visit a tavern," Kai says.

"Taverns have always been the center of gossip and political information. Has that changed during my time in the dungeons?" Nok says.

"Let him go." I slap the stone back into Kai's hand.

Right as the stone leaves my hand, I hear the echo of Okiari Forest behind me. When I look, Jupp is calmly standing in place of the trees, which I could almost smell.

"No...Kai and I will visit the temple, but it's better if Jupp is inside somewhere. Preferably sitting down." I smile and pat Jupp on his shoulder, which is above the top of my head.

"Go to the tavern. We'll meet you there at dusk," I say.

The streets are patterned with a mosaic design. One road has a blue arrow outlined in little white squares that points to an ornate painting of a grand building with a few brown squares to represent the copper roof.

"I've never entered a basilica of the Trinity." I pace alongside Kai.

I keep my face covered and turned away as three city guards pass us.

"Nor have I. I've studied them enough, but I'm coming to find studying is very different from experiencing." Kai taps the end of his staff on the tiles as he walks.

The front of the basilica is decorated with flowered reefs and twined gold. The mosaic tiles end where the chiseled steps of the temple begin.

"Shall we?" Kai leads us up the steps to the entrance of the basilica.

We peer down the long hall into the heart of the structure.

Beyond the sunlight cutting the shadow diagonally is darkness and more faint shadows. As we draw deeper inside, women greet us.

"Here, my dear." An elderly woman hands me a plain cloth.

"Oh," I say.

She directs me to attach the veil around my head. Normally, I would never wear a religious garment in vain. However, the convenience of covering my face is the kind of protection I cannot deny under these circumstances.

"Thank you," Kai says.

We shuffle into the sanctuary. We can see the inside of the copper dome above our heads. The light penetrates the folds in the metal, creating a pattern of hexagons on the ground. Worshippers notice us, but they don't adjust their practices. They pray and meditate on their mats against the walls. Their religion is one of solitude and private training. We turn down a hall that expands away from the main sanctuary.

"There should be an Ear somewhere around here," Kai whispers.

The Ears are priests who listen to both the Trinity and the people. Most of them keep vows of silence for years.

"Let's go down here." I nudge Kai.

We walk by two women dressed in black and weeping in silence. Their attire says they are mourning for a loved one. Besides their weeping, the entire basilica holds an eerie silence, interrupted by the occasional whisper. At the end of the hall, we reach a doorway with the door nearly shut but still allowing candlelight to escape from the other side. Kai and I look at each other through the haze until I pull the door back and enter.

Inside, there are two elderly women and one elder man. The man looks up from his prayers against the wall. He is the Ear. The women continue to pray as the man steps forward and tries to usher us back through the door. His hands are riddled with age spots.

"Wait." I stop his hand from guiding us out.

"Please, gracious Ear. I'm an apprentice of Summer's Light." Kai steps in front of me.

The man frowns and tries to usher us out again.

"This will only take a moment of your time. Do you have any parchment we can use to trade words?" Kai says.

With a heavy sigh, the Ear waves at us to follow him as he steps farther into the room. We walk past the women praying, around a bookshelf, and down a short hall to a small study.

The Ear urges us to sit in one of his small carved-wood seats.

"We've come in search of an ancient relic, which we redis-covered in the scrolls," Kai says.

The man slowly blinks.

"Our masters sent us here to seek out the gateways, and we thought your ear might have heard of these ancient constructs. These gateways are said to take people across large swaths. The scrolls say there are many throughout Elybion, but no city is more spoken of than the Crossing." Kai shifts in his seat.

The man holds an ugly face. It's like he knows something, and he's trying not to give it away. However, I'm much better at this game than he is.

"Master..." I look at Kai.

"Master NcTully," Kai says.

"Has asked us to come in his place to meet the great Ear of the Crossing and see the beautiful basilica he labors for. Master NcTully said that if anyone in the city were wise enough to know about the gateways, it would be the Ear of the Crossing." I smile.

The Ear transforms his expression into one of slight curi-osity. He shrugs his shoulders and shows his palms. He knows something, but he won't say. We hold a short staring contest until the Ear stands to show us out.

"Well, thank you for listening." Kai respectfully follows

him out.

As he follows, the man grabs the stone hanging in the leather pouch around Kai's neck.

"You aren't from the temple." His voice is scratched dry.

"You speak?" I say.

"Of course I can speak. The vow of silence is a convenient myth people tell each other." The Ear squeezes Kai's leather pouch.

"Please, release him." I slide my dagger from its concealed slit on the small of my back.

"You are not the first ones I've seen with a stone in a pouch," the Ear says. "Nearly twenty years ago, a woman appeared in my city with a baby and a stone like this one. A baby with the same icy-blue eyes sitting in your head." The Ear points a digit at Kai.

"My mother?" Kai says.

The Ear turns to fumble through piles of loose parchment. Kai leans his hand against a wall.

"Do you know anything about this?" I say.

"No, but...I can almost feel an echo of the encounter." Kai grabs the stone.

The Ear sends a questioning glance at Kai.

"If you could explain how they arrived, we would leave right away." I place my daggers back into their positions.

"Your mother was confused about how she arrived at the Crossing. She tried to explain how she was in the desert only hours before I found her," the Ear says.

"Where did you find her?" I say.

The Ear hands us a tattered piece of parchment. On the parchment is a description of a man, along with a man's handprint pressed into ink. Underneath the hand, it indicates his exalted status, and the royal emblem of Magnavoz is stamped below. The Ear presses his hand over the ink mark to prove its match.

"Before your mother came, I was an Underling, a slave to the rulers of the great Bridge City."

"Underling? A canyon dweller?" Kai says.

"Yes. The lowest class in Magnavoz. So low that we are often forgotten. When I found your mother, and she told me all the impossible things she had experienced, I started to believe I could do something unbelievable for myself. So I worked until I earned enough to buy my place in the city and Magnavoz." The Ear opens his shirt to show the brand of an Underling burned below his right collarbone.

"You do know where the gateway rests," I say.

"Perhaps, but it wouldn't be safe to travel there now. I'll show you what I can tomorrow." The Ear scratches his chin. "Meet me at the Climber at dawn. Now go."

The Ear escorts us out of the sanctuary. We exit the basilica and descend the steps.

"Can we trust him?" I say.

"I don't know, but I think we can trust the stone," Kai says.

●

Later Kai and I arrive at the meeting place. The tavern is well lit, clean, and welcoming. The decorations are formed from the skulls of exotic game from all around Elybion. There are elk, buffalo, and enormous boar tusks from Illitaww. The owner is a burly man with a huge gut and beard. His smile shines below his mustache when I enter. He holds a cuddled-up fur wad in one arm while he pours mugs with the other. The lump of fur covers a spoiled, fat cat.

I examine the room until I find Nok with his arm around

the bard. They seem like old friends. Nok is the least of my concern. Jupp sits at a table in the corner of the room. A few unat-
tached women are gawking over him, but he gives them little, if
any, attention. He remains vigilant, while everyone else relaxes.
Jupp nods when I locate him. He knows, as I do, the danger is
right on the other side of a door.

"Lifia." Nok releases his arm from around the singer, picks
up a mug of drink, and walks over to me.

Nok smiles and spins around with his knees outward, away
from his body, while his hands remain flat. His action results in
gasps from patrons behind him.

"What are you doing?" I return a glare.

"I'm conforming to their customs, of course," Nok says.

Nok fills us in on what he has learned from eavesdropping. There has been no word of the army coming close to the
Crossing. The locals say the military is north, along the western
border of Palon Dur.

"How about a few rounds?" Chunks of meat pie fall from
Nok's mouth as he speaks.

"We don't have the luxury of loosening with a drink, nor
the coin to buy it," I say.

"Surely we can have a few drinks." Nok pulls a fist-sized
satchel of coins out from under his shirt.

Kai and I trade expressions of confusion. Nok takes a few
and flips them in the air. The bartender places Nok's drink down
as we pretend to be casual.

"What did you find?" Nok leans in.

"We have a lead to follow an Ear to the Climber." I check
behind Nok. "We will leave before dawn."

"Yes, I've heard the same." Nok takes a sip of his drink.

"What have you heard?" Kai whispers.

"Well, just that the locals speak about peculiar things happening down below. The Underlings would be my guess for people who might dabble in the mystical." Nok slaps his cup on the

table. "How about a turnover?"

"A turnover? What is that?" I say.

"Yes. You would be quite good at this game." Nok waves at the bartender.

"A game? I don't have time for this." I push myself away from the bar.

Jupp rises and overshadows the room from the corner. I walk over to meet him and shoo away the women beside him.

"Marr has climbed to the other side now," Jupp says.

"You share a rare connection," I say.

"We have trained and lived together since the beginning. Marr is as much my blade as I am his shield," Jupp says.

The only connection I've ever felt like theirs was with Bulba. I can't sense him like Jupp seems to sense Marr, but I hope he is climbing somewhere in the canopy of the Okiari Forest. Jupp takes a drink.

"We will leave before daybreak. I'm afraid Nok has made himself too popular for us to sneak out without being noticed. Make sure he doesn't get any louder," I say.

Jupp nods as I walk away.

The stars are shining in the stillness of the night. I turn right out of the tavern door and take a few steps toward the side of the building, into the narrow walkway between. The tavern door opens and closes behind me. I carefully make several right turns until I'm at the back of the tavern. Inside the inn, the chattering is elevated with singing. Footsteps follow the path behind me. It's Kai, and I'm glad he pursues. I equip my scowl and tighten my lips. His steps pause on the other side of the corner. He seems to change his mind, and he goes back the other way. This is my opportunity. I slip around the corner and sneak up behind him. As he turns, I push him against the wall.

"The baby whale never learns, does he? Always getting lost." I pull myself close to his face, hoping he will kiss me.

When he doesn't, I release my grip and turn away.

Has something changed since our hunt together? I take a step away, alone, where I belong.

"Where are you going? We should stay together," Kai says.

"I need to look around the city to ease my mind of threats," I say.

Kai takes a few quick strides up behind me and reaches for my hand. He grabs my hand gently and pulls me back toward him.

"We should be together. We can't trust anyone in this city," Kai says.

"You're afraid to be alone?" I say.

I'm moving closer to him again, to give him one more chance to kiss me.

"Magnavoz is all around us. I'm just saying we need to be more cautious," he says.

We kiss. Pleasantly, the kiss is prolonged and less awkward than last time. I've been waiting for it since we separated our lips. I want to push it further, but when I start to think of where it will go, I lose the moment. Our lips separate, and I step away. This time, I don't hide my smile. In the night lights, Kai's face is thin, soft, and square. He doesn't know it, but he's handsome.

"Lifia," he says.

I slow my stride. The stone hung around his neck sways.

"Wait inside, rest, and I'll come for you shortly," I say.

Kai sighs and walks back to the front of the tavern.

I leap and stretch for the overhang of the roof. With the edge of the roof in hand, I kick my right leg up over the lip. The wind is brisk enough to cause the bumps on my neck to rise as I creep to the crest of the roof and unfurl my cloak to wrap around myself.

Flickering lights shine in most windows throughout the city. The only structure with substantial height in all the Crossing is the keep near the center. Lord Feechi has ruled the keep and all the people of the Crossing since King Donak gifted it to him sometime shortly after the fall of the empire. Their family was allied to the right family at the right time. Many dances are occurring in the realm, which none of us fully understand. My mother was my source for political information, and my place in the arena passed with her.

"What dance would you show me now, Mother?" I lie on my back on the cool roof.

CHAPTER THIRTY-TWO

The Fugitive

Kai

WINTER S15, 51 AE

Lifia breaks through the threshold of the tavern. The bar-man peeks from where the goods are kept. The tavern is empty besides the barman, two barmaids, a spent drunk, who remains in slumber, and us.

"The Magnavoz army is here. They're marching down the main road and searching random buildings," Lifia says.

Jupp stands and shakes his long arms lose before binding them to his shields.

"Wait. There are too many. It's not a fight we can win by

blunted assault." Lifia steps in and closes the door behind her.

"Who are you?" The barman places his cat on the table and picks up his crossbow from behind the bar. "It's the hour for you to leave."

Lifia draws her bow and directs it at the barman. I'm holding my hand out to stop Jupp from charging the man.

"Lifia, please." I motion for her to lower her bow. "Sir. I'm sorry we have brought this to your place. It was not by design. However, we cannot yet leave."

"No. You will leave, and you will take this vile woman with you." The barman directs his aim back toward the door.

Before the barman can realign his bolt, Lifia releases an arrow, knocking the crossbow free from his grasp. As it falls, a bolt is released. It punctures a wooden column in the center of the room. A barmaid screams as the splinters sprinkle the side of her face. Lifia glides to the middle of the room and covers the barmaid's mouth. Jupp rushes the barman, but the barman raises his hands in surrender. Jupp is expressionless. I fear he is waiting for an excuse to crush the man.

"I'll ask again. Who are you?" The barman lowers his hands.

"We're only travelers, seeking to continue our journey, but we can't leave now," I say.

The second barmaid stands quietly at the edge of the room. She is either too afraid to speak or wise enough to remain silent.

"We wish you no harm, and we only ask for your calm silence." Lifia releases the barmaid and pushes her toward the barman.

"I see it now. Feathered black hair, Fangourian features, and the company of mercenaries. You're the lost empress of Fangour. So the rumors are true." The barman slaps both hands on the bar. "I have no interest in the politics of this land. I don't care who rules, as long as I can serve good drinks and hunt when the season is right. If you don't leave, they will burn down my tavern and still capture or kill you all."

"We aren't mercenaries, and we wish you and your tavern no harm." I tap my staff on the wooden planks.

"Leave out the back door with my promise to hold my tongue about your visit," the barman says.

"Yes. We should leave." I turn to Lifia.

"The Magnavoz care nothing for your sentiment for this building or your desire to hunt. They want to claim it all. They allow you to sit in here and pretend it belongs to you, but they will snatch it from your grasp whenever the time is most convenient for them. Whether that is by fire or iron, they will take it." Lifia steps up to the barman.

The barman lowers his head.

"And when Fangour called us one of their countries? Was it really any better?" the barmaid says.

Lifia locks eyes with the girl.

"Wait. Where's Nok?" Lifia says.

Nok isn't here. We would've heard his opinions many times over by now if he were.

"The last I saw him, he was there, singing with the bard." I look around the room.

The bard's lute leans against a stool by the fire.

"Yes, he left with the singer," Jupp says.

"That fool," Lifia says.

Hammering fists echo from somewhere across the street, followed by cracking wood as a door is smashed in. The barman shrugs his shoulders.

"Let's go." Lifia rushes to the back exit.

"It seems you will have your deal. Thank you for your hospitality." I pass by the barman and dodge the orange cat as it streaks across our path.

The melody of men singing lofty tunes grows as we reach the stable building. Lifia is cursing under her breath.

From a distance, I see two figures with Braydenwolf. The

torches on the stable make their shadows dance as they walk and sing.

"My friends have come to hear more of your singing. Shall we give them one more ballad?" Nok stretches his back as we step up to the stable.

"Nok," Lifia says.

Lifia is expressionless. Her bow is equipped but not drawn. Jupp holds his weapons in each hand.

"Oh, has the fun come to an end?" Nok releases Braydenwolf from his tether. "Thank you for your voice. We'll sing together again someday." Nok grabs the bard by his cheeks and kisses him with a big smack.

Nok leads Braydenwolf out of the stable. The bard stands quietly as we leave to follow Nok.

"And where are we going at this ripe time that is nearer to dawn than dusk?" Nok spits.

"Fool. Do you not see the flickering torchlight in the distance? Do you not hear the pounding on doors?" Lifia says.

"I do." Nok whips Braydenwolf's rein and wraps it tightly around his wrist. "Yet that doesn't change my question."

"We're going to the Climber." I extend my staff to stop Nok from walking. "We are to meet the Ear there in the morning. He said he would show us the gateway we seek. Given the circumstances, we may need to travel down the Climber and locate the gateway by ourselves."

"And you are confident we can escape through your magical portal?" Nok says.

"Yes. I'm certain." I withdraw my staff from his pathway.

"Yes. To the Climber. It's our only chance," Lifia says.

"Sure, we'll find your gateway. Perhaps the plains will flood again." Nok pushes by me.

We cut through the city down the back roads until we reach a blockade of soldiers marching down the main road.

"The Climber is down the street here, but the path is well

occupied." I clutch the stone shaking inside the pouch. "What are you saying? What do you want?"

The others trade expressions of concern. I unwrap the stone and squeeze it between my palms.

"We are snared in, with no way out," I say.

"There's our will, and the will of the gods. One is far more refined." Jupp stretches his neck.

Lifia fingers through her bundle of arrows, which holds less than twelve.

"We cannot fight them. If Jupp could take ten men alone, more than ninety would remain. If all your arrows are guided perfectly in their release, more than eighty will remain." I look to Jupp and then Lifia.

"No, Kai. We will fight them. You will run to escape down the Climber," Lifia says.

"No. I will not," I say.

"You will, or our journey will have been for nothing. You will complete your task." Lifia places her hand on my shoulder. "Please, go."

"My task is ahead, into the fray." Jupp points at the marching soldiers. "Yet yours is another, and it's more important than any."

"Nok? Will you speak sense to them?" I say.

"I'll deliver you to the Climber while Jupp and Lifia draw the attention of their forces." Nok mounts Braydenwolf.

"Our fight will be better if we draw them into the narrower streets." Jupp draws a path in the air with his hand.

Lifia nods. They're waiting for me to jump onto Braydenwolf with Nok. With the stone still in my hands, I'm stunned. I can't leave her again.

Thunderous crashes echo from the other side of the city. Horns blare as soldiers redirect their march toward the western gates.

"What is it?" I say.

"Give me a hand." Lifia looks up to the top of the building.

"Step here." Jupp holds his shields flat so she can climb them to the edge of the roof.

Once on top, she leaps over the narrow alleyway to the building across. This building has an angled frame that reaches much higher than the surrounding dwellings.

"There's an army fighting the Magnavoz outside the gates," Lifia calls back to us. "It's still too dark to know who the formation belongs to. Wait. They carry the orange-and-green banner of the South Aptorians."

"Are you certain?" Nok shouts.

"Yes, but there's another Magnavozian regiment flanking them from the north." Lifia slides down the roof.

"What does this mean?" I say.

"It means we may yet have an alley, and that cowardice isn't a life sentence." Nok smiles and reaches for me. "Come. We'll make for the Climber while the opportunity is available."

Lifia and Jupp are running as I pull myself up behind Nok.

The city roars with terror as we roll into the center of the Crossing. City folk stampede toward the east gate, while soldiers press toward the west. The Climber is abandoned except for one man standing awkwardly next to the lever.

Braydenwolf's hooves clack on the smooth surface as we approach. A hundred feet away, I notice the red streaks pouring down his cheeks. He's the Ear we met at the temple. As we step closer, I realize his ears have been cleaved off.

"Let me off." I nudge Nok and slide off the back of Braydenwolf.

Lifia and Jupp glide up behind us. Thundering pounds en-sue down the road as people flee west to east. Yet no one seems to notice us.

"Gracious Ear, what has happened? Who did this to you?" I try to pat back the blood with my cloak, but he winces away.

Jupp turns and smashes his shields together. Lifia whips around and draws an arrow in one smooth twirl.

"Finally. You kept me waiting the whole night." A man dressed in white extends his hands as he strides to the intersec-tion.

"Vzar Musa," Nok says.

His title and name are as unique as the experience we find ourselves in. He's like a ghost or a myth from a tale, and less a person. My feet stick to the road, like they are closed in a giant clam. Who is Vzar Musa really?

"No need to apologize. I'm very patient. I would've waited a few more moments before I buried the city in the canyon." Vzar Musa treks forward.

Torches fade as he passes them. A crashing slam reverber-ates through the bridge as shouts explode from the western gate. Musa sends a soft glance to the west.

"How convenient for the rebellion to begin on this morn-ing." Musa stops. "Did you believe you were somehow saved by that pitiful army outside? There are always rebellions. Some are bolder than others, but they all fall the same."

The elegant confidence of his stride is beyond a king. He isn't afraid of Lifia's release or Jupp's charge. It's like we are children, and he's the father coming to scold us.

"What do you want?" I step in front of Lifia.

"Ah, the young watcher. Are you ready to soar against me? Has the stone shown you the way? No. It seems not. Be patient. A time will come for me to end your suffering. First, I must destroy this dynasty." He raises his hands.

Musa's eyes ignite with violet flames, which swirl around

into orbs of fire. The orbs gather and stick to his hands.

"*Drah! Drahkua! Drah, drah, drahkua!*" Jupp steps out of the space between Musa and us.

As Jupp cries his battle shout, horns blare down the street. Taking the opportunity of distraction, Lifia releases an arrow over Jupp's shoulder. Musa spins with his hands extended. The flames swirl with him, leaving fiery tails behind. Lifia's arrow flies far beyond Musa. While I'm still mesmerized by the fire, Jupp is sprinting toward the Venith.

Musa brings his hands together to combine the flames. The fire swells and bursts out like a whale spout. Jupp dodges the flames and slides across the road. I jump to cover Lifia before the blaze scorches the air above us. The flames soar before crashing into the Climber and igniting the small ropes that operate it. His flames are terrifying but less effective than the power we wit-nessed on the beach. Where is the mystic wind he spun through my fingers?

"Lifia." I pull her up.

As we run toward the Climber, Musa steps around Jupp and continues to saunter down the scorched black pathway be-hind us. Beyond the Climber, the expanse of the canyon is paint-ed with the vibrant pink sky of an early rise. The glow from Musa's eyes is gone. Lifia draws and releases an arrow. This arrow darts through the loose fabric stretched between Musa's torso and his extended arm. Musa laughs as he peers through the tiny slit at us. Then he stretches his hands out again to sum-mon more flames. More torchlight fades as the orbs of fire grow from his fingertips. His eyes reignite.

Jupp stands and looks back at the sounds coming from the western gate. Musa drops his hands and looks in that direction as well. The flames that were growing at his fingertips dissipate into the air above him. A symphony of thunderous claps and men yelling leads the charge as Aptorian riders charge down the main road. Musa directs his attention toward them, spouting a smaller flame down the western road. Many horses topple, but others continue to ride through. They are led by a stout drega-din with a gilded bow.

"*Wrekk!*" Jupp raises both shields.

Marr dashes in behind the riders.

"Marr!" Lifia points.

Horns, shouts, and smashing metal echo down the streets behind them.

"Do you hear the sound of your allies pleading for mercy as they are crushed by the might of Magnavoz?" Vzar Musa raises his palms.

Most of the riders are turning around to face the assault that chases at their heels. The dregadin with the gilded bow directs his aim at Musa.

"Hold the city!" the dregadin shouts as other riders charge beyond our vantage.

"Lifia, go with Kai down the Climber. We'll stretch as much time as we can." Nok pulls on Braydenwolf's reins.

"No. Come with us," I say.

"Until we meet again, Your Imperial Majesty." Nok bows from atop his horse.

"Jupp and Marr?" I say.

Lifia tugs at my shoulder as Braydenwolf gallops past us to meet the Aptorian riders holding Musa at their lances.

"They are exactly where they want to be." Lifia points at Jupp and Marr as they disappear down the main road.

Born for battle. I fear I'm sewn in by a different tailor.

We run to the Climber and meet the Ear.

"I'm sorry." I grab the Ear's forearm as we step into the Climber.

"We still have words to share!" Musa shouts.

"Speak to Lady Miu Miu. She'll guide you to the gate-way." The Ear grips me tightly around my arms.

He releases me and closes the wooden gate of the Climber.

Lifia and I step back against the creaking platform. The Ear pulls the lever, and we begin the descent.

As we lower below the great bridge, another flame spews across the sky. Lifia rests her hands on the outer edge of the platform, looking out into the painted canyon. As I step to meet her, the platform begins to rattle. The morning light illuminates the clay-formed dwellings below.

An explosion of fire and steel erupts above us. I reach for Lifia as she reaches for me. We catch each other and fall into an embrace as the platform comes free under our feet. I wish I could save her from all the horror of this day. Yet her in my arms is the only thing giving me hope to survive. The Climber detaches, and we crash to the ground.

☽

Rough hands tug at my limbs as I struggle to free myself from the wreckage.

"Lifia."

Wreckage of the Climber, covered in smoke, is all that I see. The Underlings lift me up. They're trying to help, but their numbers are suffocating. Ten to twenty Underlings walk alongside me as a woman with a twisted nose guides me through the crowd.

"Kai!" Lifia shouts.

My body almost shakes in relief at hearing her voice. I fight to meet her and to make sure she is unharmed. Her face is covered in black powder, but her body is whole. We reconnect our embrace, void of any restraint.

"I thought we were gone," I say.

When we fell, we were on the lower part of the descent,

but we were still several stories high.

"It was the stone. I felt it soften our fall," Lifia says.

I peel my gaze from her shoulder to find the crowd. Under-ish whispers circulate through the group. More than one hun-dred Underlings, dressed in soiled rags, stand around us. Battle cries, marching, and horns echo down the canyon from the city above.

"Why have you come here? What dragons roam the bridge on this morning?" the young woman says.

She is led by another woman, who is slightly older, thicker, and of stable feet.

"War wages above. Yet we aren't wholly involved in the battle," I say.

The woman looks past me. At first I assume she is looking above, but she isn't. Her skin is pale, while her eyes are cloudy and blind. A high-pitched reverberation sharply echoes down from above, and the young woman twitches and covers her ear closest to the city.

"Who burns the great city above, and for what cause?" She releases her guide and stands alone.

"A powerful Venith, Vzar Musa. We are his target, and he pursues us with deadly intentions," I say.

Gasps sound throughout the camp. The young woman turns away from us. Her guide grinds her teeth while glaring at us.

"And who are you?" the young woman says.

"I'm Kai, an exiled apprentice of a temple and nothing more. The Ear was to guide us down below, yet he remained above so that we could escape," I say.

"The Ear? The one who climbs?" the young woman says.

"Yes. The Ear said you would guide us the rest of the way," I say.

"Who are you? The one who carries the black bow," the young woman says.

The guide hands Lifia her bow.

"Thank you." Lifia steps close to the young woman. "I'm Lifia Evoni, daughter of Dianame, the last empress of Fangour. Lady Miu Miu, we need your help. We seek an ancient gateway, one that will allow us to travel great distances and escape the ones who pursue us."

"A gateway?" Lady Miu Miu says.

Lady Miu Miu whispers in Underish to her guide.

"Yes. You know of this gateway. Please, don't underestimate the threat of the Venith or their Magnavozian dolls." Lifia looks above.

"Your Imperial Majesty...you ask much of me and my people. What has the empire ever done for us? Your empress ruled the Crossing and all lands below for generations before the Magnavozian dolls reclaimed it. What good will come if we help a forgotten empress of a fallen empire?"

I look to Lifia. Her hands are open, and her neck is long. She conceals nothing and embodies an empress more than ever before.

"I have no power to make promises to you and your people. Fangour has fallen because our ways were imperfect. Since my home was ripped away from me, I've met others like you, strong Elybions like you. I've seen Magnavozian soldiers take from them like they've taken from me. Your people deserve peace without the tyranny and subjugation of any ruler. As long as they are not opposed, they will continue to take everything until there is nothing left for any of us," Lifia says.

Lady Miu Miu stills herself in thought.

"That's enough. If the Ear trusts you with our artifacts, then I shall too. On another day, when dragons don't fly above, I would like you to think back on my people." Lady Miu Miu reaches her hand to Lifia.

Together they are two equal pillars of power. They understand each other in ways only great leaders can. Lady Miu Miu snaps, and her people begin to move out of her pathway.

"Tullinthia. Search the wreckage and make sure everyone is well. We travel for the Borium."

"My lady? Are these outsiders welcome on our most sa‑ cred of grounds?" Tullinthia says.

"It's not for us to decide. Now come."

Lady Miu Miu leads us down the canyon alongside the eastern wall. We pass several dwellings carved into the clay walls. Children peer out of dirt houses as we pass.

"Here." Lady Miu Miu points down the narrow, dark tun‑ nel.

The tunnel is equipped with one torch. Beyond the flicker‑ ing light of the torch, the tunnel is swallowed by darkness.

"Are we to go alone?" Lifia says.

"Yes. I need to evacuate my people away from your war and the damage it causes. It's not far. Take the torch and follow the tunnel down the path until you reach the end. Do not stray from the main path. None will lead back to the trunk root," Lady Miu Miu says.

"Thank you," I say.

"Wait. The gateway does not accept everyone. Many have tried to travel through it, but most don't have the gift. There's a goat path down the Scar, beyond the three caves, and beyond the painted walls." Lady Miu Miu speaks to me.

"The painted walls?" I gaze down at the canyon floor.

"Yes, beyond the painted walls, steps lead to a trail cut into the canyon. Follow the steps up, and go north from there." Lady Miu Miu and her guide step away as we enter.

CHAPTER THIRTY-THREE

The Traveler

Kai

WINTER S15, 51 AE

The narrow tunnel opens into a spherical chamber. Stacked circles form stairs to the center, but torchlight only illuminates a small part of the sanctum. The rough tunnel floor is replaced by smooth tiles. A thick aroma of tumni sucks the moisture from my tongue. The oily tumni trees are common along the canyon above. Their sickly berries can be poisonous if not heated in water for several hours. I spit the remaining moisture onto the floor.

As we step to the center, the torchlight spreads our

shadows behind us and up the curved ceiling.

There are multiple platforms to the center. A ring of columns circles the highest platform. I extend the torch above my head to see where the pillars end. Each of their peaks falls a person's height short of meeting the ceiling.

I run my hands down a column. It is covered in seemingly random shapes.

"I recognize some of these patterns." I hold the torch closer to the column. "I've seen them before in a vision given by the stone."

Lifia glides around the stones as she traces a large triangle with her fingertip.

"They're beautiful. It's like the shapes are dancing around the pillars... Ah, and here on the next one." Lifia follows the shapes around the columns.

I follow her around to the side opposite the entrance, where the stairs begin to descend. There's a void of darkness behind us. It feels like something will reach out of the gloom and drag us away. I wave the torch behind us to illuminate anything that might be lurking. Yet nothing appears.

"What now? What does the stone tell you?" Lifia says.

I give the torch to Lifia and uncover the stone. Lifia wanders down the steps a few paces away from me. Holding the stone out into the dark void, it seems to gleam full of stars, like the night sky.

"Here." Lifia waves me over with the torch. Then she tosses the torch into a raised pit.

As I'm stepping down from the top platform, rings of fire ignite from the pit. The light spreads around the chamber in crevices within the stone. Once the flames meet, they flow up the curved wall of the chamber until they ignite large torches above us. The fire between the stones dwindles while the twelve torches burn above us.

With the entire chamber illuminated, the dark voids

disappear. In their place, colorful depictions cover the wall and ceiling. A grand battle stretches across most of the wall. Figures painted in white defend the pathway leading to the roof. Along the path, stars are connected with narrow lines. The lines form shapes, which are situated to create simple creatures. The painted pathway ends in the center of the ceiling, where moons meet. Depicted in the center of the moon, a disappointed figure looks down on the realm.

Directly below the moons, peeking between the columns, is an altar.

As we walk back up the steps between the columns, I grab Lifia's hand. Her grip is tight and more comforting than anyone's I've felt.

The altar is covered in hardened mud. The circular rings around the altar match some of the shapes that were outlined along the painted pathway. In the center of the platform is a carved notch perfectly cut to fit the stone.

I slide the stone into the notch and turn to Lifia. Her usually expressionless face is filled with worry and curiosity.

"What are you doing with that?" Vzar Musa says.

I gasp as my head starts to swim. I jerk my head around the columns to find where his voice is coming from.

"What's wrong?" Lifia says.

"Musa. He's here," I say.

"Where?" Lifia draws her last arrow.

"You aren't leaving." Musa's hot breath seeps into my ear from behind.

I swing my staff around as hard as I can, but Musa is gone, and my staff slams into a column.

"Where is he?" Lifia follows me with her arrow aligned with the column.

"He's not here, not physically at least. He's trying to stop us from using the gateway." I touch the stone.

Lifia keeps her bowstring tight against her cheek.

"Open the gateway!" I shout.

Musa's maniacal laughter echoes throughout the chamber. He appears across the platform from us.

"What does this usurper mean to you? She's nothing but the infectious remains of a stolen empire," Musa says.

"There. At the center column." I point.

Lifia releases her arrow, and Musa dissipates into a fog before the arrow can penetrate his heart.

"He can't do anything here. I feel his powers weakening," I say.

With one hand on the stone, I reach the other toward the ceiling. My hands begin to tingle with the familiar sense of being so cold that I can barely feel them. The presence matures in my body, and everything becomes balanced. A bluish light emanates from the stone. This time, I imagine a doorway opening to the Torish Desert in front of me. Geometric light beams in three distinct rays from the crest of the stone. The end of the rays outline a triangle in the space in front of us. Light bolts from the corners of the triangle, and the gateway begins to open.

Musa appears in front of the gateway. I step around the altar to meet him. His eyes flicker in contrast to the light rays forming the gateway.

"You disappoint me. It seems you are still unable to complete a simple ritual. Do you need another lesson?" His eyes ignite in violet radiance as he grabs me.

We tumble into darkness as the chamber fades away. Musa attempts to take control. His fingernails scrape through my skin, and it feels like they are ripping at my soul. A stinging pain, like a swarm of jellyfish, engulfs me. My muscles are being pulled from my bones while my mind is being uprooted from my head. We are fighting for each fiber of me. Refusing to be shucked free of my body, I push back. We are whirling through empty darkness, fighting for control. There's no ground below us or sky above us.

"You will never have control of me again," I shout.

"I will have control of you, my tender watcher. You are not ready for these powers, and you don't know who you are." Musa squeezes my arms.

It feels like the bones in my forearms are going to shatter.

"I'm Kaison Foyd, son of Joleen. I may be nothing to you, but I exist," I shout.

"Son of Joleen? The treacherous servant who stole you away? No. You are not the son of Joleen. You are one of us, and far above any empress of Elybion. Together we will vanquish her unwarranted life. Come. I'll show you the true capabilities of your powers." Musa slightly loosens his grip.

One of them? Stolen? I don't believe him. It's not true.

"No." I squeeze him as blue light explodes in the darkness around us. "I won't fall for your lies."

Everything shakes until the chamber tightens back around us.

"Kai. Kai." Lifia is shaking me.

The gateway is fully formed. Through the portal is a view from the sky down on the desert.

"Lifia. Let's go." I grab her hand.

I replace the stone in its pouch and let the necklace drop and sway around my neck as we step toward the sand blowing in.

"I'm with you," Lifia says.

I push my staff through the portal to the dry air on the other side. My shoulder follows. Right before my head enters, Lifia tugs on my other hand. When I glance back, Musa is pulling her away.

"Lifia!" I reach back for her.

Musa is grinning while his vile hands wrap around Lifia's arm. Anger grows inside me until I'm saturated, and it pours out of me like rain. My eyes narrow, and all fear leaves me. I will return the pain he has given me, if nothing else.

"Let go!" I yell.

This time, the power gushes through me. I reach through the space and grab Musa's throat. I can feel him trying to swal-low, but my squeeze is too powerful. He releases Lifia, falls from my grasp, and fades into a thin mist. When I try to step out of the portal, my weight is too much on the other side.

"Lif—" I reach.

She realizes I can't come back and jumps to grab my hand. Catching her and bringing her in is the only thing that matters. I'm screaming inside at the stone to help us. Our fingers slip past each other as I fall through.

A crackle of thunder sounds below me as I crash into the cool sand. My staff snaps in half, and the light around me fades, as does my consciousness.

CHAPTER THIRTY-FOUR

The Admirer

Nok

WINTER S15, 51 AE

A hot torch burns across the sky as I guide Braydenwolf away from Vzar Musa, down the main road, and after Kyber. Thunder crashes below the city. The Climber? It must have crashed below. The danger surrounding Lifia and Kai seems to grow with each passing moment. Kyber yanks the reins of his horse back toward us. He draws his arrow in aim at the fire god igniting behind me. Beyond Kyber, toward the western gate of the Crossing, his men fight a flood of Magnavozians. For so long I've wanted to see Kyber again. Yet now that I'm this close,

I don't want him to see me. His eyes catch my thoughts. My beard and my aged face aren't enough to hide me. Kyber relaxes and turns his aim to the road.

"Nok?" He raises his face guard to reveal his delicate features.

I want to stop, but there is no time. I urge Braydenwolf onward. Kyber releases an arrow behind me. The arrow is intercepted by a growing ball of flame that swirls around the menacing Venith. Sweat pours down my back. My scorched body remains warm from the growing monster who follows.

Instincts take control of my hands to jerk my reins to the right. We turn down a narrow street as a fireball explodes down our former path. Kyber flees by as I lead Braydenwolf in a half circle. Soldiers scream as their skin burns through their armor. The sounds are so terrifying that my joints ache.

"This is your moment, Braydenwolf. Your return to glory lies upon a path of flames." I pat the horse's neck and kick my heels into his ribs.

With a hard yank, I direct Braydenwolf through the alley and down another street heading east to west. Together we ride toward the line of Aptorian warriors.

Once I reach the back of the Aptorians, I yank the reins back to the main road. When we break through, Jupp and Marr are leading an assault against the west wall, while Kyber leads a barrage of arrows back east, toward Vzar Musa.

"Go back to your home." A large dregadin points me away as I emerge.

Other city folk flee in the direction the dregadin points in, but I remain. A wall of soldiers guards his back, and his armor is stretched into a fortress across his breast. A feathered hand is etched into the space across his chest piece. He draws his oversize bow to confirm his identity. He is the Bull of Dalveri.

The Bull releases three arrows at Musa. The arrows are all poorly aimed, and they soar high over the Venith's shoulder.

"Freden. Direct your men to the gates." Kyber situates his horse between a line of archers and the Bull.

Kyber's eyes find me again. I don't know if I should flee or fight. The walls enclose us as more Magnavozians replace the ones Jupp and Marr have cut down.

"Nok, on me." Kyber slings his bow around his back and equips his long lance.

When I motion Braydenwolf to fall in line behind Kyber, an explosion of fire engulfs the archers. Braydenwolf bucks. I squeeze my legs around him as tight as I can manage while I grip his mane. The smoke subsides, but the odor of seared flesh remains. Kyber rolls in pain on the ground with his burnt hands holding on to his face guard. His screams cut through the battle-field like a pungent herb through a bland broth. It's undeniable. I leap off Braydenwolf to help Kyber. Alerted by the screaming dregadin, Jupp fights back to our side of the attack, while Marr continues to fight alongside the Aptorians. I reach down to try to help Kyber, but he screams in more agony when I touch his face guard.

"Help us, Jupp," I say.

Jupp has a wide stance. His shield is the only thing between Musa and the rest of us. Vzar Musa is close enough to hear us speaking but far enough away to remain out of the reach of a lance. The seven fireballs fly around him like vultures around a kill. His arms stretch to the farthest sides of his reach. He's com-pletely still besides his lips, which mumble incantations.

A moment passes, and Musa remains still. Kyber has quit his screams to make low grunting moans. Jupp remains as still as Musa. Then the Bull and five other archers release their arrows. Musa reveals no flinch as the flames form a wall to intercept the arrows.

"Warrior. Take the prince and go," the Bull says.

Jupp glances back at the Bull.

"Please. The prince is everything for our cause," the

Bull says.

"He's right. This battle of fire is not your fight." I pull Kyber up and lead him to Braydenwolf.

"Rampar." The Bull grips the shoulder of one of his soldiers. "Lead them out. The prince must survive."

"You're right. His fight is with another." Jupp turns away from the mumbling man.

Musa's hands no longer extend as far as he can reach. They are pulled up tight to his throat. I push Kyber onto Braydenwolf, pull myself up, and follow Jupp and Rampar, who is now mounted on his siege horse.

"Protect the prince at all costs," the Bull says as I pass him.

Jupp slams his shields together and leads the charge, breaking through the first two soldiers to meet Marr. Then Rampar, followed by three mounted soldiers, takes over the lead. I gallop behind them all with Kyber in my arms.

CHAPTER THIRTY-FIVE

The Runner

Lifia

WINTER S15, 51 AE

The light fades in a flash, and Kai is gone, along with the triangle that he stepped through. A simple tug kept me from going through the gateway. Now I'm alone in the chamber. I can't linger. I need to find another way out. Cinching my cloak around my waist, I run around the columns, to the entrance, and into the dark tunnel. I'm running like I always have, and like I fear I always will.

CHAPTER THIRTY-SIX

The Outsider

Kai

WINTER S15, 51 AE

My ears ring as I drag my face out of the sand. I gather the broken halves of my staff in a dizzy crawl while my hearing continues to buzz. I try to stretch my jaw and crack my ears, but no relief follows. A tingling numbness in my body is replaced by cooling sensations as the breeze flows down the dunes. I cinch the edges of my cloak up to my jawline as I search over the sands. Rolling dunes break in all directions. My throat sticks as I try to swallow. I spin, trying to find my bearings. As I rotate, a dark-cloaked figure peeks from the other side of a dune.

"Lifia?" I yell.

No sound follows, but the figure ducks behind the sand and disappears. I grab my throat. I can feel the vibrations, but my ears hear nothing over the humming chime. I stretch my jaw and press my palms against my ears until they form a suction. I peel both hands away and let them fall. My fingers frantically follow the leather string draped around my neck. The stone is nestled in its pouch, more silent than ever. With or without my hearing, I need to leave, but where am I?

I start to travel east with the sun rising in my face. The breeze shifts into more powerful winds, and I cover my face with the remaining cloak.

I stretch my jaw once more. Then an explosion of bursting wind blows over me as my hearing instantly returns. I fall to one knee. Now I can hear all the swirling winds, sweeping over the dunes like a band of misfit bards. The breeze of bards relents to another sound.

"Second! Please, second!" a boy cries out behind me.

I turn to face him. He's standing at least a ship's length away. We share a staring contest. He's a young boy, no older than twelve. He's dressed in black robes, which contrast with the white sands. His soft face is the only bit of skin showing.

"Greetings." I wave.

The boy cautiously steps forward. He seems interested, but he doesn't trust me.

"Can you help me?" I say.

"Why weren't you listening to me? I was trying to tell you it's not safe to go that way," he says.

"I couldn't hear you, but now I can." I take a step forward, and he takes a step back. I open and show my palms to him. He stops his retreat.

"I don't know who you are, but I mean no harm. Where are we?" I say.

"I saw you fall from the sky," he says.

"Did you? Did anyone else fall?" I say.

"No. Just you. You fell and lay in the sand for a long time. Then you got up and started walking the wrong way, but you wouldn't listen to me," he says.

"Why is this the wrong way?" I point toward the sun.

"The storms are coming, and sandrunners will follow the storm." He walks to me. "They eat the crawlers and anything else uncovered by the winds."

Sandrunners are man-sized, flightless birds. My mother used to tell me cautionary stories about the sandrunners chasing children who wander too far from home. I'm still not sure if the creature exists outside the stories.

"Do you want to trade my directions for your goods?" the boy says.

"Trade me? What do you want?" I hold back a chuckle.

"I like your batons. We don't have strong wood like that here."

"What's your name?" I say.

"My name is Ash. Do you want to trade or not?" he says.

"These? Fine, they're yours." I pass my broken staff to him. He yanks the pieces away and shoves them into his bag.

"Follow me. The sandrunners will be here soon." He looks beyond me and then turns in the opposite direction.

I look around to nothing but sand. Then I shrug and follow behind him.

●

Their tent is enormous and appears much larger on the inside than on the outside. Many layers of thick hides cover the wooden stakes that form the tent. The interior is decorated with bright colors, which are often rare for the deserts of Ariland. A gorgeous green cactus sprouts flowers. Pale pink fairy dusters hang from fresh twigs woven into the hides. The desert flowers were my mother's favorite. She told us of them many times, but I've never seen them until now.

"They are so sweet, but you have to grind them away to get to the sweetness," she said.

In the corner of the tent, near the fire, an older man who bears a resemblance to the boys sits with his side facing me. He could be an uncle, father, or a grandfather, because his age is difficult to measure.

"The light shone in the sky, and then it faded. I followed the light to where it landed, and that's how I found him," Ash says.

"Is that so?" the woman says.

"I promise, Mother," Ash says.

His mother remains silent and shakes her head in disapproval.

"Are you thirsty?" the boy says.

Before I can answer, the man turns and stands up. The roof of the tent is well above his head, yet he is bending at his waist as he steps toward me.

"Don't start giving our camel milk to this stranger...this outsider." The man spits with rude intent.

"I don't mean to intrude. I'm only trying to find where I am so that I can leave in the direction I need to go in," I say.

"Mother, he's lost. We need to help him," Ash says.

The man grunts and waves me off before he sits back down.

"You're right in the middle of the Torish Desert. Only a fool wouldn't know where he was in the desert." He leans back and pulls a pinch of herb from his pocket. Stuffing the pinch into his pipe, he reaches out with a twig into the fire. The lit twig carries the flame to his herb-filled pipe, and white smoke begins to puff out the end. "I find it hard to believe you are out here alone. There isn't water for miles, and you don't seem to have any possessions besides your sticks."

"Torish Desert?" I look toward the opening in the tent as sand blows in.

Many moons would come and go before a traveler could go from the Crossing to the northern edge of the desert on horse-back. Ash looks at me, expecting me to explain, but I can't in a way they would understand.

"You have a funny look about you. Don't lie to me." The man points at me with his pipe, becoming angrier with me.

"My name is Kaison Foyd. I'm a traveler from the far North. I've been traveling with a few companions, including two Illitaww men, a Fangourian woman, and my new acquaintance, um...a Magnavozian man." The man scoffs as I continue to explain. "I've lost them and my direction. If this is the Torish Desert, I've found my target, though I'm not familiar with the area," I say.

"You damn sure are in the desert, and I have never heard of someone traveling with Illitaww men and living to tell of it." The man laughs.

Around the hut, there are various trinkets and glass bottles filled with herbs, and dirt.

"I'll take my leave. Thank you," I say.

"Ah, no. The dust storms are coming tonight, and your body will turn up again. Ash, get him some camel milk. The sun has taken the boy's mind. I don't want you dead in my tent today," he says. The man gets up laughing and walks out of the tent.

We drink the milk in the shelter for a while. Ash tells me how his brothers are doing his work today, since they buried him in the sand the day before.

"Did you say your name was Foyd?" Ash's mother says.

"Yes, that's right. Kaison Foyd," I say.

"I used to know some of the people named Foyd. It's a

common name though, I suppose," she says.

"You know other Foyds?" I say.

"Yes. I once knew a boy. He was a clever lad, and hand-some..." She turns away to blush.

"My mother is from the Torish Lands. Did you know her?" I say.

The woman turns back with her eyebrows raised. She studies me.

"Your face does look familiar. It's your nose. I've seen people with your narrow nose," she says.

"Her name was Joleen, Joleen Foyd. She passed last year." I take another serving of milk from Ash and chug it.

The woman stops and turns back to continue her work.

"No, I didn't know your mother. I'm sorry," she says. "Ash, get our guest some cactus fruit. I apologize for my broth-er. You can't be too careful here. There are more thieves in this land than working men these days," she continues.

"I would gratefully help you with...whatever work you need," I say.

"No, no. Thank you for your offer. We'll help you get point-ed in the right direction tomorrow, but tonight you'll be our guest. No offense, but you don't have the look of a root farmer." She smiles. "Ash, take Kaison to the water tent. There's plenty of water and a sleeping mat in the back."

Ash smiles at me with his big front teeth poking out from under his thick lips, and waves at me to follow him.

"Don't drink the water outside the tent," she says.

The sun has risen much higher since I first entered the tent. The tiny village of nine tents is abandoned except for a couple of young girls doing their chores. Vultures circle overhead. Every-thing about the village is minimalistic. Piles of roots lie outside the tents. The area is lower in the ground than the surrounding mounds. The ground is firm, consisting of less loose sand.

Young Ash leads me to the tent his mother described. The

tent is well-built. There are pits half-filled with water outside the tent. I imagine I could stand in them and have my eyes peering at the surface.

"You can stay here," Ash says.

"Thank you. I don't know where I would've gone without you," I say.

He smiles and lingers. He stares up at me with his big brown eyes, and his front teeth outshining his smaller ones.

"Why were you out there all alone?" I say.

"I'm going to be a great trader one day, like my grandfather. He traveled all over, and he was never afraid. Everyone knew him because he helped them get whatever they needed," he says.

I step back to better take it all in.

"Well, good. You will be a great trader one day," I say.

His mother calls him back, and I step into the tent. Inside, there is a different domain. It's humid, musky, and dark. I pull back the fabric covering the opening to let light in. Containers for water and milk are stacked in the back. Opposite the entrance, a raised bed stands on four legs. The bed is like a long, low table, and I'm certain it's as stiff as it seems. Yet as simple as the bed is, I'm drawn to it. My body is drained like this every time the magic leaves me.

My thoughts shift back to my companions. Did I give Lifia enough time to escape?

"She's too cunning to be captured again," I say.

My voice fades out of the tent and blows away with the sandy wind. From a gateway of lightning to a desert in Ariland? Only by days of travel would I ever be able to reach here. The gateway magic is something beyond my understanding.

I open the leather pouch containing the stone. It gleams from deep inside its core. There's more to the stone than wild magic, and the gateway helped harness it. Passing the gem from one hand to the other, I begin to examine it. I feel a connection to the stone more than ever. It's like I'm holding hands with someone. As if the stone can hear my thoughts, it shakes, and I drop it to the ground.

I don't retrieve it from its resting place on the foreign sand. Sleepiness overwhelms me, and I lie back on the firm bed.

☽

Sometime later I awake in a sweat, with feeble legs. As I'm losing my balance, Vzar Musa's eyes flash in front of me. I swat him away as I fall to my knees, my side, my face, and back to sleep.

"In here?" a stern voice says from outside the tent.

"Yes, the boy is in there," Ash's mother says.

I'm collapsed on the ground, breathing into the sand on the tent floor.

"He seems like a kind man," she says.

"Mm-hmm, yes," the stern voice responds to quiet her stammering.

The man pushes the material covering the opening. A full moon shines behind him, creating a perfect outline of the man. He is a bearded man wrapped in a hooded robe.

"He is strong-willed. It looks like he was able to gain some footing, if only for a moment," the bearded man says.

My jaw barely moves when I try to speak. It feels swollen shut. Everyone seems calm, and I don't feel in danger. Still, why would someone do this to me? I'm listening for signs of Ash or anyone who might help me.

"How much of the potion did you give him?" the bearded man says.

"Hardly any, only a few drops. It's too valuable to use any

more than that," she says.

I attempt to stand as the man comes closer to me, but my body doesn't obey. My chest is beating harder and harder, like I'm being crushed. I try to speak again, but nothing sounds. The man grabs me and lifts me up.

"It's all right, son. Your voice will come back to you," he says.

I'm screaming inside. He squats down and throws my entire body over his shoulder with a grunt and a heave.

With my vision fixed on the ground, the bearded man carries me outside. He comes to a stop a few paces from the tent, lays my body across the back of a camel, and secures me in place. All the while, I'm kicking my legs, and they aren't moving.

"I apologize if the ropes are tight. I can't lose you when we go through the sandstorms," he says.

He rubs my scalp with his hand like a man petting a dog. All the while, I'm trying to yell at him to stop or to put me down. Nothing comes out besides a shallow moan.

"The toxin was unnecessary, Lady Saiban. You Saibans have always been fond of your concoctions. Still, you have done the right thing, hailing us," he says.

"Wait. He had this with him." The sandal slapping pauses when she speaks to him.

"Yes. There it is. My old friend," he says.

We ride through the night. I fall in and out of sleep along the way. Each time I wake, I can move a little more of my body. First, I can roll my lips and my tongue. I can squeeze my fingers and almost make a fist. The man in the robe rides on his separate camel ahead of me, guiding my camel with a lead.

"Are you breathing back there?" he says.

He doesn't expect a response, but he is friendly when he speaks. My neck is heavy, and when I open my eyes, I only see sand illuminated by the bright full moons above.

Finally we come to a stop. The camels both grunt their long grumbling complaints as we slow and circle around. The bearded man dismounts and walks over to me.

"We have arrived, son." He removes the rope that tethers me to the animal.

He gathers me up, like before, and carries me on his back. I watch his feet sink into and rise out of the sand with each step he takes. I sense movement ahead, followed by a voice.

"Please let me take him," a voice says.

"No. I have him. Go tend to the camels," the bearded man says.

Without objection, feet scurry past us in the sand. We continue forward.

The ground turns from soft sand into a hard, crafted floor. The man's sandals start to clap on the floor with each step. The rocky hard floor changes to a smooth, brushed hard floor as we continue underneath a covering above us. I can smell the burning of torches, and I see the flicker of torchlight reflecting on the floor from a flame burning above. We continue down this torchlit path for a while.

We come to the end of the long path and the torchlight fades. However, there is another light growing from above. The light is of the moons, and it soaks into the mosaic stone floor. The man sits me up in a chair at the end of the path. Light seeps through an opening above me. I can't move my neck, and my vision is fixed a few feet in front of me. The man who carried me disappears into the darkness. A crowd gathers at the edge of the light of the moons. I try to yell out. This time, my voice makes a sound, and a scratchy holler rushes out.

"No need to be afraid." The man steps back out of the darkness.

He lowers his hood and reveals a bald scalp, and his face is illuminated by the light coming in through the opening above. I realize I've been here before. I was here in a vision at Simb's Point, and this must be another vision or dream.

"I am Agonok." He takes another step toward me. "And they are all your brothers and sisters."

Agonok raises his hands and swings them across the room. Some of the people step out of the darkness and closer into the light.

"Agonok, give him the stone," an elderly woman says.

He looks back at her for an extended moment, contemplating an action, and he returns to me.

"Yes. The poison... We wanted you to come here, but not like this. I'm sorry," he says.

He takes the Art Stone and unwraps it from its casing. Immediately it shines bright, brighter than I've ever seen. It absorbs the light all around it, and it grows brighter in his hands.

"Here you are. The stone will heal you if you allow it," Agonok says.

People cinch around me in curiosity as the stone glows in my lap. I can feel it attempting to connect with me, but I resist. The crowd releases elated groans as the stone flashes in a pulse.

"The stone will heal you, but you must allow it to," Agonok says.

"Wake up. Wake up." My heavy, numb tongue slurs my speech.

It's not a dream. The stone calls for me again. It's like it's calling my name through waves of silence. Is this the cradle I've been searching for? The stone pulses in response to my thoughts. Are these the Xyji? The stone pulses again. *Yes.* I understand it, and it understands me, even without words. I reach for it with my cupped hand. My first finger barely grazes its surface. The glow from the stone grows until the stone fractures into four distinct pieces and the light escapes.

No. It's like it has sacrificed itself for me. Tears pour out of my eyes, tears for the severed last connection to the people I love.

My hands loosen, and my sandy tongue flops back within my control. My lungs, which were breathing on their own, are next to come back under my control. I exhale slowly. As I let out the last pinch of the thick air, the strangers let out whispers of awe.

"He is...one of us." Agonok raises his hands.

CHAPTER THIRTY-SEVEN

The Defender

Jupp

WINTER S15, 51 AE

With the Bridge City behind us, we charge into the battle alongside northern warriors. I wasn't sure if I could trust them, but Marr believes they are honorable people. They found him and invited him into their ranks when he climbed out of the canyon. Focusing on my brother's breath, I hear a slow stream of air flowing out past his lips. A steady grip on the hilts of his blades reflects a calmness inside. The Erowkahnn elders preach about control of body and mind. Marr closes in on the prey that is his own self-control.

Marr is swifter than me now, but he still runs behind me. The great shield weighs upon my back, and the bucklers sway upon my hips, which restricts me from stretching out in stride. Yet he would still have a longer stride if we were both unencumbered.

Marr has surpassed me in every way in which an Illitaww man is judged. He knows the old ways by heart, and he was born for battle. His face is expressionless, and there are no thoughts beyond the specific task ahead. There is no one better to have alongside me.

"*Wrekk!*" I bash my shields together.

"*Wrekk!*" Marr echoes.

How did we find this most glorious of battles? A group of farm children flees from the direction the Aptorians are antagonizing in. Farther beyond, a group of Magnavozian soldiers dot the distant grasses in their crimson armor. Their colored banners distinguish them as our enemies, and their armor, which crumples easily, provides less protection than subtlety.

"Focus." I wave my shield from Marr to our Aptorian companions.

Without hesitation, Marr sprints to our new allies. I turn my attention to the children.

Closing in on the children, I send a glance to Marr right when an enemy archer lines up for a counterattack.

"Range!" I yell.

Marr intercepts an arrow with the broad side of his offhand blade. His timing is perfect. The shards of arrow sprinkle on the ground. He is more formidable with every day we spend in the North. The Aptorian archers alter their sights toward the Magnavozian archer in response.

Three stray soldiers chase the children, climbing up the hill toward me. Why would the Magnavozian soldiers chase their own people? My heart aches for the children caught in the battle. The soldiers were smart or lucky enough to avoid the

Aptorian assault, but they are still unwise enough to enter my domain.

Proclaiming my battle cry, I prepare my body for combat. With an invigorated temper, I leap over one of the children. The jump springs me into an alignment of one of the soldiers and my main-hand shield. I slam the edge of the shield into his throat, setting into motion impending suffocation. Spinning around, I catch a second soldier in the chest with my off hand, which hurls him backward off his feet. The soldier struggles to regain his breath, but the attack wasn't lethal. I sense movement, and I can smell fear over my right shoulder. The third soldier takes a hesitant step backward. He stabs at me with his long spear. Whacking his spear aside as he jabs it toward me, I locate a weakness in his attack. He drops his shoulder and twists his hand palm upward at the end of each jab. Upon his next jab, I whack his weapon to the ground with my off hand and drive my main hand down hard on the head of the spear, thus snapping the spearhead off the end. Like a beaten animal, he shifts into a flight, fleeing my grasp.

The second, small-headed soldier stands to gather himself. He is brave to continue to fight, but the gods will not favor him on this day. In the distance, behind the soldier, Marr sprints back toward me. He catches the retreating soldier with a throwing knife before I lose sight of him behind a wall of Aptorian marchers. The recovering, small-headed soldier spits blood as he curses at me.

"I'll put you down, mutt," he says.

The derogatory term, used by people from the North to brand my people as less, angers me more than I should allow. I rush the soldier, tackling him off his feet. In a fit of rage, I smash both of my shields into his chest, caving in the metal casing of his armor.

I want to keep smashing the soldier until he's buried in the ground, but the others have reached me. Marr hooks me under my shoulder to pull me up, out of my fury. As we run, Marr mumbles a battleground prayer under his breath.

Magnavozian horns sound from the farm. Nok, holding on to the Aptorian prince, pushes a stampede of Aptorian riders around the eastern plains. A pack of soldiers on horseback pursue them from the west. I shake my head in disbelief.

"May the Scalar Winds guide you." I raise my shield to salute him.

The remaining Aptorian archers are diminished in number and vigor when they reach us. Their eyes tell me they are fresh to battle, and most of them would leave it forever if given the opportunity.

"Do you have somewhere you can go?" an Aptorian archer asks the children.

The youngest one snivels as he begins to shake. Children of the North are different from ours, who scratch their way through the tundra.

The Magnavozian rulers take from everyone. They consume more than their fill, and everyone starves for it. I always knew the northerners lived poorly, but I never imagined how much they hurt each other. The Illitaww nation will not experience the tyranny of the Magnavoz. The Magnavozian armies will never be able to conquer our harsh homeland. They would perish at the sight of a real horde of warriors.

"It's a time for running and reformation," I say.

Appearing over the hill, near the origin of the altercation, a squad of soldiers blare their horns. They are advancing. The archer peers in the same direction and lets out an audible sigh. Their numbers are large, and we will not be able to protect the children and fight well enough to win.

"Marr and I will supply you the time to get them to safety," I say.

"I was hoping you would say that," Marr says.

"Still thirsty for blood, my brother?" I say.

Pure calmness emanates from him, and his eyes stare straight without a blink. He is analyzing our enemy. Now his prowess exceeds my own.

The archer begins to speak, but he stops and confirms with a nod.

"*Drah! Drahkua! Drah, drah, drahkua!*" Marr and I shout in unison as I bash my shields together, and he draws his swords of war.

The archers ride off with the strays.

"Remember the story about Sakk and Throh?" I say.

Marr glances at me with his young eyes. His teeth start to form a smile. Yet he wants nothing more than to gnash at someone.

"How could I forget? You requested the story every day from our den-mother," he says.

"Yes, my brother. Sakk and Throh were surrounded by a legion from the jungles of Fangour. If you recall, Throh used two shields for weapons, forgoing the use of an ax or sword, as is customary for an Illitaww warrior. He protected his sister while she landed devastating flanking blows. Sakk was always safe with her brother to shield her vulnerabilities." I wave my shields around in a cocky display.

"Yes, brother. You may have taken that story a bit literally," he says.

I shake my limbs loose, crack my neck, and stretch my arms wide.

"Sakk and Throh faced a great legion together that day and avoided a glorious death. Sakk was never touched, and Throh never missed a block," I say.

The Magnavozian squad is within earshot. The archers begin to take aim at us.

"And why are you repeating the legend now?" Marr swings his swords around in a taunting manner.

"When the story was retold to us, they never said how

many soldiers were in the Fangourian legion. So how do we know when we have become legends ourselves?" We let out a roar as we begin to charge forward into our heaven that is battle.

The land shifts from flat farmland to rolling hills as large mesas grow in the distance. The sky is painted with blue, heavy clouds, and sunlight cutting through. The clouds create spots of sun and shade as we step from cover to sunshine. Everything is open, and we can see for many miles all around.

As we charge, my thoughts go somewhere else. Memories of my home in past springtimes sprout in my head. Dreams of my brother, Marr, and me learning and crafting the skills we use to bring glory to our clan. Everything built us up for this day. I take notice of the great-shield resting on my back.

☾

Lakk, my father, sits comfortably in his chair adorned with tiger pelts. He holds a somber expression. We are alone in his tent while the camp remains silent and shrouded in the dark-ness of a moonless night. The great Shield of Erowkahnn leans against his chair, with a polishing silk draped over it. In the center, between us, fire burns brightly.

"Marr and I are leaving. We are going north to complete the trial," I say.

He doesn't want us to go, but this day was fated since our beginning. He created peace in our land, so we would not need to fight. Yet in peace, our hunger for glory has grown.

"Father, our path is not forged out of disrespect." I glide around the fire to meet him.

"Something to prove?" he says.

Our path is molded out of the respect for who our father is and who his sons are expected to be. As the sons of Lakk, we have always had more to prove.

"Yes. We have something to prove, but not to you or to our people. We have something to prove to ourselves," I say.

Lakk stands and heaves the great-shield up and carries it to me. My mouth clamps and my fists tighten.

"The Shield of Erowkahnn is yours to carry," he says.

His response shakes me. I stutter and struggle to find the words to respond.

"I...cannot carry the shield while you stand. It can only be carried by the strongest among us." My eyes fixate on the shield.

To me, the shield is a treasure more valuable than any other. To our people, the shield and its carrier represent an impenetrable leader.

"The old ways are fading, son, and I have already made the trade. This is only a tool. Our people have attached great value to it, but it is useless without someone to wield it." He drops the shield into my arms.

The shield is light for its size, but heavy regardless.

"Father?" I say.

"Without your mind, the tools I give you are no better given to a tortoise. The tortoise may know when to hide behind his shield, but he doesn't know how to make you focus on his shield while his mind is working out a way to counter," he says.

His words are a recurrence of knowledge he has shared many times before. His arms wrap around me in a hug.

"Listen for Sedann's words. She will guide you home," he says.

I shrug my shoulders to readjust the great-shield. Our home is very different from the rest of the world, and I didn't realize the solemnity of that truth until we left. The northern people are soft and only desire comfort and safety. Most of them are born into stations with little opportunity to rise. The farmers raise other farmers, who plant seeds to grow more farmers. In Illitaww, our station is not secured, and not perpetual.

Marr's eyes flicker at me. I turn back around, shove my hands through the leather straps of my shields, which tighten around my forearms. My blood heats, swelling my muscles.

"Together!" I shove my shield into the air without looking back at him.

Before the words leave the cords in my throat, I hear the sweet chime of his blades unsheathing from their rest. The sound is sharp, and it echoes for a moment. It's a melody that reminds me of ice and the cold.

With separation from our enemies, we slow to a walk. I shake my arms to loosen the swelling. Many soldiers draw closer.

"*Wrekk*!" Marr rolls over my back. I push him off with a grunt as he whirls his blade into an arc, brushing the sky as the tip of his blade glints in the light. The pureness of the attack is beautiful, in the way only a master of a craft could show. His arcing edge swoops down, and his second blade follows with a low horizontal sweep, cutting two men at the knees. I step back, leading with my heel to rest my back against his before I pick my next assault.

"Pace!" I shout.

The command is intended to slow Marr's assault, because I need the moment to read the field for an opportunity. They continue to march in higher numbers in the distance. I spot the trail leading up one of the smaller mesas. Marr slashes down more in front of us, giving us space to reestablish ourselves on the higher ground. My pride wants us to stay, but the tactical option prevails.

"Upland!" I shout.

Marr delivers another killing blow. Then we retreat up the trail as more Magnavozian warriors flood behind us.

Outmatched in number only, we counter every assault. Their movements are slow and predictable, making their numbers weigh less along the narrow pathway. Marr slashes through one as we climb farther up the mesa. Switching positions, I leap down, smashing my shields into the head of the chokworm. Marr claims higher ground as I defend us. One of their archers releases an arrow at us. The arrow misses us and finds a way between the creases in the armor of another soldier. The wounded soldier tumbles back down the pathway and over the edge. The archers attempt more pricks, and their attack is simple to anticipate. I absorb several arrows with one shield and smash my other shield into oncoming soldiers. My blow shatters the crimson metal covering a man's nose. His eyes roll back, and he falls into the flood of soldiers.

Marr moves elegantly with every slash. His speed has evolved to another level beyond mine. Each time I block an assault from an enemy, Marr is slicing through ahead of me. I want to tell him to slow his pace to conserve energy, but his breathing is smooth, and his movements aren't labored.

I see the glorious challenge we face as the army begins to coordinate more effectively against us. They are slower at devising war tactics and much more willing to risk the lives of their men. Yet they are not stupid.

A few well-aimed arrows ricochet off Marr's blades, and I catch a third in my shield. Marr glances at me, expecting me to give an order. We reach the highest ground of the upland. From here, we can see the long tail of the army marching from the south. We have more space from the edge than we have in the fighting pits. Today the pit walls have been replaced by a deadly fall surrounding us.

"Tighten!" I say.

Our backs meet upon the top of the hill. I heave the great-shield off my back and over my head to replace one of the smaller shields.

"*Drah! Drahkua! Drah, drah, drahkua!*" Marr shouts.

Our enemies, gathered all around, hesitate to attack us. Marr swings his swords around to loosen his grip and refocus his attack. Besides the path we climbed to reach this summit, there are two paths across the flat peak. The Magnavozian peons rush up all three tracks to meet us. From here we have the advantage, and they are limited to four or five men on our plane.

As the paths leading to our position begin to fill with crimson armor, we continue to fight with balance. They can't break our defenses in this formation. However, our attacks are slower, and Marr must time his fatal blows perfectly. We are well-conditioned, yet as I look beyond the view right in front of us, I see many more soldiers on the paths. For the first time, I question if our endurance will be enough.

I yell as I kick my foot into the chest of a soldier. He flies over the edge, disappearing below our view. Attempting to match, Marr sends a heavy boot into the face guard of another. His boot smashes into the soldier's helmet, causing it to crumple. The soldier panics, drops his weapons, and runs off the edge while fighting suffocation.

Rumblings bellow out from the sea of soldiers. Their armor clangs as they attempt to scatter. The leaders are shouting commands to run out of the way. A man rivaling me in size steps out in front of the line of soldiers on the low ground. We continue to fight off the ones right in front of us, yet as we do, he begins his climb. He shoves his allies out of his way as he ascends. Several soldiers fall over the edge in peril as he forces his way up. With warming blood, I signal to Marr, but he's already aware. We begin to fight our way toward the opening to the path that the large one climbs. He's staring us down like a bonecrusher watching an ice cat gorge on a carcass, and waiting for the right moment to strike. Behind the man, an archer steps out. Stepping in front of my brother, I manage to catch an arrow with the great-shield in time for him to roll behind me. His next move is turning back to throw his last dagger down at the archer. The pitch could have landed right in the throat of the archer, but the distance gave him enough time to duck. The knife sails over his head.

A grasp catches my ankle. One of the fallen soldiers crawls toward me with a sword in hand. His will is admirable. Not all northern men are weak, cowardly men. I try to kick off the soldier crawling toward me, but he grips my ankle. He's bleeding, and his mind fades as his breath leaves his body. I kick at him again, and he rolls backward into another body beside me. The distraction causes me to hesitate. Marr looks back at me to find the cause of my hesitation. The moment gives an opportunity to a wily soldier to lunge with his spear at Marr's head. Sensing the strike, Marr rolls away from the spear tip. He spins away and swipes the soldier across the face with a backhanded slash.

Battle-heated blood runs down my brother's cheek. The heat pouring out of his face meets the open air, causing a steady puff of steam to blow out as if it were his mouth. The wind sweeps over us from the south, bringing familiar coolness. Marr puts his hand up to his gouged cheek and wipes the blood away. For a moment, he watches the hot red escaping his body. Then he clenches his fist, gripping it so tight that the blood wrings out through the bottom hole of his tight fist. His fist thrusts into the air while his mouth turns up with a grin. The gouge will only feed him to fight more viciously. He leads with a blood-drenched fist, and I follow behind him with my shields.

For a span, we fight perfectly. I am rock, and Marr is ice. Then the large one reaches the top. Loose scree tumbles, and the other Magnavozian grunts fade behind him. His chest is exposed and scarred. Four slices from nipple to belly show remnants of past battles. His body is strong and hardened, while his face is covered. Only his eyes glare through the tiny slits in the iron. He holds a spear with a dangling red tail at its end.

"You." He points at me.

I bring my shields up so that only my eyes peer over. Most of the soldiers have stopped climbing. Many stand still, while others fight off my beast of a brother. The giant runs at me, slowly at first, then more quickly as he closes in. I wave him in like his challenge is a gift to me from the gods. My feet are squared. He jumps. The light glints off the spear tip as he eclipses the sun. He plunges his spear down toward me when my sight is failing. I block. When he lands back on the ground, he circles around me with his chest pushed out and his arms waving back and forth as he strides.

"You were at the Crossing...I saw you there, with your brother and your trickster," he says.

I raise my hands to attack. Right. Left. Right. Kick. Spin. Block. My shield blunts his spear over and over. He's faster than anyone I've fought, except Marr. I try to catch a peek at my brother to check on him, yet when I do, the giant stabs at me again.

"Your brother is fighting well. He'll kill a few more before I finish you. Illitaww men from the South... I've never met one of you, but now that I have, I believe maybe they're right. The other soldiers say I'm Illitaww. They call me the Northern Wolf. Can you see it, cousin?" He circles around me.

His words hold some truth. His rich brown skin resembles many Illitaww men, but his voice is Northern, along with his mannerisms. He comes closer to tease an attack with his spear. Letting loose a swift jab, he measures the distance between us. As he drags his outreached spear back in, I follow it. He attempts to jab back at me, but I close the distance, and his spear tip slips past me. I drag my heavy shield on the ground until I'm right in front of him. I sweep the great-shield off the ground and through the man. The blow crashes into his chest and cracks his helmet free as he flies back.

He whips his head backward, along with his thick, curly hair, released from the helm. The curls fall into his eyes, obstructing his vision. He growls at me, spits a gob of blood, and chuckles.

"I hoped you were going to give me a fight. I have grown tired of killing feeble men. You must know what I mean," he says.

"I take no pleasure in killing weak men," I say.

He freezes for a moment and stabs his spear into the ground.

"So, you know the common language? Good. Then listen to me. Northern men, southern men, and all women in between, we kill because we must." He points over to Marr carving through two men with a single swipe.

Unsheathing two blades from his boots, he rises up and walks toward me. Block. Stab. Bash. I deliver my shield into his wrist to knock his blade free. Then I lunge for another bash, but I slip on one of the fallen soldiers. The Northern Wolf sneaks a slice across the back of my knee. The wound is repairable, but it diminishes my movement advantage. I spin an attack into his jaw, which sprays red mist and bits of teeth.

In my peripheral vision, I watch a man pull back on a bow. Out of pure instinct, I hurl my shield to cut off the bowman. The shield edge crashes into the bow, cracking it in half.

"*Wrekk*!" Marr raises his blades and swings down through another man. "Flank!"

When I switch back to the Northern Wolf, I'm met with a blade piercing me below my collarbone.

CHAPTER THIRTY-EIGHT

The Hero

Jupp

WINTER S16, 51 AE

King Lakk is the first to greet us after our ascent of the mountain. He presses his thumbs firmly into the front of my shoulders. His eyes are burning cinders in his old age.

"My sons have returned." He releases one of his hands from me and swings it around Marr.

We're both silent and obedient in front of our father, careful not to assume any accomplishment.

"Go ahead. Tell me about your adventures. The sand traders tell me you have both become renowned in such a short time," he says.

We descend the southern path, toward Ruthatt's Glade.

●

When we arrive in the hall, a feast awaits us. Tables are laden with wild game and bowls full of rare berries from the west Illitaww lands. We are handed large wooden cups filled with a fermented seed as we step farther into the hall. The clan stands as we walk to the head table.

All eyes follow the king and his sons on either side. We reach the head of the table and turn to the Illitaww. They hold coy smiles and wait for the king to speak. He raises his hands to touch each of us on our shoulders nearest him.

"My sons...they have completed their task... Our season of war is over. Let this evening mark the beginning of our season of rest, peace, and love." Lakk smiles and gestures for everyone to sit.

His heavy silver ponytail hits the back of his hardwood seat with a thud. I follow my father's gesture and relax into my chair. I send a glance to Marr, who is smiling as he stares at a group of young den-mothers, who exchange giggling whispers across the room.

●

I swallow the sweet morsel of moist longtusk meat when my daughter comes up to me. She takes a step between my legs and nuzzles into my lap. Leaning her ear against the heart side *of my chest, she begins to sing.*

"Cold heart...cold heart... Only a daughter can warm a cold heart. When the mountains sweat their rain, the snows will heal your heart of pain."

My lifemate enters the tent and reaches an arm around our daughter and me to give us both a kiss.

The embrace loosens as Marr pulls away. Lakk, the greatest of us all, has passed from this world, and we all gather to mourn him. Marr is staring into my eyes to gauge my emotions. He is aged and worn in the natural ways, yet he remains handsome.

"Our father was a great man... I know he would rather have died on the battlefield, yet peace for Illitaww was worth the sacrifice," I say.

Marr smiles and steps up to meet me.

"You are king now, brother," he says.

"No. Our father was the only man great enough to be the king of Illitaww, and we shall all be stewards of the legacy he created." I raise my hands to the crowd around us.

The scent of spring blooms wafts in as I bear witness to my son's marriage. He's the most like me, but he favors others more. Closer in stature to his uncle, he favors a young version of

Marr. Yet he is kinder and softer than we were at his age. The beautiful princess from the far North stands beside him with her large crystal-blue eyes. In all my days of battle, nothing compares to the joy I feel now.

I reach down to my sweet twin brother, the last Akkimon, confined to his bed and never to rise again. We are both old, and my vision is weak, but I can see him looking up at me like he did when we fought together many years ago.

"Rest. Your battle was well fought. Let Madokk show you the path to the great lands. I'll follow you shortly, my friend." A single tear rolls down my wrinkled cheek. Before it falls, he takes his last breath and drifts away.

I shake myself free from the vision that is Madokk's grip. I rip the broad blade from my shoulder and spill thick crimson blood. I can't feel the wound, but I watch it pouring out my life. Part of me wants to give in to the grasp already pulling me under. Visions of possibilities fill my mind. Yet I ignore them all as I reach for the great-shield. Death must wait, because my brother needs me.

Marr is rushing back to meet me, but the rivers are keeping him occupied. He slashes fiercely at a speed that only he can manage. His onslaught begins to erode a path. As he carves, more of my life water pours out.

The messenger of my ending stands over me with full intention to deliver the final note. Fear scratches at the back of my mind like an old relative who remembers me from a different time. I'm afraid I won't be accepted into the heavens, and of the possibility that the great lands are only selfish desires of man. The shame of failing emerges and falls to the greater teachings from our father.

Our father would be proud of us on this day. He will hear of our battle on the upland, and he will say it was a magnificent place to fall, in open air, where all the gods can watch.

I grind my teeth so tightly that my back tooth cracks, and bloody snot squeezes from my nose. I summon all my fury. Every part of my being exists for one purpose: to fight until the final end, and not one moment premature. Marr is close enough to see my face. And the entire army is encircled around us. The Northern Wolf laughs and throws a lazy slash to test my strength.

"*Wrekk!*" I yell.

I smash the great-shield into my smaller shield. Marr joins in the battle cry. The Northern Wolf turns to the shout. Before he can complete the turn, I smash my shield into the side of his head. He stumbles back a step. After regaining balance, he returns with a vengeful hack. His power forces my shield below my chest. My arm is too feeble and numb to rise again. He smiles and swings to deliver his note.

Something interrupts his swing. The Northern Wolf bares his teeth and screams. Marr's message is delivered by his blade Harmony. The Northern Wolf spins with Marr's weapon lodged through his back and out of his chest. I step forward to finish the fight, but I collapse with my shield falling to cover me.

In the next moment, the Northern Wolf crashes behind me. His stiff body is the last thing I see before the light leaves my eyes. I hear Marr shouting, but everything else fades, and darkness surrounds me.

CHAPTER THIRTY·NINE

The Wayfarer

Lifia

SPRING M13, 51 AE

The peak of the obsidian pillar juts above the canopies. The rare black glass structure screams power, and it stood for nothing less for centuries.

"We'll depart in two days." The captain, a pale, red-haired man, offers me his hand as I step from the deck to the small transport boat.

He's a kind man who never asked any questions, which was helpful for someone who didn't want to answer any.

The Skyfort's port stretches out a mile from the mainland.

Sparse fishermen and rugged fishing vessels sway among the docks as our transport rides the last waves onto a dark brown and speckled black shore. I grab my possessions and take a long step out of the boat. As I step out, my bundled cape snags on a nail. With my balance compromised, I fail to keep the bow from spilling from its hiding spot in the cape, and it splats onto the moist sand. I throw the cape over the bow in a feeble scramble to hide my truth. My eyes feel like they are protruding from their sockets as I try to hold my breath and analyze the area. I glance back to check if anyone witnessed the reveal. Any native could recognize the bow, and I would be found. I exhale when I realize no one seems to care.

"Do you need a hand, my lady?" A young Fangourian fisherman reaches out.

"No." I reject his offer, gather up the cape, and scurry off to the city, avoiding eye contact all the way.

The Grand Market begins miles up the cobbled road from the shore. Once, it was the center of trade for the entire realm. Cities of Arilandic caravans voyaged in masses to trade their country's crops and valuables, while the Swedans sent ships through the gulf to empty their treasures on our shores. The trading houses and ordinary homes nestled tightly in the shadow of the great Skyfort don't belong in the same painting. The fort is a solid black diamond among rubble. A high gate and wall encircle the Skyfort. Inside the walls lie memories of stairs and walkways spun around my old home. On the outside, a barracks and smaller towers form the meat of the fortress. The towers have a skybridge that leads from their top floor to the bottom half of the Skyfort. Three sibling towers form a dotted line on the back side of the fort, which leads to the forest. All five towers are cold, dark children of the mother in the center. None are as inspiring.

As I draw nearer to the gate, I see two soldiers in dark red armor standing on each side of the entrance to the Grand

Market. I jolt off the path before I'm noticed.

●

Once the sun retreats below the horizon, I walk around the wall to the southern side of the market. Where someone might hope for an entrance, a looming wall impedes further travel. It reaches twenty feet or more from the ground.

Can I climb? Many nights have absorbed many days since I climbed up these stones, but I remember the ways. I rub my hands together firmly to revive them with warmth. After warming my hands, I grab the first hold and steadily begin the climb. At the top, the lip on the wall blocks me from reaching up and over. I backtrack to a part of the wall where the top edge is more worn. On the crumbling face of the wall, the bricks are loose, and one slips away as I step up. I lose my footing and slide back down. Pieces of the wall crumble off with me. I shake my hair free of dust. The descent is a ruckus, and my calm demeanor begins to leak out with the eroding wall.

"Get up." I sprint at the wall, shift my weight into a leap, take two bounds up the brick, and catch a grip in the space where a brick has slipped out.

Boots attached to soldiers thrash through brush as torchlight illuminates my position. I swing my legs over the lip moments before they arrive.

"See, Fadel. There's nothing here. Your mind is tricking you again," one of the voices says.

I listen from the other side of the wall, hanging with both hands on the inner lip. If I let go, they will hear my feet hit the floor below.

"No. I saw something." They hold their position right on

the other side of the wall.

"Fadel, there is no beast. You need to stop speaking non-sense. The others are starting to say things," the soldier says.

"What are they saying?" Fadel says.

Silence follows. Then a rock cracks the wall on the other side of where I am. I hear my beating heart through the veins on the left side of my neck.

"Fine. Let's go," Fadel says.

The torchlight fades as they continue their patrol. I wait a moment before I release my grip and slide down into the market. My heart skips and continues its normal rhythm as I descend.

The market is absent of life. The buildings have broken windows and collapsed roofs, but nothing reeks more of death than the putrid smell of the streets. To the north, the Skyfort towers over the broken city. Yet the Skyfort is separate, whole, and far out of reach.

Traveling down the empty market streets, I replace the existing decay with memories. One building is long, with a raised walkway extending over the road. This building used to house medicines and herbs. On one side of the walkway, there were ground herbs and blended tea leaves. On the other side, flowers bloomed out of the open windows. Now the windows are broken, and nothing living sprouts from them.

Lamps are sprinkled throughout the city, but few are lit, leaving more darkness than light.

"That's mine." A withered man yanks something away from a child.

"Nok?" I whisper.

I'm mistaken. The vagrant isn't Nok or anyone familiar. He's only a poor, sad man with no possessions and little life to enjoy. I sneak behind a building before they see me.

Finally I find the building I've been looking for.

"The Wailing Snake."

The hanging sign is faded, and the paint is mostly washed

away. There is an anvil painted in black on the sign, which suggests there could be a weaponsmith. I'm out of arrowheads, and my bowstring is tattered and frayed. However, I'm not here by chance. My mother took me here to buy my first staff. I roll my possessions into my cloak and hide them under the corner of the building before I enter.

The room falls silent as I pass the threshold. A man fills a row of mugs for three men dressed in dark leather. Other patrons occupy sparse tables away from the bar. At one table, a man sits facing a woman. They whisper as I stride to the bar. At another table, a man is sprawled out with his belly peeking out from under his shirt. His neck is cocked back over the backrest of his chair, and he seems content being asleep in public. The interior is different from the extraordinary shop I remember. The display of exquisite weapons from around the realm has been replaced by a crumbling bar.

"Are you the weaponsmith?" I say.

The barman frowns, an expression full of pity.

I grab a few coins from my bag and slap them down to prove to him that I'm not a beggar.

"Do you have any space? Also, we're in need of a craftsman. Your sign suggests you have the skill," I say.

"'We'?" The barman looks outside.

"Yes. The rest of my crew will be here soon," I lie.

"Yes. I have rooms," the man says.

Around the room, eyes start to flicker to me. The man who passed out over his chair awakes and looks up at me. I reach for my daggers at the small of my back. The barman hands out the drinks to the three figures sitting at the bar. He encourages them to drink, and they turn back away from me.

"You should not be here," the man says.

As he speaks, I slide my weapons free. Everyone can see the glint of light reflecting from the edges of my blades, yet they remain calm. No one moves. I begin a retreat through the door.

Exhaling to calm myself, I'm ready to end anyone who attempts to stop me.

"Well, just because you shouldn't be here doesn't mean I don't have a room for you," the man says.

"What?" My feet stick to the dark wooden floors.

"The room is on me." The man who was asleep when I entered stands.

"You don't have the coin, Soda. How about you pay off your debts before you offer rooms at my establishment?" The barman shakes his head.

Soda sits back into his seat. My wrists loosen on my daggers, and I look firmly at the barman.

"Your Imperial Majesty, please have a seat." The barman points to a stool.

My heart feels like it's dropping out of my chest.

"My name is Hiro Geotakhashni. I served the late empress," he says.

In an instant, I recall his name. He is the type of man I hoped to find here, but where does his loyalty lie now?

"Lord Hiro?" I say.

I never saw a clear sight of his face, but his voice is stout, and it rings back from my memories. It was a great honor to be a throne guard, and only the most loyal families had a representative enlisted.

"What armor did you wear?" I say.

"The boa," he says.

"Yes."

His rich voice matches a voice from my memories. It was the same rich voice that sang from the watchful guard who wore the snake helm. I look around, wondering if the other occupants are to be as easily trusted.

"Don't worry, they are allies. We are all allies here. It seems you've wandered into the only building in the city full of loyal Fangourians. I don't believe this is by chance," he says.

Soda raises himself and bows to me. He's goofy, and I struggle not to smile at his sloppy bow.

"There aren't many in the city who are still loyal to the Evoni," Hiro says.

"How did you know?" I say.

He chuckles. For a simple man, his laugh is bold.

"You look exactly like Her Imperial Majesty the Empress Dianame. There is no one else you could be, and I would not forget a face like yours," he says.

The others stand, take a step forward, and bow. One of the soldiers from the bar steps up. They swarm my personal space, making me want to run, but they mean no harm.

"My name is Takahan, son of Hiro," he says.

He doesn't look much like his father, but his voice makes the resemblance. In body, he resembles a southwestern Magnavozian, who are known for their mahogany skin and thick jawlines.

"It's an honor to visit you, but please..." I lift my hands, urging them to stand upright.

"This is Yosgo and Hakon. They've served underneath my father since before..." Takahan waves a hand to each man beside him.

"Yosgo. Hakon." I nod.

They each present a humble bow, causing a thick lump to form in my throat. I turn to others in the room, and Soda bows again. I want to cry. After all my time absent, I didn't expect this sort of welcome.

"Your Imperial Majesty, it's such an honor to see you. We didn't know if you were still out there." Soda bows for the fourth time.

Finally, the woman and the man who whispered when I entered rise.

"We are of the Awnhoto family. We've been builders for the empire since the beginning. Our family has been loyal to the

Evoni since before the empire was formed," the man says.

"Our families built the empire together," the woman says.

"I'm privileged to meet the descendants of the great builders, the sons of Fangourian warriors, and the noble guardians
of the throne." I circle around to view them all. "I've not come
here on this day to claim your loyalty. I only wish for a night to
stay and to hear more of each of your stories."

For them, it's a declaration of their loyalty to the Evoni.
For me, it's a terrifying confrontation with my reality. Still, they
each look to me for more. They explain their roles in the empire,
before and after my absence. Their tales of Fangourian suffering
bring tears to the edges of my eyes, but my plain face prevails.

I spend the night listening to their dances of sacrifice, until
Hiro asks everyone to leave.

Hiro steps into the back and returns with a cloth covering
a thin object.

"Do you still have the bow?"

"Yes," I say.

"I was there when your mother returned for it," Hiro says.

My remaining defenses fade. I'll trade anything to hear
more about her.

"You were... What happened?" I say.

"We should have known something was wrong. They traveled with many more soldiers than necessary for a diplomatic
meeting," he says.

"When did she return?" I say.

"We were going to fight them off as long as we could, to
give you time. When your mother returned, we followed her
away from the throne to get the bow. We lost a lot of great
Fangourians along the way, but we saved the Evoni Bow and
our future." He grabs my hand.

My mother would be glad I'm here with Hiro. A few tears
roll down my cheek.

"Thank you, Hiro," I say.

"Wait, I have something for you. We left before we could get to the arrows. But I went back for them." Hiro unfurls the cloth, revealing three black arrows.

"The arrows..." I glide my hands down the shafts.

Crafted by the same weaponsmith as the bow, the arrows are flawless. I'm reminded of a sense of pride to be Fangourian, one that I've forgotten in my exile.

"They belong to you. They belong to the Evoni." He rolls them up in the cloth and hands them to me.

Tears swell in the old man's eyes. Takahan stands up beside his father. Hiro pats his son's hands, and he motions me to follow him. They lead me to a room with a large bed and canopy cloths. It's a luxury I haven't experienced in many seasons. Noticing me eager to enter, Takahan takes his father by the arm.

"Sleep well, Your Imperial Majesty," Hiro says.

"She's alive. It was all worth it," Takahan says as they walk down the hall.

●

Several days later I'm alone in the Okiari Forest. I'm searching for something lost. I reach the sitting stones, but I can't linger for long. I've missed all the features of the forest. The smell of the earth is intoxicating as I sink closer to the ground. I glide my hands over moss growing up the sitting stones. This is where I belong. I kick off my boots and slide my feet into the ground. The grass tickles my feet like a fresh kiss. I leave all my possessions as I begin to venture farther.

Beyond the thicker line of trees, I avoid the light shining through the treetops, stepping only in the shade. The games I played during my youth are more exciting than ever. Before I left, I thought I was growing too old to enjoy the forest. I laugh at how foolish I was.

A powerful presence finds me, and I can't keep my throat from clenching. Twigs crack below my feet, and the presence grows stronger as I become the prey. Yet I continue onward, because my destination is worth the risk.

A branch cracks above me, followed by a padded thud on the forest floor.

"There you are." I open my hands to embrace my friend.

Yet it's not my friend. This one is younger, smaller, and more feral than Bulba. The tiger circles around me. There's nowhere for me to escape. The excitement of another tiger fights the fear of one in my thoughts.

"Who are you?" I say.

The tiger's ears twitch. She snarls in refusal at my words. She's serious, and I'm trespassing. Suddenly she crouches like she is going to pounce. I reach for the dagger at the small of my back, but the tiger remains crouched. Then I feel another presence in my bones before my other senses react. Another tiger saunters around the trees. He's somehow larger now, but it's Bulba. His front paws meet, and he stares at me. I need to hug him around his neck to really feel at home. The night we fought together and I lost my mother flashes back from my memories.

"Bulba?" I sob.

His eyes narrow, and his tail flicks. The younger tiger snarls, and Bulba growls back at her. She crouches back to the ground, lowering her head.

I drop my dagger onto the forest floor as I step to meet him. His head remains high when I press my forehead into his neck. For a moment, he remains still. Then I feel a shaking tremble through his body, followed by a gentle nuzzle on the top of my head.

The End.